THE SITTAFORD MYSTERY

D1347137

Agatha Christie®

The Sittaford Mystery

HarperCollins*Publishers*

HarperCollins*Publishers* Ltd
1 London Bridge Street
London SE1 9GF
www.harpercollins.co.uk

This paperback edition 2017

HarperCollins*Publishers*
Macken House, 39/40 Mayor Street Upper
Dublin 1, D01 C9W8, Ireland

First published in Great Britain by
Collins, The Crime Club 1931
13

The Sittaford Mystery™ is a trade mark of Agatha Christie Limited
and Agatha Christie® and the Agatha Christie Signature are
registered trade marks of Agatha Christie Limited in the UK and elsewhere.
Copyright © 1931 Agatha Christie Limited. All rights reserved.
www.agathachristie.com

A catalogue record for this book is available from the British Library

ISBN 978-0-00-819623-3 (PB)
ISBN 978-0-00-825561-9 (POD PB)

Set in Sabon LT Std by Palimpsest Book Production Limited, Falkirk, Stirlingshire
Printed and bound in the UK using 100% renewable electricity at CPI Group (UK) Ltd

All rights reserved. No part of this publication may be reproduced,
stored in a retrieval system, or transmitted, in any form or by any means,
electronic, mechanical, photocopying, recording or otherwise, without the
prior written permission of the publishers.

MIX
Paper | Supporting
responsible forestry
FSC™ C007454

This book is produced from independently certified FSC™ paper
to ensure responsible forest management.

For more information visit: www.harpercollins.co.uk/green

To M.E.M.
with whom I discussed the plot of this book,
to the alarm of those around us.

Contents

CHAPTER 1

Sittaford House

Major Burnaby drew on his gum boots, buttoned his overcoat collar round his neck, took from a shelf near the door a hurricane lantern, and cautiously opened the front door of his little bungalow and peered out.

The scene that met his eyes was typical of the English countryside as depicted on Christmas cards and in old-fashioned melodramas. Everywhere was snow, deep drifts of it—no mere powdering an inch or two thick. Snow had fallen all over England for the last four days, and up here on the fringe of Dartmoor it had attained a depth of several feet. All over England householders were groaning over burst pipes, and to have a plumber friend (or even a plumber's mate) was the most coveted of all distinctions.

Up here, in the tiny village of Sittaford, at all times remote from the world, and now almost completely cut off, the rigours of winter were a very real problem.

Major Burnaby, however, was a hardy soul. He snorted twice, grunted once, and marched resolutely out into the snow.

His destination was not far away. A few paces along a winding lane, then in at a gate, and so up a drive partially swept clear of snow to a house of some considerable size built of granite.

The door was opened by a neatly clad parlourmaid. The Major was divested of his British Warm, his gum boots and his aged scarf.

A door was flung open and he passed through it into a room which conveyed all the illusion of a transformation scene.

Although it was only half past three the curtains had been drawn, the electric lights were on and a huge fire blazed cheerfully on the hearth. Two women in afternoon frocks rose to greet the staunch old warrior.

'Splendid of you to turn out, Major Burnaby,' said the elder of the two.

'Not at all, Mrs Willett, not at all. Very good of you to ask me.' He shook hands with them both.

'Mr Garfield is coming,' went on Mrs Willett, 'and Mr Duke, and Mr Rycroft *said* he would come—but one can hardly expect him at his age in such weather. Really, it is *too* dreadful. One feels one *must* do something to keep oneself cheerful. Violet, put another log on the fire.'

The Major rose gallantly to perform this task.

'Allow me, Miss Violet.'

He put the log expertly in the right place and returned once more to the armchair his hostess had indicated. Trying not to appear as though he were doing so, he cast surreptitious glances round the room. Amazing how a couple of women could alter the whole character of a room—and without doing anything very outstanding that you could put your finger on.

Sittaford House had been built ten years ago by Captain Joseph Trevelyan, R.N., on the occasion of his retirement from the Navy. He was a man of substance, and he had always had a great hankering to live on Dartmoor. He had placed his choice on the tiny hamlet of Sittaford. It was not in a valley like most of the villages and farms, but perched right on the shoulder of the moor under the shadow of Sittaford Beacon. He had purchased a large tract of ground, had built a comfortable house with its own electric light plant and an electric pump to save labour in pumping water. Then, as a speculation, he had built six small bungalows, each in its quarter acre of ground, along the lane.

The first of these, the one at his very gates, had been allotted to his old friend and crony, John Burnaby—the others had by degrees been sold, there being still a few people who from choice or necessity like to live right out of the world. The village itself consisted of three picturesque but dilapidated cottages, a forge and a combined post office and sweet shop. The nearest town was Exhampton, six miles away, a steady descent which necessitated the sign, 'Motorists engage your lowest gear', so familiar on the Dartmoor roads.

Captain Trevelyan, as has been said, was a man of substance. In spite of this—or perhaps because of it—he was a man who was inordinately fond of money. At the end of October a house agent in Exhampton wrote to him asking if he would consider letting Sittaford House. A

Agatha Christie

tenant had made inquiries concerning it, wishing to rent it for the winter.

Captain Trevelyan's first impulse was to refuse, his second to demand further information. The tenant in question proved to be a Mrs Willett, a widow with one daughter. She had recently arrived from South Africa and wanted a house on Dartmoor for the winter.

'Damn it all, the woman must be mad,' said Captain Trevelyan. 'Eh, Burnaby, don't you think so?'

Burnaby did think so, and said so as forcibly as his friend had done.

'Anyway, you don't want to let,' he said. 'Let the fool woman go somewhere else if she wants to freeze. Coming from South Africa too!'

But at this point Captain Trevelyan's money complex asserted itself. Not once in a hundred times would you get a chance of letting your house in mid-winter. He demanded what rent the tenant was willing to pay.

An offer of twelve guineas a week clinched matters. Captain Trevelyan went into Exhampton, rented a small house on the outskirts at two guineas a week, and handed over Sittaford House to Mrs Willett, half the rent to be paid in advance.

'A fool and her money are soon parted,' he growled.

But Burnaby was thinking this afternoon as he scanned Mrs Willett covertly, that she did not look a fool. She was a tall woman with a rather silly manner—but her physiognomy was shrewd rather than foolish. She was inclined to overdress, had a distinct Colonial accent, and seemed perfectly content with the transaction. She was clearly very

4

well off, and that—as Burnaby had reflected more than once—really made the whole affair more odd. She was not the kind of woman one would credit with a passion for solitude.

As a neighbour she had proved almost embarrassingly friendly. Invitations to Sittaford House were rained on everybody. Captain Trevelyan was constantly urged to 'Treat the house as though we hadn't rented it.' Trevelyan, however, was not fond of women. Report went that he had been jilted in his youth. He persistently refused all invitations.

Two months had passed since the installation of the Willetts and the first wonder at their arrival had passed away.

Burnaby, naturally a silent man, continued to study his hostess, oblivious to any need for small talk. Liked to make herself out a fool, but wasn't really. So he summed up the situation. His glance shifted to Violet Willett. Pretty girl—scraggy, of course—they all were nowadays. What was the good of a woman if she didn't look like a woman? Papers said curves were coming back. About time too.

He roused himself to the necessity of conversation.

'We were afraid at first that you wouldn't be able to come,' said Mrs Willett. 'You said so, you remember. We were so pleased when you said that after all you would.'

'Friday,' said Major Burnaby, with an air of being explicit.

Mrs Willett looked puzzled.

'Friday?'

'Every Friday go to Trevelyan's. Tuesday he comes to me. Both of us done it for years.'

'Oh! I see. Of course, living so near—'

'Kind of habit.'

'But do you still keep it up? I mean now that he is living in Exhampton—'

'Pity to break a habit,' said Major Burnaby. 'We'd both of us miss those evenings.'

'You go in for competitions, don't you?' asked Violet. 'Acrostics and crosswords and all those things.'

Burnaby nodded.

'I do crosswords. Trevelyan does acrostics. We each stick to our own line of country. I won three books last month in a crossword competition,' he volunteered.

'Oh! really. How nice. Were they interesting books?'

'Don't know. Haven't read them. Looked pretty hopeless.'

'It's the winning them that matters, isn't it?' said Mrs Willett vaguely.

'How do you get to Exhampton?' asked Violet. 'You haven't got a car.'

'Walk.'

'What? Not really? Six miles.'

'Good exercise. What's twelve miles? Keeps a man fit. Great thing to be fit.'

'Fancy! Twelve miles. But both you and Captain Trevelyan were great athletes, weren't you?'

'Used to go to Switzerland together. Winter sports in winter, climbing in summer. Wonderful man on ice, Trevelyan. Both too old for that sort of thing nowadays.'

'You won the Army Racquets Championship, too, didn't you?' asked Violet.

The Major blushed like a girl.

'Who told you that?' he mumbled.

'Captain Trevelyan.'

'Joe should hold his tongue,' said Burnaby. 'He talks too much. What's the weather like now?'

Respecting his embarrassment, Violet followed him to the window. They drew the curtain aside and looked out over the desolate scene.

'More snow coming,' said Burnaby. 'A pretty heavy fall too, I should say.'

'Oh! how thrilling,' said Violet. 'I do think snow is so romantic. I've never seen it before.'

'It isn't romantic when the pipes freeze, you foolish child,' said her mother.

'Have you lived all your life in South Africa, Miss Willett?' asked Major Burnaby.

Some of the girl's animation dropped away from her. She seemed almost constrained in her manner as she answered.

'Yes—this is the first time I've ever been away. It's all most frightfully thrilling.'

Thrilling to be shut away like this in a remote moorland village? Funny ideas. He couldn't get the hang of these people.

The door opened and the parlourmaid announced:

'Mr Rycroft and Mr Garfield.'

There entered a little elderly, dried-up man and a fresh-coloured, boyish young man. The latter spoke first.

'I brought him along, Mrs Willett. Said I wouldn't let him be buried in a snowdrift. Ha, ha. I say, this all looks simply marvellous. Yule logs burning.'

'As he says, my young friend very kindly piloted me here,' said Mr Rycroft as he shook hands somewhat ceremoniously. 'How do you do, Miss Violet? Very seasonable weather—rather too seasonable, I fear.'

He moved to the fire talking to Mrs Willett. Ronald Garfield buttonholed Violet.

'I say, can't we get up any skating anywhere? Aren't there some ponds about?'

'I think path digging will be your only sport.'

'I've been at it all the morning.'

'Oh! you he-man.'

'Don't laugh at me. I've got blisters all over my hands.'

'How's your aunt?'

'Oh! she's always the same—sometimes she says she's better and sometimes she says she's worse, but I think it's all the same really. It's a ghastly life, you know. Each year, I wonder how I can stick it—but there it is—if one doesn't rally round the old bird for Christmas—why, she's quite capable of leaving her money to a Cat's Home. She's got five of them, you know. I'm always stroking the brutes and pretending I dote upon them.'

'I like dogs much better than cats.'

'So do I. Any day. What I mean is a dog is—well, a dog's a dog, you know.'

'Has your aunt always been fond of cats?'

'I think it's just a kind of thing old maids grow into. Ugh! I hate the brutes.'

'Your aunt's very nice, but rather frightening.'

'I should think she was frightening. Snaps my head off sometimes. Thinks I've got no brains, you know.'

'Not really?'

'Oh! look here, don't say it like that. Lots of fellows look like fools and are laughing underneath.'

'Mr Duke,' announced the parlourmaid.

Mr Duke was a recent arrival. He had bought the last of the six bungalows in September. He was a big man, very quiet and devoted to gardening. Mr Rycroft who was an enthusiast on birds and who lived next door to him had taken him up, overruling the section of thought which voiced the opinion that of course Mr Duke was a very nice man, quite unassuming, but was he, after all, quite—well, quite? Mightn't he, just possibly, be a retired tradesman?

But nobody liked to ask him—and indeed it was thought better not to know. Because if one did know, it might be awkward, and really in such a small community it was best to know everybody.

'Not walking to Exhampton in this weather?' he asked of Major Burnaby.

'No, I fancy Trevelyan will hardly expect me tonight.'

'It's awful, isn't it?' said Mrs Willett with a shudder. 'To be buried up here, year after year—it must be ghastly.'

Mr Duke gave her a quick glance. Major Burnaby too stared at her curiously.

But at that moment tea was brought in.

CHAPTER 2

The Message

After tea, Mrs Willett suggested bridge.

'There are six of us. Two can cut in.'

Ronnie's eyes brightened.

'You four start,' he suggested. 'Miss Willett and I will cut in.'

But Mr Duke said that he did not play bridge.

Ronnie's face fell.

'We might play a round game,' said Mrs Willett.

'Or table-turning,' suggested Ronnie. 'It's a spooky evening. We spoke about it the other day, you remember. Mr Rycroft and I were talking about it this evening as we came along here.'

'I am a member of the Psychical Research Society,' explained Mr Rycroft in his precise way. 'I was able to put my young friend right on one or two points.'

'Tommy rot,' said Major Burnaby very distinctly.

'Oh! but it's great fun, don't you think?' said Violet Willett. 'I mean, one doesn't believe in it or anything. It's just an amusement. What do you say, Mr Duke?'

'Anything you like, Miss Willett.'

'We must turn the lights out, and we must find a suitable table. No—not that one, Mother. I'm sure it's much too heavy.'

Things were settled at last to everyone's satisfaction. A small round table with a polished top was brought from an adjoining room. It was set in front of the fire and everyone took their places round it with the lights switched off.

Major Burnaby was between his hostess and Violet. On the other side of the girl was Ronnie Garfield. A cynical smile creased the Major's lips. He thought to himself:

'In my young days it was Up Jenkins.' And he tried to recall the name of a girl with fluffy fair hair whose hand he had held beneath the table at considerable length. A long time ago that was. But Up Jenkins had been a good game.

There were all the usual laughs, whispers, stereotyped remarks.

'The spirits are a long time.'

'Got a long way to come.'

'Hush—nothing will happen unless we are serious.'

'Oh! do be quiet—everyone.'

'Nothing's happening.'

'Of course not—it never does at first.'

'If only you'd all be quiet.'

At last, after some time, the murmur of talk died away. A silence.

'This table's dead as mutton,' murmured Ronnie Garfield disgustedly.

'Hush.'

A tremor ran through the polished surface. The table began to rock.

'Ask it questions. Who shall ask? You, Ronnie.'

'Oh—er—I say—what do I ask it?'

'Is a spirit present?' prompted Violet.

'Oh! Hullo—is a spirit present?'

A sharp rock.

'That means yes,' said Violet.

'Oh! er—who are you?'

No response.

'Ask it to spell its name.'

'How can it?'

'We count the number of rocks.'

'Oh! I see. Will you please spell your name.'

The table started rocking violently.

'*A B C D E F G H I*—I say, was that *I* or *J*?'

'Ask it. Was that I?'

One rock.

'Yes. Next letter, please.'

The spirit's name was Ida.

'Have you a message for anyone here?'

'Yes.'

'Who is it for? Miss Willett?'

'No.'

'Mrs Willett?'

'No.'

'Mr Rycroft?'

'No.'

'Me?'

'Yes.'

'It's for you, Ronnie. Go on. Make it spell it out.'

The table spelt 'Diana'.

'Who's Diana? Do you know anyone called Diana?'

'No, I don't. At least—'

'There you are. He does.'

'Ask her if she's a widow?'

The fun went on. Mr Rycroft smiled indulgently. Young people must have their jokes. He caught one glance of his hostess's face in a sudden flicker of the firelight. It looked worried and abstracted. Her thoughts were somewhere far away.

Major Burnaby was thinking of the snow. It was going to snow again this evening. Hardest winter he ever remembered.

Mr Duke was playing very seriously. The spirits, alas, paid very little attention to him. All the messages seemed to be for Violet and Ronnie.

Violet was told she was going to Italy. Someone was going with her. Not a woman. A man. His name was Leonard.

More laughter. The table spelt the name of the town. A Russian jumble of letters—not in the least Italian.

The usual accusations were levelled.

'Look here, Violet,' ('Miss Willett' had been dropped) 'you are shoving.'

'I'm not. Look, I take my hands right off the table and it rocks just the same.'

'I like raps. I'm going to ask it to rap. Loud ones.'

'There should be raps.' Ronnie turned to Mr Rycroft. 'There ought to be raps, oughtn't there, sir?'

'Under the circumstances, I should hardly think it likely,' said Mr Rycroft dryly.

There was a pause. The table was inert. It returned no answer to questions.

'Has Ida gone away?'

One languid rock.

'Will another spirit come, please?'

Nothing. Suddenly the table began to quiver and rock violently.

'Hurrah. Are you a new spirit?'

'Yes.'

'Have you a message for someone?'

'Yes.'

'For me?'

'No.'

'For Violet?'

'No.'

'For Major Burnaby?'

'Yes.'

'It's for you, Major Burnaby. Will you spell it out, please?'

The table started rocking slowly.

'T R E V—are you sure it's V? It can't be. T R E V—it doesn't make sense.'

'Trevelyan, of course,' said Mrs Willett. 'Captain Trevelyan.'

'Do you mean Captain Trevelyan?'

'Yes.'

'You've got a message for Captain Trevelyan?'

'No.'

'Well, what is it then?'

The table began to rock—slowly, rhythmically. So slowly that it was easy to count the letters.

'*D*—' a pause. '*E—AD.*'

'Dead.'

'Somebody is dead?'

Instead of Yes or No, the table began to rock again till it reached the letter *T*.

'*T*—do you mean Trevelyan?'

'Yes.'

'You don't mean Trevelyan is dead?'

'Yes.'

A very sharp rock. 'Yes.'

Somebody gasped. There was a faint stir all round the table.

Ronnie's voice as he resumed his questions held a different note—an awed uneasy note.

'You mean—that Captain Trevelyan is dead?'

'Yes.'

There was a pause. It was as though no one knew what to ask next, or how to take this unexpected development.

And in the pause, the table started rocking again. Rhythmically and slowly Ronnie spelled out the letters aloud . . .

M-U-R-D-E-R . . .

Mrs Willett gave a cry and took her hands off the table. 'I won't go on with this. It's horrible. I don't like it.'

Mr Duke's voice rang out, resonant and clear. He was questioning the table.

'Do you mean—that Captain Trevelyan has been murdered?'

The last word had hardly left his lips when the answer

came. The table rocked so violently and assertively that it nearly fell over. One rock only.

'Yes . . .'

'Look here,' said Ronnie. He took his hands from the table. 'I call this a rotten joke.' His voice trembled.

'Turn up the lights,' said Mr Rycroft.

Major Burnaby rose and did so. The sudden glare revealed a company of pale uneasy faces.

Everyone looked at each other. Somehow—nobody quite knew what to say.

'All rot, of course,' said Ronnie with an uneasy laugh.

'Silly nonsense,' said Mrs Willett. 'Nobody ought to—to make jokes like that.'

'Not about people dying,' said Violet. 'It's—oh! I don't like it.'

'I wasn't shoving,' said Ronnie, feeling unspoken criticism levelled at him. 'I swear I wasn't.'

'I can say the same,' said Mr Duke. 'And you, Mr Rycroft?'

'Certainly not,' said Mr Rycroft warmly.

'You don't think I'd make a joke of that kind, do you?' growled Major Burnaby. 'Rotten bad taste.'

'Violet dear—'

'I didn't, Mother. Indeed, I didn't. I wouldn't do such a thing.' The girl was almost tearful.

Everyone was embarrassed. A sudden blight had come over the cheerful party.

Major Burnaby pushed back his chair, went to the window and pulled aside the curtain. He stood there looking out with his back to the room.

'Twenty-five minutes past five,' said Mr Rycroft glancing

up at the clock. He compared it with his own watch and somehow everyone felt the action was significant in some way.

'Let me see,' said Mrs Willett with forced cheerfulness. 'I think we'd better have cocktails. Will you ring the bell, Mr Garfield?'

Ronnie obeyed.

Ingredients for cocktails were brought and Ronnie was appointed mixer. The situation grew a little easier.

'Well,' said Ronnie, raising his glass. 'Here's how.'

The others responded—all but the silent figure by the window.

'Major Burnaby. Here's your cocktail.'

The Major roused himself with a start. He turned slowly.

'Thank you, Mrs Willett. Not for me.' He looked once more out into the night, then came slowly back to the group by the fire. 'Many thanks for a very pleasant time. Good night.'

'You're not going?'

'Afraid I must.'

'Not so soon. And on a night like this.'

'Sorry, Mrs Willett—but it's got to be done. If there were only a telephone.'

'A telephone?'

'Yes—to tell you the truth—I'm—well, I'd like to be sure that Joe Trevelyan's all right. Silly superstition and all that—but there it is. Naturally, I don't believe in this tommy rot—but—'

'But you can't telephone from anywhere. There's not such a thing in Sittaford.'

'That's just it. As I can't telephone, I'll have to go.'

'Go—but you couldn't get a car down that road! Elmer wouldn't take his car out on such a night.'

Elmer was the proprietor of the sole car in the place, an aged Ford, hired at a handsome price by those who wished to go into Exhampton.

'No, no—car's out of the question. My two legs will take me there, Mrs Willett.'

There was a chorus of protest.

'Oh! Major Burnaby—it's *impossible*. You said yourself it was going to snow.'

'Not for an hour—perhaps longer. I'll get there, never fear.'

'Oh! you can't. We can't allow it.'

She was seriously disturbed and upset.

But argument and entreaty had no more effect on Major Burnaby than if he were a rock. He was an obstinate man. Once his mind was made up on any point, no power on earth could move him.

He had determined to walk to Exhampton and see for himself that all was well with his old friend, and he repeated that simple statement half a dozen times.

In the end they were brought to realize that he meant it. He wrapped himself up in his overcoat, lighted the hurricane lantern, and stepped out into the night.

'I'll just drop in to my place for a flask,' he said cheerily, 'and then push straight on. Trevelyan will put me up for the night when I get there. Ridiculous fuss, I know. Everything sure to be all right. Don't worry, Mrs Willett. Snow or no snow—I'll get there in a couple of hours. Good night.'

He strode away. The others returned to the fire.

Rycroft had looked up at the sky.

'It *is* going to snow,' he murmured to Mr Duke. 'And it will begin long before he gets to Exhampton. I—I hope he gets there all right.'

Duke frowned.

'I know. I feel I ought to have gone with him. One of us ought to have done so.'

'Most distressing,' Mrs Willett was saying, 'most distressing. Violet, I will not have that silly game ever played again. Poor Major Burnaby will probably plunge into a snow-drift—or if he doesn't he'll die of the cold and exposure. At his age, too. Very foolish of him to go off like that. Of course, Captain Trevelyan is perfectly all right.'

Everyone echoed:

'Of course.'

But even now they did not feel really too comfortable.

Supposing something had happened to Captain Trevelyan . . .

Supposing . . .

CHAPTER 3

Five and Twenty Past Five

Two and a half hours later, just before eight o'clock, Major Burnaby, hurricane lantern in hand, his head dropped forward so as not to meet the blinding drive of snow, stumbled up the path to the door of Hazelmoor, the small house tenanted by Captain Trevelyan.

The snow had begun to fall about an hour ago—great blinding flakes of it. Major Burnaby was gasping, emitting the loud sighing gasps of an utterly exhausted man. He was numbed with cold. He stamped his feet, blew, puffed, snorted and applied a numbed finger to the bell push.

The bell trilled shrilly.

Burnaby waited. After a pause of a few minutes, as nothing happened, he pushed the bell again.

Once more there was no stir of life.

Burnaby rang a third time. This time he kept his finger on the bell.

It trilled on and on—but there was still no sign of life in the house.

There was a knocker on the door. Major Burnaby

seized it and worked it vigorously, producing a noise like thunder.

And still the little house remained silent as the dead.

The Major desisted. He stood for a moment as though perplexed—then he slowly went down the path and out at the gate, continuing on the road he had come towards Exhampton. A hundred yards brought him to the small police station.

He hesitated again, then finally made up his mind and entered.

Constable Graves, who knew the Major well, rose in astonishment.

'Well, I never, sir, fancy you being out on a night like this.'

'Look here,' said Burnaby curtly. 'I've been ringing and knocking at the Captain's house and I can't get any answer.'

'Why, of course, it's Friday,' said Graves who knew the habits of the two pretty well. 'But you don't mean to say you've actually come down from Sittaford on a night like this? Surely the Captain would never expect you.'

'Whether he's expected me or not, I've come,' said Burnaby testily. 'And as I'm telling you, I can't get in. I've rung and knocked and nobody answers.'

Some of his uneasiness seemed to communicate itself to the policeman.

'That's odd,' he said, frowning.

'Of course, it's odd,' said Burnaby.

'It's not as though he's likely to be out—on a night like this.'

Agatha Christie

'Of course he's not likely to be out.'

'It *is* odd,' said Graves again.

Burnaby displayed impatience at the man's slowness.

'Aren't you going to do something?' he snapped.

'Do something?'

'Yes, do something.'

The policeman ruminated.

'Think he might have been taken bad?' His face brightened. 'I'll try the telephone.' It stood at his elbow. He took it up and gave the number.

But to the telephone, as to the front door bell, Captain Trevelyan gave no reply.

'Looks as though he had been taken bad,' said Graves as he replaced the receiver. 'And all alone in the house, too. We'd best got hold of Dr Warren and take him along with us.'

Dr Warren's house was almost next door to the police station. The doctor was just sitting down to dinner with his wife and was not best pleased at the summons. However, he grudgingly agreed to accompany them, drawing on an aged British Warm and a pair of rubber boots and muffling his neck with a knitted scarf.

The snow was still falling.

'Damnable night,' murmured the doctor. 'Hope you haven't brought me out on a wild goose chase. Trevelyan's as strong as a horse. Never has anything the matter with him.'

Burnaby did not reply.

Arriving at Hazelmoor once more, they rang again and knocked, but elicited no response.

The doctor then suggested going round the house to one of the back windows.

'Easier to force than the door.'

Graves agreeing, they went round the back. There was a side door which they tried on the way, but it too was locked, and presently they emerged on the snow-covered lawn that led up to the back windows. Suddenly, Warren uttered an exclamation.

'The window of the study—it's open.'

True enough, the window, a French one, was standing ajar. They quickened their steps. On a night like this, no one in their senses would open a window. There was a light in the room that streamed out in a thin yellow band.

The three men arrived simultaneously at the window—Burnaby was the first man to enter, the constable hard on his heels.

They both stopped dead inside and something like a muffled cry came from the ex-soldier. In another moment Warren was beside them, and saw what they had seen.

Captain Trevelyan lay on the floor, face downwards. His arms sprawled widely. The room was in confusion—drawers of the bureau pulled out, papers lying about the floor. The window beside them was splintered where it had been forced near the lock. Beside Captain Trevelyan was a dark green baize tube about two inches in diameter.

Warren sprang forward. He knelt down by the prostrate figure.

One minute sufficed. He rose to his feet, his face pale.

'He's dead?' asked Burnaby.

The doctor nodded.

Then he turned to Graves.

'It's for you to say what's to be done. I can do nothing except examine the body and perhaps you'd rather I didn't do that until the Inspector comes. I can tell you the cause of death now. Fracture of the base of the skull. And I think I can make a guess at the weapon.'

He indicated the green baize tube.

'Trevelyan always had them along the bottom of the door—to keep the draught out,' said Burnaby.

His voice was hoarse.

'Yes—a very efficient form of sandbag.'

'My God!'

'But this here—' the constable broke in, his wits arriving at the point slowly. 'You mean—this here is murder.'

The policeman stepped to the table on which stood a telephone.

Major Burnaby approached the doctor.

'Have you any idea,' he said, breathing hard, 'how long he's been dead?'

'About two hours, I should say, or possibly three. That's a rough estimate.'

Burnaby passed his tongue over dry lips.

'Would you say,' he asked, 'that he might have been killed at five twenty-five?'

The doctor looked at him curiously.

'If I had to give a time definitely, that's just about the time I would suggest.'

'Oh! my God,' said Burnaby.

Warren stared at him.

The Major felt his way blindly to a chair, collapsed on

to it and muttered to himself whilst a kind of staring terror overspread his face.

'*Five and twenty past five*—Oh! my God, then it *was* true after all.'

CHAPTER 4

Inspector Narracott

It was the morning after the tragedy, and two men were standing in the little study of Hazelmoor.

Inspector Narracott looked round him. A little frown appeared upon his forehead.

'Ye-es,' he said thoughtfully. 'Ye-es.'

Inspector Narracott was a very efficient officer. He had a quiet persistence, a logical mind and a keen attention to detail which brought him success where many another man might have failed.

He was a tall man with a quiet manner, rather far-away grey eyes, and a slow, soft Devonshire voice.

Summoned from Exeter to take charge of the case, he had arrived on the first train that morning. The roads had been impassable for cars, even with chains, otherwise he would have arrived the night before. He was standing now in Captain Trevelyan's study having just completed his examination of the room. With him was Sergeant Pollock of the Exhampton police.

'Ye-es,' said Inspector Narracott.

A ray of pale wintry sunshine came in through the window. Outside was the snowy landscape. There was a fence about a hundred yards from the window and beyond it the steep ascending slope of the snow-covered hillside.

Inspector Narracott bent once more over the body which had been left for his inspection. An athletic man himself, he recognized the athlete's type, the broad shoulders, narrow flanks, and the good muscular development. The head was small and well set on the shoulders, and the pointed naval beard was carefully trimmed. Captain Trevelyan's age, he had ascertained, was sixty, but he looked not much more than fifty-one or two.

'It's a curious business,' said Inspector Narracott.

'Ah!' said Sergeant Pollock.

The other turned on him.

'What is your view of it?'

'Well—' Sergeant Pollock scratched his head. He was a cautious man, unwilling to advance further than necessary.

'Well,' he said, 'as I see it, sir, I should say that the man came to the window, forced the lock, and started rifling the room. Captain Trevelyan, I suppose, must have been upstairs. Doubtless the burglar thought the house was empty—'

'Where is Captain Trevelyan's bedroom situated?'

'Upstairs, sir. Over this room.'

'At the present time of year it is dark at four o'clock. If Captain Trevelyan was up in his bedroom the electric light would have been on, the burglar would have seen it as he approached this window.'

'You mean he'd have waited.'

'No man in his senses would break into a house with a

27

light in it. If anyone forced this window—he did it because
he thought the house was empty.'

Sergeant Pollock scratched his head.

'Seems a bit odd, I admit. But there it is.'

'We'll let it pass for the moment. Go on.'

'Well, suppose the Captain hears a noise downstairs. He
comes down to investigate. The burglar hears him coming.
He snatches up that bolster arrangement, gets behind the
door, and as the Captain enters the room strikes him down
from behind.'

Inspector Narracott nodded.

'Yes, that's true enough. He was struck down when he
was facing the window. But all the same, Pollock, I don't
like it.'

'No, sir?'

'No, as I say, I don't believe in houses that are broken
into at five o'clock in the afternoon.'

'We-ell, he may have thought it a good opportunity—'

'It is not a question of opportunity—slipping in because
he found a window unlatched. It was deliberate house-
breaking—look at the confusion everywhere—what would
a burglar go for first? The pantry where the silver is kept.'

'That's true enough,' admitted the Sergeant.

'And this confusion—this chaos,' continued Narracott,
'these drawers pulled out and their contents scattered. Pah!
It's bunkum.'

'Bunkum?'

'Look at the window, Sergeant. *That window was not
locked and forced open!* It was merely shut and then splintered from the outside to give the appearance of forcing.'

Pollock examined the latch of the window closely, uttering an ejaculation to himself as he did so.

'You are right, sir,' he said with respect in his voice. 'Who'd have thought of that now!'

'Someone who wishes to throw dust in our eyes—and hasn't succeeded.'

Sergeant Pollock was grateful for the 'our'. In such small ways did Inspector Narracott endear himself to his subordinates.

'Then it wasn't burglary. You mean, sir, it was an inside job.'

Inspector Narracott nodded. 'Yes,' he said. 'The only curious thing is, though, that I think the murderer did actually enter by the window. As you and Graves reported, and as I can still see for myself, there are damp patches still visible where the snow melted and was trodden in by the murderer's boots. These damp patches are only in this room. Constable Graves was quite positive that there was nothing of the kind in the hall when he and Dr Warren passed through it. In this room he noticed them immediately. In that case it seems clear that the murderer was admitted by Captain Trevelyan through the window. Therefore it must have been someone whom Captain Trevelyan knew. You are a local man, Sergeant, can you tell me if Captain Trevelyan was a man who made enemies easily?'

'No, sir, I should say he hadn't an enemy in the world. A bit keen on money, and a bit of a martinet—wouldn't stand for any slackness or incivility—but bless my soul he was respected for that.'

'No enemies,' said Narracott thoughtfully.

'Not here, that is.'

'Very true—we don't know what enemies he may have made during his naval career. It's my experience, Sergeant, that a man who makes enemies in one place will make them in another, but I agree that we can't put that possibility entirely aside. We come logically now to the next motive—the most common motive for every crime—gain. Captain Trevelyan was, I understand, a rich man?'

'Very warm indeed by all accounts. But close. Not an easy man to touch for a subscription.'

'Ah!' said Narracott thoughtfully.

'Pity it snowed as it did,' said the Sergeant. 'But for that we'd have had his footprints as something to go on.'

'There was no one else in the house?' asked the Inspector.

'No. For the last five years Captain Trevelyan has only had one servant—retired naval chap. Up at Sittaford House a woman came in daily, but this chap, Evans, cooked and looked after his master. About a month ago he got married—much to the Captain's annoyance. I believe that's one of the reasons he let Sittaford House to this South African lady. He wouldn't have any woman living in the house. Evans lives just round the corner here in Fore Street with his wife, and comes in daily to do for his master. I've got him here now for you to see. His statement is that he left here at half past two yesterday afternoon, the Captain having no further need for him.'

'Yes, I shall want to see him. He may be able to tell us something—useful.'

Sergeant Pollock looked at his superior officer curiously. There was something so odd about his tone.

'You think—' he began.

'I think,' said Inspector Narracott deliberately, 'that there's a lot more in this case than meets the eye.'

'In what way, sir?'

But the Inspector refused to be drawn.

'You say this man, Evans, is here now?'

'He's waiting in the dining-room.'

'Good. I'll see him straight away. What sort of a fellow is he?'

Sergeant Pollock was better at reporting facts than at descriptive accuracy.

'He's a retired naval chap. Ugly customer in a scrap, I should say.'

'Does he drink?'

'Never been the worse for it that I know of.'

'What about this wife of his? Not a fancy of the Captain's or anything of that sort?'

'Oh! no, sir, nothing of that kind about Captain Trevelyan. He wasn't that kind at all. He was known as a woman hater, if anything.'

'And Evans was supposed to be devoted to his master?'

'That's the general idea, sir, and I think it would be known if he wasn't. Exhampton's a small place.'

Inspector Narracott nodded.

'Well,' he said, 'there's nothing more to be seen here. I'll interview Evans and I'll take a look at the rest of the house and after that we will go over to the Three Crowns and see this Major Burnaby. That remark of his about the time was curious. Twenty-five past five, eh? He must know something he hasn't told, or why should he suggest the time of the crime so accurately?'

The two men moved towards the door.

'It's a rum business,' said Sergeant Pollock, his eye wandering to the littered floor. 'All this burglary fake!'

'It's not that that strikes me as odd,' said Narracott, 'under the circumstances it was probably the natural thing to do. No—what strikes me as odd is the window.'

'The window, sir?'

'Yes. Why should the murderer go to the window? Assuming it was someone Trevelyan knew and admitted without question, why not go to the front door? To get round to this window from the road on a night like last night would have been a difficult and unpleasant proceeding with the snow lying as thick as it does. Yet there must have been some reason.'

'Perhaps,' suggested Pollock, 'the man didn't want to be seen turning in to the house from the road.'

'There wouldn't be many people about yesterday afternoon to see him. Nobody who could help it was out of doors. No—there's some other reason. Well, perhaps it will come to light in due course.'

CHAPTER 5

Evans

They found Evans waiting in the dining-room. He rose respectfully on their entrance.

He was a short thick-set man. He had very long arms and a habit of standing with his hands half clenched. He was clean shaven with small, rather pig-like eyes, yet he had a look of cheerfulness and efficiency that redeemed his bulldog appearance.

Inspector Narracott mentally tabulated his impressions.

'Intelligent. Shrewd and practical. Looks rattled.'

Then he spoke:

'You're Evans, eh?'

'Yes, sir.'

'Christian names?'

'Robert Henry.'

'Ah! Now what do you know about this business?'

'Not a thing, sir. It's fair knocked me over. To think of the Capting being done in!'

'When did you last see your master?'

'Two o'clock I should say it was, sir. I cleared away the lunch things and laid the table here as you see for supper. The Capting, he told me as I needn't come back.'

'What do you usually do?'

'As a general rule, I come back about seven for a couple of hours. Not always—sometimes the Capting would say as I needn't.'

'Then you weren't surprised when he told you that yesterday you wouldn't be wanted again?'

'No, sir. I didn't come back the evening before either—on account of the weather. Very considerate gentleman, the Capting was, as long as you didn't try to shirk things. I knew him and his ways pretty well.'

'What exactly did he say?'

'Well, he looked out of the window and he says, "Not a hope of Burnaby today". "Shouldn't wonder," he says, "if Sittaford isn't cut off altogether. Don't remember such a winter since I was a boy." That was his friend Major Burnaby over to Sittaford that he was referring to. Always comes on a Friday, he does, he and the Capting play chess and do acrostics. And on Tuesdays the Capting would go to Major Burnaby's. Very regular in his habits was the Capting. Then he said to me: "You can go now, Evans, and you needn't come till tomorrow morning." '

'Apart from his reference to Major Burnaby, he didn't speak of expecting anyone that afternoon?'

'No, sir, not a word.'

'There was nothing unusual or different in any way in his manner?'

'No, sir, not that I could see.'

'Ah! Now I understand, Evans, that you have lately got married.'

'Yes, sir. Mrs Belling's daughter at the Three Crowns. Matter of two months ago, sir.'

'And Captain Trevelyan was not overpleased about it.'

A very faint grin appeared for a moment on Evans's face.

'Cut up rough about it, he did, the Capting. My Rebecca is a fine girl, sir, and a very good cook. And I hoped we might have been able to do for the Capting together, but he—he wouldn't hear of it. Said he wouldn't have women servants about his house. In fact, sir, things were rather at a deadlock when this South African lady came along and wanted to take Sittaford House for the winter. The Capting he rented this place, I came in to do for him every day, and I don't mind telling you, sir, that I had been hoping that by the end of the winter the Capting would have come round to the idea; and that me and Rebecca would go back to Sittaford with him. Why, he would never even know she was in the house. She would keep to the kitchen, and she would manage so that he would never meet her on the stairs.'

'Have you any idea what lay behind Captain Trevelyan's dislike of women?'

'Nothing to it, sir. Just an 'abit, sir, that's all. I have seen many a gentleman like it before. If you ask me, it's nothing more or less than shyness. Some young lady or other gives them a snub when they are young—and they gets the 'abit.'

'Captain Trevelyan was not married?'

'No, indeed, sir.'

'What relations had he? Do you know?'

'I believe he had a sister living at Exeter, sir, and I think I have heard him mention a nephew or nephews.'

'None of them ever came to see him?'

'No, sir. I think he quarrelled with his sister at Exeter.'

'Do you know her name?'

'Gardner, I think, sir, but I wouldn't be sure.'

'You don't know her address?'

'I'm afraid I don't, sir.'

'Well, doubtless we shall come across that in looking through Captain Trevelyan's papers. Now, Evans, what were you yourself doing from four o'clock onwards yesterday afternoon?'

'I was at home, sir.'

'Where's home?'

'Just round the corner, sir, 85 Fore Street.'

'You didn't go out at all?'

'Not likely, sir. Why, the snow was coming down a fair treat.'

'Yes, yes. Is there anyone who can support your statement?'

'Beg pardon, sir.'

'Is there anyone who knows that you were at home during that time?'

'My wife, sir.'

'She and you were alone in the house?'

'Yes, sir.'

'Well, well, I have no doubt that's all right. That will be all for the present, Evans.'

The ex-sailor hesitated. He shifted from one foot to the other.

'Anything I can do here, sir—in the way of tidying up?'

'No—the whole place is to be left exactly as it is for the present.'

'I see.'

'You had better wait, though, until I have had a look round,' said Narracott, 'in case there might be any question I want to ask you.'

'Very good, sir.'

Inspector Narracott transferred his gaze from Evans to the room.

The interview had taken place in the dining-room. On the table an evening meal was set out. A cold tongue, pickles, a Stilton cheese and biscuits, and on a gas ring by the fire a saucepan containing soup. On the sideboard was a tantalus, a soda water siphon, and two bottles of beer. There was also an immense array of silver cups and with them—a rather incongruous item, three very new-looking novels.

Inspector Narracott examined one or two of the cups and read the inscriptions on them.

'Bit of a sportsman, Captain Trevelyan,' he observed.

'Yes, indeed, sir,' said Evans. 'Been an athlete all his life, he had.'

Inspector Narracott read the titles of the novels. *Love Turns the Key*, *The Merry Men of Lincoln*, *Love's Prisoner*.

'H'm,' he remarked. 'The Captain's taste in literature seems somewhat incongruous.'

'Oh! that, sir.' Evans laughed. 'That's not for reading, sir. That's the prizes he won in these Railway Pictures

Names Competitions. Ten solutions the Capting sent in under different names, including mine, because he said 85 Fore Street was a likely address to give a prize to! The commoner your name and address the more likely you were to get a prize in the Capting's opinion. And sure enough a prize I got—but not the £2,000, only three new novels—and the kind of novels, in my opinion, that no one would ever pay money for in a shop.'

Narracott smiled, then again mentioning that Evans was to wait, he proceeded on his tour of inspection. There was a large kind of cupboard in one corner of the room. It was almost a small room in itself. Here, packed in unceremoniously, were two pairs of skis, a pair of sculls mounted, ten or twelve hippopotamus tusks, rods and lines and various fishing tackle including a book of flies, a bag of golf clubs, a tennis racket, an elephant's foot stuffed and mounted and a tiger skin. It was clear that, when Captain Trevelyan had let Sittaford House furnished, he had removed his most precious possessions, distrustful of female influence.

'Funny idea—to bring all this with him,' said the Inspector. 'The house was only let for a few months, wasn't it?'

'That's right, sir.'

'Surely these things could have been locked up at Sittaford House?'

For the second time in the course of the interview, Evans grinned.

'That would have been much the easiest way of doing it,' he agreed. 'Not that there *are* many cupboards at

Sittaford House. The architect and the Capting planned it together, and it takes a female to understand the value of cupboard room. Still, as you say, sir, that would have been the commonsense thing to do. Carting them down here was a job—I should say it was a job! But there, the Capting couldn't bear the idea of anyone messing around with his things. And lock things up as you will, he says, a woman will always find a way of getting in. It's curiosity, he says. Better not lock them up at all if you don't want her to handle them, he says. But best of all, take them along, and then you're sure to be on the safe side. So take 'em along we did, and as I say, it was a job, and came expensive too. But there, those things of the Capting's was like his children.'

Evans paused, out of breath.

Inspector Narracott nodded thoughtfully. There was another point on which he wanted information, and it seemed to him that this was a good moment when the subject had arisen naturally.

'This Mrs Willett,' he said casually. 'Was she an old friend or acquaintance of the Captain's?'

'Oh no, sir, she was quite a stranger to him.'

'You are sure of that?' said the Inspector, sharply.

'Well—' the sharpness took the old sailor aback. 'The Capting never actually said so—but—Oh! yes, I'm sure of it.'

'I ask,' explained the Inspector, 'because it is a very curious time of year for a let. On the other hand, if this Mrs Willett was acquainted with Captain Trevelyan and knew the house, she might have written to him and suggested taking it.'

Evans shook his head.

''Twas the agents—Williamsons—that wrote, said they had an offer from a lady.'

Inspector Narracott frowned. He found this business of letting Sittaford House distinctly odd.

'Captain Trevelyan and Mrs Willett met, I suppose?' he asked.

'Oh! yes. She came to see the house and he took her over it.'

'And you're positive they hadn't met before?'

'Oh! quite, sir.'

'Did they—er—' the Inspector paused, as he tried to frame the question naturally. 'Did they get on well together? Were they friendly?'

'The lady was.' A faint smile crossed Evans's lips. 'All over him, as you might say. Admiring the house, and asking him if he'd planned the building of it. Altogether laying it on thick, as you might say.'

'And the Captain?'

The smile broadened.

'That sort of gushing lady wasn't likely to cut any ice with him. Polite he was, but nothing more. And declined her invitations.'

'Invitations?'

'Yes, to consider the house as his own any time, and drop in, that's how she put it—drop in. You don't drop in to a place when you're living six miles away.'

'She seemed anxious to—well—to see something of the Captain?'

Narracott was wondering. Was that the reason for the

taking of the house? Was it only a prelude to the making of Captain Trevelyan's acquaintance? Was that the real game? It would probably not have occurred to her that the Captain would have gone as far as Exhampton to live. She might have calculated on his moving into one of the small bungalows, perhaps sharing Major Burnaby's.

Evans's answer was not very helpful.

'She's a very hospitable lady, by all accounts. Someone in to lunch or dinner every day.'

Narracott nodded. He could learn no more here. But he determined to seek an interview with this Mrs Willett at an early date. Her abrupt arrival needed looking into.

'Come on, Pollock, we'll go upstairs now,' he said.

They left Evans in the dining-room and proceeded to the upper storey.

'All right, do you think?' asked the Sergeant in a low voice, jerking his head over his shoulder in the direction of the closed dining-room door.

'He seems so,' said the Inspector. 'But one never knows. He's no fool, that fellow, whatever else he is.'

'No, he's an intelligent sort of chap.'

'His story seems straightforward enough,' went on the Inspector. 'Perfectly clear and above board. Still, as I say, one never knows.'

And with this pronouncement, very typical of his careful and suspicious mind, the Inspector proceeded to search the rooms on the first floor.

There were three bedrooms and a bathroom. Two of the bedrooms were empty and had clearly not been entered for some weeks. The third, Captain Trevelyan's own room, was in exquisite and apple-pie order. Inspector Narracott moved about in it, opening drawers and cupboards. Everything was in its right place. It was the room of a man almost fanatically tidy and neat in his habits. Narracott finished his inspection and glanced into the adjoining bathroom. Here, too, everything was in order. He gave a last glance at the bed, neatly turned down, with folded pyjamas laid ready.

Then he shook his head.

'Nothing here,' he said.

'No, everything seems in perfect order.'

'There are the papers in the desk in the study. You had better go through those, Pollock. I'll tell Evans that he can go. I may call round and see him at his own place later.'

'Very good, sir.'

'The body can be removed. I shall want to see Warren, by the way. He lives near here, doesn't he?'

'Yes, sir.'

'This side of the Three Crowns or the other?'

'The other, sir.'

'Then I'll take the Three Crowns first. Carry on, Sergeant.'

Pollock went to the dining-room to dismiss Evans. The Inspector passed out of the front door and walked rapidly in the direction of the Three Crowns.

CHAPTER 6

At the Three Crowns

Inspector Narracott was not destined to see Major Burnaby until he had had a protracted interview with Mrs Belling—licensed proprietor of the Three Crowns. Mrs Belling was fat and excitable, and so voluble that there was nothing to be done but to listen patiently until such time as the stream of conversation should dry up.

'And such a night as never was,' she ended up. 'And little did any of us think what was happening to the poor dear gentleman. Those nasty tramps—if I've said it once, I've said it a dozen times, I can't abear those nasty tramps. Do anybody in they would. The Captain had not so much as a dog to protect him. Can't abear a dog, tramps can't. Ah, well, you never know what is happening within a stone's throw.

'Yes, Mr Narracott,' she proceeded in answer to his question, 'the Major is having his breakfast now. You will find him in the coffee-room. And what kind of a night he has passed with no pyjamas or anything, and me a widow woman with nothing to lend him, I can't say, I am sure. Said it made no matter he did—all upset and queer he was—and no wonder with his best friend murdered. Very nice gentlemen the two of them, though the Captain had the reputation of being close with his money. Ah, well, well, I have always thought it dangerous to live up to Sittaford, miles away from anywhere, and here's the Captain struck down in Exhampton itself. It's always what you don't expect in this life that happens, isn't it, Mr Narracott?'

The Inspector said that undoubtedly it was. Then he added:

'Who did you have staying here yesterday, Mrs Belling? Any strangers?'

'Now let me see. There was Mr Moresby and Mr Jones— commercial gentlemen they are, and there was a young gentleman from London. Nobody else. It stands to reason there wouldn't be this time of year. Very quiet here in the winter. Oh, and there was another young gentleman— arrived by the last train. Nosey young fellow I call him. He isn't up yet.'

'The last train?' said the Inspector. 'That gets in at ten o'clock, eh? I don't think we need trouble ourselves about him. What about the other—the one from London? Did you know him?'

'Never seen him before in my life. Not a commercial gentleman, oh, no—a cut above that. I can't remember his name for the moment—but you'll find it in the register. Left on the first train to Exeter this morning, he did. Six ten. Rather curious. What did he want down here anyway, that's what I'd like to know.'

'He didn't mention his business?'

'Not a word.'

'Did he go out at all?'

'Arrived at lunch time, went out about half past four and came in about twenty past six.'

'Where did he go when he went out?'

'I haven't the remotest idea, sir. May have been just for a stroll like. That was before the snow came, but it wasn't what you might call a pleasant day for walking.'

'Went out at half past four and returned about twenty past six,' said the Inspector thoughtfully. 'That's rather odd. He didn't mention Captain Trevelyan?'

Mrs Belling shook her head decisively.

'No, Mr Narracott, he didn't mention anybody at all. Kept himself to himself he did. A nice looking young fellow—but worried, I should say.'

The Inspector nodded and stepped across to inspect the register.

'James Pearson, London,' said the Inspector. 'Well—that doesn't tell us much. We'll have to make a few inquiries about Mr James Pearson.'

Then he strode off to the coffee-room in search of Major Burnaby.

The Major was the only occupant of the room. He was drinking some rather muddy-looking coffee and *The Times* was propped up in front of him.

'Major Burnaby?'

'That's my name.'

'I am Inspector Narracott from Exeter.'

'Good morning, Inspector. Any forrarder?'

'Yes, sir. I think we are a little forrarder. I think I can safely say that.'

'Glad to hear it,' said the Major drily. His attitude was one of resigned disbelief.

'Now there are just one or two points I would like some information on, Major Burnaby,' said the Inspector, 'and I think you can probably tell me what I want to know.'

'Do what I can,' said Burnaby.

'Had Captain Trevelyan any enemies to your knowledge?'

'Not an enemy in the world.' Burnaby was decisive.

'This man, Evans—do you yourself consider him trustworthy?'

'Should think so. Trevelyan trusted him, I know.'

'There was no ill feeling about this marriage of his?'

'Not ill feeling, no. Trevelyan was annoyed—didn't like his habits upset. Old bachelor, you know.'

'Talking of bachelors, that's another point. Captain Trevelyan was unmarried—do you know if he made a will? And in the event of there being no will, have you any idea who would inherit his estate?'

'Trevelyan made a will,' said Burnaby promptly.

'Ah—you know that.'

'Yes. Made me executor. Told me so.'

'Do you know how he left his money?'

'That I can't say.'

'I understand he was very comfortably off?'

'Trevelyan was a rich man,' replied Burnaby. 'I should say he was much better off than anyone around here suspected.'

'What relations had he—do you know?'

'He'd a sister and some nephews and nieces, I believe. Never saw much of any of them, but there was no quarrel.'

'About this will, do you know where he kept it?'

'It's at Walters & Kirkwood—the solicitors here in Exhampton. They drew it up for him.'

'Then perhaps, Major Burnaby, as you are executor, I wonder if you would come round to Walters & Kirkwood with me now. I should like to have an idea of the contents of that will as soon as possible.'

Burnaby looked up alertly.

'What's in the wind?' he said. 'What's the will got to do with it?'

Inspector Narracott was not disposed to show his hand too soon.

'The case isn't such plain sailing as we thought,' he said. 'By the way, there's another question I want to ask you. I understand, Major Burnaby, that you asked Dr Warren whether death had occurred at five and twenty minutes past five?'

'Well,' said the Major gruffly.

'What made you select that exact time, Major?'

'Why shouldn't I?' said Burnaby.

'Well—something must have put it into your head.'

There was quite a pause before Major Burnaby replied. Inspector Narracott's interest was aroused. The Major had something he quite patently wished to conceal. To watch him doing so was almost ludicrous.

'Why shouldn't I say twenty-five past five?' he demanded truculently, 'or twenty-five to six—or twenty past four, for that matter?'

'Quite so, sir,' said Inspector Narracott soothingly.

He did not wish to antagonize the Major just at this moment. He promised himself that he would get to the bottom of the matter before the day was out.

'There's one thing that strikes me as curious, sir,' he went on.

'Yes?'

'This business of the letting of Sittaford House. I don't know what you think about it, but it seems to me a curious thing to have happened.'

'If you ask me,' said Burnaby, 'it's damned odd.'

'That's your opinion?'

'It's everyone's opinion.'

'In Sittaford?'

'In Sittaford and Exhampton too. The woman must be mad.'

'Well, I suppose there's no accounting for tastes,' said the Inspector.

'Damned odd taste for a woman of that kind.'

'You know the lady?'

'I know her. Why, I was at her house when—'

'When what?' asked Narracott as the Major came to an abrupt halt.

'Nothing,' said Burnaby.

Inspector Narracott looked at him keenly. There was something here he would have liked to get at. The Major's obvious confusion and embarrassment did not escape him. He had been on the point of saying—what?

'All in good time,' said Narracott to himself. 'Now isn't the moment to rub him up the wrong way.'

Aloud he said innocently:

'You were at Sittaford House, you say, sir. The lady has been there now—about how long?'

'A couple of months.'

The Major was eager to escape the result of his imprudent words. It made him more loquacious than usual.

'A widow lady with her daughter?'

'That's it.'

'Does she give any reason for her choice of residence?'

'Well—' the Major rubbed his nose dubiously. 'She talks a lot, she's that kind of woman—beauties of nature—out of the world—that sort of thing. But—'

He paused rather helplessly. Inspector Narracott came to his rescue.

'It didn't strike you as natural on her part?'

'Well, it's like this. She's a fashionable sort of woman. Dressed up to the nines—daughter's a smart, pretty girl. Natural thing would be for them to be staying at the Ritz or Claridge's, or some other big hotel somewhere. You know the sort.'

Narracott nodded.

'They don't keep themselves to themselves, do they?' he asked. 'You don't think they are—well—hiding?'

Major Burnaby shook his head positively.

'Oh! no, nothing of that kind. They're very sociable—a bit too sociable. I mean, in a little place like Sittaford, you can't have previous engagements, and when invitations are showered on you it's a bit awkward. They're exceedingly kind, hospitable people, but a bit too hospitable for English ideas.'

'The Colonial touch,' said the Inspector.

'Yes, I suppose so.'

'You've no reason to think they were previously acquainted with Captain Trevelyan?'

'Sure they weren't.'

'You seem very positive?'

'Joe would have told me.'

'And you don't think their motive could have been—well—to scrape acquaintance with the Captain?'

This was clearly a new idea to the Major. He pondered over it for some minutes.

'Well, I never thought of that. They were very gushing to him, certainly. Not that they got any change out of Joe. But no, I think it was just their usual manner. Over friendly, you know, like Colonials are,' added the super-insular soldier.

'I see. Now, as to the house itself. Captain Trevelyan built that, I understand?'

'Yes.'

'And nobody else has ever lived in it? I mean, it's not been let before?'

'Never.'

'Then it doesn't seem as though it could be anything in the house itself that was the attraction. It's a puzzle. Ten to one it's got nothing to do with the case, but it just struck me as an odd coincidence. This house that Captain Trevelyan took, Hazelmoor, whose property was that?'

'Miss Larpent's. Middle-aged woman, she's gone to a boarding house at Cheltenham for the winter. Does every year. Usually shuts the house up, but lets it if she can, which isn't often.'

There seemed nothing promising there. The Inspector shook his head in a discouraged fashion.

'Williamsons were the agents, I understand?' he said.

'Yes.'

'Their office is in Exhampton?'

'Next door to Walters & Kirkwood.'

'Ah! then, perhaps, if you don't mind, Major, we might just drop in on our way.'

'Not at all. You won't find Kirkwood at his office before ten anyway. You know what lawyers are.'

'Then, shall we go?'

The Major, who had finished his breakfast some time ago, nodded assent and rose.

CHAPTER 7

The Will

An alert-looking young man rose to receive them in the office of Messrs Williamson.

'Good morning, Major Burnaby.'

'Morning.'

'Terrible business, this,' said the young man chattily. 'Not been such a thing in Exhampton for years.'

He spoke with gusto and the Major winced.

'This is Inspector Narracott,' he said.

'Oh! yes,' said the young man, pleasurably excited.

'I want some information that I think you can give me,' said the Inspector. 'I understand that you put through this let of Sittaford House.'

'To Mrs Willett? Yes, we did.'

'Can you give me full details, please, of how that came about? Did the lady apply personally, or by letter?'

'By letter. She wrote, let me see—' He opened a drawer and turned up a file. 'Yes, from the Carlton Hotel, London.'

'Did she mention Sittaford House by name?'

'No, she merely said she wanted to rent a house for the

winter, it must be right on Dartmoor and have at least eight bedrooms. Being near a railway station or town was of no consequence.'

'Was Sittaford House on your books?'

'No, it was not. But as a matter of fact it was the only house in the neighbourhood that at all fulfilled the requirements. The lady mentioned in her letter that she would be willing to go to twelve guineas, and in these circumstances I thought it worth while writing to Captain Trevelyan and asking whether he would consider letting. He replied in the affirmative, and we fixed the thing up.'

'Without Mrs Willett seeing the house?'

'She agreed to take it without seeing it, and signed the agreement. Then she came down here one day, drove up to Sittaford, saw Captain Trevelyan, arranged with him about plate and linen, etc., and saw over the house.'

'She was quite satisfied?'

'She came in and said she was delighted with it.'

'And what did you think?' asked Inspector Narracott, eyeing him keenly.

The young man shrugged his shoulders.

'You learn never to be surprised at anything in the house business,' he said.

On this note of philosophy they left, the Inspector thanking the young man for his help.

'Not at all, a pleasure, I'm sure.'

He accompanied them politely to the door.

The offices of Messrs Walters and Kirkwood were, as Major Burnaby had said, next door to the estate agents.

On reaching there, they were told that Mr Kirkwood had just arrived and they were shown into his room.

Mr Kirkwood was an elderly man with a benign expression. He was a native of Exhampton and had succeeded his father and grandfather in the firm.

He rose, put on his mourning face, and shook hands with the Major.

'Good morning, Major Burnaby,' he said. 'This is a very shocking affair. Very shocking indeed. Poor Trevelyan.'

He looked inquiringly at Narracott and Major Burnaby explained his presence in a few succinct words.

'You are in charge of the case, Inspector Narracott?'

'Yes, Mr Kirkwood. In pursuance of my investigations, I have come to ask you for certain information.'

'I shall be happy to give you any information if it is proper for me to do so,' said the lawyer.

'It concerns the late Captain Trevelyan's will,' said Narracott. 'I understand the will is here in your office.'

'That is so.'

'It was made some time ago?'

'Five or six years ago. I cannot be sure of the exact date at the moment.'

'Ah! I am anxious, Mr Kirkwood, to know the contents of that will as soon as possible. It may have an important bearing on the case.'

'Indeed?' said the lawyer. 'Indeed! I should not have thought that, but naturally you know your own business best, Inspector. Well—' he glanced across at the other man. 'Major Burnaby and myself are joint executors of the will. If he has no objection—'

'None.'

'Then I see no reason why I should not accede to your request, Inspector.'

Taking a telephone that stood on his desk he spoke a few words down it. In two or three minutes a clerk entered the room and laid a sealed envelope in front of the lawyer. The clerk left the room, Mr Kirkwood picked up the envelope, slit it open with a paper knife and drew out a large and important-looking document, cleared his throat and began to read—

'I, Joseph Arthur Trevelyan, of Sittaford House, Sittaford, in the County of Devon, declare this to be my last will and testament which I make this thirteenth day of August nineteen hundred and twenty-six.

'(1) I appoint John Edward Burnaby of 1 The Cottages, Sittaford, and Frederick Kirkwood of Exhampton, to be the executors and trustees of this, my will.

'(2) I give to Robert Henry Evans, who has served me long and faithfully, the sum of £100 (one hundred pounds) free of legacy duty for his own benefit absolutely, provided that he is in my service at the time of my death and not under notice to leave whether given or received.

'(3) I give the said John Edward Burnaby, as a token of our friendship and of my affection and regard for him, all my trophies of sport, including my collection of heads and pelts of big game as well as any challenge cups and prizes awarded to me in any department of sport and any spoils of the chase in my possession.

'(4) I give all my real and personal property, not

otherwise disposed of by this, my will, or any codicil hereto, to my Trustees upon Trust that my Trustees shall sell, call in and convert the same into money.

'(5) My Trustees shall out of the moneys to arise out of such sale, calling in and conversion pay any funeral and testamentary expenses and debts, and the legacies given by this, my will, or any codicil hereto and all death duties and other moneys.

'(6) My Trustees shall hold the residue of such moneys or the investments for the time being, representing the same upon Trust to divide the same into four equal parts or shares.

'(7) Upon such division as aforesaid my Trustees shall hold one such equal fourth part or share upon Trust to pay the same to my sister Jennifer Gardner for her own use and enjoyment absolutely.

'And my Trustees shall hold the remaining three such equal fourth parts or shares upon Trust to pay one such equal fourth part or share to each of the three children of my deceased sister, Mary Pearson, for the benefit of each such child absolutely.

'In Witness whereof I, the said Joseph Arthur Trevelyan, have hereunto set my hand the day and year first above written.

'Signed by the above named Testator as his last will in the presence of us both present at the same time, who in his presence and at his request and in the presence of each other have hereunto subscribed our names as witness.'

Mr Kirkwood handed the document to the Inspector. 'Witnessed by two of my clerks in this office.'

The Inspector ran his eye over the will thoughtfully.

'"My deceased sister, Mary Pearson",' he said. 'Can you tell me anything about Mrs Pearson, Mr Kirkwood?'

'Very little. She died about ten years ago, I believe. Her husband, a stockbroker, had predeceased her. As far as I know, she never visited Captain Trevelyan here.'

'Pearson,' said the Inspector again. Then he added: 'One thing more. The amount of Captain Trevelyan's estate is not mentioned. To what sum do you think it will amount?'

'That is difficult to say exactly,' said Mr Kirkwood, enjoying, like all lawyers, making the reply to a simple question difficult. 'It is a question of real or personal estate. Besides Sittaford House, Captain Trevelyan owns some property in the neighbourhood of Plymouth, and various investments he made from time to time have fluctuated in value.'

'I just want an approximate idea,' said Inspector Narracott.

'I should not like to commit myself—'

'Just the roughest estimate as a guide. For instance would twenty thousand pounds be out of the way?'

'Twenty thousand pounds. My dear sir! Captain Trevelyan's estate will be worth at least four times as much as that. Eighty or even ninety thousand pounds will be much nearer the mark.'

'I told you Trevelyan was a rich man,' said Burnaby.

Inspector Narracott rose.

'Thank you very much, Mr Kirkwood,' he said, 'for the information you have given me.'

'You think you will find it helpful, eh?'

The lawyer very clearly was agog with curiosity, but Inspector Narracott was in no mood to satisfy it at present.

'In a case like this we have to take everything into account,' he said, noncommittally. 'By the way, have you the names and addresses of this Jennifer Gardner and of the Pearson family?'

'I know nothing of the Pearson family. Mrs Gardner's address is The Laurels, Waldon Road, Exeter.'

The Inspector noted it down in his book.

'That will do to get on with,' he said. 'You don't know how many children the late Mrs Pearson left?'

'Three, I fancy. Two girls and a boy—or possibly two boys and a girl—I cannot remember which.'

The Inspector nodded and put away his notebook and thanked the lawyer once more and took his departure.

When they had reached the street, he turned suddenly and faced his companion.

'And now, sir,' he said, 'we'll have the truth about the twenty-five past five business.'

Major Burnaby's face reddened with annoyance.

'I have told you already—'

'That won't go down with me. Withholding information, that is what you are doing, Major Burnaby. You must have had some idea in mentioning that specific time to Dr Warren—and I think I have a very good idea of what that something is.'

'Well, if you know about it, why ask me?' growled the Major.

'I take it that you were aware that a certain person had

an appointment with Captain Trevelyan somewhere about that time. Now, isn't that so?'

Major Burnaby stared at him in surprise.

'Nothing of the kind,' he snarled, 'nothing of the kind.'

'Be careful, Major Burnaby. What about Mr James Pearson?'

'James Pearson? James Pearson, who's he? Do you mean one of Trevelyan's nephews?'

'I presume it would be a nephew. He had one called James, hadn't he?'

'Not the least idea. Trevelyan had nephews—I know that. But what their names were, I haven't the vaguest idea.'

'The young man in question was at the Three Crowns last night. You probably recognized him there.'

'I didn't recognize anybody,' growled the Major. 'Shouldn't anyway—never saw any of Trevelyan's nephews in my life.'

'But you knew that Captain Trevelyan was expecting a nephew to call upon him yesterday afternoon?'

'I did not,' roared the Major.

Several people in the street turned round to stare at him.

'Damn it, won't you take plain truth! I knew nothing about any appointment. Trevelyan's nephews may have been in Timbuctoo for all I knew about them.'

Inspector Narracott was a little taken aback. The Major's vehement denial bore the mark of truth too plainly for him to be deceived.

'Then why this twenty-five past five business?'

'Oh! well—I suppose I had better tell you,' the Major coughed in an embarrassed fashion. 'But mind you—the whole thing is damned foolishness! Tommy rot, sir. How any thinking man can believe such nonsense!'

Agatha Christie

Inspector Narracott looked more and more surprised. Major Burnaby was looking more uncomfortable and ashamed of himself every minute.

'You know what it is, Inspector. You have to join in these things to please a lady. Of course, I never thought there was anything in it.'

'In what, Major Burnaby?'

'Table-turning.'

'*Table-turning?*'

Whatever Narracott had expected he had not expected this. The Major proceeded to explain himself. Haltingly, and with many disclaimers of his own belief in the thing, he described the events of the previous afternoon and the message that had purported to come through for himself.

'You mean, Major Burnaby, that the table spelt out the name of Trevelyan and informed you that he was dead— murdered?'

Major Burnaby wiped his forehead.

'Yes, that's what happened. I didn't believe in it— naturally, I didn't believe in it.' He looked ashamed. 'Well—it was Friday and I thought after all I would make sure and go along and see if everything was all right.'

The Inspector reflected on the difficulties of that six mile walk, with the piled-up snowdrifts and the prospect of a heavy snowfall, and he realized that deny it as he would Major Burnaby must have been deeply impressed by the spirit message. Narracott turned it over in his mind. A queer thing to happen—a very queer thing to happen. The sort of thing you couldn't explain satisfactorily. There might be something in this spirit business after all. It was the first well-authenticated case he had come across.

A very queer business altogether but, as far as he could see, though it explained Major Burnaby's attitude, it had no practical bearing on the case as far as he himself was concerned. He had to deal with the physical world and not the psychic.

It was his job to track down the murderer.

And to do that he required no guidance from the spirit world.

CHAPTER 8

Mr Charles Enderby

Glancing at his watch, the Inspector realized he could just catch the train for Exeter if he hurried off. He was anxious to interview the late Captain Trevelyan's sister as soon as possible and obtain from her the addresses of the other members of the family. So, with a hurried word of farewell to Major Burnaby, he raced off to the station. The Major retraced his steps to the Three Crowns. He had hardly put a foot across the doorstep when he was accosted by a bright young man with a very shiny head and a round, boyish face.

'Major Burnaby?' said the young man.

'Yes.'

'Of No. I Sittaford Cottages?'

'Yes,' said Major Burnaby.

'I represent the *Daily Wire*,' said the young man, 'and I—'

He got no further. In true military fashion of the old school, the Major exploded.

'Not another word,' he roared. 'I know you and your

kind. No decency. No reticence. Clustering round a murder like vultures round a carcass, but I can tell you, young man, you will get no information from me. Not a word. No story for your damned paper. If you want to know anything, go and ask the police, and have the decency to leave the friends of the dead man alone.'

The young man seemed not a whit taken aback. He smiled more encouragingly than ever.

'I say, sir, you know you have got hold of the wrong end of the stick. I know nothing about this murder business.'

This was not, strictly speaking, the truth. No one in Exhampton could pretend ignorance of the event that had shaken the quiet moorland town to its core.

'I am empowered on behalf of the *Daily Wire*,' went on the young man, 'to hand you this cheque for £5,000 and congratulate you on sending in the only correct solution of our football competition.'

Major Burnaby was completely taken aback.

'I have no doubt,' continued the young man, 'that you have already received our letter yesterday morning informing you of the good news.'

'Letter?' said Major Burnaby. 'Do you realize, young man, that Sittaford is about ten feet deep in snow? What chance do you think we have had in the last few days of a regular delivery of letters?'

'But doubtless you saw your name announced as winner in the *Daily Wire*, this morning?'

'No,' said Major Burnaby. 'I haven't glanced at the paper this morning.'

'Ah! of course not,' said the young man. 'This sad business. The murdered man was a friend of yours, I understand.'

'My best friend,' said the Major.

'Hard lines,' said the young man tactfully averting his eyes. Then he drew from his pocket a small folded piece of mauve paper and handed it to Major Burnaby with a bow.

'With the compliments of the *Daily Wire*,' he said.

Major Burnaby took it and said the only thing possible under the circumstances.

'Have a drink, Mr—er—?'

'Enderby, Charles Enderby my name is. I got here last night,' he explained. 'Made inquiries about getting to Sittaford. We make it a point to hand cheques to winners personally. Always publish a little interview. Interests our readers. Well, everyone told me it was out of the question— the snow was falling and it simply couldn't be done, and then with the greatest good luck I find you are actually here, staying at the Three Crowns.' He smiled. 'No difficulty about identification. Everybody seems to know everybody else in this part of the world.'

'What will you have?' said the Major.

'Beer for me,' said Enderby.

The Major ordered two beers.

'The whole place seems off its head with this murder,' remarked Enderby. 'Rather a mysterious business by all accounts.'

The Major grunted. He was in something of a quandary. His sentiments towards journalists remained unchanged, but a man who has just handed you a cheque for £5,000 is in a privileged position. You cannot very well tell him to go to the devil.

'No enemies, had he?' asked the young man.

'No,' said the Major.

'But I hear the police don't think it is robbery,' went on Enderby.

'How do you know that?' asked the Major.

Mr Enderby, however, did not reveal the source of his information.

'I hear it was you who actually discovered the body, sir,' said the young man.

'Yes.'

'It must have been an awful shock.'

The conversation proceeded. Major Burnaby was still determined to give no information, but he was no match for the adroitness of Mr Enderby. The latter made statements with which the Major was forced to agree or disagree, thereby providing the information the young man wanted. So pleasant was his manner, however, that the process was really not painful at all and the Major found himself taking quite a liking to the ingenuous young man.

Presently, Mr Enderby rose and observed that he must go along to the post office.

'If you will just give me a receipt for that cheque, sir.'

The Major went across to the writing table, wrote a receipt and handed it to him.

'Splendid,' said the young man and slipped it into his pocket.

'I suppose,' said Major Burnaby, 'that you are off back to London today?'

'Oh! no,' said the young man. 'I want to take a few photographs, you know, of your cottage at Sittaford, and of you feeding the pigs, or hoeing up the dandelions, or doing anything characteristic that you fancy. You have no idea how our readers appreciate that sort of thing. Then I would like to have a few words from you on "What I intend to do with the £5,000". Something snappy. You have no idea how disappointed our readers would be if they didn't get that sort of thing.'

'Yes, but look here—it's impossible to get to Sittaford in this weather. The fall of snow was exceptionally heavy. No vehicle has been able to take the road for three days anyway, and it may be another three before the thaw sets in properly.'

'I know,' said the young man, 'it *is* awkward. Well, well, one will just have to resign oneself to kicking up one's heels in Exhampton. They do you pretty well at the Three Crowns. So long, sir, see you later.'

He emerged into the main street of Exhampton and made his way to the post office and wired his paper that by the greatest of good luck he would be able to supply them with tasty and exclusive information on the Exhampton Murder Case.

He reflected on his next course of action and decided on interviewing the late Captain Trevelyan's servant, Evans, whose name Major Burnaby had incautiously let slip during their conversation.

A few inquiries brought him to 85 Fore Street. The

servant of the murdered man was a person of importance today. Everyone was willing and anxious to point out where he lived.

Enderby beat a smart rat-tat on the door. It was opened by a man so typically an ex-sailor that Enderby had no doubt of his identity.

'Evans, isn't it?' said Enderby cheerfully. 'I have just come along from Major Burnaby.'

'Oh—' Evans hesitated a moment. 'Will you come in, sir.'

Enderby accepted the invitation. A buxom young woman with dark hair and red cheeks hovered in the background. Enderby judged her as the newly-wed Mrs Evans.

'Bad thing about your late master,' said Enderby.

'It's shocking, sir, that's what it is.'

'Who do you think did it?' demanded Enderby with an ingenuous air of seeking information.

'One of those low-down tramps, I suppose,' said Evans.

'Oh! no, my dear man. That theory is quite exploded.'

'Eh?'

'That's all a put-up job. The police saw through that at once.'

'Who told you that, sir?'

Enderby's real informant had been the housemaid at the Three Crowns whose sister was the legal spouse of Constable Graves, but he replied:

'Had a tip from headquarters. Yes, the burglary idea was all a put-up job.'

'Who do they think did it then?' demanded Mrs Evans, coming forward. Her eyes looked frightened and eager.

'Now, Rebecca, don't you take on so,' said her husband.

'Cruel stupid the police are,' said Mrs Evans. 'Don't mind who they take up as long as they get hold of someone.' She cast a quick glance at Enderby.

'Are you connected with the police, sir?'

'Me? Oh! no. I am from a newspaper, the *Daily Wire*. I came down to see Major Burnaby. He has just won our Free Football Competition for £5,000.'

'What?' cried Evans. 'Damn it all, then these things are square after all.'

'Didn't you think they were?' asked Enderby.

'Well, it's a wicked world, sir.' Evans was a little confused, feeling that his exclamation had been wanting in tact. 'I have heard there's a lot of trickery concerned. The late Capting used to say that a prize never went to a good address. That's why he used mine time and again.'

With a certain naïveté he described the Captain's winning of three new novels.

Enderby encouraged him to talk. He saw a very good story being made out of Evans. The faithful servant—old sea dog touch. He wondered just a little why Mrs Evans seemed so nervous; he put it down to the suspicious ignorance of her class.

'You find the skunk that done it,' said Evans. 'Newspapers can do a lot, they say, in hunting down criminals.'

'It was a burglar,' said Mrs Evans. 'That's what it was.'

'Of course, it was a burglar,' said Evans. 'Why, there's no one in Exhampton would want to harm the Capting.'

Enderby rose.

'Well,' he said. 'I must be going. I will run in now and

then and have a little chat if I may. If the Captain won three new novels in a *Daily Wire* Competition, the *Daily Wire* ought to make it a personal matter to hunt down his murderer.'

'You can't say fairer than that, sir. No, you can't say fairer than that.'

Wishing them a cheery good day, Charles Enderby took his leave.

'I wonder who really did the beggar in?' he murmured to himself. 'I don't think our friend Evans. Perhaps it *was* a burglar! Very disappointing, if so. Doesn't seem any woman in the case, which is a pity. We've got to have some sensational development soon or the case will fade into insignificance. Just my luck, if so. First time I have ever been on the spot in a matter of this kind. I must make good. Charles, my boy, your chance in life has come. Make the most of it. Our military friend will, I see, soon be eating out of my hand if I remember to be sufficiently respectful and call him "sir" often enough. Wonder if he was in the Indian Mutiny. No, of course not, not old enough for that. The South African War, that's it. Ask him about the South African War, that will tame him.'

And pondering these good resolutions in his mind Mr Enderby sauntered back to the Three Crowns.

CHAPTER 9

The Laurels

It takes about half an hour from Exhampton to Exeter by train. At five minutes to twelve Inspector Narracott was ringing the front door bell of The Laurels.

The Laurels was a somewhat dilapidated house, badly in need of a new coat of paint. The garden round it was unkempt and weedy and the gate hung askew on its hinges.

'Not too much money about here,' thought Inspector Narracott to himself. 'Evidently hard up.'

He was a very fair-minded man, but inquiries seemed to indicate that there was very little possibility of the Captain's having been done to death by an enemy. On the other hand, four people, as far as he could make out, stood to gain a considerable sum by the old man's death. The movements of each of these four people had got to be inquired into. The entry in the hotel register was suggestive, but after all Pearson was quite a common name. Inspector Narracott was anxious not to come to any decision too rapidly and to keep a perfectly open mind whilst covering the preliminary ground as rapidly as possible.

A somewhat slatternly-looking maid answered the bell.

'Good afternoon,' said Inspector Narracott. 'I want to see Mrs Gardner, please. It is in connection with the death of her brother, Captain Trevelyan, at Exhampton.'

He purposely did not hand his official card to the maid. The mere fact of his being a police officer, as he knew by experience, would render her awkward and tongue-tied.

'She's heard of her brother's death?' asked the Inspector casually as the maid drew back to let him into the hall.

'Yes, got a telegram she did. From the lawyer, Mr Kirkwood.'

'Just so,' said Inspector Narracott.

The maid ushered him into the drawing-room—a room which, like the outside of the house, was badly in need of a little money spent upon it, but yet had, with all that, an air of charm which the Inspector felt without being able to particularize the why and wherefore of it.

'Must have been a shock to your mistress,' he observed.

The girl seemed a little vague about that, he noticed.

'She didn't see much of him,' was her answer.

'Shut the door and come here,' said Inspector Narracott. He was anxious to try the effect of a surprise attack.

'Did the telegram say that it was murder?' he asked.

'Murder!'

The girl's eyes opened wide, a mixture of horror and intense enjoyment in them. 'Murdered, was he?'

'Ah!' said Inspector Narracott, 'I thought you hadn't heard that. Mr Kirkwood didn't want to break the news too abruptly to your mistress, but you see, my dear—what is your name, by the way?'

'Beatrice, sir.'

'Well, you see, Beatrice, it will be in the evening papers tonight.'

'Well, I never,' said Beatrice. 'Murdered, 'orrible, isn't it? Did they bash his head in or shoot him or what?'

The Inspector satisfied her passion for detail, then added casually, 'I believe there was some idea of your mistress going over to Exhampton yesterday afternoon. But I suppose the weather was too bad for her.'

'I never heard anything about it, sir,' said Beatrice. 'I think you must have made a mistake. The mistress went out in the afternoon to do some shopping and then she went to the pictures.'

'What time did she get in?'

'About six o'clock.'

So that let Mrs Gardner out.

'I don't know much about the family,' he went on in a casual voice. 'Is Mrs Gardner a widow?'

'Oh, no, sir, there's master.'

'What does he do?'

'He doesn't do anything,' said Beatrice staring. 'He can't. He's an invalid.'

'An invalid, is he? Oh, I'm sorry. I hadn't heard.'

'He can't walk. He lies in bed all day. Got a nurse always in the house we have. It isn't every girl what stays on with an 'ospital nurse in the house the whole time. Always wanting trays carried up and pots of tea made.'

'Must be very trying,' said the Inspector soothingly. 'Now, will you go and tell your mistress, please, that I am here from Mr Kirkwood of Exhampton.'

Beatrice withdrew, and a few minutes later the door opened and a tall, rather commanding woman came into the room. She had an unusual-looking face, broad about the brows, and black hair with a touch of grey at the temples, which she wore combed straight back from her forehead. She looked at the Inspector inquiringly.

'You have come from Mr Kirkwood at Exhampton?'

'Not exactly, Mrs Gardner. I put it that way to your maid. Your brother, Captain Trevelyan, was murdered yesterday afternoon and I am Divisional Inspector Narracott in charge of the case.'

Whatever else Mrs Gardner might be she was certainly a woman of iron nerve. Her eyes narrowed and she drew in her breath sharply, then motioning the Inspector to a chair and sitting down herself she said:

'Murdered! How extraordinary! Who in the world would want to murder Joe?'

'That is what I'm anxious to find out, Mrs Gardner.'

'Of course. I hope I shall be able to help you in some way, but I doubt it. My brother and I have seen very little of each other in the last ten years. I know nothing of his friends or of any ties he has formed.'

'You'll excuse me, Mrs Gardner, but had you and your brother quarrelled?'

'No—not quarrelled. I think estranged would be a better word to describe the position between us. I don't want to go into family details, but my brother rather resented my marriage. Brothers, I think, seldom approve of their sisters' choice, but usually, I fancy, they conceal it better than my brother did. My brother, as perhaps you know, had a large fortune left him by an aunt. Both my sister and myself married poor men. When my husband was invalided out of the army after the war with shell shock, a little financial assistance would have been a wonderful relief—would have enabled me to give him an expensive course of treatment which was otherwise denied to him. I asked my brother for a loan which he refused. That, of course, he was perfectly entitled to do. But since then we have met at very rare intervals, and hardly corresponded at all.'

It was a clear succinct statement.

An intriguing personality, this Mrs Gardner's, the Inspector thought. Somehow, he couldn't quite make her out. She seemed unnaturally calm, unnaturally ready with her recital of facts. He also noticed that, with all her surprise, she asked for no details of her brother's death. That struck him as extraordinary.

'I don't know if you want to hear what exactly occurred—at Exhampton,' he began.

She frowned.

'Must I hear it? My brother was killed—painlessly, I hope.'

'Quite painlessly, I should say.'

'Then please spare me any revolting details.'

'Unnatural,' thought the Inspector, 'decidedly unnatural.'

As though she had read his mind she used the word that he had spoken to himself.

'I suppose you think that very unnatural, Inspector, but—I have heard a good many horrors. My husband has told me things when he has had one of his bad turns—' she shivered. 'I think you would understand if you knew my circumstances better.'

'Oh! quite so, quite so, Mrs Gardner. What I really came for was to get a few family details from you.'

'Yes?'

'Do you know how many relatives living your brother has besides yourself?'

'Of near relations, only the Pearsons. My sister Mary's children.'

'And they are?'

'James, Sylvia and Brian.'

'James?'

'He is the eldest. He works in an insurance office.'

'What age is he?'

'Twenty-eight.'

'Is he married?'

'No, but he is engaged—to a very nice girl, I believe. I've not yet met her.'

'And his address?'

'21 Cromwell Street, S.W.3.'

The Inspector noted it down.

'Yes, Mrs Gardner?'

'Then there's Sylvia. She's married to Martin Dering— you may have read his books. He's a moderately successful author.'

'Thank you, and their address?'

'The Nook, Surrey Road, Wimbledon.'

'Yes?'

'And the youngest is Brian—but he is out in Australia. I am afraid I don't know his address, but either his brother or sister would know.'

'Thank you, Mrs Gardner. Just a matter of form, do

you mind my asking you how you spent yesterday afternoon?'

She looked surprised.

'Let me see. I did some shopping—yes—then I went to the pictures. I came home about six and lay down on my bed until dinner, as the pictures had given me rather a headache.'

'Thank you, Mrs Gardner.'

'Is there anything else?'

'No, I don't think I have anything further to ask you. I will now get into communication with your nephew and niece. I don't know if Mr Kirkwood has informed you of the fact yet, but you and the three young Pearsons are the joint inheritors of Captain Trevelyan's money.'

The colour came into her face in a slow, rich blush.

'That will be wonderful,' she said quietly. 'It has been so difficult—so terribly difficult—always skimping and saving and wishing.'

She started up as a man's rather querulous voice came floating down the stairs.

'Jennifer, Jennifer, I want you.'

'Excuse me,' she said.

As she opened the door the call came again, louder and more imperiously.

'Jennifer, where are you? I want you, Jennifer.'

The Inspector had followed her to the door. He stood in the hall looking after her as she ran up the stairs.

'I am coming, dear,' she called.

A hospital nurse who was coming down the stairs stood aside to let her pass up.

'Please go to Mr Gardner, he is getting very excited. You always manage to calm him.'

Inspector Narracott stood deliberately in the nurse's way as she reached the bottom of the stairs.

'May I speak to you for a moment?' he said. 'My conversation with Mrs Gardner was interrupted.'

The nurse came with alacrity into the drawing-room.

'The news of the murder has upset my patient,' she explained, adjusting a well-starched cuff. 'That foolish girl, Beatrice, came running up and blurted it all out.'

'I am sorry,' said the Inspector. 'I am afraid that was my fault.'

'Oh, of course, you couldn't be expected to know,' said the nurse graciously.

'Is Mr Gardner dangerously ill?' inquired the Inspector.

'It's a sad case,' said the nurse. 'Of course, in a manner of speaking, there's nothing the matter with him really. He's lost the use of his limbs entirely through nervous shock. There's no visible disability.'

'He had no extra strain or shock yesterday afternoon?' inquired the Inspector.

'Not that I know of,' the nurse looked somewhat surprised.

'You were with him all the afternoon?'

'I intended to be, but, well—as a matter of fact, Captain Gardner was very anxious for me to change two books for him at the library. He had forgotten to ask his wife before she went out. So, to oblige him I went out with them, and he asked me at the same time to get one or two little things for him—presents for his wife as a matter of fact. Very nice about it he was, and told me I was to have tea at his expense at Boots. He said nurses never liked missing their tea. His little joke, you know. I didn't get out until past four, and what with the shops being so full just before Christmas, and one thing and another, I didn't get back until after six, but the poor fellow had been quite comfortable. In fact, he told me he had been asleep most of the time.'

'Mrs Gardner was back by then?'

'Yes, I believe she was lying down.'

'She's very devoted to her husband, isn't she?'

'She worships him. I really do believe that woman would do anything in the world for him. Quite touching, and very different from some of the cases I have attended. Why, only last month—'

But Inspector Narracott fended off the impending scandal of last month with considerable skill. He glanced at his watch and gave a loud exclamation.

'Goodness gracious,' he cried, 'I shall miss my train. The station is not far away, is it?'

'St David's is only three minutes' walk, if it's St David's you want, or did you mean Queen Street?'

'I must run,' said the Inspector, 'tell Mrs Gardner I am sorry not to have seen her to say goodbye. Very pleased to have had this little chat with you, nurse.'

The nurse bridled ever so slightly.

'Rather a good-looking man,' she said to herself as the front door shut after the Inspector. 'Really quite good-looking. Such a nice sympathetic manner.'

And with a slight sigh she went upstairs to her patient.

CHAPTER 10

The Pearson Family

Inspector Narracott's next move was to report to his superior, Superintendent Maxwell.

The latter listened with interest to the Inspector's narrative.

'It's going to be a big case,' he said thoughtfully. 'There'll be headlines in the papers over this.'

'I agree with you, sir.'

'We've got to be careful. We don't want to make any mistake. But I think you're on the right track. You must get after this James Pearson as soon as possible—find out where he was yesterday afternoon. As you say, it's a common enough name, but there's the Christian name as well. Of course, his signing his own name openly like that shows there wasn't any premeditation about it. He'd hardly have been such a fool otherwise. It looks to me like a quarrel and a sudden blow. If it is the man, he must have heard of his uncle's death that night. And if so, why did he sneak off by the six train in the morning without a word to anyone? No, it looks bad. Always granting that the whole thing's not a coincidence. You must clear that up as quickly as possible.'

'That's what I thought, sir. I'd better take the 1.45 to town. Some time or other I want to have a word with this Willett woman who rented the Captain's house. There's something fishy there. But I can't get to Sittaford at present, the roads are impassable with snow. And anyway, she can't have any direct connection with the crime. She and her daughter were actually—well—table-turning at the time the crime was committed. And, by the way, rather a queer thing happened—'

The Inspector narrated the story he had heard from Major Burnaby.

'That's a rum go,' ejaculated the Superintendent. 'Think this old fellow was telling the truth? That's the sort of story that gets cooked up afterwards by those believers in spooks and things of that kind.'

'I fancy it's true all right,' said Narracott with a grin. 'I had a lot of difficulty getting it out of him. *He's* not a believer—just the opposite—old soldier, all damned nonsense attitude.'

The Superintendent nodded his comprehension.

'Well, it's odd, but it doesn't get us anywhere,' was his conclusion.

'Then I'll take the 1.45 to London.'

The other nodded.

On arrival in town Narracott went straight to 21 Cromwell Street. Mr Pearson, he was told, was at the office. He would be back for certain about seven o'clock.

Narracott nodded carelessly as though the information were of no value to him.

'I'll call back if I can,' he said. 'It's nothing of importance,' and departed quickly without leaving a name.

He decided not to go to the insurance office, but to visit Wimbledon instead and have an interview with Mrs Martin Dering, formerly Miss Sylvia Pearson.

There were no signs of shabbiness about The Nook. 'New and shoddy,' was how Inspector Narracott described it to himself.

Mrs Dering was at home. A rather pert-looking maid dressed in lilac colour showed him into a rather over-crowded drawing-room. He gave her his official card to take to her mistress.

Mrs Dering came to him almost immediately, his card in her hand.

'I suppose you have come about poor Uncle Joseph,' was her greeting. 'It's shocking—really shocking! I am so dreadfully nervous of burglars myself. I had two extra bolts put on the back door last week, and new patent catches on the windows.'

Sylvia Dering, the Inspector knew from Mrs Gardner, was only twenty-five, but she looked considerably over thirty. She was small and fair and anaemic-looking, with a worried and harassed expression. Her voice had that faintly complaining note in it which is about the most annoying sound a human voice can contain. Still not allowing the Inspector to speak, she went on:

'If there's anything I can do to help you in any way, of course, I shall be only too glad to do so, but one hardly ever saw Uncle Joseph. He wasn't a very nice man—I am sure he couldn't have been. Not the sort of person one could go to in trouble, always carping and criticizing. Not the sort of man who had any knowledge of what literature meant. Success—true success is not always measured in terms of money, Inspector.'

At last she paused, and the Inspector, to whom those remarks had opened certain fields of conjecture, was given his turn to speak.

'You've heard of the tragedy very quickly, Mrs Dering.'

'Aunt Jennifer wired it to me.'

'I see.'

'But I suppose it will be in the evening papers. Dreadful, isn't it?'

'I gather you've not seen your uncle of late years.'

'I have only seen him twice since my marriage. On the second occasion he was really very rude to Martin. Of course he was a regular philistine in every way—devoted to sport. No appreciation, as I said just now, of literature.'

'Husband applied to him for a loan and got refused,' was Inspector Narracott's private comment on the situation.

'Just as a matter of form, Mrs Dering, will you tell me what your movements were yesterday afternoon?'

'My movements? What a very queer way of putting it, Inspector. I played bridge most of the afternoon and a friend came in and spent the evening with me, as my husband was out.'

'Out, was he? Away from home altogether?'

'A literary dinner,' explained Mrs Dering with importance. 'He lunched with an American publisher and had this dinner in the evening.'

'I see.'

That seemed quite fair and above board. He went on.

'Your younger brother is in Australia, I believe, Mrs Dering?'

'Yes.'

'You have his address?'

'Oh, yes, I can find it for you if you wish—rather a peculiar name—I've forgotten it for the minute. Somewhere in New South Wales.'

'And now, Mrs Dering, your elder brother?'

'Jim?'

'Yes. I shall want to get in touch with him.'

Mrs Dering hastened to supply him with the address—the same as that which Mrs Gardner had already given him.

Then, feeling there was no more to be said on either side, he cut the interview short.

Glancing at his watch, he noted that by the time he had returned to town it would be seven o'clock—a likely time, he hoped, for finding Mr James Pearson at home.

The same superior-looking, middle-aged woman opened the door of No. 21. Yes, Mr Pearson was at home now. It was on the second floor, if the gentleman would walk up.

She preceded him, tapped at a door, and in a murmured and apologetic voice said: 'The gentleman to see you, sir.' Then, standing back, allowed the Inspector to enter.

A young man in evening dress was standing in the middle of the room. He was good-looking, indeed handsome, if you took no account of the rather weak mouth and the irresolute slant of the eye. He had a haggard, worried look and an air of not having had much sleep of late.

He looked inquiringly at the Inspector as the latter advanced.

'I am Detective Inspector Narracott,' he began—but got no further.

With a hoarse cry the young man dropped on to a chair, flung his arms out in front of him on the table, bowing his head on them and muttering:

'Oh! my God! It's come.'

After a minute or two he lifted his head and said, 'Well, why don't you get on with it, man?'

Inspector Narracott looked exceedingly stolid and unintelligent.

'I am investigating the death of your uncle, Captain Joseph Trevelyan. May I ask you, sir, if you have anything to say?'

The young man rose slowly to his feet and said in a low strained voice:

'Are you—arresting me?'

'No, sir, I am not. If I was arresting you I would give you the customary caution. I am simply asking you to account for your movements yesterday afternoon. You may reply to my questions or not as you see fit.'

'And if I don't reply to them—it will tell against me. Oh, yes, I know your little ways. You've found out then that I was down there yesterday?'

'You signed your name in the hotel register, Mr Pearson.'

'Oh, I suppose there's no use denying it. I *was* there—why shouldn't I be?'

'Why indeed?' said the Inspector mildly.

'I went down there to see my uncle.'

'By appointment?'

'What do you mean, by appointment?'

'Did your uncle know you were coming?'

'I—no—he didn't. It—it was a sudden impulse.'

'No reason for it?'

'I—reason? No—no, why should there be? I—I just wanted to see my uncle.'

'Quite so, sir. And you did see him?'

There was a pause—a very long pause. Indecision was written on every feature of the young man's face. Inspector Narracott felt a kind of pity as he watched him. Couldn't the boy see that his palpable indecision was as good as an admission of the fact?

At last Jim Pearson drew a deep breath. 'I—I suppose I had better make a clean breast of it. Yes—I did see him. I asked at the station how I could get to Sittaford. They told me it was out of the question. The roads were impassable for any vehicle. I said it was urgent.'

'Urgent?' murmured the Inspector.

'I—I wanted to see my uncle very much.'

'So it seems, sir.'

'The porter continued to shake his head and say that it was impossible. I mentioned my uncle's name and at once his face cleared up, and he told me my uncle was actually in Exhampton, and gave me full directions as to how to find the house he had rented.'

'This was at what time, sir?'

'About one o'clock, I think. I went to the inn—the Three Crowns—booked a room and had some lunch there. Then afterwards I—I went out to see my uncle.'

'Immediately afterwards?'

'No, not immediately.'

'What time was it?'

'Well, I couldn't say for certain.'

'Half past three? Four o'clock? Half past four?'

'I—I—' he stammered worse than ever. 'I don't think it could have been as late as that.'

'Mrs Belling, the proprietress, said you went out at half past four.'

'Did I? I—I think she's wrong. It couldn't have been as late as that.'

'What happened next?'

'I found my uncle's house, had a talk with him and came back to the inn.'

'How did you get into your uncle's house?'

'I rang the bell and he opened the door to me himself.'

'Wasn't he surprised to see you?'

'Yes—yes—he was rather surprised.'

'How long did you remain with him, Mr Pearson?'

'A quarter of an hour—twenty minutes. But look here, he was perfectly all right when I left him. Perfectly all right. I swear it.'

'And what time *did* you leave him?'

The young man lowered his eyes. Again, the hesitation was palpable in his tone. 'I don't know exactly.'

'I think you do, Mr Pearson.'

The assured tone had its effect. The boy replied in a low tone.

'It was a quarter past five.'

'You returned to the Three Crowns at a quarter to six.

At most it could only take you seven or eight minutes to walk over from your uncle's house.'

'I didn't go straight back. I walked about the town.'

'In that icy weather—in the snow!'

'It wasn't actually snowing then. It came on to snow later.'

'I see. And what was the nature of your conversation with your uncle?'

'Oh! nothing in particular. I—I just wanted to talk to the old boy, look him up, that sort of thing, you know.'

'He's a poor liar,' thought Inspector Narracott to himself. 'Why, I could manage better than that myself.'

Aloud he said:

'Very good, sir. Now, may I ask you why, on hearing of your uncle's murder, you left Exhampton without disclosing your relationship to the murdered man?'

'I was scared,' said the young man frankly. 'I heard he had been murdered round about the time I left him. Now, dash it all, that's enough to scare anyone, isn't it? I got the wind up and left the place by the first available train. Oh, I dare say I was a fool to do anything of the sort. But you know what it is when you are rattled. And anyone might have been rattled under these circumstances.'

'And that's all you have to say, sir?'

'Yes—yes, of course.'

'Then, perhaps you'll have no objection, sir, to coming round with me and having this statement taken down in writing, after which you will have it read over to you, and you will sign it.'

'Is—is that all?'

'I think it possible, Mr Pearson, that it may be necessary to detain you until after the inquest.'

'Oh! my God,' said Jim Pearson. 'Can nobody help me?'

At that moment the door opened and a young woman walked into the room.

She was, as the observant Inspector Narracott noted at once, a very exceptional kind of young woman. She was not strikingly beautiful, but she had a face which was arresting and unusual, a face that having once seen you could not forget. There was about her an atmosphere of common sense, *savoir faire*, invincible determination and a most tantalizing fascination.

'Oh! Jim,' she exclaimed. 'What's happened?'

'It's all over, Emily,' said the young man. 'They think I murdered my uncle.'

'Who thinks so?' demanded Emily.

The young man indicated his visitor by a gesture.

'This is Inspector Narracott,' he said, and he added with a dismal attempt at introduction, 'Miss Emily Trefusis.'

'Oh!' said Emily Trefusis.

She studied Inspector Narracott with keen hazel eyes.

'Jim,' she said, 'is a frightful idiot. But he doesn't murder people.'

The Inspector said nothing.

'I expect,' said Emily, turning to Jim, 'that you've been saying the most frightfully imprudent things. If you read the papers a little better than you do, Jim, you would know that you must never talk to policemen unless you have a strong solicitor sitting beside you making objections to every word. What's happened? Are you arresting him, Inspector Narracott?'

Inspector Narracott explained technically and clearly exactly what he was doing.

'Emily,' cried the young man, 'you won't believe I did it? You never will believe it, will you?'

'No, darling,' said Emily kindly. 'Of course not.' And she added in a gentle meditative tone, 'You haven't got the guts.'

'I don't feel as if I had a friend in the world,' groaned Jim.

'Yes, you have,' said Emily. 'You've got me. Cheer up, Jim, look at the winking diamonds on the third finger of my left hand. Here stands the faithful fiancée. Go with the Inspector and leave everything to me.'

Jim Pearson rose, still with a dazed expression on his face. His overcoat was lying over a chair and he put it on. Inspector Narracott handed him a hat which was lying on a bureau near by. They moved towards the door and the Inspector said politely:

'Good evening, Miss Trefusis.'

'Au revoir, Inspector,' said Emily sweetly.

And if he had known Miss Emily Trefusis better he would have known that in these three words lay a challenge.

CHAPTER 11

Emily Sets to Work

The inquest on the body of Captain Trevelyan was held on Monday morning. From the point of view of sensation it was a tame affair, for it was almost immediately adjourned for a week, thus disappointing large numbers of people. Between Saturday and Monday Exhampton had sprung into fame. The knowledge that the dead man's nephew had been detained in connection with the murder made the whole affair spring from a mere paragraph in the back pages of the newspapers to gigantic headlines. On the Monday, reporters had arrived at Exhampton in large numbers. Mr Charles Enderby had reason once more to congratulate himself on the superior position he had obtained from the purely fortuitous chance of the football competition prize.

It was the journalist's intention to stick to Major Burnaby like a leech, and under the pretext of photographing the latter's cottage, to obtain exclusive information of the inhabitants of Sittaford and their relations with the dead man.

It did not escape Mr Enderby's notice that at lunch time a small table near the door was occupied by a very attractive girl. Mr Enderby wondered what she was doing in Exhampton. She was well dressed in a demure and provocative style, and did not appear to be a relation of the deceased, and still less could be labelled as one of the idle curious.

'I wonder how long she's staying?' thought Mr Enderby. 'Rather a pity I am going up to Sittaford this afternoon. Just my luck. Well, you can't have it both ways, I suppose.'

But shortly after lunch, Mr Enderby received an agreeable surprise. He was standing on the steps of the Three Crowns observing the fast melting snow, and enjoying the sluggish rays of wintry sunshine, when he was aware of a voice, an extremely charming voice, addressing him.

'I beg your pardon—but could you tell me—if there is anything to see in Exhampton?'

Charles Enderby rose to the occasion promptly.

'There's a castle, I believe,' he said. 'Not much to it—but there it is. Perhaps you would allow me to show you the way to it.'

'That would be frightfully kind of you,' said the girl. 'If you are sure you are not too busy—'

Charles Enderby disclaimed immediately the notion of being busy.

They set out together.

'You are Mr Enderby, aren't you?' said the girl.

'Yes. How did you know?'

'Mrs Belling pointed you out to me.'

'Oh, I see.'

'My name is Emily Trefusis. Mr Enderby—I want you to help me.'

'To help you?' said Enderby. 'Why, certainly—but—'

'You see, I am engaged to Jim Pearson.'

'Oh!' said Mr Enderby, journalistic possibilities rising before his mind.

'And the police are going to arrest him. I know they are. Mr Enderby, I *know* that Jim didn't do this thing. I am down here to prove he didn't. But I must have someone to help me. One can't do anything without a man. Men know so much, and are able to get information in so many ways that are simply impossible to women.'

'Well—I—yes, I suppose that is true,' said Mr Enderby complacently.

'I was looking at all these journalists this morning,' said Emily. 'Such a lot of them I thought had such stupid faces. I picked you out as the one really clever one among them.'

'Oh! I say. I don't think that's true, you know,' said Mr Enderby still more complacently.

'What I want to propose,' said Emily Trefusis, 'is a kind of partnership. There would, I think, be advantages on both sides. There are certain things I want to investigate— to find out about. There you in your character of journalist can help me. I want—'

Emily paused. What she really wanted was to engage Mr Enderby as a kind of private sleuth of her own. To go where she told him, to ask the questions she wanted asked, and in general to be a kind of bond slave. But she was aware of the necessity of couching these proposals in terms at once flattering and agreeable. The whole point was that she was to be the boss, but the matter needed managing tactfully.

'I want,' said Emily, 'to feel that I can *depend* upon you.'

She had a lovely voice, liquid and alluring. As she uttered the last sentence a feeling rose in Mr Enderby's bosom that this lovely helpless girl could depend upon him to the last ditch.

'It must be ghastly,' said Mr Enderby, and taking her hand he squeezed it with fervour.

'But you know,' he went on with a journalistic reaction, 'my time is not entirely my own. I mean, I have got to go where I am sent, and all that.'

'Yes,' said Emily. 'I have thought of that, and that you see is where I come in. Surely I am what you call a "scoop", aren't I? You can do an interview with me every day, you can make me say anything that you think your readers will like. *Jim Pearson's fiancée. Girl who believes passionately in his innocence. Reminiscences of his childhood which she supplies.* I don't really know about his childhood, you know,' she added, 'but that doesn't matter.'

'I think,' said Mr Enderby, 'that you are marvellous. You really are marvellous.'

'And then,' said Emily pursuing her advantage, 'I have access naturally to Jim's relations. I can get you in there as a friend of mine, where quite possibly you might have the door shut in your face any other way.'

'Don't I know that only too well,' said Mr Enderby with feeling, recalling various rebuffs of the past.

A glorious prospect opened out before him. He had been

in luck over this affair all round. First the lucky chance of the football competition, and now this.

'It's a deal,' he said fervently.

'Good,' said Emily becoming brisk and business-like. 'Now, what's the first move?'

'I'm going up to Sittaford this afternoon.'

He explained the fortunate circumstance which had put him in such an advantageous position with regard to Major Burnaby. 'Because, mind you, he is the kind of old buffer that hates newspaper men like poison. But you can't exactly push a chap in the face who has just handed you £5,000, can you?'

'It would be awkward,' said Emily. 'Well, if you are going to Sittaford, I am coming with you.'

'Splendid,' said Mr Enderby. 'I don't know, though, if there's anywhere to stay up there. As far as I know there's only Sittaford House and a few odd cottages belonging to people like Burnaby.'

'We shall find something,' said Emily. 'I always find something.'

Mr Enderby could well believe that. Emily had the kind of personality that soars triumphantly over all obstacles.

They had arrived by now at the ruined castle, but paying no attention to it, they sat down on a piece of wall in the so-called sunshine and Emily proceeded to develop her ideas.

'I am looking at this, Mr Enderby, in an absolutely unsentimental and business-like way. You've got to take it from me to begin with that Jim didn't do the murder. I'm not saying that simply because I am in love with him, or believe in his beautiful character or anything like that. It's just well—knowledge. You see I have been on my own pretty well since I was sixteen. I have never come into contact with many women and I know very little about them, but I know a lot about men. And unless a girl can size up a man pretty accurately, and know what she's got to deal with, she will never get on. I have got on. I work as a mannequin at Lucie's, and I can tell you, Mr Enderby, that to arrive there is a Feat.

'Well, as I was saying, I can size up men pretty accurately. Jim is rather a weak character in many ways. I am not sure,' said Emily, forgetting for a moment her rôle of admirer of strong men, 'that that's not why I like him. The feeling that I can run him and make something of him. There are quite a lot of—well—even criminal things that I can imagine him doing if pushed to it—but not murder. He simply couldn't pick up a sandbag and hit an old man on the back of the neck with it. He would make a bosh shot and hit him in the wrong place if he did. He is a—he is a *gentle* creature, Mr Enderby. He doesn't even like killing wasps. He always tries to put them out of a window without hurting them and usually gets stung. However, it's no good my going on like this. You've got to take my word for it and start on the assumption that Jim is innocent.'

'Do you think that somebody is deliberately trying to fasten the crime on him?' asked Charles Enderby in his best journalistic manner.

'I don't think so. You see nobody knew about Jim coming down to see his uncle. Of course, one can't be certain, but I should put that down as just a coincidence and bad luck. What we have to find is someone else with a motive for killing Captain Trevelyan. The police are quite certain that this is not what they call an "outside job"—I mean, it wasn't a burglar. The broken open window was faked.'

'Did the police tell you all this?'

'Practically,' said Emily.

'What do you mean by practically?'

'The chambermaid told me, and her sister is married to Constable Graves, so, of course, she knows everything the police think.'

'Very well,' said Mr Enderby, 'it wasn't an outside job. It was an inside one.'

'Exactly,' said Emily. 'The police—that is Inspector Narracott who, by the way, I should think is an awfully sound man, have started investigating to find who benefits by Captain Trevelyan's death, and with Jim sticking out a mile, so to speak, they won't bother to go on with other investigations much. Well, that's got to be our job.'

'What a scoop it would be,' said Mr Enderby, 'if you and I discovered the real murderer. The crime expert of the *Daily Wire*—that's the way I should be described. But it's too good to be true,' he added despondently. 'That sort of thing only happens in books.'

'Nonsense,' said Emily, 'it happens with me.'

'You're simply marvellous,' said Enderby again.

Emily brought out a little notebook.

'Now let's put things down methodically. Jim himself, his brother and sister, and his Aunt Jennifer benefit equally by Captain Trevelyan's death. Of course Sylvia—that's Jim's sister—wouldn't hurt a fly, but I wouldn't put it past her husband, he's what I call a nasty kind of brute. You know—

the artistic nasty kind, has affairs with women—all that sort of thing. Very likely to be in a hole financially. The money they'd come into would actually be Sylvia's, but that wouldn't matter to him. He would soon manage to get it out of her.'

'He sounds a most unpleasant person,' said Mr Enderby.

'Oh! yes. Good-looking in a bold sort of way. Women talk about sex with him in corners. Real men hate him.'

'Well, that's suspect No. 1,' said Mr Enderby, also writing in a little book. 'Investigate his movements on Friday— easily done under the guise of interview with popular novelist connected with the crime. Is that all right?'

'Splendid,' said Emily. 'Then there's Brian, Jim's younger brother. He's supposed to be in Australia, but he might quite easily have come back. I mean, people do sometimes without saying.'

'We could send him a cable.'

'We will. I suppose Aunt Jennifer is out of it. From all I've heard she's a rather wonderful person. She's got character. Still, after all, she wasn't very far away, she was only at Exeter. She *might* have come over to see her brother, and he *might* have said something nasty about her husband whom she adores, and she *might* have seen red and snatched up a sandbag and biffed him one.'

'Do you really think so?' said Mr Enderby dubiously.

'No, not really. But one never *knows*. Then, of course, there's the batman. He only gets £100 under the will and he seems all right. But there again, one never knows. His wife is Mrs Belling's niece. You know Mrs Belling who keeps the Three Crowns. I think I shall weep on her shoulder when I get back. She looks rather a motherly and romantic soul. I think she would be terribly sorry for me with my young man probably going to prison, and she might let slip something useful. And then, of course, there's Sittaford House. Do you know what struck me as queer?'

'No, what?'

'These people, the Willetts. The ones that took Captain Trevelyan's house furnished in the middle of winter. It's an awfully queer thing to do.'

'Yes, it is odd,' agreed Mr Enderby. 'There might be something at the bottom of that—something to do with Captain Trevelyan's past life.

'That *séance* business was queer too,' he added. 'I'm thinking of writing that up for the paper. Get opinions from Sir Oliver Lodge and Sir Arthur Conan Doyle and a few actresses and people about it.'

'What *séance* business?'

Mr Enderby recounted it with gusto. There was nothing connected with the murder that he had not managed somehow or other to hear.

'Bit odd, isn't it?' he finished. 'I mean, it makes you think and all that. May be something in these things. First time I've really ever come across anything authentic.'

Emily gave a slight shiver. 'I hate supernatural things,' she said. 'Just for once, as you say, it does look as though there was something in it. But how—how gruesome!'

'This *séance* business never seems very practical, does it? If the old boy could get through and say he was dead, why couldn't he say who murdered him? It ought to be all so simple.'

'I feel there may be a clue in Sittaford,' said Emily thoughtfully.

'Yes, I think we ought to investigate there thoroughly,' said Enderby. 'I've hired a car and I'm starting there in about half an hour's time. You had better come along with me.'

'I will,' said Emily. 'What about Major Burnaby?'

'He's going to tramp it,' said Enderby. 'Started immediately after the inquest. If you ask me, he wanted to get out of having my company on the way there. Nobody could like trudging there through all this slush.'

'Will the car be able to get up all right?'

'Oh! yes. First day a car has been able to get through though.'

'Well,' said Emily rising to her feet. 'It's about time we went back to the Three Crowns, and I will pack my suitcase and do a short weeping act on Mrs Belling's shoulder.'

'Don't you worry,' said Mr Enderby rather fatuously. 'You leave everything to me.'

'That's just what I mean to do,' said Emily with a complete lack of truth. 'It's so wonderful to have someone you can really rely on.'

Emily Trefusis was really a very accomplished young woman.

CHAPTER 12

The Arrest

On her return to the Three Crowns, Emily had the good fortune to run right into Mrs Belling who was standing in the hallway.

'Oh! Mrs Belling,' she exclaimed. 'I am leaving this afternoon.'

'Yes, Miss. By the four ten train to Exeter, Miss?'

'No, I am going up to Sittaford.'

'To Sittaford?'

Mrs Belling's countenance showed the most lively curiosity.

'Yes, and I wanted to ask you if you knew of anywhere there where I could stay.'

'You want to stay up there?'

The curiosity was heightened.

'Yes, that is—Oh! Mrs Belling, is there somewhere I could speak to you privately for a moment?'

With something like alacrity Mrs Belling led the way to her own private sanctum. A small comfortable room with a large fire burning.

'You won't tell anyone, will you?' began Emily, knowing well that of all openings on earth this one is the most certain to provoke interest and sympathy.

'No, indeed, Miss, that I won't,' said Mrs Belling, her dark eyes aglitter with interest.

'You see, Mr Pearson—you know—'

'The young gentleman that stayed here on Friday? And that the police have arrested?'

'Arrested? Do you mean really arrested?'

'Yes, Miss. Not half an hour ago.'

Emily had gone very white.

'You—you're sure of that?'

'Oh! yes, Miss. Our Amy had it from the Sergeant.'

'It's too awful!' said Emily. She had been expecting this, but it was none the better for that. 'You see, Mrs Belling, I—I'm engaged to him. And he didn't do it, and, oh dear, it's all too dreadful!'

And here Emily began to cry. She had, earlier in the day, announced her intention to Charles Enderby of doing so, but what appalled her so was with what ease the tears came. To cry at will is not an easy accomplishment. There was something much too real about these tears. It frightened her. She mustn't really give way. Giving way wasn't the least use to Jim. To be resolute, logical and clear-sighted—these were the qualities that were going to count in this game. Sloppy crying had never helped anyone yet.

But it was a relief, all the same, to let yourself go. After all she had meant to cry. Crying would be an undeniable passport to Mrs Belling's sympathy and help. So why not have a good cry while she was about it? A real orgy of weeping in which all her troubles, doubts and unacknowledged fears might find vent and be swept away.

'There, there, my dear, don't ee take on so,' said Mrs Belling.

She put a large motherly arm round Emily's shoulders and patted her consolingly.

'Said from the start I have that he didn't do it. A regular nice young gentleman. A lot of chuckle-heads the police are, and so I've said before now. Some thieving tramp is a great deal more likely. Now, don't ee fret, my dear, it'll all come right, you see if it don't.'

'I am so dreadfully fond of him,' wailed Emily.

Dear Jim, dear, sweet, boyish, helpless, impractical Jim. So utterly to be depended on to do the wrong thing at the wrong moment. What possible chance had he got against that steady, resolute Inspector Narracott?

'We *must* save him,' she wailed.

'Of course we will. Of course we will,' Mrs Belling consoled her.

Emily dabbed her eyes vigorously, gave one last sniff and gulp, and raising her head demanded fiercely:

'Where can I stay at Sittaford?'

'Up to Sittaford? You're set on going there, my dear?'

'Yes,' Emily nodded vigorously.

'Well, now,' Mrs Belling cogitated the matter. 'There's only one place for ee to stay. There's not much to Sittaford. There's the big house, Sittaford House, which Captain Trevelyan built, and that's let now to a South African lady. And there's the six cottages he built, and No. 5 of them cottages has got Curtis, what used to be gardener at Sittaford House, in it, and Mrs Curtis. She lets rooms in the summer time, the Captain allowing her to do so. There's nowhere else you could stay and that's a fact. There's the blacksmith's and the post office, but Mary Hibbert, she's got six children and her sister-in-law living with her, and the blacksmith's wife she's expecting her eighth, so there won't be so much as a corner there. But how are you going to get up to Sittaford, Miss? Have you hired a car?'

'I am going to share Mr Enderby's.'

'Ah, and where will he be staying, I wonder?'

'I suppose he will have to be put up at Mrs Curtis's too. Will she have room for both of us?'

'I don't know that that will look quite right for a young lady like you,' said Mrs Belling.

'He's my cousin,' said Emily.

On no account, she felt, must a sense of propriety intervene to work against her in Mrs Belling's mind.

The landlady's brow cleared. 'Well, that may be all right then,' she allowed grudgingly, 'and likely as not if you're not comfortable with Mrs Curtis they would put you up at the big house.'

'I'm sorry I've been such an idiot,' said Emily, mopping once more at her eyes.

'It's only natural, my dear. And you feel better for it.'

'I do,' said Emily truthfully. 'I feel much better.'

'A good cry and a cup of tea—there's nothing to beat them, and a nice cup of tea you shall have at once, my dear, before you start off on that cold drive.'

'Oh, thank you, but I don't think I really want—'

'Never mind what you want, it's what you're going to have,' said Mrs Belling, rising with determination and moving towards the door. 'And you tell Amelia Curtis from me that she's to look after you and see you take your food proper and see you don't fret.'

'You *are* kind,' said Emily.

'And what's more I shall keep my eyes and ears open down here,' said Mrs Belling, entering with relish into her part of the romance. 'There's many a little thing that I hear that never goes to the police. And anything I do hear I'll pass on to you, Miss.'

'Will you really?'

'That I will. Don't ee worry, my dear, we'll have your young gentleman out of his trouble in no time.'

'I must go and pack,' said Emily, rising.

'I'll send the tea up to you,' said Mrs Belling.

Emily went upstairs, packed her few belongings into her suitcase, sponged her eyes with cold water and applied a liberal allowance of powder.

'You *have* made yourself look a sight,' she apostrophized herself in the glass. She added more powder and a touch of rouge.

'Curious,' said Emily, 'how much better I feel. It's worth the puffy look.'

She rang the bell. The chambermaid (the sympathetic sister-in-law of Constable Graves) came promptly. Emily presented her with a pound note and begged her earnestly to pass on any information she might acquire in roundabout ways from police circles. The girl promised readily.

'Mrs Curtis's up to Sittaford? I will indeed, Miss. Do

anything, that I will. We all feel for you, Miss, more than I can say. All the time I keep saying to myself, "Just fancy if it was you and Fred," I keep saying. I would be distracted—that I would. The least thing I hears I'll pass it on to you, Miss.'

'You angel,' said Emily.

'Just like a sixpenny I got at Woolworth's the other day, *The Syringa Murders* it was called. And do you know what led them to find the real murderer, Miss? Just a bit of common sealing wax. Your gentleman *is* good-looking, Miss, isn't he? Quite unlike his picture in the papers. I'm sure I'll do anything I can, Miss, for you and for him.'

Thus the centre of romantic attention, Emily left the Three Crowns, having duly gulped down the cup of tea prescribed by Mrs Belling.

'By the way,' she said to Enderby as the aged Ford sprang forward, 'you are my cousin, don't forget.'

'Why?'

'They've got such pure minds in the country,' said Emily. 'I thought it would be better.'

'Splendid. In that case,' said Mr Enderby, rising to his opportunities, 'I had better call you Emily.'

'All right, cousin—what's your name?'

'Charles.'

'All right, Charles.'

The car went upwards on the Sittaford road.

CHAPTER 13

Sittaford

Emily was rather fascinated by her first view of Sittaford. Turning off the main road about two miles from Exhampton, they went upwards over a rough moorland road until they reached a village that was situated right on the edge of the moor. It consisted of a smithy, and a combined post office and sweet shop. From there they followed a lane and came to a row of newly built small granite bungalows. At the second of these the car stopped and the driver volunteered the information that this was Mrs Curtis's.

Mrs Curtis was a small, thin, grey-haired woman, energetic and shrewish in disposition. She was all agog with the news of the murder which had only penetrated to Sittaford that morning.

'Yes, of course I can take you in, Miss, and your cousin too, if he can just wait until I shift a few duds. You won't mind having your meals along of us, I don't suppose? Well, who would have believed it! Captain Trevelyan murdered and an inquest and all! Cut off from the world we've been since Friday morning, and this morning when the news came you could have knocked me down with a feather. "The Captain's dead," I said to Curtis, "that *shows* you the wickedness there is in the world nowadays." But I'm keeping you talking here, Miss. Come away in and the gentleman too. I have got the kettle on and you shall have a cup of tea immediately, for you must be perished by the drive up, though of course, it's warmer today after what it's been. Eight and ten feet the snow has been hereabout.'

Drowned in this sea of talk, Emily and Charles Enderby were shown their new quarters. Emily had a small square room, scrupulously clean, looking out and up to the slope of Sittaford Beacon. Charles's room was a small slit facing the front of the house and the lane, containing a bed and a microscopic chest of drawers and washstand.

'The great thing is,' he observed after the driver of the car had disposed his suitcase upon the bed, and had been duly paid and thanked, 'that we are here. If we don't know all there is to be known about everyone living in Sittaford within the next quarter of an hour, I'll eat my hat.'

Ten minutes later, they were sitting downstairs in the comfortable kitchen being introduced to Curtis, a rather gruff-looking, grey-haired old man, and being regaled with strong tea, bread and butter, Devonshire cream and hard-boiled eggs. While they ate and drank they listened. Within half an hour they knew everything there was to be known about the inhabitants of the small community.

First there was Miss Percehouse, who lived in No. 4, The Cottages, a spinster of uncertain years and temper who had come down here to die, according to Mrs Curtis, six years ago.

'But believe it or not, Miss, the air of Sittaford is that healthy that she picked up from the day she came. Wonderfully pure air for lungs it is.

'Miss Percehouse has a nephew who occasionally comes down to see her,' she went on, 'and indeed he's staying with her at the present time. Seeing to it that the money doesn't go out of the family, that's what he's doing. Very dull for a young gentleman at this time of year. But there, there's more ways than one of amusing yourself, and his coming has been a providence for the young lady at Sittaford House. Poor young thing, the idea of bringing her to that great barrack of a house in the winter time. Selfish is what some mothers are. A very pretty young lady, too. Mr Ronald Garfield is up there as often as he can be without neglecting Miss Percehouse.'

Charles Enderby and Emily exchanged glances. Charles remembered that Ronald Garfield had been mentioned as one of the party present at the table-turning.

'The cottage this side of mine, No. 6,' continued Mrs Curtis, 'has only just been took. Gentleman of the name of Duke. That is if you would call him a gentleman. Of course, he may be and he may not. There's no saying, folks aren't so particular nowadays as they used to be. He's been made free of the place in the heartiest manner. A bashful sort of gentleman he is—might be a military gentleman from the look of him, but somehow he hasn't got the manner. Not like Major Burnaby, that you would know as a military gentleman the first time you clapped eyes on him.

'No. 3, that's Mr Rycroft's, little elderly gentleman. They do say that he used to go after birds to outlandish parts for the British Museum. What they call a naturalist he is. Always out and roaming over the moor when the weather permits. And he has a very fine library of books. His cottage is nearly all bookcases.

'No. 2, is an invalid gentleman's, a Captain Wyatt with an Indian servant. And, poor fellow, he does feel the cold, he does. The servant I mean, not the Captain. Coming from warm outlandish parts, it's no wonder. The heat they keep up inside the house would frighten you. It's like walking into an oven.

'No. 1, is Major Burnaby's cottage. Lives by himself he does, and I go in to do for him early mornings. He is a very neat gentleman, he is, and very particular. He and Captain Trevelyan were as thick as thieves. Friends of a lifetime they were. And they both have the same kind of outlandish heads stuck up on the walls.

'As for Mrs Willett and Miss Willett, that's what no one can make out. Plenty of money there. Amos Parker at Exhampton they deal with, and he tells me their weekly book comes to well over eight pounds or nine pounds. You wouldn't believe the eggs that goes into that house! Brought their maidservants from Exeter with them, they did, but they don't like it and want to leave, and I'm sure I don't blame them. Mrs Willett, she sends them into Exeter twice a week in her car, and what with that and the living being so good, they agreed to stop on, but if you ask me it's a queer business, burying yourself in the country like this, a smart lady like that. Well, well, I suppose I had better be clearing away these tea things.'

She drew a deep breath and so did Charles and Emily. The flow of information loosened with so little difficulty had almost overwhelmed them.

Charles ventured to put a question.

'Has Major Burnaby got back yet?' he asked.

Mrs Curtis paused at once, tray in hand. 'Yes, indeed, sir, came tramping in just the same as ever about half an hour before you arrived. "Why, sir," I cried to him. "You've never walked all the way from Exhampton?" And he says in his stern way, "Why not? If a man has got two legs he doesn't need four wheels. I do it once a week anyway as you know, Mrs Curtis." "Oh, yes, sir, but this is different. What with the shock and the murder and the inquest it's wonderful you've got the strength to do it." But he only grunted like and walked on. He looks bad though. It's a miracle he ever got through on Friday night. Brave I call it at his age. Tramping off like that and three miles of it in a snowstorm. You may say what you like, but nowadays the young gentlemen aren't a patch on the old ones. That Mr Ronald Garfield he would never have done it, and it's my opinion, and it's the opinion of Mrs Hibbert at the post office, and it's the opinion of Mr Pound, the blacksmith, that Mr Garfield ought never to have let him go off alone the way he did. He should have gone with him. If Major Burnaby had been lost in a snowdrift, everybody would have blamed Mr Garfield. And that's a fact.'

She disappeared triumphantly into the scullery amid a clatter of tea things.

Mr Curtis thoughtfully removed an aged pipe from the right side of his mouth to the left side.

'Women,' he said, 'talk a lot.'

He paused and then murmured:

'And half the time they don't know the truth of what they are talking about.'

Emily and Charles received this announcement in silence. Seeing that no more was coming, however, Charles murmured approvingly:

'That's very true—yes, very true.'

'Ah!' said Mr Curtis, and relapsed into a pleasant and contemplative silence.

Charles rose. 'I think I'll go round and see old Burnaby,' he said, 'tell him the camera parade will be tomorrow morning.'

'I'll come with you,' said Emily. 'I want to know what he really thinks about Jim and what ideas he has about the crime in general.'

'Have you got any rubber boots or anything? It's awfully slushy.'

'I bought some Wellingtons in Exhampton,' said Emily.

'What a practical girl you are. You think of everything.'

'Unfortunately,' said Emily, 'that's not much help to you in finding out who's done a murder. It might help one to do a murder,' she added reflectively.

'Well, don't murder me,' said Mr Enderby.

They went out together. Mrs Curtis immediately returned.

'They be gone round to the Major's,' said Mr Curtis.

'Ah!' said Mrs Curtis. 'Now, what do you think? Are they sweethearting, or are they not? A lot of harm comes of cousins marrying, so they say. Deaf and dumbs and half wits and a lot of other evils. He's sweet on her, that you can see easily enough. As for her, she's a deep one like my Great Aunt Sarah's Belinda, she is. Got a way with her and with the men. I wonder what she's after now? Do you know what I think, Curtis?'

Mr Curtis grunted.

'This young gentleman that the police are holding on account of the murder, it's my belief that he's the one she's set on. And she's come up here to nose about and see what she can find out. And mark my words,' said Mrs Curtis, rattling china, 'if there's anything *to* find out she will find it!'

CHAPTER 14

The Willetts

At the same moment that Charles and Emily started out
to visit Major Burnaby, Inspector Narracott was seated in
the drawing-room of Sittaford House, trying to formulate
an impression of Mrs Willett.

He had not been able to interview her sooner as the
roads had been impassable until this morning. He had
hardly known what he had expected to find, but certainly
not what he had found. It was Mrs Willett who had taken
charge of the situation, not he.

She had come rushing into the room, thoroughly business-
like and efficient. He saw a tall woman, thin-faced and
keen-eyed. She was wearing rather an elaborate knitted silk
jumper suit that was just over the border line of unsuitability
for country wear. Her stockings were of very expensive
gossamer silk, her shoes high-heeled patent leather. She wore
several valuable rings and rather a large quantity of very
good and expensive imitation pearls.

'Inspector Narracott?' said Mrs Willett. 'Naturally, you
want to come over the house. What a shocking tragedy! I

could hardly believe it. We only heard about it this morning, you know. We were terribly shocked. Sit down, won't you, Inspector? This is my daughter, Violet.'

He had hardly noticed the girl who had followed her in, and yet she was a very pretty girl, tall and fair with big blue eyes.

Mrs Willett herself took a seat.

'Is there any way in which I can help you, Inspector? I knew very little of poor Captain Trevelyan, but if there is anything you can think of—'

The Inspector said slowly:

'Thank you, madam. Of course, one never knows what may be useful or what may not.'

'I quite understand. There may possibly be something in the house that may throw light upon this sad business, but I rather doubt it. Captain Trevelyan removed all his personal belongings. He even feared I should tamper with his fishing rods, poor, dear man.'

She laughed a little.

'You were not acquainted with him?'

'Before I took the house, you mean? Oh! no. I've asked him here several times since, but he never came. Terribly shy, poor dear. That was what was the matter with him. I've known dozens of men like it. They are called women haters and all sorts of silly things, and really all the time it's only shyness. If I could have got at him,' said Mrs Willett with determination, 'I'd soon have got over all that nonsense. That sort of man only wants bringing out.'

Inspector Narracott began to understand Captain Trevelyan's strongly defensive attitude towards his tenants.

'We both asked him,' continued Mrs Willett. 'Didn't we, Violet?'

'Oh! yes, Mother.'

'A real simple sailor at heart,' said Mrs Willett. 'Every woman loves a sailor, Inspector Narracott.'

It occurred to Inspector Narracott at this juncture that the interview so far had been run entirely by Mrs Willett. He was convinced that she was an exceedingly clever woman. She might be as innocent as she appeared. On the other hand she might not.

'The point I am anxious to get information about is this,' he said and paused.

'Yes, Inspector?'

'Major Burnaby, as you doubtless know, discovered the body. He was led to do so by an accident that occurred in this house.'

'You mean?'

'I mean, the table-turning. I beg your pardon—'

He turned sharply.

A faint sound had come from the girl.

'Poor Violet,' said her mother. 'She was terribly upset—indeed we all were! Most unaccountable. I'm not superstitious, but really it was the most unaccountable thing.'

'It did occur then?'

Mrs Willett opened her eyes very wide.

'Occur? Of course it occurred. At the time I thought it was a joke—a most unfeeling joke and one in very bad taste. I suspected young Ronald Garfield—'

'Oh! no, Mother. I'm sure he didn't. He absolutely swore he didn't.'

'I'm saying what I thought at the time, Violet. What could one think it but a joke?'

'It was curious,' said the Inspector slowly. 'You were very upset, Mrs Willett?'

'We all were. Up to then it had been, oh, just light-hearted fooling. You know the sort of thing. Good fun on a winter's evening. And then suddenly—this! I was very angry.'

'Angry?'

'Well, naturally. I thought someone was doing it deliberately—for a joke, as I say.'

'And now?'

'Now?'

'Yes, what do you think now?'

Mrs Willett spread her hands out expressively.

'I don't know what to think. It—it's uncanny.'

'And you, Miss Willett?'

'I?'

The girl started.

'I—I don't know. I shall never forget it. I *dream* of it. I shall never dare to do table-turning again.'

'Mr Rycroft would say it was genuine, I suppose,' said her mother. 'He believes in all that sort of thing. Really I'm inclined to believe in it myself. What other explanation is there except that it was a genuine message from a spirit?'

The Inspector shook his head. The table-turning had been his red herring. His next remark was most casual sounding.

'Don't you find it very bleak here in winter, Mrs Willett?'

'Oh, we love it. Such a change. We're South Africans, you know.'

116

Her tone was brisk and ordinary.

'Really? What part of South Africa?'

'Oh! the Cape. Violet has never been in England before. She is enchanted with it—finds the snow most romantic. This house is really most comfortable.'

'What led you to come to this part of the world?'

There was just gentle curiosity in his voice.

'We've read so many books on Devonshire, and especially on Dartmoor. We were reading one on the boat—all about Widdecombe Fair. I've always had a hankering to see Dartmoor.'

'What made you fix on Exhampton? It's not a very well known little town.'

'Well—we were reading these books as I told you, and there was a boy on board who talked about Exhampton— he was so enthusiastic about it.'

'What was his name?' asked the Inspector. 'Did he come from this part of the world?'

'Now, what was his name? Cullen—I think. No—it was Smythe. How stupid of me. I really can't remember. You know how it is on board ship, Inspector, you get to know people so well and plan to meet again—and a week after you've landed, you can't even be sure of their names!'

She laughed.

'But he was such a nice boy—not good-looking, reddish hair, but a delightful smile.'

'And on the strength of that you decided to take a house in these parts?' said the Inspector smiling.

'Yes, wasn't it mad of us?'

Clever, thought Narracott. Distinctly clever. He began

to realize Mrs Willett's methods. She always carried the war into the enemy's country.

'So you wrote to the house agents and inquired about a house?'

'Yes—and they sent us particulars of Sittaford. It sounded just what we wanted.'

'It wouldn't be my taste at this time of year,' said the Inspector with a laugh.

'I daresay it wouldn't be ours if we lived in England,' said Mrs Willett brightly.

The Inspector rose.

'How did you know the name of a house agent to write to in Exhampton?' he asked. 'That must have presented a difficulty.'

There was a pause. The first pause in the conversation. He thought he caught a glimpse of vexation, more, of anger in Mrs Willett's eyes. He had hit upon something to which she had not thought out the answer. She turned towards her daughter.

'How did we, Violet? I can't remember.'

There was a different look in the girl's eyes. She looked frightened.

'Why, of course,' said Mrs Willett. 'Delfridges. Their information bureau. It's too wonderful. I always go and inquire there about everything. I asked them the name of the best agent here and they told me.'

'Quick,' thought the Inspector. 'Very quick. But not quite quick enough. I had you there, madam.'

He made a cursory examination of the house. There was nothing there. No papers, no locked drawers or cupboards.

Mrs Willett accompanied him talking brightly. He took his leave, thanking her politely.

As he departed he caught a glimpse of the girl's face over her shoulder. There was no mistaking the expression on her face.

It was fear he saw on her countenance. Fear written there plainly at this moment when she thought herself unobserved.

Mrs Willett was still talking.

'Alas. We have one grave drawback here. The domestic problem, Inspector. Servants will not stand these country places. All of mine have been threatening to leave us for some time, and the news of the murder seems to have unsettled them utterly. I don't know what I shall do. Perhaps men servants would answer the case. That is what the Registry Office in Exeter advised.'

The Inspector answered mechanically. He was not listening to her flow of talk. He was thinking of the expression he had surprised on the girl's face.

Mrs Willett had been clever—but not quite clever enough.

He went away cogitating on his problem.

If the Willetts had nothing to do with Captain Trevelyan's death, why was Violet Willett afraid?

He fired his last shot. With his foot actually over the threshold of the front door he turned back.

'By the way,' he said, 'you know young Pearson, don't you?'

There was no doubt of the pause this time. A dead silence of about a second. Then Mrs Willett spoke:

'Pearson?' she said. 'I don't think—'

She was interrupted. A queer sighing breath came from the room behind her and then the sound of a fall. The Inspector was over the threshold and into the room in a flash.

Violet Willett had fainted.

'Poor child,' cried Mrs Willett. 'All this strain and shock. That dreadful table-turning business and the murder on the top of it. She isn't strong. Thank you so much, Inspector. Yes, on the sofa please. If you would ring the bell. No, I don't think there is anything more you can do. Thank you so much.'

The Inspector went down the drive with his lips set in a grim line.

Jim Pearson was engaged, he knew, to that extremely charming-looking girl he had seen in London.

Why then should Violet Willett faint at the mention of his name? What was the connection between Jim Pearson and the Willetts?

He paused indecisively as he emerged from the front gate. Then he took from his pocket a small notebook. In it was entered a list of the inhabitants of the six bungalows built by Captain Trevelyan with a few brief remarks against each name. Inspector Narracott's stubby forefinger paused at the entry against No. 6 The Cottages.

'Yes,' he said to himself. 'I'd better see him next.'

He strode briskly down the lane and beat a firm rat-tat on the knocker of No. 6—the bungalow inhabited by Mr Duke.

CHAPTER 15

Visit to Major Burnaby

Leading the way up the path to the Major's front door, Mr
Enderby rapped upon it in a cheery fashion. The door was
flung open almost immediately and Major Burnaby, red in
the face, appeared on the threshold.

'It's you, is it?' he observed with no very great fervour
in his voice, and was about to go on in the same strain
when he caught sight of Emily and his expression altered.

'This is Miss Trefusis,' said Charles with the air of
one producing the ace of trumps. 'She was very anxious
to see you.'

'May I come in?' said Emily with her sweetest smile.

'Oh! yes. Certainly. Of course—Oh, yes, of course.'

Stumbling in his speech the Major backed into the
living-room of his cottage and began pulling forward chairs
and pushing aside tables.

Emily, as was her fashion, came straight to the point.

'You see, Major Burnaby, I am engaged to Jim—Jim
Pearson, you know. And naturally I am terribly anxious
about him.'

Agatha Christie

In the act of pushing a table the Major paused with his mouth open.

'Oh dear,' he said, 'that's a bad business. My dear young lady, I am more sorry about it than I can say.'

'Major Burnaby, tell me honestly. Do you yourself believe he is guilty? Oh, you needn't mind saying if you do. I would a hundred times rather people didn't lie to me.'

'No, I do *not* think him guilty,' said the Major in a loud assertive voice. He hit a cushion once or twice vigorously, and then sat down facing Emily. 'The chap is a nice young chap. Mind you, he might be a bit weak. Don't be offended if I say that he's the kind of young fellow that might easily go wrong if temptation came in his way. But murder—no. And mind you, I know what I am talking about—a lot of subalterns have passed through my hands in my time. It's the fashion to poke fun at retired army officers nowadays, but we know a thing or two all the same, Miss Trefusis.'

'I'm sure you do,' said Emily. 'I'm awfully grateful to you for saying what you've done.'

'Have—have a whisky and soda?' said the Major. 'I'm afraid there's nothing else,' he said apologetically.

'No, thank you, Major Burnaby.'

'Some plain soda then?'

'No, thank you,' said Emily.

'I ought to be able to produce tea,' said the Major with a touch of wistfulness.

'We've had it,' said Charles. 'At Mrs Curtis's,' he added.

'Major Burnaby,' said Emily, 'who do you think did it—have you any idea at all?'

'No. I am damned—er—bothered—if I have,' said the

Major. 'Took it for granted it was some chap that broke in, but now the police say that can't be so. Well, it's their job, and I suppose they know best. They say nobody broke in, so I suppose nobody did break in. But all the same it beats me, Miss Trefusis. Trevelyan hadn't an enemy in the world as far as I know.'

'And *you* would know if anybody did,' said Emily.

'Yes, I suppose I knew more of Trevelyan than many of his relations did.'

'And you can't think of anything—anything that would help, in any way?' asked Emily.

The Major pulled at his short moustache.

'I know what you're thinking. Like in books there ought to be some little incident that I should remember that would be a clue. Well, I'm sorry, but there isn't any such thing. Trevelyan just led an ordinary life. Got very few letters and wrote less. There were no female complications in his life, I am sure of that. No, it beats me, Miss Trefusis.'

All three were silent.

'What about that servant of his?' asked Charles.

'Been with him for years. Absolutely faithful.'

'He had married lately,' said Charles.

'Married a perfectly decent respectable girl.'

'Major Burnaby,' said Emily, 'forgive me putting it this way—but didn't you get the wind up rather easily about him?'

The Major rubbed his nose with the embarrassed air that always came over him when the table-turning was mentioned.

'Yes, there's no denying it, I did. I knew the whole thing was tommy rot and yet—'

'You felt somehow it wasn't,' said Emily helpfully.

The Major nodded.

'That's why I wonder—' said Emily.

The two men looked at her.

'I can't quite put what I mean in the way I want,' said Emily. 'What I mean is this: You say that you don't believe in all this table-turning business—and yet, in spite of the awful weather and what must have seemed to you the absurdity of the whole thing—you felt so uneasy that you had to set out, no matter what the weather conditions, and see for yourself that Captain Trevelyan was all right. Well, don't you think that may have been because—because there was something in the atmosphere?

'I mean,' she continued desperately as she saw no trace of comprehension in the Major's face, 'that there was something in someone else's mind as well as yours. And that somehow or other you felt it.'

'Well, I don't know,' said the Major. He rubbed his nose again. 'Of course,' he added hopefully, 'women do take these things seriously.'

'Women!' said Emily. 'Yes,' she murmured softly to herself, 'I believe somehow or other that's it.'

She turned abruptly to Major Burnaby.

'What are they like, these Willetts?'

'Oh, well,' Major Burnaby cast about in his mind, he was clearly no good at personal descriptions. 'Well—they are very kind, you know—very helpful and all that.'

'Why do they want to take a house like Sittaford House at this time of year?'

'I can't imagine,' said the Major. 'Nobody does,' he added.

'Don't you think it's very queer?' persisted Emily.

'Of course, it's queer. However, there's no accounting for tastes. That's what the Inspector said.'

'That's nonsense,' said Emily. 'People don't do things without a reason.'

'Well, I don't know,' said Major Burnaby cautiously. 'Some people don't. You wouldn't, Miss Trefusis. But some people—' He sighed and shook his head.

'You are sure they hadn't met Captain Trevelyan before?'

The Major scouted the idea. Trevelyan would have said something to him. No, he was as astonished himself as anyone could be.

'So *he* thought it queer?'

'Of course, I've just told you we all did.'

'What was Mrs Willett's attitude towards Captain Trevelyan?' asked Emily. 'Did she try and avoid him?'

A faint chuckle came from the Major.

'No, indeed she didn't. Pestered the life out of him— always asking him to come and see them.'

'Oh!' said Emily thoughtfully. She paused and then said, 'So she might—just possibly she might have taken Sittaford House just on purpose to get acquainted with Captain Trevelyan.'

'Well,' the Major seemed to turn it over in his mind. 'Yes, I suppose she might have. Rather an expensive way of doing things.'

'I don't know,' said Emily. 'Captain Trevelyan wouldn't have been an easy person to get to know otherwise.'

'No, he wouldn't,' agreed the late Captain Trevelyan's friend.

'I wonder,' said Emily.

'The Inspector thought of that too,' said Burnaby.

Emily felt a sudden irritation against Inspector Narracott. Everything that she thought of seemed to have already been thought of by the Inspector. It was galling to a young woman who prided herself on being sharper than other people.

She rose and held out her hand.

'Thank you very much,' she said simply.

'I wish I could help you more,' said the Major. 'I'm rather an obvious sort of person—always have been. If I were a clever chap I might be able to hit upon something that might be a clue. At any rate count on me for anything you want.'

'Thank you,' said Emily. 'I will.'

'Goodbye, sir,' said Enderby. 'I shall be along in the morning with my camera, you know.'

Burnaby grunted.

Emily and Charles retraced their steps to Mrs Curtis's.

'Come into my room, I want to talk to you,' said Emily.

She sat on the one chair and Charles sat on the bed. Emily plucked off her hat and sent it spinning into a corner of the room.

'Now, listen,' she said. 'I think I've got a kind of starting point. I may be wrong and I may be right, at any rate it's an idea. I think a lot hinges on this table-turning business. You've done table-turning, haven't you?'

'Oh, yes, now and then. Not serious, you know.'

'No, of course not. It's the kind of thing one does on a wet afternoon, and everyone accuses everyone else of shoving. Well, if you've played it you know what happens. The table starts spelling out, say, a name, well, it's a name somebody knows. Very often they recognize it at once and hope it isn't going to be that, and all the time unconsciously they are what one calls shoving. I mean sort of recognizing things makes one give an involuntary jerk when the next letter comes and stops the thing. And the less you want to do that sometimes the more it happens.'

'Yes, that's true,' agreed Mr Enderby.

'I don't believe for a moment in spirits or anything like that. But supposing that one of those people who were playing knew that Captain Trevelyan was being murdered at that minute—'

'Oh, I say,' protested Charles, 'that's awfully far fetched.'

'Well, it needn't be quite so crude as that. Yes, I think it must be. We are just taking a hypothesis—that's all. We are asserting that somebody knew that Captain Trevelyan was dead and absolutely couldn't hide their knowledge. The table betrayed them.'

'It's awfully ingenious,' said Charles, 'but I don't believe for a minute it's true.'

'We'll assume that it is true,' said Emily firmly. 'I am sure that in detection of crime you mustn't be afraid to assume things.'

'Oh, I'm quite agreeable,' said Mr Enderby. 'We'll assume that it is true—anything you like.'

'So what we have to do,' said Emily, 'is to consider very carefully the people who were playing. To begin with there's Major Burnaby and Mr Rycroft. Well, it seems wildly unlikely that either of them should have an accomplice who was the murderer. Then there is this Mr Duke. Well, for the moment we know nothing about him. He has only just arrived here lately and of course, he might be a sinister stranger—part of a gang or something. We will put X against his name. And now we come to the Willetts. Charles, there is something awfully mysterious about the Willetts.'

'What on earth have they got to gain from Captain Trevelyan's death?'

'Well, on the face of it, nothing. But if my theory is correct there must be a connection somewhere. We've got to find what is the connection.'

'Right,' said Mr Enderby. 'And supposing it's all a mare's nest?'

'Well, we'll have to start all over again,' said Emily.

'Hark!' cried Charles suddenly.

He held up his hand. Then he went over to the window and opened it, and Emily too, heard the sound which had aroused his attention. It was the far-off booming of a great bell.

As they stood listening, Mrs Curtis's voice called excitedly from below:

'Do you hear the bell, Miss—do you hear it?'

Emily opened the door.

'D'you hear it? Plain as plain, isn't it? Well now, to think of that!'

'What is it?' asked Emily.

'It's the bell at Princetown, Miss, near to twelve mile away. It means that a convict's escaped. George, George, where is that man? D'you hear the bell? There's a convict loose.'

Her voice died away as she went through the kitchen.

Charles shut the window and sat down on the bed again.

'It's a pity that things happen all wrong,' he said dispassionately. 'If only this convict had escaped on Friday, why, there would be our murderer nicely accounted for. No farther to look. Hungry man, desperate criminal breaks in. Trevelyan defends his Englishman's castle—and desperate criminal biffs him one. All so simple.'

'It would have been,' said Emily with a sigh.

'Instead of which,' said Charles, 'he escapes three days too late. It's—it's hopelessly inartistic.'

He shook his head sadly.

CHAPTER 16

Mr Rycroft

Emily woke early the next morning. Being a sensible young woman, she realized there was little possibility of Mr Enderby's collaboration until the morning was well advanced. So, feeling restless and unable to lie still she set out for a brisk walk along the lane in the opposite direction from which they had come last night.

She passed the gates of Sittaford House on her right and shortly after that the lane took a sharp turn to the right and ran steeply uphill and came out on the open moor where it degenerated into a grass track and soon petered out altogether. The morning was a fine one, cold and crisp, and the view was lovely. Emily ascended to the very top of Sittaford Tor, a pile of grey rock of a fantastic shape. From this height she looked down over an expanse of moorland, unbroken as far as she could see without any habitation or any road. Below her, on the opposite side of the Tor, were grey masses of granite boulders and rocks. After considering the scene for a minute or two she turned to view the prospect to the north from which she had come. Just below her lay Sittaford, clustering on the flank of the hill, the square grey blob of Sittaford House, and the dotted cottages beyond it. In the valley below she could see Exhampton.

'One ought,' thought Emily confusedly, 'to see things better when you are high up like this. It ought to be like lifting off the top of a doll's house and peering in.'

She wished with all her heart that she had met the dead man even if only once. It was so hard to get an idea of people you had never seen. You had to rely on other people's judgment, and Emily had never yet acknowledged that any other person's judgment was superior to her own. Other people's impressions were no good to you. They might be just as true as yours but you couldn't act on them. You couldn't, as it were, use another person's angle of attack.

Meditating vexedly on these questions, Emily sighed impatiently and shifted her position.

She had been so lost in her own thoughts that she had been oblivious to her immediate surroundings. It was with a shock of surprise that she realized that a small elderly gentleman was standing a few feet away from her, his hat held courteously in his hand, while he breathed rather fast.

'Excuse me,' he said. 'Miss Trefusis, I believe?'

'Yes,' said Emily.

'My name is Rycroft. You must forgive me speaking to you, but in this little community of ours the smallest detail is known, and your arrival here yesterday has naturally gone the round. I can assure you that everyone feels a deep sympathy with your position, Miss Trefusis. We are all, one and all, anxious to assist you in any way we can.'

Agatha Christie

'That's very kind of you,' said Emily.

'Not at all, not at all,' said Mr Rycroft. 'Beauty in distress, you will pardon my old-fashioned manner of putting it. But seriously, my dear young lady, do count on me if there is any way in which I can possibly assist you. Beautiful view from up here, is it not?'

'Wonderful,' agreed Emily. 'The moor is a wonderful place.'

'You know that a prisoner must have escaped last night from Princetown.'

'Yes. Has he been recaptured?'

'Not yet, I believe. Ah, well, poor fellow, he will no doubt be recaptured soon enough. I believe I am right in saying that no one has escaped successfully from Princetown for the last twenty years.'

'Which direction is Princetown?'

Mr Rycroft stretched out his arm and pointed southwards over the moor.

'It lies over there, about twelve miles as the crow flies over unbroken moorland. It's sixteen miles by road.'

Emily gave a faint shiver. The idea of the desperate hunted man impressed her powerfully. Mr Rycroft was watching her and gave a little nod.

'Yes,' he said. 'I feel the same myself. It's curious how one's instincts rebel at the thought of a man being hunted down, and yet these men at Princetown are all dangerous and violent criminals, the kind of men whom probably you and I would do our utmost to put there in the first place.'

He gave a little apologetic laugh.

'You must forgive me, Miss Trefusis, I am deeply

interested in the study of crime. A fascinating study. Ornithology and criminology are my two subjects.' He paused and then went on:

'That's the reason why, if you will allow me to do so, I should like to associate myself with you in this matter. To study a crime at first hand has long been an unrealized dream of mine. Will you place your confidence in me, Miss Trefusis, and allow me to place my experience at your disposal? I have read and studied this subject deeply.'

Emily was silent for a minute. She was congratulating herself on the way events were playing into her hand. Here was first-hand knowledge being offered her of life as it had been lived at Sittaford. 'Angle of attack,' Emily repeated the phrase that had crept into her mind so short a time before. She had had Major Burnaby's angle—matter of fact—simple—direct. Taking cognizance of facts and completely oblivious of subtleties. Now, she was being offered another angle which she suspected might open up a very different field of vision. This little, shrivelled, dried-up gentleman had read and studied deeply, was well versed in human nature, had that devouring interested curiosity in life displayed by the man of reflection as opposed to the man of action.

'Please help me,' she said simply. 'I am so very worried and unhappy.'

'You must be, my dear, you must be. Now, as I understand the position, Trevelyan's eldest nephew has been arrested or detained—the evidence against him being of a somewhat simple and obvious nature. I, of course, have an open mind. You must allow me that.'

'Of course,' said Emily. 'Why should you believe in his innocence when you know nothing about him?'

'Most reasonable,' said Mr Rycroft. 'Really, Miss Trefusis, you yourself are a most interesting study. By the way, your name—is it Cornish like our poor friend Trevelyan?'

'Yes,' said Emily. 'My father was Cornish, my mother was Scottish.'

'Ah!' said Mr Rycroft, 'very interesting. Now to approach our little problem. On the one hand we assume that young Jim—the name is Jim, is it not? We assume that young Jim had a pressing need of money, that he came down to see his uncle, that he asked for money, that his uncle refused, that in a moment of passion he picked up a sandbag that was lying at the door and that he hit his uncle over the head. The crime was unpremeditated—was in fact a foolish irrational affair most deplorably conducted. Now, all that may be so, on the other hand he may have parted with his uncle in anger and some other person may have stepped in shortly afterwards and committed the crime. That is what you believe—and to put it a little differently, that is what I hope. I do not want your fiancé to have committed the crime, for from my point of view it is so uninteresting that he should have done so. I am therefore backing the other horse. The crime was committed by someone else. We will assume that and go at once to a most important point. Was that someone else aware of the quarrel that had just taken place? Did that quarrel, in fact, actually precipitate the murder? You see my point? Someone is meditating doing away with Captain Trevelyan and seized this opportunity, realizing that suspicion is bound to fall on young Jim.'

Emily considered the matter from this angle.

'In that case,' she said slowly—

Mr Rycroft took the words out of her mouth.

'In that case,' he said briskly, 'the murderer would have to be a person in close association with Captain Trevelyan. He would have to be domiciled in Exhampton. In all probability he would have to be in the house, either during or after the quarrel. And since we are not in a court of law and can bandy about names freely, the name of the servant, Evans, leaps to our minds as a person who could satisfy our conditions. A man who quite possibly might have been in the house, have overheard the quarrel and seized the opportunity. Our next point is to discover whether Evans benefits in any way from his master's death.'

'I believe he gets a small legacy,' said Emily.

'That may or may not constitute a sufficient motive. We shall have to discover whether or not Evans had a pressing need of money. We must also consider Mrs Evans—there is a Mrs Evans of recent date, I understand. If you had studied criminology, Miss Trefusis, you would realize the curious effect caused by inbreeding, especially in country districts. There are at least four young women in Broadmoor, pleasant in manner, but with that curious kink in their dispositions that human life is of little or no account to them. No—we must not leave Mrs Evans out of account.'

'What do you think about this table-turning business, Mr Rycroft?'

'Now, that is very strange. Most strange. I confess, Miss Trefusis, that I am powerfully impressed by it. I am, as perhaps you may have heard, a believer in psychic things.

To a certain degree I am a believer in spiritualism. I have already written out a full account and sent it up to the Society of Psychical Research. A well-authenticated and amazing case. Five people present, none of whom could have the least idea or suspicion that Captain Trevelyan was murdered.'

'You don't think—'

Emily stopped. It was not so easy to suggest her own idea to Mr Rycroft that one of the five people might have guilty foreknowledge, as he himself had been one of them. Not that she suspected for a moment that there was anything whatever to connect Mr Rycroft with the tragedy. Still she felt that the suggestion might not be wholly tactful. She pursued her object in a more roundabout manner.

'It all interested me very much, Mr Rycroft, it is, as you say, an amazing occurrence. You don't think that any of the people present, with the exception of yourself, of course, were in any way psychic?'

'My dear young lady, I myself am not psychic. I have no powers in that direction. I am only a very deeply interested observer.'

'What about this Mr Garfield?'

'A nice lad,' said Mr Rycroft, 'but not remarkable in any way.'

'Well off, I suppose,' said Emily.

'Stony broke, I believe,' said Mr Rycroft. 'I hope I am using that idiom correctly. He comes down here to dance attendance on an aunt, from whom he has what I call "expectations". Miss Percehouse is a very sharp lady and I think she knows what these attentions are worth. But as she has a sardonic form of humour of her own she keeps him dancing.'

'I should like to meet her,' said Emily.

'Yes, you must certainly meet her. She will no doubt insist on meeting you. Curiosity—alas, my dear Miss Trefusis—curiosity.'

'Tell me about the Willetts,' said Emily.

'Charming,' said Mr Rycroft, 'quite charming. Colonial, of course. No real poise, if you understand me. A little too lavish in their hospitality. Everything a shade on the ornate side. Miss Violet is a charming girl.'

'A funny place to come for the winter,' said Emily.

'Yes, very odd, is it not? But after all it is only logical. We ourselves living in this country long for the sunshine, hot climates, waving palm trees. People who live in Australia or South Africa are enchanted with the idea of an old-fashioned Christmas with snow and ice.'

'I wonder which of them,' said Emily to herself, 'told him that.'

She reflected that it was not necessary to bury yourself in a moorland village in order to obtain an old-fashioned Christmas with snow and ice. Clearly, Mr Rycroft did not see anything suspicious in the Willetts' choice of a winter resort. But that, she reflected, was perhaps natural in one who was an ornithologist and a criminologist. Sittaford clearly appeared an ideal residence to Mr Rycroft, and he could not conceive of it as an unsuitable environment to someone else.

They had been slowly descending the slope of the hillside and were now wending their way down the lane.

'Who lives in that cottage?' asked Emily abruptly.

'Captain Wyatt—he is an invalid. Rather unsociable, I fear.'

'Was he a friend of Captain Trevelyan's?'

'Not an intimate friend in any way. Trevelyan merely made a formal visit to him every now and then. As a matter of fact Wyatt doesn't encourage visitors. A surly man.'

Emily was silent. She was reviewing the possibility of how she herself might become a visitor. She had no intention of allowing any angle of attack to remain unexplored.

She suddenly remembered the hitherto unmentioned member of the *séance*.

'What about Mr Duke?' she asked brightly.

'What about him?'

'Well, who is he?'

'Well,' said Mr Rycroft slowly, 'that is what nobody knows.'

'How extraordinary,' said Emily.

'As a matter of fact,' said Mr Rycroft, 'it isn't. You see, Duke is such an entirely unmysterious individual. I should imagine that the only mystery about him was his social origin. Not—not quite, if you understand me. But a very solid good fellow,' he hastened to add.

Emily was silent.

'This is my cottage,' said Mr Rycroft pausing, 'perhaps you will do me the honour of coming in and inspecting it.'

'I should love to,' said Emily.

They went up the small path and entered the cottage. The interior was charming. Bookcases lined the walls.

Emily went from one to the other glancing curiously at

the titles of the books. One section dealt with occult phenomena, another with modern detective fiction, but by far the greater part of the bookcase was given up to criminology and to the world's famous trials. Books on ornithology held a comparatively small portion.

'I think it's all delightful,' said Emily. 'I must get back now. I expect Mr Enderby will be up and waiting for me. As a matter of fact I haven't had breakfast yet. We told Mrs Curtis half past nine, and I see it's ten o'clock. I shall be dreadfully late—that's because you've been so interesting—and so very helpful.'

'Anything I can do,' burbled Mr Rycroft as Emily turned a bewitching glance on him. 'You can count on me. We are collaborators.'

Emily gave him her hand and squeezed his warmly.

'It's so wonderful,' she said, using the phrase that in the course of her short life she had found so effectual, 'to feel that there's someone on whom one can really rely.'

CHAPTER 17

Miss Percehouse

Emily returned to find eggs and bacon, and Charles waiting for her.

Mrs Curtis was still agog with excitement over the escape of the convict.

'Two years it is since last one escaped,' she said, 'and three days it was before they found him. Near to Moretonhampstead he was.'

'Do you think he'll come this way?' asked Charles.

Local knowledge vetoed this suggestion.

'They never comes this way, all bare moorland it is and only small towns when you do come off the moor. He'll make for Plymouth, that's the most likely. But they'll catch him long before that.'

'You could find a good hiding place among these rocks on the other side of the Tor,' said Emily.

'You're right, Miss, and there *is* a hiding place there, the Pixie's Cave they call it. As narrow an opening between two rocks as you could find, but it widens out inside. They say one of King Charles's men hid there once

140

for a fortnight with a serving maid from a farm bringing him food.'

'I must take a look at that Pixie's Cave,' said Charles.

'You'll be surprised how hard it is to find, sir. Many a picnic party in summer looks for it the whole afternoon and doesn't find it, but if you do find it be sure you leave a pin inside it for luck.'

'I wonder,' said Charles when breakfast was over and he and Emily had strolled out into the small bit of garden, 'if I ought to go off to Princetown? Amazing how things pile up once you have a bit of luck. Here I am—I start with a simple football competition prize, and before I know where I am I run straight into an escaped convict and a murderer. Marvellous!'

'What about this photographing of Major Burnaby's cottage?'

Charles looked up at the sky.

'H'm,' he said. 'I think I shall say the weather is wrong. I have got to hang on to my *raison d'être* of being in Sittaford as long as possible, and it's coming over misty. Er—I hope you don't mind, I have just posted off an interview with you?'

'Oh! that's all right,' said Emily mechanically. 'What have you made me say?'

'Oh, the usual sort of things people like to hear,' said Mr Enderby. 'Our special representative records his interview with Miss Emily Trefusis, the fiancée of Mr James Pearson who has been arrested by the police and charged with the murder of Captain Trevelyan—Then my impression of you as a high-spirited, beautiful girl.'

'Thank you,' said Emily.

'Shingled,' went on Charles.

'What do you mean by shingled?'

'You are,' said Charles.

'Well, of course I am,' said Emily. 'But why mention it?'

'Women readers always like to know,' said Charles Enderby. 'It was a splendid interview. You've no idea what fine womanly touching things you said about standing by your man, no matter if the whole world was against him.'

'Did I really say that?' said Emily wincing slightly.

'Do you mind?' said Mr Enderby anxiously.

'Oh! no,' said Emily. 'Enjoy yourself, darling.'

Mr Enderby looked slightly taken aback.

'It's all right,' said Emily. 'That's a quotation. I had it on my bib when I was small—my Sunday bib. The weekday one had "Don't be a glutton" on it.'

'Oh! I see. I put in a very good bit about Captain Trevelyan's sea career and just a hint at foreign idols looted and a possibility of a strange priest's revenge—only a hint, you know.'

'Well, you seem to have done your day's good deed,' said Emily.

'What have you been up to? You were up early enough, heaven knows.'

Emily described her meeting with Mr Rycroft.

She broke off suddenly and Enderby, glancing over his shoulder and following the direction of her eyes, became aware of a pink, healthy-looking young man leaning over the gate and making various apologetic noises to attract their attention.

'I say,' said the young man, 'frightfully sorry to butt in and all that. I mean, it is awfully awkward, but my aunt sent me along.'

Emily and Charles both said, 'Oh,' in an inquiring tone, not being much the wiser for the explanation.

'Yes,' said the young man. 'To tell the truth my aunt's rather a Tartar. What she says *goes*, if you know what I mean. Of course, I think it's frightfully bad form coming along at a time like this, but if you knew my aunt—and if you do as she wants, you will know her in a few minutes—'

'Is your aunt Miss Percehouse?' broke in Emily.

'That's right,' said the young man, much relieved. 'So you know all about her? Old Mother Curtis has been talking, I suppose. She can wag a tongue, can't she? Not that she's a bad sort, mind you. Well, the fact is, my aunt said she wanted to see you, and I was to come along and tell you so. Compliments, and all that, and would it be troubling you too much—she was an invalid and quite unable to get out and it would be a great kindness—well, you know the sort of thing. I needn't say it all. It's curiosity really, of course, and if you say you've got a headache, or have got letters to write, it will be quite all right and you needn't bother.'

'Oh, but I should like to bother,' said Emily. 'I'll come with you at once. Mr Enderby has got to go along and see Major Burnaby.'

'Have I?' said Enderby in a low voice.

'You have,' said Emily firmly.

She dismissed him with a brief nod and joined her new friend in the road.

'I suppose you're Mr Garfield,' she said.

'That's right. I ought to have told you.'

'Oh, well,' said Emily, 'it wasn't very difficult to guess.'

'Splendid of you coming along like this,' said Mr Garfield. 'Lots of girls would have been awfully offended. But you know what old ladies are.'

'You don't live down here, do you, Mr Garfield?'

'You bet your life I don't,' said Ronnie Garfield with fervour. 'Did you ever see such a god-forsaken spot? Not so much as the pictures to go to. I wonder someone doesn't commit a murder to—'

He paused, appalled by what he had said.

'I say, I *am* sorry. I am the most unlucky devil that ever lived. Always coming out with the wrong thing. I never meant it for a moment.'

'I'm sure you didn't,' said Emily soothingly.

'Here we are,' said Mr Garfield. He pushed open a gate, and Emily passed through and went up the path leading to a small cottage identical with the rest. In the living-room giving on the garden was a couch, and on it was lying an elderly lady with a thin wrinkled face and with one of the sharpest and most interrogative noses that Emily had ever seen. She raised herself on an elbow with a little difficulty.

'So you've brought her,' she said. 'Very kind of you, my dear, to come along to see an old woman. But you know what it is when you are an invalid. You must have a finger in every pie going and if you can't go to the pie, then the pie has got to come to you. And you needn't think it's all curiosity—it's more than that. Ronnie, go out and paint the garden furniture. In the shed at the end of the garden.

144

Two basket chairs and a bench. You'll find the paint there all ready.'

'Right oh, Aunt Caroline.'

The obedient nephew disappeared.

'Sit down,' said Miss Percehouse.

Emily sat on the chair indicated. Strange to say she had immediately felt conscious of a distinct liking and sympathy for this rather sharp-tongued middle-aged invalid. She felt indeed a kind of kinship with her. 'Here is someone,' thought Emily, 'who goes straight to the point and means to have her own way and bosses everybody she can. Just like me, only I happen to be rather good-looking, and she has to do it all by force of character.'

'I understand you are the girl who is engaged to Trevelyan's nephew,' said Miss Percehouse. 'I've heard all about you and now I have seen you I understand exactly what you are up to. And I wish you good luck.'

'Thank you,' said Emily.

'I hate a slobbering female,' said Miss Percehouse. 'I like one who gets up and does things.'

She looked at Emily sharply.

'I suppose you pity me—lying here never able to get up and walk about?'

'No,' said Emily thoughtfully. 'I don't know that I do. I suppose that one can, if one has the determination, always get something out of life. If you can't get it in one way you get it in another.'

'Quite right,' said Miss Percehouse. 'You've got to take life from a different angle, that's all.'

'Angle of attack,' murmured Emily.

'What's that you say?'

As clearly as she was able, Emily outlined the theory that she had evolved that morning and the application of it she had made to the matter in hand.

'Not bad,' said Miss Percehouse nodding her head. 'Now, my dear—we will get down to business. Not being a born fool, I suppose you've come up to this village to find out what you can about the people here, and to see if what you find out has any bearing on the murder. Well, if there's anything you want to know about the people here, I can tell it to you.'

Emily wasted no time. Concise and business-like she came to the point.

'Major Burnaby?' she asked.

'Typical retired army officer, narrow-minded and limited in outlook, jealous disposition. Credulous in money matters. Kind of man who invests in a South Sea Bubble because he can't see a yard in front of his own nose. Likes to pay his debts promptly and dislikes people who don't wipe their feet on the mat.'

'Mr Rycroft?' said Emily.

'Queer little man, enormous egotist. Cranky. Likes to think himself a wonderful fellow. I suppose he has offered to help you solve the case aright owing to his wonderful knowledge of criminology.'

Emily admitted that that was the case.

'Mr Duke?' she asked.

'Don't know a thing about the man—and yet I ought to. Most ordinary type. I ought to know—and yet I don't. It's queer. It's like a name on the tip of your tongue and yet for the life of you, you can't remember it.'

'The Willetts?' asked Emily.

'Ah! the Willetts!' Miss Percehouse hoisted herself up on an elbow again in some excitement. 'What about the Willetts indeed? Now, I'll tell you something about them, my dear. It may be useful to you, or it may not. Go over to my writing table there and pull out the little top drawer—the one to the left—that's right. Bring me the blank envelope that's there.'

Emily brought the envelope as directed.

'I don't say it's important—it probably isn't,' said Miss Percehouse. 'Everybody tells lies one way or another, and Mrs Willett is perfectly entitled to do the same as everybody else.'

She took the envelope and slipped her hand inside.

'I will tell you all about it. When the Willetts arrived here, with their smart clothes and their maids and their innovation trunks, she and Violet came up in Forder's car and the maids and the innovation trunks came by the station bus. And naturally, the whole thing being an event as you might say, I was looking out as they passed, and I saw a coloured label blow off from one of the trunks and dive down on to one of my borders. Now, if there is one thing I hate more than another it is a litter of paper or mess of any kind, so I sent Ronnie out to pick it up, and I was going to throw it away when it struck me it was a bright, pretty thing, and I might as well keep it for the scrapbooks I make for the children's hospital. Well, I wouldn't have thought about it again except for Mrs Willett deliberately mentioning on two or three occasions that Violet had never been out of South Africa and that she herself had only been to South Africa, England, and the Riviera.'

'Yes?' said Emily.

'Exactly. Now—look at this.'

Miss Percehouse thrust a luggage label into Emily's hand. It bore the inscription, Mendle's Hotel, Melbourne.

'Australia,' said Miss Percehouse, 'isn't South Africa—or it wasn't in my young days. I daresay it isn't important, but there it is for what it is worth. And I'll tell you another thing. I have heard Mrs Willett calling to her daughter, and she called Coo-ee, and that again is more typical of Australia than South Africa. And what I say is, it is queer. Why shouldn't you wish to admit that you come from Australia if you do?'

'It's certainly curious,' said Emily. 'And it's curious that they should come to live here in winter time as they have.'

'That leaps to the eye,' said Miss Percehouse. 'Have you met them yet?'

'No. I thought of going there this morning. Only—I didn't know quite what to say.'

'I'll provide you with an excuse,' said Miss Percehouse briskly. 'Fetch me my fountain pen and some notepaper and an envelope. That's right. Now, let me see.' She paused deliberately, then without the least warning raised her voice in a hideous scream.

'Ronnie, Ronnie, Ronnie! Is the boy deaf? Why can't he come when he's called? Ronnie! Ronnie!'

Ronnie arrived at a brisk trot, paint brush in hand.

'Is there anything the matter, Aunt Caroline?'

'What should be the matter? I was calling you, that was

all. Did you have any particular cake for tea when you were at the Willetts' yesterday?'

'Cake?'

'Cake, sandwiches—anything. How slow you are, boy. What did you have to eat for tea?'

'There was coffee cake,' said Ronnie very much puzzled, 'and some *pâté* sandwiches—'

'Coffee cake,' said Miss Percehouse. 'That'll do.' She began to write briskly. 'You can go back to your painting, Ronnie. Don't hang about, and don't stand there with your mouth open. You had your adenoids out when you were eight years old, so there is no excuse for it.'

She continued to write:

Dear Mrs Willett,—I hear you had the most delicious coffee cake for tea yesterday afternoon. Will you be so very kind as to give me the recipe for it? I know you'll not mind my asking you this—an invalid has so little variety except in her diet. Miss Trefusis has kindly promised to take this note for me as Ronnie is busy this morning. Is not this news about the convict too dreadful?

Yours very sincerely,
Caroline Percehouse.

She put it in an envelope, sealed it down and addressed it.

'There you are, young woman. You will probably find the doorstep littered with reporters. A lot of them passed along the lane in Forder's charabanc. I saw them. But you ask for Mrs Willett and say you have brought a note from me and you'll sail in. I needn't tell you to keep your eyes open and make the most you can of your visit. You will do that anyway.'

'You are kind,' said Emily. 'You really are.'

'I help those who can help themselves,' said Miss Percehouse. 'By the way, you haven't asked me what I think of Ronnie yet. I presume he is on your list of the village. He is a good lad in his way, but pitifully weak. I am sorry to say he would do almost anything for money. Look at what he stands from me! And he hasn't got the brains to see that I would like him just ten times better if he stood up to me now and again, and told me to go to the devil.

'The only other person in the village is Captain Wyatt. He smokes opium, I believe. And he's easily the worst-tempered man in England. Anything more you want to know?'

'I don't think so,' said Emily. 'What you have told me seems pretty comprehensive.'

CHAPTER 18

Emily Visits Sittaford House

As Emily walked briskly along the lane she noticed once more how the character of the morning was changing. The mist was closing up and round.

'What an awful place to live in England is,' thought Emily. 'If it isn't snowing or raining or blowing it's misty. And if the sun does shine it's so cold that you can't feel your fingers or toes.'

She was interrupted in these reflections by a rather hoarse voice speaking rather close to her right ear.

'Excuse me,' it said, 'but do you happen to have seen a bull terrier?'

Emily started and turned. Leaning over a gate was a tall thin man with a very brown complexion, bloodshot eyes and grey hair. He was propped up with a crutch one side, and was eyeing Emily with enormous interest. She had no difficulty in identifying him as Captain Wyatt, the invalid owner of No. 2 The Cottages.

'No, I haven't,' said Emily.

'She's got out,' said Captain Wyatt. 'An affectionate

creature, but an absolute fool. With all these cars and things—'

'I shouldn't think many motors come up this lane,' said Emily.

'Charabancs do in the summer time,' said Captain Wyatt grimly. 'It's the three and sixpenny morning run from Exhampton. Ascent of Sittaford Beacon with a halt halfway up from Exhampton for light refreshments.'

'Yes, but this isn't summer time,' said Emily.

'All the same a charabanc came along just now. Reporters, I suppose, going to have a look at Sittaford House.'

'Did you know Captain Trevelyan well?' asked Emily.

She was of the opinion that the incident of the bull terrier had been a mere subterfuge on Captain Wyatt's part dictated by a very natural curiosity. She was, she was well aware, the principal object of attention in Sittaford at present, and it was only natural that Captain Wyatt should wish to have a look at her as well as everyone else.

'I don't know about well,' said Captain Wyatt. 'He sold me this cottage.'

'Yes,' said Emily encouragingly.

'A skinflint, that's what he was,' said Captain Wyatt. 'The arrangement was that he was to do the place up to suit the purchaser's taste, and just because I had the window sashes in chocolate picked out in lemon, he wanted me to pay half. Said the arrangement was for uniform colour.'

'You didn't like him,' said Emily.

'I was always having rows with him,' said Captain Wyatt. 'But I always have rows with everyone,' he added as an afterthought. 'In a place like this you have to teach people to leave a man alone. Always knocking at the door and dropping in and chattering. I don't mind seeing people when I am in the mood—but it has got to be my mood, not theirs. No good Trevelyan giving me his Lord of the Manor airs and dropping in whenever he felt like it. There's not a soul in the place comes near me now,' he added with satisfaction.

'Oh!' said Emily.

'That's the best of having a native servant,' said Captain Wyatt. 'They understand orders. Abdul!' he roared.

A tall Indian in a turban came out of the cottage and waited attentively.

'Come in and have something,' said Captain Wyatt. 'And see my little cottage.'

'I'm sorry,' said Emily, 'but I have to hurry on.'

'Oh, no, you haven't,' said Captain Wyatt.

'Yes, I have,' said Emily. 'I've got an appointment.'

'Nobody understands the art of living nowadays,' said Captain Wyatt. 'Catching trains, making appointments, fixing times for everything—all nonsense. Get up with the sun, I say, have your meals when you feel like it, and never tie yourself to a time or a date. I could teach people how to live if they would listen to me.'

The results of this exalted idea of living were not too hopeful, Emily reflected. Anything more like a battered wreck of a man than Captain Wyatt she had never seen. However, feeling that his curiosity had been sufficiently satisfied for the time being, she insisted once more on her appointment and went on her way.

Sittaford House had a solid oak front door, a neat bell

pull, an immense wire mat, and a brilliantly polished brass letter box. It represented, as Emily could not fail to see, comfort and decorum. A neat and conventional parlourmaid answered the bell.

Emily deduced the journalist evil had been before her as the parlourmaid said at once in a distant tone, 'Mrs Willett is not seeing anyone this morning.'

'I have brought a note from Miss Percehouse,' said Emily.

This clearly altered matters. The parlourmaid's face expressed indecision, then she shifted her ground.

'Will you come inside, please.'

Emily was ushered into what house agents describe as 'a well-appointed hall', and from there into a large drawing-room. A fire was burning brightly and there were traces of feminine occupation in the room. Some glass tulips, an elaborate workbag, a girl's hat, and a Pierrot doll with very long legs, were lying about. There were, she noticed, no photographs.

Having taken in all there was to see, Emily was warming her hands in front of the fire when the door opened and a girl about her own age came in. She was a very pretty girl, Emily noticed, smartly and expensively dressed, and she also thought that she had never seen a girl in a greater state of nervous apprehension. Not that this was apparent on the surface, however. Miss Willett was making a gallant appearance of being entirely at her ease.

'Good morning,' she said advancing and shaking hands. 'I'm so sorry Mother isn't down, but she's spending the morning in bed.'

'Oh, I am sorry, I'm afraid I have come at an unfortunate time.'

'No, of course not. The cook is writing out the recipe for that cake now. We are only too delighted for Miss Percehouse to have it. Are you staying with her?'

Emily reflected with an inward smile that this was perhaps the only house in Sittaford whose members were not exactly aware of who she was and why she was there. Sittaford House had a definite regime of employers and employed. The employed might know about her—the employers clearly did not.

'I am not exactly staying with her,' said Emily. 'In fact, I'm at Mrs Curtis's.'

'Of course the cottage is terribly small, and she has her nephew, Ronnie, with her, hasn't she? I suppose there wouldn't be room for you too. She's a wonderful person, isn't she? So much character, I always think, but I am rather afraid of her really.'

'She's a bully, isn't she?' agreed Emily cheerfully. 'But it's an awful temptation to be a bully, especially if people won't stand up to you.'

Miss Willett sighed.

'I wish I could stand up to people,' she said. 'We've had the most awful morning absolutely pestered by reporters.'

'Oh, of course,' said Emily. 'This is Captain Trevelyan's house really, isn't it?—the man who was murdered at Exhampton.'

She was trying to determine the exact cause of Violet Willett's nervousness. The girl was clearly on the jump. Something was frightening her—and frightening her badly. She mentioned Captain Trevelyan's name bluntly on purpose. The girl didn't noticeably react to it in any way, but then she was probably expecting some such reference.

'Yes, wasn't it dreadful?'

'Do tell me—that's if you don't mind talking about it?'

'No—no—of course not—why should I?'

'There's something very wrong with this girl,' thought Emily. 'She hardly knows what she's saying. What has made her get the wind up this morning particularly?'

'About that table-turning,' went on Emily. 'I heard about it in a casual sort of way and it seemed to me so frightfully interesting—I mean so absolutely gruesome.'

Girlish thrills, she thought to herself, that's my line.

'Oh, it was horrid,' said Violet. 'That evening—I shall never forget it! We thought, of course, that it was somebody just fooling—only it seemed a very nasty kind of joke.'

'Yes?'

'I shall never forget when we turned the lights on—everybody looked so queer. Not Mr Duke and Major Burnaby—they are the stolid kind, they would never like to admit that they were impressed by anything of that kind. But you could see that Major Burnaby was really awfully rattled by it. I think that actually he believed in it more than anybody else. But I thought poor little Mr Rycroft was going to have a heart attack or something, yet he must be used to that kind of thing because he does a lot of psychic research, and as for Ronnie, Ronnie Garfield you know—he looked as though he had seen a ghost—actually seen one. Even Mother was awfully upset—more than I have ever seen her before.'

'It must have been most spooky,' said Emily. 'I wish I had been there to see.'

'It was rather horrid really. We all pretended that it was—just fun, you know, but it didn't seem like that. And then Major Burnaby suddenly made up his mind to go over to Exhampton and we all tried to stop him, and said he would be buried in a snowdrift, but he would go. And there we sat, after he had gone, all feeling dreadful and worried. And then, last night—no, yesterday morning, we got the news.'

'You think it was Captain Trevelyan's spirit?' said Emily in an awed voice. 'Or do you think it was clairvoyance or telepathy?'

'Oh, I don't know. But I shall never, never laugh at these things again.'

The parlourmaid entered with a folded piece of paper on a salver which she handed to Violet.

The parlourmaid withdrew and Violet unfolded the paper, glanced over it and handed it to Emily.

'There you are,' she said. 'As a matter of fact you are just in time. This murder business has upset the servants. They think it's dangerous to live in this out of the way part. Mother lost her temper with them yesterday evening and has sent them all packing. They are going after lunch. We are going to get two men instead—a house-parlourman and a kind of butler-chauffeur. I think it will answer much better.'

'Servants are silly, aren't they?' said Emily.

'It isn't even as if Captain Trevelyan had been killed in this house.'

'What made you think of coming to live here?' asked Emily, trying to make the question sound artless and girlishly natural.

'Oh, we thought it would be rather fun,' said Violet.

'Don't you find it rather dull?'

'Oh, no, I love the country.'

But her eyes avoided Emily's. Just for a moment she looked suspicious and afraid.

She stirred uneasily in her chair and Emily rose rather reluctantly to her feet.

'I must be going now,' she said. 'Thank you so much, Miss Willett. I do hope your mother will be all right.'

'Oh, she's quite well really. It's only the servants—and all the worry.'

'Of course.'

Adroitly, unperceived by the other, Emily managed to discard her gloves on a small table. Violet Willett accompanied her to the front door and they took leave of each other with a few pleasant remarks.

The parlourmaid who had opened the door to Emily had unlocked it, but as Violet Willett closed it behind her retreating guest Emily caught no sound of the key being turned. When she reached the gate, therefore, she retraced her steps slowly.

Her visit had more than confirmed the theories she held about Sittaford House. There was something queer going on here. She didn't think Violet Willett was directly implicated—that is unless she was a very clever actress indeed. But there was something wrong, and that something *must* have a connection with the tragedy. There *must* be some link between the Willetts and Captain Trevelyan, and in that link there might lie the clue to the whole mystery.

She came up to the front door, turned the handle very gently and passed across the threshold. The hall was deserted. Emily paused, uncertain what to do next. She had her excuse—the gloves left thoughtfully behind in the drawing-room. She stood stock still listening. There was no sound anywhere except a very faint murmur of voices from upstairs. As quietly as possible Emily crept to the foot of the stairs and stood looking up. Then, very gingerly she ascended a step at a time. This was rather more risky. She could hardly pretend that her gloves had walked of their own accord to the first floor, but she had a burning desire to overhear something of the conversation that was going on upstairs. Modern builders never made their doors fit well, in Emily's opinion. You could hear a murmur of voices down here. Therefore, if you reached the door itself you would hear plainly the conversation that was going on inside the room. Another step—one more again . . . Two women's voices—Violet and her mother without doubt.

Suddenly there was a break in the conversation—a sound of a footstep. Emily retreated rapidly.

When Violet Willett opened her mother's door and came down the stairs she was surprised to find her late guest standing in the hall peering about her in a lost dog kind of way.

'My gloves,' she explained. 'I must have left them. I came back for them.'

'I expect they are in here,' said Violet.

They went into the drawing-room and there, sure enough, on a little table near where Emily had been sitting lay the missing gloves.

'Oh, thank you,' said Emily. 'It's so stupid of me. I am always leaving things.'

'And you want gloves in this weather,' said Violet. 'It's so cold.' Once again they parted at the hall door, and this time Emily heard the key being turned in the lock.

She went down the drive with plenty to think about, for, as that door on the upper landing had opened, she had heard distinctly one sentence spoken in an older woman's fretful and plaintive voice.

'*My God,*' the voice had wailed, '*I can't bear it. Will tonight never come?*'

CHAPTER 19

Theories

Emily arrived back at the cottage to find her boy friend absent. He had, Mrs Curtis explained, gone off with several other young gentlemen, but two telegrams had come for the young lady. Emily took them, opened them, and put them in the pocket of her sweater, Mrs Curtis eyeing them hungrily the while.

'Not bad news, I hope?' said Mrs Curtis.

'Oh, no,' said Emily.

'Always gives me a turn, a telegram does,' said Mrs Curtis.

'I know,' said Emily. 'Very disturbing.'

At the moment she felt disinclined for anything but solitude. She wanted to sort out and arrange her own ideas. She went up to her own room, and taking pencil and notepaper she set to work on a system of her own. After twenty minutes of this exercise she was interrupted by Mr Enderby.

'Hullo, hullo, hullo, there you are. Fleet Street has been hard on your tracks all morning but they have just missed

161

you everywhere. Anyway they have had it from me that you are not to be worried. As far as you're concerned, I am the big noise.'

He sat down on the chair—Emily was occupying the bed—and chuckled.

'Envy and malice isn't in it!' he said. 'I have been handing them out the goods. I know everyone and I am right in it. It's too good to be true. I keep pinching myself and feeling I will wake up in a minute. I say, have you noticed the fog?'

'It won't stop me going to Exeter this afternoon, will it?' said Emily.

'Do you want to go to Exeter?'

'Yes. I have to meet Mr Dacres there. My solicitor, you know—the one who is undertaking Jim's defence. He wants to see me. And I think I shall pay a visit to Jim's Aunt Jennifer, while I am there. After all, Exeter is only half an hour away.'

'Meaning she might have nipped over by train and batted her brother over the head and nobody would have noticed her absence.'

'Oh, I know it sounds rather improbable, but one has to go into everything. Not that I want it to be Aunt Jennifer—I don't. I would much rather it was Martin Dering. I hate the sort of man who presumes on going to be a brother-in-law and does things in public that you can't smack his face for.'

'Is he that kind?'

'Very much that kind. He's an ideal person for a murderer—always getting telegrams from bookmakers and losing money on horses. It's annoying that he's got such a good alibi. Mr Dacres told me about it. A publisher and a literary dinner seems so very unbreakable and respectable.'

'A literary dinner,' said Enderby. 'Friday night. Martin Dering—let me see—Martin Dering—why, yes—I am almost sure of it. Dash it all, I am quite sure of it, but I can clinch things by wiring to Carruthers.'

'What are you talking about?' said Emily.

'Listen. You know I came down to Exhampton on Friday evening. Well, there was a bit of information I was going to get from a pal of mine, another newspaper man, Carruthers his name is. He was coming round to see me about half past six if he could—before he went on to some literary dinner—he is rather a big bug, Carruthers, and if he couldn't make it he would send me a line to Exhampton. Well, he didn't make it and he did send me a line.'

'What *has* all this got to do with it?' said Emily.

'Don't be so impatient, I am coming to the point. The old chap was rather screwed when he wrote it—done himself well at the dinner—after giving me the item I wanted, he went on to waste a good bit of juicy description on me. You know—about the speeches, and what asses so and so, a famous novelist and a famous playwright, were. And he said he had been rottenly placed at dinner. There was an empty seat on one side of him where Ruby McAlmott, that awful best-seller woman, ought to have sat and an empty place on the other side of him where the sex specialist, Martin Dering, ought to have been, but he moved up nearer to a poet, who is very well known in Blackheath, and tried to make the best of things. Now, do you see the point?'

'Charles! Darling!' Emily became lyrical with excitement. 'How marvellous. Then the brute wasn't at the dinner at all?'

'Exactly.'

'You are sure you've remembered the name right?'

'I'm positive. I have torn up the letter, worse luck, but I can always wire to Carruthers to make sure. But I absolutely know that I'm not mistaken.'

'There's the publisher still, of course,' said Emily. 'The one he spent the afternoon with. But I rather think it was a publisher who was just going back to America, and if so, that looks fishy. I mean it looks as though he had selected someone who couldn't be asked without rather a lot of trouble.'

'Do you really think we have hit it?' said Charles Enderby.

'Well, it looks like it. I think the best thing to be done is—to go straight to that nice Inspector Narracott and just tell him these new facts. I mean, we can't tackle an American publisher who is on the *Mauretania* or the *Berengaria* or somewhere. That's a job for the police.'

'My word, if this comes off. What a scoop!' said Mr Enderby. 'If it does, I should think the *Daily Wire* couldn't offer me less than—'

Emily broke ruthlessly into his dreams of advancement.

'But we mustn't lose our heads,' she said, 'and throw everything else to the wind. I must go to Exeter. I don't suppose I shall be able to be back here until tomorrow. But I've got a job for you.'

'What kind of a job?'

Emily described her visit to the Willetts and the strange sentence she had overheard on leaving.

'We have got absolutely and positively to find out what is going to happen tonight. There's something in the wind.'

'What an extraordinary thing!'

'Wasn't it? But of course it may be a coincidence. Or it may not—but you observe that the servants are being cleared out of the way. Something queer is going to happen there tonight, and *you* have to be on the spot to see what it is.'

'You mean I have to spend the whole night shivering under a bush in the garden?'

'Well, you don't mind that, do you? Journalists don't mind what they do in a good cause.'

'Who told you that?'

'Never mind who told me, I know it. You will do it, won't you?'

'Oh, rather,' said Charles. 'I am not going to miss anything. If anything queer goes on at Sittaford House tonight, I shall be in it.'

Emily then told him about the luggage label.

'It's odd,' said Mr Enderby. 'Australia is where the third Pearson is, isn't it?—the youngest one. Not, of course, that that means anything, but still it—well, there might be a connection.'

'H'm,' said Emily. 'I think that's all. Have you anything to report on your side?'

'Well,' said Charles, 'I've got an idea.'

'Yes?'

'The only thing is I don't know how you'll like it.'

'What do you mean—how I'll like it?'

'You won't fly out over it, will you?'

'I don't suppose so. I mean I hope I can listen sensibly and quietly to anything.'

'Well, the point is,' said Charles Enderby eyeing her doubtfully, 'don't think I mean to be offensive or anything like that, but do you think that lad of yours is to be depended on for the strict truth?'

'Do you mean,' said Emily, 'that he did murder him after all? You are quite welcome to that view if you like. I said to you at the beginning that that was the natural view to take, but I said we had to work on the assumption that he didn't.'

'I don't mean that,' said Enderby. 'I am with you in assuming that he didn't do the old boy in. What I mean is, how far is his own story of what happened true? He says that he went there, had a chat with the old fellow, and came away leaving him alive and well.'

'Yes.'

'Well, it just occurred to me, you don't think it's possible that he went there and actually found the old man dead? I mean, he might have got the wind up and been scared and not liked to say so.'

Charles had propounded this theory rather dubiously, but he was relieved to find that Emily showed no signs of flying out at him over it. Instead, she frowned and creased her brow in thought.

'I am not going to pretend,' she said. 'It *is* possible. I hadn't thought of it before. I know Jim wouldn't murder anyone, but he might quite well get rattled and tell a silly lie and then, of course, he would have to stick to it. Yes, it is quite possible.'

'The awkward thing is that you can't go and ask him about it now. I mean they wouldn't let you see him alone, would they?'

'I can put Mr Dacres on to him,' said Emily. 'You see your solicitor alone, I believe. The worst of Jim is that he is frightfully obstinate, if he has once said a thing he sticks to it.'

'That's my story and I'm going to stick to it,' said Mr Enderby comprehendingly.

'Yes. I am glad you mentioned that possibility to me, Charles, it hadn't occurred to me. We have been looking for someone who came in *after* Jim had left—but if it was *before*—'

She paused, lost in thought. Two very different theories stretched out in opposite directions. There was the one suggested by Mr Rycroft, in which Jim's quarrel with his uncle was the determining point. The other theory, however, took no cognizance of Jim whatsoever. The first thing to do, Emily felt, was to see the doctor who had first examined the body. If it were possible that Captain Trevelyan had been murdered at—say—four o'clock, it might make a considerable difference to the question of alibis. And the other thing to do was to make Mr Dacres urge most strongly on his client the absolute necessity of speaking the truth on this point.

She rose from the bed.

'Well,' she said, 'you had better find out how I can get to Exhampton. The man at the smithy has a car of a kind, I believe. Will you go and settle with him about it? I'll start immediately after lunch. There's a train at three ten to Exeter. That will give me time to see the doctor first. What's the time now?'

'Half past twelve,' said Mr Enderby, consulting his watch.

'Then we will both go up and fix up about that car,' said Emily. 'And there's just one other thing I want to do before leaving Sittaford.'

'What's that?'

'I am going to pay a call on Mr Duke. He's the only person in Sittaford I haven't seen. And he was one of the people at the table-turning.'

'Oh, we'll pass his cottage on the way to the smithy.'

Mr Duke's cottage was the last of the row. Emily and Charles unlatched the gate and walked up the path. And then something rather surprising occurred. For the door opened and a man came out. And that man was Inspector Narracott.

He, too, looked surprised and, Emily fancied, embarrassed.

Emily abandoned her original intention.

'I am so glad to have met you, Inspector Narracott,' she said. 'There are one or two things I want to talk to you about if I may.'

'Delighted, Miss Trefusis.' He drew out a watch. 'I'm afraid you will have to look sharp. I've a car waiting. I've got to go back to Exhampton almost immediately.'

'How extraordinarily fortunate,' said Emily. 'You might give me a lift, will you, Inspector?'

The Inspector said rather woodenly that he would be very pleased to do so.

'You might go and get my suitcase, Charles,' said Emily. 'It's packed up and ready.'

Charles departed immediately.

'It's a great surprise meeting you here, Miss Trefusis,' said Inspector Narracott.

'I said *au revoir*,' Emily reminded him.

'I didn't notice it at the time.'

'You've not seen the last of me by a long way,' said Emily candidly. 'You know, Inspector Narracott, you've made a mistake. Jim's not the man you're after.'

'Indeed!'

'And what's more,' said Emily, 'I believe in your heart that you agree with me.'

'What makes you think that, Miss Trefusis?'

'What were you doing in Mr Duke's cottage?' retaliated Emily.

Narracott looked embarrassed, and she was quick to follow it up.

'You're doubtful, Inspector—that's what you are—doubtful. You thought you had got the right man and now you are not so sure, and so you are making a few investigations. Well, I have got something to tell you that may help. I'll tell it to you on the way to Exhampton.'

Footsteps sounded down the road, and Ronnie Garfield appeared. He had the air of a truant, breathless and guilty.

'I say, Miss Trefusis,' he began. 'What about a walk this afternoon? While my aunt has a nap, you know.'

'Impossible,' said Emily. 'I'm going away. To Exeter.'

'What, not really! For good, you mean?'

'Oh, no,' said Emily. 'I shall be back again tomorrow.'

'Oh, that's splendid.'

Emily took something from the pocket of her sweater

and handed it to him. 'Give that to your aunt, will you? It's a recipe for coffee cake, and tell her that she was just in time, the cook is leaving today and so are the other servants. Be sure to tell her, she will be interested.'

A far-off scream was borne on the breeze. 'Ronnie,' it said, 'Ronnie, Ronnie.'

'There's my aunt,' said Ronnie starting nervously. 'I had better go.'

'I think you had,' said Emily. 'You've got green paint on your left cheek,' she called after him. Ronnie Garfield disappeared through his aunt's gate.

'Here's my boy friend with my suitcase,' said Emily. 'Come on, Inspector. I'll tell you everything in the car.'

CHAPTER 20

Visit to Aunt Jennifer

At half past two Dr Warren received a call from Emily. He took an immediate fancy to this business-like and attractive girl. Her questions were blunt and to the point.

'Yes, Miss Trefusis, I see exactly what you mean. You'll understand that contrary to the popular belief in novels it is extremely difficult to fix the time of death accurately. I saw the body at eight o'clock. I can say decidedly that Captain Trevelyan had been dead at least two hours. How much longer than that would be difficult to say. If you were to tell me that he was killed at four o'clock, I should say that it was possible, though my own opinion inclines to a later time. On the other hand he could certainly not have been dead for much longer than that. Four and a half hours would be the outside limit.'

'Thank you,' said Emily, 'that's all I wanted to know.'

She caught the three-ten train at the station and drove straight to the hotel where Mr Dacres was staying.

Their interview was business-like and unemotional. Mr Dacres had known Emily since she was a small child

171

and had managed her affairs for her since she came of age.

'You must prepare yourself for a shock, Emily,' he said. 'Things are much worse for Jim Pearson than we imagined.'

'Worse?'

'Yes. It's no good beating about the bush. Certain facts have come to light which are bound to show him up in a most unfavourable light. It is those facts which led the police actually to charge him with the crime. I should not be acting in your interests if I withheld these facts from you.'

'Please tell me,' said Emily.

Her voice was perfectly calm and composed. Whatever the inward shock she might have felt, she had no intention of making an outward display of her feelings. It was not feelings that were going to help Jim Pearson, it was brains. She must keep all her wits about her.

'There is no doubt that he was in urgent and immediate need of money. I am not going to enter into the ethics of the situation at the moment. Pearson had apparently before now occasionally borrowed money—to use a euphemism—from his firm—I may say without their knowledge. He was fond of speculating in shares, and on one occasion previously, knowing that certain dividends were to be paid into his account in a week's time, he anticipated them by using the firm's money to buy certain shares which he had pretty certain knowledge were bound to go up. The transaction was quite satisfactory, the money was replaced and Pearson really doesn't seem to have had any doubts as to the honesty of the transaction. Apparently he repeated this just over a week ago. This time an unforeseen thing occurred. The books of the firm were examined at certain stated times, but for some reason or other this date was advanced, and Pearson was faced with a very unpleasant dilemma. He was quite aware of the construction that would be put on his action and he was quite unable to raise the sum of money involved. He admits himself that he had tried in various quarters and failed when as a last resource he rushed down to Devonshire to lay the matter before his uncle and persuade him to help him. This Captain Trevelyan absolutely refused to do.

'Now, my dear Emily, we shall be quite unable to prevent these facts from being brought to light. The police have already unearthed the matter. And you see, don't you, that we have here a very pressing and urgent motive for the crime? The moment Captain Trevelyan was dead Pearson could easily have obtained the necessary sum as an advance from Mr Kirkwood and saved himself from disaster and possibly criminal prosecution.'

'Oh, the idiot,' said Emily helplessly.

'Quite so,' said Mr Dacres dryly. 'It seems to me that our only chance lies in proving that Jim Pearson was quite unaware of the provisions of his uncle's will.'

There was a pause while Emily considered the matter. Then she said quietly:

'I'm afraid that's impossible. All three of them knew— Sylvia, Jim and Brian. They often discussed it and laughed and joked about the rich uncle in Devonshire.'

'Dear, dear,' said Mr Dacres. 'That's unfortunate.'

'You don't think him guilty, Mr Dacres?' asked Emily.

'Curiously enough I do not,' replied the lawyer. 'In some ways Jim Pearson is a most transparent young man. He hasn't, if you will allow me to say so, Emily, a very high standard of commercial honesty, but I do not believe for one minute that his hand sandbagged his uncle.'

'Well, that's a good thing,' said Emily. 'I wish the police thought the same.'

'Quite so. Our own impressions and ideas are of no practical use. The case against him is unfortunately strong. I am not going to disguise from you, my dear child, that the outlook is bad. I should suggest Lorimer, K.C., as the defence. Forlorn hope man they call him,' he added cheerfully.

'There is one thing I should like to know,' said Emily. 'You have, of course, seen Jim?'

'Certainly.'

'I want you to tell me honestly if you think he has told the truth in other respects.' She outlined to him the idea that Enderby had suggested to her.

The lawyer considered the matter carefully before replying.

'It's my impression,' he said, 'that he is speaking the truth when he describes his interview with his uncle. But there is little doubt that he has got the wind up badly, and if he went round to the window, entered that way and came across his uncle's dead body—he might just possibly be too scared to admit the fact and have concocted this other story.'

'That's what I thought,' said Emily. 'Next time you see him, Mr Dacres, will you urge him to speak the truth? It may make the most tremendous difference.'

'I will do so. All the same,' he said after a moment or two's pause, 'I think you are mistaken in this idea. The news of Captain Trevelyan's death was bandied around in Exhampton about eight thirty. At that time the last train had left for Exeter, but Jim Pearson got the first train available in the morning—a thoroughly unwise proceeding, by the way, as it called attention to his movements which otherwise would not have been aroused if he had left by a train at a more conventional hour. Now if, as you suggest, he discovered his uncle's dead body some time after half past four, I think he would have left Exhampton straight away. There's a train which leaves shortly after six and another at a quarter to eight.'

'That's a point,' admitted Emily, 'I didn't think of that.'

'I have questioned him narrowly about his method of entering his uncle's house,' went on Mr Dacres. 'He says that Captain Trevelyan made him remove his boots, and leave them on the doorstep. That accounts for no wet marks being discovered in the hall.'

'He doesn't speak of having heard any sound—anything at all—that gives him the idea that there might have been someone else in the house?'

'He didn't mention it to me. But I will ask him.'

'Thank you,' said Emily. 'If I write a note can you take it to him?'

'Subject to its being read, of course.'

'Oh, it will be a very discreet one.'

She crossed to the writing table and scribbled a few words.

'Dearest Jim,—Everything's going to be all right, so cheer up. I am working like the worst kind of slave to find out the truth. What an idiot you've been, darling.

Love from
Emily.'

'There,' she said.

Mr Dacres read it but made no comment.

'I have taken pains with my handwriting,' said Emily, 'so that the prison authorities can read it easily. Now, I must be off.'

'You will allow me to offer you a cup of tea?'

'No, thank you, Mr Dacres. I have no time to lose. I am going to see Jim's Aunt Jennifer.'

At The Laurels, Emily was informed that Mrs Gardner was out but would be home shortly.

Emily smiled upon the parlourmaid.

'I'll come in and wait then.'

'Would you like to see Nurse?'

Emily was always ready to see anybody. 'Yes,' she said promptly.

A few minutes later Nurse Davis, starched and curious, arrived.

'How do you do,' said Emily. 'I am Emily Trefusis—a kind of niece of Mrs Gardner's. That is, I am going to be a niece, but my fiancé, Jim Pearson, has been arrested, as I expect you know.'

'Oh, it's been too dreadful,' said Nurse Davis. 'We saw it all in the papers this morning. What a terrible business!

You seem to be bearing up wonderfully, Miss Trefusis—
really wonderfully.'

There was a faint note of disapproval in the nurse's
voice. Hospital nurses, she implied, were able to bear up
owing to their force of character, but lesser mortals were
expected to *give way*.

'Well, one mustn't sag at the knees,' said Emily. 'I hope
you don't mind very much. I mean, it must be awkward
for you to be associated with a family that has got a murder
in it.'

'It's very unpleasant, of course,' said Nurse Davis,
unbending at this proof of consideration. 'But one's duty
to one's patient comes before everything.'

'How splendid,' said Emily. 'It must be wonderful for
Aunt Jennifer to feel she has somebody upon whom she
can rely.'

'Oh, really,' said the nurse, whispering, 'you are too kind.
But, of course, I have had curious experiences before this.
Why, at the last case I attended—' Emily listened patiently
to a long and scandalous anecdote comprising complicated
divorce and paternity questions. After complimenting Nurse
Davis on her tact, discretion and *savoir faire*, Emily slid
back to the topic of the Gardners.

'I don't know Aunt Jennifer's husband at all,' she said. 'I've
never met him. He never goes away from home, does he?'

'No, poor fellow.'

'What exactly is the matter with him?'

Nurse Davis embarked on the subject with professional
gusto.

'So, really he might get well again any minute,' Emily murmured thoughtfully.

'He would be terribly weak,' said the nurse.

'Oh, of course. But it makes it seem more hopeful, doesn't it?'

The nurse shook her head with firm professional despondency.

'I don't suppose there will be any cure in his case.'

Emily had copied down in her little notebook the timetable of what she called Aunt Jennifer's alibi. She now murmured tentatively:

'How queer it seems to think that Aunt Jennifer was actually at the pictures when her brother was being killed.'

'Very sad, isn't it?' said Nurse Davis. 'Of course, she couldn't tell—but it gives one such a shock afterwards.'

Emily cast about in her mind to find out what she wanted to know without asking a direct question.

'Didn't she have some queer kind of vision or premonition?' she inquired. 'Wasn't it you who met her in the hall when she came in and exclaimed that she looked quite queer?'

'Oh, no,' said the nurse. 'It wasn't me. I didn't see her until we were sitting down to dinner together, and she seemed quite her ordinary self then. How very interesting.'

'I expect I am mixing it up with something else,' said Emily.

'Perhaps it was some other relation,' suggested Nurse Davis. 'I came in rather late myself. I felt rather guilty about leaving my patient so long, but he himself had urged me to go.'

She suddenly looked at her watch.

'Oh, dear. He asked me for another hot water bottle. I must see about it at once. Will you excuse me, Miss Trefusis?'

Emily excused her and going over to the fireplace, she put her finger on the bell.

The slipshod maid came with rather a frightened face.

'What's your name?' said Emily.

'Beatrice, Miss.'

'Oh, Beatrice, I may not be able to wait to see my aunt, Mrs Gardner, after all—I wanted to ask her about some shopping she did on Friday. Do you know if she brought a big parcel back with her?'

'No, Miss, I didn't see her come in.'

'I thought you said she came in at six o'clock.'

'Yes, Miss, she did. I didn't see her come in, but when I went to take some hot water to her room at seven o'clock it gave me a shock to find her lying in the dark on the bed. "Well, ma'am," I said to her, "You gave me quite a shock." "I came in quite a long time ago. At six o'clock," she said. I didn't see a big parcel anywhere,' said Beatrice, trying her hardest to be helpful.

'It's all very difficult,' thought Emily. 'One has to invent so many things. I've already invented a premonition and a big parcel, but so far as I can see one has to invent something if one doesn't want to sound suspicious.' She smiled sweetly and said:

'That's all right, Beatrice, it doesn't matter.'

Beatrice left the room. Emily took a small local time-table out of her handbag and consulted it.

'Leave Exeter, St David's, three ten,' she murmured, 'Arrive Exhampton, three forty-two. Time allowed for going to brother's house and murdering him—how beastly and cold-blooded it sounds—and such nonsense too—say half an hour to three quarters. What are the trains back? There's one at four twenty-five and there's one Mr Dacres mentioned at six ten, that gets in at twenty-three minutes to seven. Yes, it's actually possible either way. It's a pity there's nothing to suspect the nurse for. She was out all the afternoon and nobody knows where she was. But you can't have a murder without any motive at all. Of course, I don't really believe anybody in this house murdered Captain Trevelyan, but in a way it's comforting to know that they could have. Hello—there's the front door.'

There was a murmur of voices in the hall and the door opened and Jennifer Gardner came into the room.

'I'm Emily Trefusis,' said Emily. 'You know—the one who is engaged to Jim Pearson.'

'So you are Emily,' said Mrs Gardner, shaking hands. 'Well, this is a surprise.'

Suddenly Emily felt very weak and small. Rather like a little girl in the act of doing something very silly. An extraordinary person, Aunt Jennifer. Character—that was what it was. Aunt Jennifer had about enough character for two and three quarter people instead of one.

'Have you had tea, my dear? No? Then we'll have it here. Just a moment—I must go up and see Robert first.'

A strange expression flitted over her face as she mentioned her husband's name. The hard, beautiful voice softened. It was like a light passing over dark ripples of water.

'She adores him,' thought Emily, left alone in the drawing-room. 'All the same there's something frightening about Aunt Jennifer. I wonder if Uncle Robert likes being adored quite as much as that.'

When Jennifer Gardner returned, she had taken off her hat. Emily admired the smooth sweep of the hair back from her forehead.

'Do you want to talk about things, Emily, or don't you? If you don't I shall quite understand.'

'It isn't much good talking about them, is it?'

'We can only hope,' said Mrs Gardner, 'that they will find the real murderer quickly. Just press the bell, will you, Emily? I'll send Nurse's tea up to her. I don't want her chattering down here. How I hate hospital nurses.'

'Is she a good one?'

'I suppose she is. Robert says she is anyway. I dislike her intensely and always have. But Robert says she's far and away the best nurse we've had.'

'She's rather good-looking,' said Emily.

'Nonsense. With her ugly beefy hands?'

Emily watched her aunt's long white fingers as they touched the milk jug and the sugar tongs.

Beatrice came, took the cup of tea and a plate of eatables and left the room.

'Robert has been very upset over all this,' said Mrs Gardner. 'He works himself into such curious states. I suppose it's all part of his illness really.'

'He didn't know Captain Trevelyan well, did he?'

Jennifer Gardner shook her head.

'He neither knew him nor cared about him. To be honest, I myself can't pretend any great sorrow over his death. He was a cruel, grasping man, Emily. He knew the struggle we have had. The poverty! He knew that a loan of money at the right time might have given Robert special treatment that would have made all the difference. Well, retribution has overtaken him.'

She spoke in a deep brooding voice.

'What a strange woman she is,' thought Emily. 'Beautiful and terrible, like something out of a Greek play.'

'It may still not be too late,' said Mrs Gardner. 'I wrote to the lawyers at Exhampton today, to ask them if I could have a certain sum of money in advance. The treatment I am speaking of is in some respects what they would call a quack remedy, but it has been successful in a large number of cases. Emily—how wonderful it will be if Robert is able to walk again.'

Her face was glowing, lit up as though by a lamp.

Emily was tired. She had had a long day, little or nothing to eat, and she was worn out by suppressed emotion. The room kept going away and coming back again.

'Aren't you feeling well, dear?'

'It's all right,' gasped Emily, and to her own surprise, annoyance and humiliation, burst into tears.

Mrs Gardner did not attempt to rise and console her, for which Emily was grateful. She just sat silently until Emily's tears should subside. She murmured in a thoughtful voice:

'Poor child. It's very unlucky that Jim Pearson should have been arrested—very unlucky. I wish—something could be done about it.'

CHAPTER 21

Conversations

Left to his own devices Charles Enderby did not relax his efforts. To familiarize himself with life as lived in Sittaford village he had only to turn on Mrs Curtis much as you would turn on the tap of a hydrant. Listening slightly dazed to a stream of anecdote, reminiscence, rumours, surmise and meticulous detail he endeavoured valiantly to sift the grain from the chaff. He then mentioned another name and immediately the force of the water was directed in that direction. He heard all about Captain Wyatt, his tropical temper, his rudeness, his quarrels with his neighbours, his occasional amazing graciousness, usually to personable young women. The life he led his Indian servant, the peculiar times he had his meals and the exact diet that composed them. He heard about Mr Rycroft's library, his hair tonics, his insistence on strict tidiness and punctuality, his inordinate curiosity over other people's doings, his recent selling of a few old prized personal possessions, his inexplicable fondness for birds, and the prevalent idea that Mrs Willett was setting her cap at him. He heard about Miss Percehouse and her tongue and the way she bullied her nephew, and of the rumours of the gay life that same nephew led in London. He heard all over again of Major Burnaby's friendship with Captain Trevelyan, their reminiscences of the past and their fondness for chess. He heard everything that was known about the Willetts, including the belief that Miss Violet Willett was leading on Mr Ronnie Garfield and that she didn't really mean to have him. It was hinted that she made mysterious excursions to the moor and that she had been seen walking there with a young man. And it was doubtless for that reason, so Mrs Curtis had surmised, that they had come to this desolate spot. Her mother had taken her right away, 'to get right over it like'. But there—'girls can be far more artful than ladies ever dream of'. About Mr Duke, there was curiously little to hear. He had been there only a short time and his activities seemed to be solely horticultural.

It was half past three, and, with his head spinning from the effects of Mrs Curtis's conversation, Mr Enderby went out for a stroll. His intention was to cultivate the acquaintance of Miss Percehouse's nephew more closely. Prudent reconnaissance in the neighbourhood of Miss Percehouse's cottage proved unavailing, but by a stroke of good fortune he ran into that young man just as he was emerging disconsolately from the gates of Sittaford House. He had all the appearance of having been sent away with a flea in his ear.

'Hello,' said Charles. 'I say, isn't that Captain Trevelyan's house?'

'That's right,' said Ronnie.

'I was hoping to get a snapshot of it this morning. For my paper, you know,' he added. 'But this weather is hopeless for photography.'

Ronnie accepted this statement in all good faith without reflecting that if photography was only possible on days of brilliant sunshine, the pictures appearing in the daily papers would be few.

'It must be a very interesting job—yours,' he said.

'A dog's life,' said Charles, faithful to the convention of never showing enthusiasm about one's work. He looked over his shoulder at Sittaford House. 'Rather a gloomy place I should imagine.'

'No end of a difference there since the Willetts moved in,' said Ronnie. 'I was down here last year about the same time, and really you would hardly take it for the same place, and yet, I don't know quite what they have done. Moved the furniture about a bit, I suppose, got cushions and things of that sort about. It's been a godsend to me their being there, I can tell you.'

'Can't be a very jolly spot as a rule, I suppose,' said Charles.

'Jolly? If I lived here a fortnight I should pass out altogether. How my aunt manages to cling on to life in the way she does beats me. You haven't seen her cats, have you? I had to comb one of them this morning and look at the way the brute scratched me.' He held out a hand and an arm for inspection.

'Rather rough luck,' said Charles.

'I should say it was. I say, are you doing any sleuthing? If so, can I help? Be the Watson to your Sherlock, or anything of that kind?'

'Any clues in Sittaford House?' inquired Charles casually. 'I mean did Captain Trevelyan leave any of his things there?'

'I don't think so. My aunt was saying he moved lock, stock and barrel. Took his elephant's trotters and his hippopotamus's toothy pegs and all the sporting rifles and what nots.'

'Almost as though he didn't mean to come back,' said Charles.

'I say—that's an idea. You don't think it was suicide, do you?'

'A man who can hit himself correctly on the back of the head with a sandbag would be something of an artist in the suicide world,' said Charles.

'Yes, I thought there wasn't much in that idea. Looks as if he had a premonition though.' Ronnie's face brightened. 'Look here, what about this? Enemies on his track, he knows they're coming, so he clears out and passes the buck, as it were, to the Willetts.'

'The Willetts were a bit of a miracle by themselves,' said Charles.

'Yes, I can't make it out. Fancy planting yourself down here in the country like this. Violet doesn't seem to mind—actually says she likes it. I don't know what's the matter with her today. I suppose it's the domestic trouble. I can't think why women worry so about servants. If they cut up nasty, just push them out.'

'That's just what they have done, isn't it?' said Charles.

'Yes, I know. But they are in a great stew about it all. Mother lying down with screaming hysterics or something and daughter snapping like a turtle. Fairly pushed me out just now.'

'They haven't had the police here, have they?'

Ronnie stared.

'The police, no, why would they?'

'Well, I wondered. Seeing Inspector Narracott in Sittaford this morning.'

Ronnie dropped his stick with a clatter and stooped to pick it up.

'Who did you say was in Sittaford this morning— Inspector Narracott?'

'Yes.'

'Is he—is he the man in charge of the Trevelyan case?'

'That's right.'

'What was he doing in Sittaford? Where did you see him?'

'Oh, I suppose he was just nosing about,' said Charles, 'checking up Captain Trevelyan's past life, so to speak.'

'You think that's all?'

'I suppose so.'

'He doesn't think anyone in Sittaford had anything to do with it?'

'That would be very unlikely, wouldn't it?'

'Oh, frightfully. But then you know what the police are—always butting in on the wrong tack. At least that's what it says in detective novels.'

'I think they are really rather an intelligent body of men,' said Charles. 'Of course, the Press does a lot to help them.' he added. 'But if you really read a case carefully it's amazing the way they track down murderers with practically no evidence to go on.'

'Oh—well—it's nice to know that, isn't it? They have certainly got on to this man Pearson pretty quick. It seems a pretty clear case.'

'Crystal clear,' said Charles. 'A good thing it wasn't you or me, eh? Well, I must be sending off a few wires. They don't seem very used to telegrams in this place. If you send more than half a crown's worth at one go they seem to think you are an escaped lunatic.'

Charles sent his telegrams, bought a packet of cigarettes, a few doubtful-looking bull's eyes and two very aged paper-backed novelettes. He then returned to the cottage, threw himself on his bed and slept peacefully, blissfully unaware that he and his affairs, particularly Miss Emily Trefusis, were being discussed in various places all around him.

It is fairly safe to say that there were only three topics of conversation at present in Sittaford. One was the murder, one was the escape of the convict, and the other was Miss Emily Trefusis and her cousin. Indeed at a certain moment, four separate conversations were going on with her as their main theme.

Conversation No. 1 was at Sittaford House, where Violet Willett and her mother had just washed up their own tea things owing to the domestic retreat.

'It was Mrs Curtis who told me,' said Violet.

She still looked pale and wan.

'It's almost a disease the way that woman talks,' said her mother.

'I know. It seems the girl is actually stopping there with a cousin or something. She did mention this morning that she was at Mrs Curtis's, but I thought that that was simply

188

because Miss Percehouse hadn't room for her. And now it seems that she'd never even seen Miss Percehouse till this morning!'

'I dislike that woman intensely,' said Mrs Willett.

'Mrs Curtis?'

'No, no, the Percehouse woman. That kind of woman is dangerous. They live for what they can find out about other people. Sending that girl along here for a recipe for coffee cake! I'd like to have sent her a poisoned cake. That would have stopped her interfering for good and all!'

'I suppose I ought to have realized—' began Violet. But her mother interrupted her.

'How could you, my dear! And anyway what harm is done?'

'Why do you think she came here?'

'I don't suppose she had anything definite in mind. She was just spying out the land. Is Mrs Curtis sure about her being engaged to Jim Pearson?'

'That girl told Mr Rycroft so, I believe. Mrs Curtis said she suspected it from the first.'

'Well, then the whole thing's natural enough. She's just looking about aimlessly for something that might help.'

'You didn't see her, Mother,' said Violet. 'She isn't aimless.'

'I wish I had seen her,' said Mrs Willett. 'But my nerves were all to pieces this morning. Reaction, I suppose, after that interview with the police inspector yesterday.'

'You were wonderful, Mother. If only I hadn't been such an utter fool—to go and *faint*. Oh! I'm ashamed of myself for giving the whole show away. And there were you perfectly calm and collected—not turning a hair.'

'I'm in pretty good training,' said Mrs Willett in a hard dry voice. 'If you'd been through what I've been through—but there, I hope you never will, my child. I trust and believe that you've got a happy, peaceful life ahead of you.'

Violet shook her head.

'I'm afraid—I'm afraid—'

'Nonsense—and as for saying you gave the show away by fainting yesterday—nothing of the kind. Don't worry.'

'But that Inspector—he's bound to think—'

'That it was the mention of Jim Pearson made you faint? Yes—he'll think that all right. He's no fool, that Inspector Narracott. But what if he does? He'll suspect a connection—and he'll look for it—*and he won't find it.*'

'You think not?'

'Of course not! How can he? Trust me, Violet dear. That's cast-iron certainty and, in a way, perhaps that faint of yours was a lucky happening. We'll think so anyway.'

Conversation No. 2 was in Major Burnaby's cottage. It was a somewhat one-sided one, the brunt of it being borne by Mrs Curtis, who had been poised for departure for the last half hour, having dropped in to collect Major Burnaby's laundry.

'Like my Great Aunt Sarah's Belinda, that's what I said to Curtis this morning,' said Mrs Curtis triumphantly. 'A deep one—and one that can twist all the men round her little finger.'

A great grunt from Major Burnaby.

'Engaged to one young man and carrying on with another,' said Mrs Curtis. 'That's my Great Aunt Sarah's Belinda all over. And not for the fun of it, mark you. It's not just flightiness—she's a deep one. And now young Mr Garfield—she'll have him roped in before you can say knife. Never have I seen a young gentleman look more like a sheep than he did this morning—and that's a sure sign.'

She paused for breath.

'Well, well,' said Major Burnaby. 'Don't let me keep you, Mrs Curtis.'

'Curtis will be wanting his tea and that's a fact,' said Mrs Curtis without moving. 'I was never one to stand about gossiping. Get on with your job—that's what I say. And talking about jobs, what do you say, sir, to a good turn out?'

'No!' said Major Burnaby with force.

'It's a month since it's been done.'

'No. I like to know where to lay my hand on everything. After one of these turn outs nothing's ever put back in its place.'

Mrs Curtis sighed. She was an impassioned cleaner and turner out.

'It's Captain Wyatt as could do with a spring cleaning,' she observed. 'That nasty native of his—what does he know about cleaning, I should like to know? Nasty black fellow.'

'Nothing better than a native servant,' said Major Burnaby. 'They know their job and they don't talk.'

Any hint the last sentence might have contained was lost on Mrs Curtis. Her mind had reverted to a former topic.

'Two telegrams she got—two arriving in half an hour. Gave me quite a turn it did. But she read them as cool as anything. And then she told me she was going to Exeter and wouldn't be back till tomorrow.'

Agatha Christie

'Did she take her young man with her?' inquired the Major with a gleam of hope.

'No, he's still here. A pleasant spoken young gentleman. He and she'd make a nice pair.'

Grunt from Major Burnaby.

'Well,' said Mrs Curtis. 'I'll be getting along.'

The Major hardly dared breathe for fear he might distract her from her purpose. But this time Mrs Curtis was as good as her word. The door closed behind her.

With a sigh of relief the Major drew forth a pipe and began to peruse a prospectus of a certain mine which was couched in terms so blatantly optimistic that it would have aroused suspicion in any heart but that of a widow or a retired soldier.

'Twelve per cent,' murmured Major Burnaby. 'That sounds pretty good . . .'

Next door Captain Wyatt was laying down the law to Mr Rycroft.

'Fellows like you,' he said, 'don't know anything of the world. You've never lived. You've never roughed it.'

Mr Rycroft said nothing. It was so difficult not to say the wrong thing to Captain Wyatt that it was usually safer not to reply at all.

The Captain leaned over the side of his invalid chair.

'Where's that bitch got to? Nice-looking girl,' he added.

The association of ideas in his mind was quite natural. It was less so to Mr Rycroft, who looked at him in a scandalized fashion.

'What's she doing here? That's what I want to know?' demanded Captain Wyatt. 'Abdul!'

'Sahib?'

'Where's Bully? Has she got out again?'

'She in kitchen, Sahib.'

'Well, don't feed her.' He sank back in his chair again and proceeded on his second tack. 'What does she want here? Who's she going to talk to in a place like this? All you old fogies will bore her stiff. I had a word with her this morning. Expect she was surprised to find a man like me in a place like this.'

He twisted his moustache.

'She's James Pearson's fiancée,' said Mr Rycroft. 'You know—the man who has been arrested for Trevelyan's murder.'

Wyatt dropped a glass of whisky he was just raising to his lips with a crash upon the floor. He immediately roared for Abdul and cursed him in no measured terms for not placing a table at a convenient angle to his chair. He then resumed the conversation.

'So that's who she is. Too good for a counter-jumper like that. A girl like that wants a real man.'

'Young Pearson is very good-looking,' said Mr Rycroft.

'Good-looking—good-looking—a girl doesn't want a barber's block. What does that sort of young man who works in an office every day know of life? What experience has he had of reality?'

'Perhaps the experience of being tried for murder will be sufficient reality to last him for some time,' said Mr Rycroft dryly.

'Police sure he did it, eh?'

'They must be fairly sure or they wouldn't have arrested him.'

'Country bumpkins,' said Captain Wyatt contemptuously.

'Not quite,' said Mr Rycroft. 'Inspector Narracott struck me this morning as an able and efficient man.'

'Where did you see him this morning?'

'He called at my house.'

'He didn't call at mine,' said Captain Wyatt in an injured fashion.

'Well, you weren't a close friend of Trevelyan's or anything like that.'

'I don't know what you mean. Trevelyan was a skinflint and I told him so to his face. He couldn't come bossing it over me. I didn't kowtow to him like the rest of the people here. Always dropping in—dropping in—too much dropping in. If I don't choose to see anyone for a week, or a month, or a year, that's my business.'

'You haven't seen anyone for a week now, have you?' said Mr Rycroft.

'No, and why should I?' The irate invalid banged the table. Mr Rycroft was aware, as usual, of having said the wrong thing. 'Why the bloody hell should I? Tell me that?'

Mr Rycroft was prudently silent. The Captain's wrath subsided.

'All the same,' he growled, 'if the police want to know about Trevelyan I'm the man they should have come to. I've knocked about the world, and I've got judgment. I can size a man up for what he's worth. What's the good of going to a lot of dodderers and old women? What they want is a *man's* judgment.'

He banged the table again.

'Well,' said Mr Rycroft, 'I suppose they think they know themselves what they are after.'

'They inquired about me,' said Captain Wyatt. 'They would naturally.'

'Well—er—I don't quite remember,' said Mr Rycroft cautiously.

'Why can't you remember? You're not in your dotage yet.'

'I expect I was—er—rattled,' said Mr Rycroft soothingly.

'Rattled, were you? Afraid of the police? I'm not afraid of the police. Let 'em come here. That's what I say. I'll show them. Do you know I shot a cat at a hundred yards the other night?'

'Did you?' said Mr Rycroft.

The Captain's habit of letting off a revolver at real or imaginary cats was a sore trial to his neighbours.

'Well, I'm tired,' said Captain Wyatt suddenly. 'Have another drink before you go?'

Rightly interpreting this hint, Mr Rycroft rose to his feet. Captain Wyatt continued to urge a drink upon him.

'You'd be twice the man if you drank a bit more. A man who can't enjoy a drink isn't a man at all.'

But Mr Rycroft continued to decline the offer. He had already consumed one whisky and soda of most unusual strength.

'What tea do you drink?' asked Wyatt. 'I don't know anything about tea. Told Abdul to get some. Thought that girl might like to come in to tea one day. Darned pretty girl. Must do something for her. She must be bored to death in a place like this with no one to talk to.'

'There's a young man with her,' said Mr Rycroft.

'The young men of the present day make me sick,' said Captain Wyatt. 'What's the good of them?'

This being a difficult query to answer suitably, Mr Rycroft did not attempt it, he took his departure.

The bull terrier bitch accompanied him to the gate and caused him acute alarm.

In No. 4, The Cottages, Miss Percehouse was speaking to her nephew, Ronald.

'If you like to moon about after a girl who doesn't want you, that is your affair, Ronald,' she was saying. 'Better stick to the Willett girl. You may have a chance there, though I think it is extremely unlikely.'

'Oh, I say,' protested Ronnie.

'The other thing I have to say is, that if there was a police officer in Sittaford I should have been informed of it. Who knows, I might have been able to give him valuable information.'

'I didn't know about it myself till after he had gone.'

'That is so like you, Ronnie. Absolutely typical.'

'Sorry, Aunt Caroline.'

'And when you are painting the garden furniture, there is no need to paint your face as well. It doesn't improve it and it wastes the paint.'

'Sorry, Aunt Caroline.'

'And now,' said Miss Percehouse, closing her eyes, 'don't argue with me any more. I'm tired.'

Ronnie shuffled his feet and looked uncomfortable.

'Well?' said Miss Percehouse sharply.

'Oh! nothing—only—'

'Yes?'

'Well, I was wondering if you'd mind if I blew in to Exeter tomorrow.'

'Why?'

'Well, I want to meet a fellow there.'

'What kind of a fellow?'

'Oh! just a fellow.'

'If a young man wishes to tell lies, he should do so well,' said Miss Percehouse.

'Oh! I say—but—'

'Don't apologize.'

'It's all right then? I can go?'

'I don't know what you mean by saying, "I can go?" as though you were a small child. You are over twenty-one.'

'Yes, but what I mean is, I don't want—'

Miss Percehouse closed her eyes again.

'I have asked you once before not to argue. I am tired and wish to rest. If the "fellow" you are meeting in Exeter wears skirts and is called Emily Trefusis, more fool you—that is all I have to say.'

'But look here—'

'I am tired, Ronald. That's enough.'

CHAPTER 22

Nocturnal Adventures of Charles

Charles was not looking forward with any relish to the prospect of his night's vigil. He privately considered that it was likely to be a wild goose chase. Emily, he considered, was possessed of a too vivid imagination.

He was convinced that she had read into the few words she had overheard a meaning that had its origin in her own brain. Probably sheer weariness had induced Mrs Willett to yearn for night to come.

Charles looked out of his window and shivered. It was a piercingly cold night, raw and foggy—the last night one would wish to spend in the open hanging about and waiting for something, very nebulous in nature, to happen.

Still he dared not yield to his intense desire to remain comfortably indoors. He recalled the liquid melodiousness of Emily's voice as she said, 'It's wonderful to have someone you can really rely on.'

She relied on him, Charles, and she should not rely in vain. What? Fail that beautiful, helpless girl? Never.

Besides, he reflected as he donned all the spare underclothes he possessed before encasing himself in two pullovers and his overcoat, things were likely to be deucedly unpleasant if Emily on her return found out that he had not carried out his promise.

She would probably say the most unpleasant things. No, he couldn't risk it. But as for anything happening—

And anyway, when and how was it going to happen? He couldn't be everywhere at once. Probably whatever was going to happen would happen inside Sittaford House and he would never know a thing about it.

'Just like a girl,' he grumbled to himself, 'waltzing off to Exeter and leaving me to do the dirty work.'

And then he remembered once more the liquid tones of Emily's voice as she expressed her reliance on him, and he felt ashamed of his outburst.

He completed his toilet, rather after the model of Tweedledee, and effected a surreptitious exit from the cottage.

The night was even colder and more unpleasant than he had thought. Did Emily realize all he was about to suffer on her behalf? He hoped so.

His hand went tenderly to a pocket and caressed a hidden flask concealed in a near pocket.

'The boy's best friend,' he murmured. 'It *would* be a night like this, of course.'

With suitable precautions he introduced himself into the grounds of Sittaford House. The Willetts kept no dog, so there was no fear of alarm from that quarter. A light in the gardener's cottage showed that it was inhabited. Sittaford House itself was in darkness save for one lighted window on the first floor.

'Those two women are alone in the house,' thought Charles. 'I shouldn't care for that myself. A bit creepy!'

He supposed Emily had really overheard that sentence, '*Will tonight never come?*' What did it really mean?

'I wonder,' he thought to himself, 'if they mean to do a flit? Well, whatever happens, little Charles is going to be here to see it.'

He circled the house at a discreet distance. Owing to the foggy nature of the night he had no fears of being observed. Everything as far as he could see appeared to be as usual. A cautious visiting of the outbuildings showed them to be locked.

'I hope something does happen,' said Charles as the hours passed. He took a prudent sip from his flask. 'I've never known anything like this cold. "What did you do in the Great War, Daddy?" can't have been any worse than this.'

He glanced at his watch and was surprised to find that it was still only twenty minutes to twelve. He had been convinced that it must be nearly dawn.

An unexpected sound made him prick up his ears excitedly. It was the sound of a bolt being very gently drawn back in its socket, and it came from the direction of the house. Charles made a noiseless sprint from bush to bush. Yes, he had been quite right, the small side door was slowly opening. A dark figure stood on the threshold. It was peering anxiously out into the night.

'Mrs or Miss Willett,' said Charles to himself. 'The fair Violet, I think.'

After waiting a minute or two, the figure stepped out on the path and closed the door noiselessly behind her and started to walk away from the house in the opposite direction to the front drive. The path in question led up behind Sittaford House, passing through a small plantation of trees and so out on to the open moor.

The path wound quite near the bushes where Charles was concealed, so near that Charles was able to recognize the woman as she passed. He had been quite right, it was Violet Willett. She was wearing a long dark coat and had a beret on her head.

She went on up, and as quietly as possible Charles followed her. He had no fears of being seen, but he was alive to the danger of being overheard. He was particularly anxious not to alarm the girl. Owing to his care in this respect she outdistanced him. For a moment or two he was afraid lest he should lose her, but as he in his turn wound his way anxiously through the plantation of trees he saw her standing a little way ahead of him. Here the low wall which surrounded the estate was broken by a gate. Violet Willett was standing by this gate, leaning over it peering out into the night.

Charles crept up as near as he dared and waited. The time passed. The girl had a small pocket torch with her and once she switched it on for a moment or two, directing it, Charles thought, to see the time by the wrist watch she was wearing, then she leant over the gate again in the same attitude of expectant interest. Suddenly, Charles heard a low whistle twice repeated.

He saw the girl start to sudden attention. She leant farther over the gate and from her lips came the same signal—a low whistle twice repeated.

Then with startling suddenness a man's figure loomed out of the night. A low exclamation came from the girl. She moved back a pace or two, the gate swung inward and the man joined her. She spoke to him in a low hurried voice. Unable to catch what they said, Charles moved forward somewhat imprudently. A twig snapped beneath his feet. The man swung round instantly.

'What's that?' he said.

He caught sight of Charles's retreating figure.

'Hie, you, stop! What are you doing here?'

With a bound he sprang after Charles. Charles turned and tackled him adroitly. The next moment they were rolling over and over together locked in a tight embrace.

The tussle was a short one. Charles's assailant was by far the heavier and stronger of the two. He rose to his feet jerking his captive with him.

'Switch on that light, Violet,' he said, 'let's have a look at this fellow.'

The girl, who had been standing terrified a few paces away, came forward and switched on the torch obediently.

'It must be the man who is staying in the village,' she said. 'A journalist.'

'A journalist, eh?' exclaimed the other. 'I don't like the breed. What are you doing, you skunk, nosing round private grounds at this time of night?'

The torch wavered in Violet's hand. For the first time Charles was given a full view of his antagonist. For a few minutes he had entertained the wild idea that the visitor might have been the escaped convict. One look at the other dispelled any such fancy. This was a young man not more than twenty-four or-five years of age. Tall, good-looking and determined, with none of the hunted criminal about him.

'Now then,' he said sharply, 'what's your name?'

'My name is Charles Enderby,' said Charles. 'You haven't told me yours,' he continued.

'Confound your cheek!'

A sudden flash of inspiration came to Charles. An inspired guess had saved him more than once. It was a long shot, but he believed that he was right.

'I think, however,' he said quietly, 'that I can guess it.'

'Eh?'

The other was clearly taken aback.

'I think,' said Charles, 'that I have the pleasure of addressing Mr Brian Pearson from Australia. Is that so?'

There was a silence—rather a long silence. Charles had a feeling that the tables were turned.

'How the devil you knew that I can't think,' said the other at last, 'but you're right. My name *is* Brian Pearson.'

'In that case,' said Charles, 'supposing we adjourn to the house and talk things over!'

CHAPTER 23

At Hazelmoor

Major Burnaby was doing his accounts or—to use a more Dickens-like phrase—he was looking into his affairs. The Major was an extremely methodical man. In a calf-bound book he kept a record of shares bought, shares sold and the accompanying loss or profit—usually a loss, for in common with most retired army men the Major was attracted by a high rate of interest rather than a modest percentage coupled with safety.

'These oil wells looked all right,' he was muttering. 'Seems as though there ought to have been a fortune in it. Almost as bad as that diamond mine! Canadian land, that ought to be sound now.'

His cogitations were interrupted as the head of Mr Ronald Garfield appeared at the open window.

'Hello,' said Ronnie cheerfully, 'I hope I'm not butting in?'

'If you are coming in go round to the front door,' said Major Burnaby. 'Mind the rock plants. I believe you are standing on them at the moment.'

Ronnie retreated with an apology and presently presented himself at the front door.

'Wipe your feet on the mat, if you don't mind,' cried the Major.

He found young men extremely trying. Indeed, the only young man towards whom he had felt any kindliness for a long time was the journalist, Charles Enderby.

'A nice young chap,' the Major had said to himself. 'And very interested, too, in what I have told him about the Boer War.'

Towards Ronnie Garfield the Major felt no such kindliness. Practically everything that the unfortunate Ronnie said or did managed to rub the Major up the wrong way. Still, hospitality is hospitality.

'Have a drink?' said the Major, loyal to that tradition.

'No thanks. As a matter of fact I just dropped in to see if we couldn't get together. I wanted to go to Exhampton today and I hear Elmer is booked to take you in.'

Burnaby nodded.

'Got to go over Trevelyan's things,' he explained. 'The police have done with the place now.'

'Well, you see,' said Ronnie rather awkwardly, 'I particularly wanted to go into Exhampton today. I thought if we could get together and share and share alike as it were. Eh? What about it?'

'Certainly,' said the Major. 'I am agreeable. Do you a lot more good to walk,' he added. 'Exercise. None of you young chaps nowadays take any exercise. A brisk six miles there and a brisk six miles back would do you all the good in the world. If it weren't that I needed the car to bring some of Trevelyan's things back here, I should be walking myself. Getting soft—that's the curse of the present day.'

'Oh, well,' said Ronnie, 'I don't believe in being strenuous myself. But I'm glad we've settled that all right. Elmer said you were starting at eleven o'clock. Is that right?'

'That's it.'

'Good. I'll be there.'

Ronnie was not quite so good as his word. His idea of being on the spot was to be ten minutes late, and he found Major Burnaby fuming and fretting and not at all inclined to be placated by a careless apology.

'What a fuss old buffers make,' thought Ronnie to himself. 'They have no idea what a curse they are to everybody with their punctuality, and everything done on the dot of the minute, and their cursed exercise and keeping fit.'

His mind played agreeably for a few minutes with the idea of a marriage between Major Burnaby and his aunt. Which, he wondered, would get the better of it? He thought his aunt every time. Rather amusing to think of her clapping her hands and uttering piercing cries to summon the Major to her side.

Banishing these reflections from his mind he proceeded to enter into cheerful conversation.

'Sittaford has become a pretty gay spot—what? Miss Trefusis and this chap Enderby and the lad from Australia—by the way, when did he blow in? There he was as large as life this morning and nobody knew where he had come from. It's been worrying my aunt blue in the face.'

'He is staying with the Willetts,' said Major Burnaby tartly.

'Yes, but where did he blow in from? Even the Willetts

haven't got a private aerodrome. You know, I think there's something deuced mysterious about this lad Pearson. He's got what I call a nasty gleam in his eye—a very nasty glint. It's my impression that he's the chap who did in poor old Trevelyan.'

The Major made no reply.

'The way I look at it is this,' continued Ronnie, 'fellows that go off to the Colonies are usually bad hats. Their relations don't like them and push them out there for that reason. Very well then—there you are. The bad hat comes back, short of money, visits wealthy uncle in the neighbourhood of Christmas time, wealthy relative won't cough up to impecunious nephew—and impecunious nephew bats him one. That's what I call a theory.'

'You should mention it to the police,' said Major Burnaby.

'I thought you might do that,' said Mr Garfield. 'You're Narracott's little pal, aren't you? By the way he hasn't been nosing about Sittaford again, has he?'

'Not that I know about.'

'Not meeting you at the house today, is he?'

'No.'

The shortness of the Major's answers seemed to strike Ronnie at last.

'Well,' he said vaguely, 'that's that,' and relapsed into a thoughtful silence.

At Exhampton the car drew up outside the Three Crowns. Ronnie alighted and after arranging with the Major that they would rendezvous there at half past four for the return journey, he strode off in the direction of such shops as Exhampton offered.

The Major went first to see Mr Kirkwood. After a brief conversation with him, he took the keys and started off for Hazelmoor.

He had told Evans to meet him there at twelve o'clock, and he found the faithful retainer waiting on the doorstep. With a rather grim face, Major Burnaby inserted the key into the front door and passed into the empty house, Evans at his heels. He had not been in it since the night of the tragedy, and in spite of his iron determination to show no weakness, he gave a slight shiver as he passed the drawing-room.

Evans and the Major worked together in sympathy and silence. When either of them made a brief remark it was duly appreciated and understood by the other.

'Unpleasant job this, but it has to be done,' said Major Burnaby, and Evans, sorting out socks into neat piles, and counting pyjamas, responded.

'It seems rather unnatural like, but as you say, sir, it's got to be done.'

Evans was deft and efficient at his work. Everything was neatly sorted and arranged and classified in heaps. At one o'clock they repaired to the Three Crowns for a short mid-day meal. When they returned to the house the Major suddenly caught Evans by the arm as the latter closed the front door behind him.

'Hush,' he said. 'Do you hear that footstep overhead? It's—it's in Joe's bedroom.'

'My Gawd, sir. So it is.'

A kind of superstitious terror held them both for a minute, and then, breaking loose from it, and with an angry squaring of the shoulders, the Major strode to the foot of the stairs and shouted in a stentorian voice:

'Who's that? Come out of there, I say.'

To his intense surprise and annoyance and yet, be it confessed, to his slight relief, Ronnie Garfield appeared at the top of the stairs. He looked embarrassed and sheepish.

'Hello,' he said. 'I have been looking for you.'

'What do you mean, looking for me?'

'Well, I wanted to tell you that I shan't be ready at half past four. I've got to go into Exeter. So don't wait for me. I'll have to get a car up from Exhampton.'

'How did you get into this house?' asked the Major.

'The door was open,' exclaimed Ronnie. 'Naturally I thought you were here.'

The Major turned to Evans sharply.

'Didn't you lock it when you came out?'

'No, sir, I hadn't got the key.'

'Stupid of me,' muttered the Major.

'You don't mind, do you?' said Ronnie. 'I couldn't see anyone downstairs so I went upstairs and had a look round.'

'Of course, it doesn't matter,' snapped the Major. 'You startled me, that's all.'

'Well,' said Ronnie airily, 'I shall be pushing along now. So long.'

The Major grunted. Ronnie came down the stairs.

'I say,' he said boyishly, 'do you mind telling me—er—er—where it happened?'

The Major jerked a thumb in the direction of the drawing-room.

'Oh, may I look inside?'

'If you like,' growled the Major.

Ronnie opened the drawing-room door. He was absent a few minutes and then returned.

The Major had gone up the stairs, but Evans was in the hall. He had the air of a bulldog on guard, his small deep-set eyes watched Ronnie with a somewhat malicious scrutiny.

'I say,' said Ronnie. 'I thought you could never wash out bloodstains. I thought, however much you washed them, they always came back. Oh, of course—the old fellow was sandbagged, wasn't he? Stupid of me. It was one of these, wasn't it?' He took up a long narrow bolster that lay against one of the other doors. He weighed it thoughtfully and balanced it in his hand. 'Nice little toy, eh?' He made a few tentative swings with it in the air.

Evans was silent.

'Well,' said Ronnie, realizing that the silence was not a wholly appreciative one, 'I'd better be getting along. I'm afraid I've been a bit tactless, eh?' He jerked his head towards the upper storey. 'I forgot about them being such pals and all that. Two of a kind, weren't they? Well, I'm really going now. Sorry if I've said all the wrong things.'

He walked across the hall and out through the front door. Evans stayed impassively in the hall, and only when he had heard the latch of the gate close behind Mr Garfield did he mount the stairs and rejoin Major Burnaby. Without any word or comment he resumed where he had left off, going straight across the room and kneeling down in front of the boot cupboard.

At half past three their task was finished. One trunk of clothes and underclothes was allotted to Evans, and another was strapped up ready to be sent to the Seamen's Orphanage. Papers and bills were packed into an attaché case and Evans was given instructions to see a local firm of removers about the storage of the various sporting trophies and heads, as there was no room for them in Major Burnaby's cottage. Since Hazelmoor was only rented furnished no other questions arose.

When all this was settled Evans cleared his throat nervously once or twice and then said:

'Beg pardon, sir, but—I'll be wanting a job to look after a gentleman, same as I did to look after the Capting.'

'Yes, yes, you can tell anyone to apply to me for a recommendation. That will be quite all right.'

'Begging your pardon, sir, that wasn't quite what I meant. Rebecca and me, sir, we've talked it over and we was wondering if, sir—if maybe you would give us a trial?'

'Oh! but—well—I look after myself as you know. That old what's her name comes in and cleans for me once a day and cooks a few things. That's—er—about all I can afford.'

'It isn't the money that matters so much, sir,' said Evans quickly. 'You see, sir, I was very fond of the Capting and—well, if I could do for you, sir, the same as I did for him, well, it would be almost like the same thing, if you know what I mean.'

The Major cleared his throat and averted his eyes.

'Very decent of you, 'pon my word. I'll—I'll think about it.' And escaping with alacrity he almost bolted down the

211

road. Evans stood looking after him, an understanding smile upon his face.

'Like as two peas, him and the Capting,' he murmured.

And then a puzzled expression came over his face.

'Where can they have got to?' he murmured. 'It's a bit queer that. I must ask Rebecca what she thinks.'

CHAPTER 24

Inspector Narracott Discusses the Case

'I am not entirely happy about it, sir,' said Inspector Narracott.

The Chief Constable looked at him inquiringly.

'No,' said Inspector Narracott. 'I'm not nearly as happy about it as I was.'

'You don't think we've got the right man?'

'I'm not satisfied. You see, to start with, everything pointed the one way but now—it's different.'

'The evidence against Pearson remains the same.'

'Yes, but there's a good deal of further evidence come to light, sir. There's the other Pearson—Brian. Feeling that we had no further to look I accepted the statement that he was in Australia. Now, it turns out that he was in England all the time. It seems he arrived back in England two months ago—travelled on the same boat as these Willetts apparently. Looks as though he had got sweet on the girl on the voyage. Anyway, for whatever reason he didn't communicate with any of his family. Neither his

213

sister nor his brother had any idea he was in England. On Thursday of last week he left the Ormsby Hotel in Russell Square and drove to Paddington. From there until Tuesday night, when Enderby ran across him, he refuses to account for his movements in any way.'

'You pointed out to him the gravity of such a course of action?'

'Said he didn't give a damn. He had had nothing to do with the murder and it was up to us to prove he had. The way he had employed his time was his own business and none of ours, and he declined definitely to state where he had been and what he had been doing.'

'Most extraordinary,' said the Chief Constable.

'Yes, sir. It's an extraordinary case. You see, there's no use getting away from the facts, this man's far more the type than the other. There's something incongruous about James Pearson hitting an old man on the head with a sandbag—but in a manner of speaking it might be all in the day's work to Brian Pearson. He's a hot-tempered, high-handed young man—and he profits to exactly the same extent, remember.

'Yes—he came over with Mr Enderby this morning, very bright and breezy, quite square and above-board, that was his attitude. But it won't wash, sir, it won't wash.'

'H'm—you mean—'

'It isn't borne out by the facts. Why didn't he come forward before? His uncle's death was in the papers Saturday. His brother was arrested Monday. And he doesn't give a sign of life. And he wouldn't have either, if that journalist hadn't run across him in the garden of Sittaford House at midnight last night.'

'What was he doing there? Enderby, I mean?'

'You know what journalists are,' said Narracott, 'always nosing round. They're uncanny.'

'They are a darned nuisance very often,' said the Chief Constable. 'Though they have their uses too.'

'I fancy it was the young lady put him up to it,' said Narracott.

'The young lady?'

'Miss Emily Trefusis.'

'How did she know anything about it?'

'She was up at Sittaford nosing around. And she's what you'd call a sharp young lady. There's not much gets past her.'

'What was Brian Pearson's own account of his movements?'

'Said he came to Sittaford House to see his young lady, Miss Willett, that is. She came out of the house to meet him when everyone was asleep because she didn't want her mother to know about it. That's their story.'

Inspector Narracott's voice expressed distinct disbelief.

'It's my belief, sir, that if Enderby hadn't run him to earth, he never would have come forward. He'd have gone back to Australia and claimed his inheritance from there.'

A faint smile crossed the Chief Constable's lips.

'How he must have cursed these pestilential prying journalists,' he murmured.

'There's something else come to light,' continued the Inspector. 'There are three Pearsons, you remember, and Sylvia Pearson is married to Martin Dering, the novelist. He told me that he lunched and spent the afternoon with

215

an American publisher and went to a literary dinner in the evening, but now it seems that he wasn't at the dinner at all.'

'Who says so?'

'Enderby again.'

'I think I must meet Enderby,' said the Chief Constable. 'He appears to be one of the live wires of this investigation. No doubt about it, the *Daily Wire* does have some bright young men on their staff.'

'Well, of course, that may mean little or nothing,' continued the Inspector. 'Captain Trevelyan was killed before six o'clock, so where Dering spent his evening is really of no consequence—but why should he have deliberately lied about it? I don't like it, sir.'

'No,' agreed the Chief Constable. 'It seems a little unnecessary.'

'It makes one think that the whole thing may be false. It's a far-fetched supposition, I suppose, but Dering *might* have left Paddington by the twelve ten train—arrived at Exhampton some time after five, have killed the old man, got the six ten train and been back home again before midnight. At any rate it's got to be looked into, sir. We've got to investigate his financial position, see if he was desperately hard up. Any money his wife came into he would have the handling of— you've only got to look at her to know that. We've got to make perfectly sure that the afternoon alibi holds water.'

'The whole thing is extraordinary,' commented the Chief Constable. 'But I still think the evidence against Pearson is pretty conclusive. I see that you don't agree with me— you've a feeling you've got hold of the wrong man.'

'The evidence is all right,' admitted Inspector Narracott, 'circumstantial and all that, and any jury ought to convict on it. Still, what you say is true enough—I don't see him as a murderer.'

'And his young lady is very active in the case,' said the Chief Constable.

'Miss Trefusis, yes, she's a one and no mistake. A real fine young lady. And absolutely determined to get him off. She's got hold of that journalist, Enderby, and she's working him for all she's worth. She's a great deal too good for Mr James Pearson. Beyond his good looks I wouldn't say there was much to him in the way of character.'

'But if she's a managing young woman that's what she likes,' said the Chief Constable.

'Ah well,' said Inspector Narracott, 'there's no accounting for tastes. Well, you agree, sir, that I had better take up this alibi of Dering's without any more delay.'

'Yes, get on to it at once. What about the fourth interested party in the will? There's a fourth, isn't there?'

'Yes, the sister. That's perfectly all right. I have made inquiries there. She was at home at six o'clock all right, sir. I'll get right on with the Dering business.'

It was about five hours later that Inspector Narracott found himself once more in the small sitting-room of The Nook. This time Mr Dering was at home. He couldn't be disturbed as he was writing, the maid had said at first, but the Inspector had produced an official card and bade her take it to her master without delay. Whilst waiting he strode up and down the room. His mind was working actively. Every now and then he picked up a small object from a

table, looked at it almost unseeingly, and then replaced it.
The cigarette box of Australian fiddleback—a present from
Brian Pearson possibly. He picked up a rather battered old
book. *Pride and Prejudice*. He opened the cover and saw
scrawled on the fly-leaf in rather faded ink the name,
Martha Rycroft. Somehow, the name of Rycroft seemed
familiar, but he could not for the moment remember why.
He was interrupted as the door opened and Martin Dering
came into the room.

The novelist was a man of middle height with thick
rather heavy chestnut hair. He was good-looking in a somewhat heavy fashion, with lips that were rather full and red.

Inspector Narracott was not prepossessed by his
apppearance.

'Good morning, Mr Dering. Sorry to trouble you all
here again.'

'Oh, it doesn't matter, Inspector, but really I can't tell
you any more than you've been told already.'

'We were led to understand that your brother-in-law,
Mr Brian Pearson, was in Australia. Now, we find that he
has been in England for the last two months. I might have
been given an inkling of that, I think. Your wife distinctly
told me that he was in New South Wales.'

'Brian in England!' Dering seemed genuinely astonished.
'I can assure you, Inspector, that I had no knowledge of
that fact—nor, I'm sure, had my wife.'

'He has not communicated with you in any way?'

'No, indeed, I know for a fact that Sylvia has twice
written him letters to Australia during that time.'

'Oh, well, in that case I apologize, sir. But naturally I

thought he would have communicated with his relations and I was a bit sore with you for holding out on me.'

'Well, as I tell you we knew nothing. Have a cigarette, Inspector? By the way, I see you've recaptured your escaped convict.'

'Yes, got him late Tuesday night. Rather bad luck for him the mist coming down. He walked right round in a circle. Did about twenty miles to find himself about half a mile from Princetown at the end of it.'

'Extraordinary how everyone goes round in circles in a fog. Good thing he didn't escape on the Friday. I suppose he would have had this murder put down to him as a certainty.'

'He's a dangerous man. Fremantle Freddy, they used to call him. Robbery with violence, assault—led the most extraordinary double life. Half the time he passed as an educated, respectable wealthy man. I am not at all sure myself that Broadmoor wasn't the place for him. A kind of criminal mania used to come over him from time to time. He would disappear and consort with the lowest characters.'

'I suppose many people don't escape from Princetown?'

'It's well-nigh impossible, sir. But this particular escape was extraordinarily well planned and carried out. We haven't nearly got to the bottom of it yet.'

'Well,' Dering rose and glanced at his watch, 'if there's nothing more, Inspector—I'm afraid I am rather a busy man—'

'Oh, but there *is* something more, Mr Dering. I want to know why you told me that you were at a literary dinner at the Cecil Hotel on Friday night?'

'I—I don't understand you, Inspector.'

'I think you do, sir. You weren't at that dinner, Mr Dering.'

Martin Dering hesitated. His eyes ran uncertainly from the Inspector's face, up to the ceiling, then to the door, and then to his feet.

The Inspector waited, calm and stolid.

'Well,' said Martin Dering at last, 'supposing I wasn't. What the hell has that got to do with you? What have my movements, five hours after my uncle was murdered, got to do with you or anyone else?'

'You made a certain statement to us, Mr Dering, and I want that statement verified. Part of it has already proved to be untrue. I've got to check up on the other half. You say you lunched and spent the afternoon with a friend.'

'Yes—my American publisher.'

'His name?'

'Rosenkraun, Edgar Rosenkraun.'

'Ah, and his address?'

'He's left England. He left last Saturday.'

'For New York?'

'Yes.'

'Then he'll be on the sea at the present moment. What boat is he on?'

'I—I really can't remember.'

'You know the line? Was it a Cunard or White Star?'

'I—I really don't remember.'

'Ah well,' said the Inspector, 'we'll cable his firm in New York. They'll know.'

'It was the *Gargantua*,' said Dering sullenly.

'Thank you, Mr Dering, I thought you could remember if you tried. Now, your statement is that you lunched with Mr Rosenkraun and that you spent the afternoon with him. At what time did you leave him?'

'About five o'clock, I should say.'

'And then?'

'I decline to state. It's no business of yours. That's all you want, surely.'

Inspector Narracott nodded thoughtfully. If Rosenkraun confirmed Dering's statement then any case against Dering must fall to the ground. Whatever his mysterious activities had been that evening could not affect the case.

'What are you going to do?' demanded Dering uneasily.

'Wireless Mr Rosenkraun on board the *Gargantua*.'

'Damn it all,' cried Dering, 'you'll involve me in all sorts of publicity. Look here—'

He went across to his desk, scribbled a few words on a bit of paper, then took it to the Inspector.

'I suppose you've got to do what you're doing,' he said ungraciously, 'but at least you might do it in my way. It's not fair to run a chap in for a lot of trouble.'

On the sheet of paper was written:

Rosenkraun S.S. 'Gargantua.' Please confirm my statement I was with you lunch-time until five o'clock Friday 14th. Martin Dering.

'Have the reply sent straight to you—I don't mind. But don't have it sent to Scotland Yard or a police station. You don't know what these Americans are like. Any hint of me being mixed up in a police case and this new contract that I've been discussing will go to the winds. Keep it a private matter, Inspector.'

'I've no objection to that, Mr Dering. All I want is the truth. I'll send this reply paid, the reply to be sent to my private address in Exeter.'

'Thank you, you are a good chap. It's not such easy going earning your living by literature, Inspector. You'll see the answer will be all right. I did tell you a lie about the dinner, but as a matter of fact I had told my wife that that was where I had been, and I thought I might as well stick to the same story to you. Otherwise I would have let myself in for a lot of trouble.'

'If Mr Rosenkraun confirms your statement, Mr Dering, you will have nothing else to fear.'

'An unpleasant character,' the Inspector thought, as he left the house. 'But he seems pretty certain that this American publisher will confirm the truth of his story.'

A sudden remembrance came to the Inspector, as he hopped into the train which would take him back to Devon.

'Rycroft,' he said, 'of course—that's the name of the old gentleman who lives in one of the cottages at Sittaford. A curious coincidence.'

CHAPTER 25

At Deller's Café

Emily Trefusis and Charles Enderby were seated at a small table in Deller's Café in Exeter. It was half past three, and at that hour there was comparative peace and quiet. A few people were having a quiet cup of tea, but the restaurant on the whole was deserted.

'Well,' said Charles, 'what do you think of him?'

Emily frowned.

'It's difficult,' she said.

After his interview with the police, Brian Pearson had lunched with them. He had been extremely polite to Emily, rather too polite in her opinion.

To that astute girl it seemed a shade unnatural. Here was a young man conducting a clandestine love affair and an officious stranger butts in.

Brian Pearson had taken it like a lamb; had fallen in with Charles's suggestion of having a car and driving over to see the police.

Why this attitude of meek acquiescence? It seemed to

Emily entirely untypical of the natural Brian Pearson as she read his character.

'I'll see you in hell first!' would, she felt sure, have been far more his attitude.

This lamb-like demeanour was suspicious. She tried to convey something of her feelings to Enderby.

'I get you,' said Enderby. 'Our Brian has got something to conceal, therefore he can't be his natural high-handed self.'

'That's it exactly.'

'Do you think he might possibly have killed old Trevelyan?'

'Brian,' said Emily thoughtfully, 'is—well, a person to be reckoned with. He is rather unscrupulous, I should think, and if he wanted anything, I don't think he would let ordinary conventional standards stand in his way. He's not plain tame English.'

'Putting all personal considerations on one side, he's a more likely starter than Jim?' said Enderby.

Emily nodded.

'Much more likely. He would carry a thing through well—because he would never lose his nerve.'

'Honestly, Emily, do you think he did it?'

'I—I don't know. He fulfils the conditions—the only person who does.'

'What do you mean by fulfils the conditions?'

'Well, (1) *Motive*.' She ticked off the items on her fingers. 'The same motive. Twenty thousand pounds. (2) *Opportunity*. Nobody knows where he was on Friday afternoon, and if he was anywhere that he could say—well—surely he would say it? So we assume that he was actually in the neighbour-hood of Hazelmoor on Friday.'

'They haven't found anyone who saw him in Exhampton,' Charles pointed out, 'and he's a fairly noticeable person.'

Emily shook her head scornfully.

'He wasn't in Exhampton. Don't you see, Charles, if he committed the murder, he planned it beforehand. It's only poor innocent Jim who came down like a mug and stayed there. There's Lydford and Chagford or perhaps Exeter. He might have walked over from Lydford—that's a main road and the snow wouldn't have been impassable. It would have been pretty good going.'

'I suppose we ought to make inquiries all round.'

'The police are doing that,' said Emily, 'and they'll do it a lot better than we shall. All public things are much better done by the police. It's private and personal things like listening to Mrs Curtis and picking up a hint from Miss Percehouse and watching the Willetts—that's where we score.'

'Or don't, as the case may be,' said Charles.

'To go back to Brian Pearson fulfilling the conditions,' said Emily. 'We've done two, motive and opportunity, and there's the third—the one that in a way I think is the most important of all.'

'What's that?'

'Well, I have felt from the beginning that we couldn't ignore that queer business of the table-turning. I have tried to look at it as logically and clear-sightedly as possible. There are just three solutions of it. (1) That it was super-natural. Well, of course, that may be so, but personally I am ruling it out. (2) That it was deliberate—someone did it on purpose, but as one can't arrive at any conceivable reason, we can rule that out also. (3) Accidental. Someone gave themselves away without meaning to do so—indeed quite against his will. An unconscious piece of self-revelation. If so, someone among those six people either knew definitely that Captain Trevelyan was going to be killed at a certain time that afternoon, or that someone was having an interview with him from which violence might result. None of those six people could have been the actual murderer, but one of them must have been in collusion with the murderer. There's no link between Major Burnaby and anybody else, or Mr Rycroft and anybody else, or Ronald Garfield and anybody else, but when we come to the Willetts it's different. There's a link between Violet Willett and Brian Pearson. Those two are on very intimate terms and that girl was all on the jump after the murder.'

'You think she knew?' said Charles.

'She or her mother—one or other of them.'

'There's one person you haven't mentioned,' said Charles. 'Mr Duke.'

'I know,' said Emily. 'It's queer. He's the one person we know absolutely nothing about. I've tried to see him twice and failed. There seems no connection between him and Captain Trevelyan, or between him and any of Captain Trevelyan's relations, there's absolutely nothing to connect him with the case in any way, and yet—'

'Well?' said Charles Enderby as Emily paused.

'And yet we met Inspector Narracott coming out of his cottage. What does Inspector Narracott know about him that we don't? I wish I knew.'

'You think—'

'Supposing Duke is a suspicious character and the police know it. Supposing Captain Trevelyan had found out something about Duke. He was particular about his tenants, remember, and supposing he was going to tell the police what he knew. And Duke arranges with an accomplice to have him killed. Oh, I know it all sounds dreadfully melodramatic put like that, and yet, after all, something of the kind might be possible.'

'It's an idea certainly,' said Charles slowly.

They were both silent, each one deep in thought.

Suddenly Emily said:

'Do you know that queer feeling you get when somebody is looking at you? I feel now as though someone's eyes were burning the back of my neck. Is it all fancy or is there really someone staring at me now?'

Charles moved his chair an inch or two and looked round the café in a casual manner.

'There's a woman at a table in the window,' he reported. 'Tall, dark and handsome. She's staring at you.'

'Young?'

'No, not very young. Hello!'

'What is it?'

'Ronnie Garfield. He has just come in and he's shaking hands with her and he's sitting down at her table. I think she's saying something about us.'

Emily opened her handbag. Rather ostentatiously she powdered her nose, adjusting the small pocket mirror to a convenient angle.

'It's Aunt Jennifer,' she said softly. 'They are getting up.'

'They are going,' said Charles. 'Do you want to speak to her?'

'No,' said Emily. 'I think it's better for me to pretend that I haven't seen her.'

'After all,' said Charles, 'why shouldn't Aunt Jennifer know Ronnie Garfield and ask him to tea?'

'Why should she?' said Emily.

'Why shouldn't she?'

'Oh, for goodness sake, Charles, don't let's go on and on like this, *should—shouldn't—should—shouldn't*. Of course it's all nonsense, and it doesn't mean anything! But we *were* just saying that nobody else at that *séance* had any relation with the family, and not five minutes later we see Ronnie Garfield having tea with Captain Trevelyan's sister.'

'It shows,' said Charles, 'that you never know.'

'It shows,' said Emily, 'that you are always having to begin again.'

'In more ways than one,' said Charles.

Emily looked at him.

'What do you mean?'

'Nothing at present,' said Charles.

He put his hand over hers. She did not draw it away.

'We've got to put this through,' said Charles. 'Afterwards—'

'Afterwards?' said Emily softly.

'I'd do anything for you, Emily,' said Charles. 'Simply anything—'

'Would you?' said Emily. 'That's rather nice of you, Charles dear.'

CHAPTER 26

Robert Gardner

It was just twenty minutes later when Emily rang the front door bell of The Laurels. It had been a sudden impulse.

Aunt Jennifer, she knew, would be still at Deller's with Ronnie Garfield. She smiled beamingly on Beatrice when the latter opened the door to her.

'It's me again,' said Emily. 'Mrs Gardner's out, I know, but can I see Mr Gardner?'

Such a request was clearly unusual. Beatrice seemed doubtful.

'Well, I don't know. I'll go up and see, shall I?'

'Yes, do,' said Emily.

Beatrice went upstairs, leaving Emily alone in the hall. She returned in a few minutes to ask the young lady to please step this way.

Robert Gardner was lying on a couch by the window in a big room on the first floor. He was a big man, blue-eyed and fair-haired. He looked, Emily thought, as Tristan ought to look in the third act of *Tristan and Isolde* and as no Wagnerian tenor has ever looked yet.

'Hello,' he said. 'You are the criminal's spouse to be, aren't you?'

'That's right, Uncle Robert,' said Emily. 'I suppose I *do* call you Uncle Robert, don't I?' she asked.

'If Jennifer will allow it. What's it like having a young man languishing in prison?'

A cruel man, Emily decided. A man who would take a malicious joy in giving you sharp digs in painful places. But she was a match for him. She said smilingly:

'Very thrilling.'

'Not so thrilling for Master Jim, eh?'

'Oh, well,' said Emily, 'it's an experience, isn't it?'

'Teach him life can't be all beer and skittles,' said Robert Gardner maliciously. 'Too young to fight in the Great War, wasn't he? Able to live soft and take it easily. Well, well . . . He got it in the neck from another source.'

He looked at her curiously.

'What did you want to come and see me for, eh?'

There was a tinge of something like suspicion in his voice.

'If you are going to marry into a family it's just as well to see all your relations-in-law beforehand.'

'Know the worst before it's too late. So you really think you are going to marry young Jim, eh?'

'Why not?'

'In spite of this murder charge?'

'In spite of this murder charge.'

'Well,' said Robert Gardner, 'I have never seen anybody less cast down. Anyone would think you were enjoying yourself.'

'I am. Tracking down a murderer is frightfully thrilling,' said Emily.

'Eh?'

'I said tracking down a murderer is frightfully thrilling,' said Emily.

Robert Gardner stared at her, then he threw himself back on his pillows.

'I am tired,' he said in a fretful voice. 'I can't talk any more. Nurse, where's Nurse? Nurse, I'm tired.'

Nurse Davis had come swiftly at his call from an adjoining room. 'Mr Gardner gets tired very easily. I think you had better go now if you don't mind, Miss Trefusis.'

Emily rose to her feet. She nodded brightly and said:

'Good-bye, Uncle Robert. Perhaps I'll come back some day.'

'What do you mean?'

'Au revoir,' said Emily.

She was going out of the front door when she stopped.

'Oh!' she said to Beatrice. 'I have left my gloves.'

'I will get them, Miss.'

'Oh, no,' said Emily. 'I'll do it.' She ran lightly up the stairs and entered without knocking.

'Oh,' said Emily. 'I beg your pardon. I am so sorry. It was my gloves.' She took them up ostentatiously, and smiling sweetly at the two occupants of the room who were sitting hand in hand, ran down the stairs and out of the house.

'This glove leaving is a terrific scheme,' said Emily to herself. 'This is the second time it's come off. Poor Aunt Jennifer, does she know, I wonder? Probably not. I must hurry or I'll keep Charles waiting.'

Enderby was waiting in Elmer's Ford at the agreed rendezvous.

'Any luck?' he asked as he tucked the rug round her.

'In a way, yes. I'm not sure.'

Enderby looked at her inquiringly.

'No,' said Emily in answer to his glance, 'I'm not going to tell you about it. You see, it may have nothing whatever to do with it—and if so, it wouldn't be fair.'

Enderby sighed.

'I call that hard,' he observed.

'I'm sorry,' said Emily firmly. 'But there it is.'

'Have it your own way,' said Charles coldly.

They drove on in silence—an offended silence on Charles's part—an oblivious one on Emily's.

They were nearly at Exhampton when she broke the silence by a totally unexpected remark.

'Charles,' she said, 'are you a bridge player?'

'Yes, I am. Why?'

'I was thinking. You know what they tell you to do when you're assessing the value of your hand? If you're defending—count the winners—but if you're attacking count the losers. Now, we're attacking in this business of ours—but perhaps we have been doing it the wrong way.'

'How do you mean?'

'Well, we've been counting the winners, haven't we? I mean going over the people who *could* have killed Captain Trevelyan, however improbable it seems. And that's perhaps why we've got so terribly muddled.'

'I haven't got muddled,' said Charles.

'Well, I have then. I'm so muddled I can't think at all.

Let's look at it the other way round. Let's count the losers—
the people who can't possibly have killed Captain Trevelyan.'

'Well, let's see—' Enderby reflected. 'To begin with there's
the Willetts and Burnaby and Rycroft and Ronnie—Oh!
and Duke.'

'Yes,' agreed Emily. 'We know none of them can have
killed him. Because at the time he was killed they were all
at Sittaford House and they all saw each other and they
can't all be lying. Yes, they're all out of it.'

'As a matter of fact everyone in Sittaford is out of it,'
said Enderby. 'Even Elmer,' he lowered his voice in deference to the possibility of the driver hearing him. 'Because
the road to Sittaford was impassable for cars on Friday.'

'He could have walked,' said Emily in an equally low
voice. 'If Major Burnaby could have got there that evening
Elmer could have started at lunch time—got to Exhampton
at five, murdered him, and walked back again.'

Enderby shook his head.

'I don't think he could have walked back again.
Remember the snow started to fall about half past six.
Anyway, you're not accusing Elmer, are you?'

'No,' said Emily, 'though, of course, he might be a
homicidal maniac.'

'Hush,' said Charles. 'You'll hurt his feelings if he hears
you.'

'At any rate,' said Emily, 'you can't say definitely that
he couldn't have murdered Captain Trevelyan.'

'Almost,' said Charles. 'He couldn't walk to Exhampton
and back without all Sittaford knowing about it and saying
it was queer.'

'It certainly is a place where everyone knows everything,' agreed Emily.

'Exactly,' said Charles, 'and that's why I say that everyone in Sittaford is out of it. The only ones that weren't at the Willetts—Miss Percehouse and Captain Wyatt—are invalids. They couldn't go ploughing through snowstorms. And dear old Curtis and Mrs C. If any of them did it, they must have gone comfortably to Exhampton for the weekend and come back when it was all over.'

Emily laughed.

'You couldn't be absent from Sittaford for the weekend without its being noticed, certainly,' she said.

'Curtis would notice the silence if Mrs C was,' said Enderby.

'Of course,' said Emily, 'the person it ought to be is Abdul. It would be in a book. He'd be a Lascar really, and Captain Trevelyan would have thrown his favourite brother overboard in a mutiny—something like that.'

'I decline to believe,' said Charles, 'that that wretched depressed-looking native ever murdered anybody.

'I know,' he said suddenly.

'What?' said Emily eagerly.

'The blacksmith's wife. The one who's expecting her eighth. The intrepid woman despite her condition walked all the way to Exhampton and batted him one with the sandbag.'

'And why, pray?'

'Because, of course, although the blacksmith was the father of the preceding seven, Captain Trevelyan was the father of her coming che-ild.'

'Charles,' said Emily. 'Don't be indelicate.'

'And anyway,' she added, 'it would be the blacksmith who did it, not her. A really good case there. Think how that brawny arm could wield a sandbag! And his wife would never notice his absence with seven children to look after. She wouldn't have time to notice a mere man.'

'This is degenerating into mere idiocy,' said Charles.

'It is rather,' agreed Emily. 'Counting losers hasn't been a great success.'

'What about you?' said Charles.

'Me?'

'Where were you when the crime was committed?'

'How extraordinary! I never thought of that. I was in London, of course. But I don't know that I could prove it. I was alone in my flat.'

'There you are,' said Charles. 'Motive and everything. Your young man coming into twenty thousand pounds. What more do you want?'

'You are clever, Charles,' said Emily. 'I can see that really I'm a most suspicious character. I never thought of it before.'

CHAPTER 27

Narracott Acts

Two mornings later Emily was seated in Inspector Narracott's office. She had come over from Sittaford that morning.

Inspector Narracott looked at her appraisingly. He admired Emily's pluck, her courageous determination not to give in and her resolute cheerfulness. She was a fighter, and Inspector Narracott admired fighters. It was his private opinion that she was a great deal too good for Jim Pearson, even if that young man was innocent of the murder.

'It's generally understood in books,' he said, 'that the police are intent on having a victim and don't in the least care if that victim is innocent or not as long as they have enough evidence to convict him. That's not the truth, Miss Trefusis, it's only the guilty man we want.'

'Do you honestly believe Jim to be guilty, Inspector Narracott?'

'I can't give you an official answer to that, Miss Trefusis. But I'll tell you this—that we are examining not only the evidence against him but the evidence against other people very carefully.'

'You mean against his brother—Brian?'

'A very unsatisfactory gentleman, Mr Brian Pearson. Refused to answer questions or to give any information about himself, but I think—' Inspector Narracott's slow Devonshire smile widened, 'I think I can make a pretty good guess at some of his activities. If I am right I shall know in another half hour. Then there's the lady's husband, Mr Dering.'

'You've seen him?' asked Emily curiously.

Inspector Narracott looked at her vivid face, and felt tempted to relax official caution. Leaning back in his chair he recounted his interview with Mr Dering, then from a file at his elbow he took out a copy of the wireless message he had dispatched to Mr Rosenkraun. 'That's what I sent,' he said. 'And here's the reply.'

Emily read it.

Narracott 2 Drysdale Road Exeter. Certainly confirm
Mr Dering's statement. He was in my company all Friday
afternoon. Rosenkraun.

'Oh!—bother,' said Emily, selecting a milder word than she had meant to use, knowing that the police force was old-fashioned and easily shocked.

'Ye-es,' said Inspector Narracott reflectively. 'It's annoying, isn't it?'

And his slow Devonshire smile broke out again.

'But I am a suspicious man, Miss Trefusis. Mr Dering's reasons sounded very plausible—but I thought it a pity to play into his hands too completely. So I sent another wireless message.'

Again he handed her two pieces of paper.
The first ran:

Information wanted re murder of Captain Trevelyan. Do
you support Martin Dering's statement of alibi for Friday
afternoon. Divisional Inspector Narracott Exeter.

The return message showed agitation and a reckless
disregard for expense.

Had no idea it was criminal case did not see Martin Dering
Friday. Agreed support his statement as one friend to
another believed his wife was having him watched for
divorce proceedings.

'Oh,' said Emily. 'Oh!—you *are* clever, Inspector.'
The Inspector evidently thought that he *had* been rather
clever. His smile was gentle and contented.
'How men do stick together,' went on Emily, looking
over the telegrams. 'Poor Sylvia. In some ways I
really think that men are beasts. That's why,' she added,
'it's so nice when one finds a man on whom one can
really rely.'
And she smiled admiringly at the Inspector.
'Now, all this is very confidential, Miss Trefusis,' the
Inspector warned her. 'I have gone further than I should
in letting you know about this.'
'I think it's adorable of you,' said Emily. 'I shall never,
never forget it.'

'Well, mind,' the Inspector warned her. 'Not a word to *anybody*.'

'You mean that I am not to tell Charles—Mr Enderby?'

'Journalists will be journalists,' said Inspector Narracott. 'However well you have got him tamed, Miss Trefusis—well, news is news, isn't it?'

'I won't tell him then,' said Emily. 'I think I've got him muzzled all right, but as you say newspaper men will be newspaper men.'

'Never part with information unnecessarily. That's my rule,' said Inspector Narracott.

A faint twinkle appeared in Emily's eyes, her unspoken thought being that Inspector Narracott had infringed this rule rather badly during the last half hour.

A sudden recollection came into her mind, not of course that it probably mattered now. Everything seemed to be pointing in a totally different direction. But still it would be nice to know.

'Inspector Narracott!' she said suddenly. 'Who is Mr Duke?'

'Mr Duke?'

She thought the Inspector was rather taken aback by her questions.

'You remember,' said Emily, 'we met you coming out of his cottage in Sittaford.'

'Ah, yes, yes, I remember. To tell you the truth, Miss Trefusis, I thought I would like to have an independent account of that table-turning business. Major Burnaby is not a first-rate hand at description.'

'And yet,' said Emily thoughtfully, 'if I had been you, I should have gone to somebody like Mr Rycroft for it. Why Mr Duke?'

There was a silence and then the Inspector said:

'Just a matter of opinion.'

'I wonder. I wonder if the police know something about Mr Duke.'

Inspector Narracott didn't answer. He had got his eyes fixed very steadily on the blotting paper.

'The man who leads a blameless life!' said Emily, 'that seems to describe Mr Duke awfully accurately, but perhaps he hasn't always led a blameless life? Perhaps the police know that?'

She saw a faint quiver on Inspector Narracott's face as he tried to conceal a smile.

'You like guessing, don't you, Miss Trefusis?' he said amiably.

'When people don't tell you things you have to guess!' retaliated Emily.

'If a man, as you say, is leading a blameless life,' Inspector Narracott said, 'and if it would be an annoyance and an inconvenience for him to have his past life raked up, well, the police are capable of keeping their own counsel. We have no wish to give a man away.'

'I see,' said Emily, 'but all the same—you went to see him, didn't you? That looks as though you thought, to begin with at any rate, that he might have had a hand in it. I wish—I wish I knew who Mr Duke really was? And what particular branch of criminology he indulged in in the past?'

She looked appealingly at Inspector Narracott but the latter preserved a wooden face, and realizing that on this point she could not hope to move him, Emily sighed and took her departure.

When she had gone the Inspector sat staring at the blotting pad, a trace of a smile still lingering on his lips. Then he rang the bell and one of his underlings entered.

'Well?' demanded Inspector Narracott.

'Quite right, sir. But it wasn't the Duchy at Princetown, it was the hotel at Two Bridges.'

'Ah!' The Inspector took the papers the other handed to him.

'Well,' he said. 'That settles it all right. Have you followed up the other young chap's movements on Friday?'

'He certainly arrived at Exhampton by the last train, but I haven't found out yet what time he left London. Inquiries are being made.'

Narracott nodded.

'Here is the entry from Somerset House, sir.'

Narracott unfolded it. It was the record of a marriage in 1894 between William Martin Dering and Martha Elizabeth Rycroft.

'Ah!' said the Inspector, 'anything else?'

'Yes, sir. Mr Brian Pearson sailed from Australia on a Blue Funnel Boat, the *Phidias*. She touched at Cape Town but no passengers of the name of Willett were aboard. No mother and daughter at all from South Africa. There was a Mrs and Miss Evans and a Mrs and Miss Johnson from Melbourne—the latter answer the description of the Willetts.'

'H'm,' said the Inspector—'Johnson. Probably neither Johnson nor Willett is the right name. I think I've got them taped out all right. Anything more?'

There was nothing else, it seemed.

'Well,' said Narracott, 'I think we have got enough to go on with.'

CHAPTER 28

Boots

'But, my dear young lady,' said Mr Kirkwood, 'what can you possibly expect to find at Hazelmoor? All Captain Trevelyan's effects have been removed. The police have made a thorough search of the house. I quite understand your position and your anxiety that Mr Pearson shall be—er—cleared if possible. But what can you do?'

'I don't expect to find anything,' Emily replied, 'or to notice anything that the police have overlooked. I can't explain to you, Mr Kirkwood. I want—I want to get the *atmosphere* of the place. Please let me have the key. There's no harm in it.'

'Certainly there's no harm in it,' said Mr Kirkwood with dignity.

'Then please be kind,' said Emily.

So Mr Kirkwood was kind and handed over the key with an indulgent smile. He did his best to come with her, which catastrophe was only averted by great tact and firmness on Emily's part.

That morning Emily had received a letter. It was couched in the following terms:

'*Dear Miss Trefusis,*'—wrote Mrs Belling. '*You said as how you would like to hear if anything at all should happen that was in any way out of the common even if not important, and, as this is peculiar, though not in any way important, I thought it my duty, Miss, to let you know at once, hoping this will catch you by the last post tonight or the first post tomorrow. My niece she come round and said it wasn't of any importance but peculiar which I agreed with her. The police said, and it was generally thought that nothing was taken from Captain Trevelyan's house and nothing was in a manner of speaking nothing that is of any value, but something there is missing though not noticed at the time being unimportant. But it seems, Miss, that a pair of the Captain's boots is missing which Evans noticed when he went over the things with Major Burnaby. Though I don't suppose it is of any importance, Miss, I thought you would like to know. It was a pair of boots, Miss, the thick kind you rubs oil into and which the Captain would have worn if he had gone out in the snow but as he didn't go out in the snow it doesn't seem to make sense. But missing they are, and who took them nobody knows, and though I well know it's of no importance I felt it my duty to write and hoping this finds you as it leaves me at present and hoping you are not worrying too much about the young gentleman, I remain, Miss, Yours truly—Mrs J. Belling.*'

Emily had read and re-read this letter. She had discussed it with Charles.

'Boots,' said Charles thoughtfully. 'It doesn't seem to make sense.'

'It must mean something,' Emily pointed out. 'I mean— why should a pair of boots be missing?'

'You don't think Evans is inventing?'

'Why should he? And after all if people do invent, they invent something sensible. Not a silly pointless thing like this.'

'Boots suggests something to do with footprints,' said Charles thoughtfully.

'I know. But footprints don't seem to enter into this case at all. Perhaps if it hadn't come on to snow again—'

'Yes, perhaps, but even then.

'Could he have given them to some tramp,' suggested Charles, 'and then the tramp did him in?'

'I suppose that's possible,' said Emily, 'but it doesn't sound very like Captain Trevelyan. He might perhaps have found a man some work to do or given him a shilling, but he wouldn't have pressed his best winter boots on him.'

'Well, I give it up,' said Charles.

'I'm not going to give it up,' said Emily. 'By hook or by crook I'm going to get to the bottom of it.'

Accordingly she came to Exhampton and went first to the Three Crowns, where Mrs Belling received her with great enthusiasm.

'And your young gentleman still in prison, Miss! Well, it's a cruel shame and none of us don't believe it was him, at least I would like to hear them say so when I am about. So you got my letter? You'd like to see Evans? Well, he lives right round the corner, 85 Fore Street it is. I wish I could come with you, but I can't leave the place, but you can't mistake it.'

Emily did not mistake it. Evans himself was out, but Mrs Evans received her and invited her in. Emily sat down and induced Mrs Evans to do so also and plunged straight into the matter on hand.

'I've come to talk about what your husband told Mrs Belling. I mean about a pair of Captain Trevelyan's boots being missing.'

'It's an odd thing, to be sure,' said the girl.

'Your husband is quite certain about it?'

'Oh, yes. Wore these boots most of the time in winter, the Captain did. Big ones they were, and he wore a couple of pairs of socks inside them.'

Emily nodded.

'They can't have gone to be mended or anything like that?' she suggested.

'Not without Evans knowing, they couldn't,' said his wife boastfully.

'No, I suppose not.'

'It's queer like,' said Mrs Evans, 'but I don't suppose it had anything to do with the murder, do you, Miss?'

'It doesn't seem likely,' agreed Emily.

'Have they found out anything new, Miss?' The girl's voice was eager.

'Yes, one or two things—nothing very important.'

'Seeing as that the Inspector from Exeter was here again today, I thought as though they might.'

'Inspector Narracott?'

'Yes, that's the one, Miss.'

'Did he come by my train?'

'No, he came by car. He went to the Three Crowns first and asked about the young gentleman's luggage.'

'What young gentleman's luggage?'

'The gentleman you go about with, Miss.'

Emily stared.

'They asked Tom,' went on the girl, 'I was passing by just after and he told me about it. He's a one for noticing is Tom. He remembered there were two labels on the young gentleman's luggage, one to Exeter and one to Exhampton.'

A sudden smile illuminated Emily's face as she pictured the crime being committed by Charles in order to provide a scoop for himself. One could, she decided, write a gruesome little story on that theme. But she admired Inspector Narracott's thoroughness in checking every detail to do with anyone, however remote their connection with the crime. He must have left Exeter almost immediately after his interview with her. A fast car would easily beat the train, and in any case she had lunched in Exeter.

'Where did the Inspector go afterwards?' she asked.

'To Sittaford, Miss. Tom heard him tell the driver.'

'To Sittaford House?'

Brian Pearson was, she knew, still staying at Sittaford House with the Willetts.

'No, Miss, to Mr Duke's.'

Duke again. Emily felt irritated and baffled. Always Duke—the unknown factor. She ought, she felt, to be able to deduce him from the evidence, but he seemed to have produced the same effect on everyone—a normal, ordinary, pleasant man.

'I've got to see him,' said Emily to herself. 'I'll go straight there as soon as I get back to Sittaford.'

Then she had thanked Mrs Evans, gone on to Mr Kirkwood's and obtained the key, and was now standing in the hall of Hazelmoor and wondering how and what she had expected to feel there.

She mounted the stairs slowly and went into the first room at the top of the stairs. This was quite clearly Captain Trevelyan's bedroom. It had, as Mr Kirkwood had said, been emptied of personal effects. Blankets were folded in a neat pile, the drawers were empty, there was not so much as a hanger left in the cupboard. The boot cupboard showed a row of bare shelves.

Emily sighed and then turned and went downstairs. Here was the sitting-room where the dead man had lain, the snow blowing in from the open window.

She tried to visualize the scene. Whose hand had struck Captain Trevelyan down, and why? Had he been killed at five and twenty past five as everyone believed—or had Jim really lost his nerve and lied? Had he failed to make anyone hear at the front door and gone round to the window, looked in and seen his dead uncle's body and dashed away in an agony of fear? If only she knew. According to Mr Dacres, Jim stuck to his story. Yes—but Jim might have lost his nerve. She couldn't be sure.

Had there been, as Mr Rycroft had suggested, someone else in the house—someone who had overheard the quarrel and seized his chance?

If so—did that throw any light on the boot problem? Had someone been upstairs—perhaps in Captain Trevelyan's bedroom? Emily passed through the hall again. She took a quick look into the dining-room; there were a couple of trunks there neatly strapped and labelled. The sideboard was bare. The silver cups were at Major Burnaby's bungalow.

She noticed, however, that the prize of three new novels, an account of which Charles had had from Evans and had reported with amusing embellishments to her, had been forgotten and lay dejectedly on a chair.

She looked round the room and shook her head. There was nothing here.

She went up the stairs again and once more entered the bedroom.

She *must* know why these boots were missing! Until she could concoct some theory reasonably satisfactory to herself which would account for their disappearance, she felt powerless to put them out of her mind. They were soaring to ridiculous proportions, dwarfing everything else to do with the case. Was there *nothing* to help her?

She took each drawer out and felt behind it. In detective stories there was always an obliging scrap of paper. But evidently in real life one could not expect such fortunate accidents, or else Inspector Narracott and his men had been wonderfully thorough. She felt for loose boards, she felt round the edge of the carpet with her fingers. She investigated the spring mattress. What she expected to find in all these places she hardly knew, but she went on looking with dogged perseverance.

And then, as she straightened her back and stood upright, her eye was caught by the one incongruous touch in this room of apple-pie order, a little pile of soot in the grate.

Emily looked at it with the fascinated gaze of a bird for a snake. She drew nearer, eyeing it. It was no logical deduction, no reasoning of cause and effect, it was simply that the sight of soot as such suggested a certain possibility. Emily rolled up her sleeves and thrust both arms up the chimney.

A moment later she was staring with incredulous delight at a parcel wrapped neatly in newspaper. One shake detached the newspaper and there, before her, were the missing pair of boots.

'But why?' said Emily. 'Here they are. But why? Why? Why? Why?'

She stared at them. She turned them over. She examined them outside and inside and the same question beat monotonously in her brain. Why?

Granted that someone had removed Captain Trevelyan's boots and hidden them up the chimney. Why had they done so?

'Oh!' cried Emily desperately, 'I shall go mad!'

She put the boots carefully in the middle of the floor, and drawing up a chair opposite them she sat down. And then deliberately she set herself to think out things from the beginning, going over every detail that she knew herself or had learned by hearsay from other people. She considered every actor in the drama and outside the drama.

And suddenly, a queer nebulous idea began to take shape—an idea suggested by that pair of innocent boots that stood there dumbly on the floor.

'But if so,' said Emily—'if so—'

She picked up the boots in her hand and hurried downstairs. She pushed open the dining-room door and went to the cupboard in the corner. Here was Captain Trevelyan's motley array of sporting trophies and sporting outfits, all the things he had not trusted within reach of the female tenants. The skis, the sculls, the elephant's foot, the tusks, the fishing rods—everything still waiting for Messrs Young and Peabody to pack them expertly for store.

Emily bent down, boots in hand.

In a minute or two she stood upright, flushed, incredulous.

'So that was it,' said Emily. 'So that was it.'

She sank into a chair. There was still much that she did not understand.

After some minutes she rose to her feet. She spoke aloud.

'I know who killed Captain Trevelyan,' she said. 'But I don't know *why*. I still can't think *why*. But I mustn't lose time.'

She hurried out of Hazelmoor. To find a car to drive her to Sittaford was the work of a few minutes. She ordered it to take her to Mr Duke's bungalow. Here she paid the man and then walked up the path as the car drove away.

She lifted the knocker and gave a loud rat-tat.

After a moment or two's interval the door was opened by a big burly man with a rather impassive face.

For the first time, Emily met Mr Duke face to face.

'Mr Duke?' she asked.

'Yes.'

'I am Miss Trefusis. May I come in, please?'

There was a momentary hesitation. Then he stood aside to let her pass. Emily walked into the living-room. He closed the front door and followed her.

'I want to see Inspector Narracott,' said Emily. 'Is he here?'

Again there was a pause. Mr Duke seemed uncertain how to answer. At last he appeared to make up his mind. He smiled—a rather curious smile.

'Inspector Narracott is here,' he said. 'What do you want to see him about?'

Emily took the parcel she was carrying and unwrapped it. She took out a pair of boots and placed them on the table in front of him.

'I want,' she said, 'to see him about those boots.'

CHAPTER 29

The Second Séance

'Hullo, hullo, hullo,' said Ronnie Garfield.

Mr Rycroft, slowly ascending the steep slope of the lane from the post office, paused, till Ronnie overtook him.

'Been to the local Harrods, eh?' said Ronnie. 'Old Mother Hibbert.'

'No,' said Mr Rycroft. 'I have been for a short walk along past the forge. Very delightful weather today.'

Ronnie looked up at the blue sky.

'Yes, a bit of a difference from last week. By the way, you're going to the Willetts', I suppose?'

'I am. You also?'

'Yes. Our bright spot in Sittaford—the Willetts. Mustn't let yourself get downhearted, that's their motto. Carry on as usual. My aunt says it is unfeeling of them to ask people to tea so soon after the funeral and all that, but that's all bunkum. She just says that because she's feeling rattled about the Emperor of Peru.'

'The Emperor of Peru?' said Mr Rycroft, surprised.

'One of the blinking cats. It's turned out to be an Empress

253

instead and Aunt Caroline's naturally annoyed about it. She doesn't like these sex problems—so, as I say, she got her feelings off her chest by making catty remarks about the Willetts. Why shouldn't they ask people to tea? Trevelyan wasn't a relation, or anything like that.'

'Very true,' said Mr Rycroft, turning his head and examining a bird which flew past and in which he thought he recognized a rare species.

'How annoying,' he murmured. 'I haven't got my glasses with me.'

'Eh! I say, talking of Trevelyan, do you think Mrs Willett can have known the old boy better than she says?'

'Why do you ask that?'

'Because of the change in her. Have you ever seen anything like it? She's aged about twenty years in the last week. You must have noticed it.'

'Yes,' said Mr Rycroft. 'I have noticed it.'

'Well, there you are. Trevelyan's death must have been the most frightful shock to her in some way or other. Queer if she turned out to be the old man's long lost wife whom he deserted in his youth and didn't recognize.'

'I hardly think that likely, Mr Garfield.'

'Bit too much of a movie stunt, eh? All the same very odd things happen. I've read some really amazing things in the *Daily Wire*—things you wouldn't credit if a newspaper didn't print them.'

'Are they any more to be credited on that account?' inquired Mr Rycroft acidly.

'You have got a down on young Enderby, haven't you?' said Ronnie.

'I dislike ill-bred nosing into affairs that do not concern you,' said Mr Rycroft.

'Yes, but then they do concern him,' Ronnie persisted. 'I mean nosing about is the poor chap's job. He seems to have tamed old Burnaby all right. Funny, the old boy can hardly bear the sight of me. I'm like a red rag to a bull to him.'

Mr Rycroft did not reply.

'By Jove,' said Ronnie again glancing up at the sky. 'Do you realize it's Friday? Just a week ago today at about this time we were trudging up to the Willetts' just as we are now. But a bit of a change in the weather.'

'A week ago,' said Mr Rycroft. 'It seems infinitely longer.'

'More like a bally year, doesn't it? Hullo, Abdul.'

They were passing Captain Wyatt's gate over which the melancholy Indian was leaning.

'Good afternoon, Abdul,' said Mr Rycroft. 'How's your master?'

The Indian shook his head.

'Master bad today, Sahib. Not see anyone. Not see anyone for long time.'

'You know,' said Ronnie as they passed on, 'that chap could murder Wyatt quite easily and no one would know. He could go on for weeks shaking his head and saying the master wouldn't see anyone and no one would think it the least odd.'

Mr Rycroft admitted the truth of the statement.

'But there would still be the problem of the disposal of the body,' he pointed out.

'Yes, that's always the snag, isn't it? Inconvenient thing, a human body.'

They passed Major Burnaby's cottage. The Major was in his garden looking sternly at a weed which was growing where no weed should be.

'Good afternoon, Major,' said Mr Rycroft. 'Are you also coming to Sittaford House?'

Burnaby rubbed his nose.

'Don't think so. They sent a note asking me. But—well—I don't feel like it. Expect you'll understand.'

Mr Rycroft bowed his head in token of understanding.

'All the same,' he said. 'I wish you'd come. I've got a reason.'

'A reason. What sort of reason?'

Mr Rycroft hesitated. It was clear that the presence of Ronnie Garfield constrained him. But Ronnie, completely oblivious of the fact, stood his ground listening with ingenuous interest.

'I'd like to try an experiment,' he said at last slowly.

'What sort of experiment?' demanded Burnaby. Mr Rycroft hesitated.

'I'd rather not tell you beforehand. But if you come, I'll ask you to back me up in anything I suggest.'

Burnaby's curiosity was aroused.

'All right,' he said. 'I'll come. You can count on me. Where's my hat?'

He rejoined them in a minute, hat on head, and all three turned in at the gates of Sittaford House.

'Hear you are expecting company, Rycroft,' said Burnaby conversationally.

A shade of vexation passed over the older man's face.

'Who told you that?'

'That chattering magpie of a woman, Mrs Curtis. She's

clean and she's honest, but her tongue never stops, and she pays no attention to whether you listen or whether you don't.'

'It's quite true,' admitted Mr Rycroft. 'I am expecting my niece, Mrs Dering, and her husband, tomorrow.'

They had arrived at the front door by now, and on pressing the bell it was opened to them by Brian Pearson.

As they removed their overcoats in the hall, Mr Rycroft observed the tall broad-shouldered young man with an interested eye.

'Fine specimen,' he thought. 'Very fine specimen. Strong temper. Curious angle of the jaw. Might be a nasty customer to tackle in certain circumstances. What you might call a dangerous young man.'

A queer feeling of unreality stole over Major Burnaby as he entered the drawing-room, and Mrs Willett rose to greet him.

'Splendid of you to turn out.'

The same words as last week. The same blazing fire on the hearth. He fancied, but was not sure, the same gowns on the two women.

It did give one a queer feeling. As though it were last week again—as though Joe Trevelyan hadn't died—as though nothing had happened or were changed. Stop, that was wrong. The Willett woman had changed. A wreck, that was the only way of describing her. No longer the prosperous determined woman of the world, but a broken nervy creature making an obvious and pathetic effort to appear as usual.

'But I'm hanged if I can see what Joe's death meant to her,' thought the Major.

For the hundredth time he registered the impression that there was something deuced odd about the Willetts.

As usual, he awoke to the realization that he was being silent and that someone was speaking to him.

'Our last little gathering, I am afraid,' Mrs Willett was saying.

'What's that?' Ronnie Garfield looked up suddenly.

'Yes.' Mrs Willett shook her head with a would-be smile. 'We have got to forego the rest of the winter in Sittaford. Personally, of course, I love it—the snow and the tors and the wildness of it all. But the domestic problem! The domestic problem is too difficult—it defeats me!'

'I thought you were going to get a chauffeur-butler and a handyman,' said Major Burnaby.

A sudden shiver shook Mrs Willett's frame.

'No,' she said, 'I—I have had to give up that idea.'

'Dear, dear,' said Mr Rycroft. 'This is a great blow to us all. Very sad indeed. We will sink back into our little rut after you have gone. When do you go, by the way?'

'On Monday, I expect,' said Mrs Willett. 'Unless I can get away tomorrow. It's so very awkward with no servants. Of course, I must arrange things with Mr Kirkwood. I took the house for four months.'

'You are going to London?' inquired Mr Rycroft.

'Yes, probably, to start with anyway. Then I expect we shall go abroad to the Riviera.'

'A great loss,' said Mr Rycroft bowing gallantly.

Mrs Willett gave a queer aimless little titter.

'Too kind of you, Mr Rycroft. Well, shall we have tea?'

Tea was laid ready. Mrs Willett poured out. Ronnie and

Brian handed things. A queer kind of embarrassment lay over the party.

'What about you?' said Burnaby abruptly to Brian Pearson. 'You off too?'

'To London, yes. Naturally I shan't go abroad till this business is over.'

'This business?'

'I mean until my brother is cleared of this ridiculous charge.'

He flung the words at them defiantly in such a challenging manner that nobody knew quite what to say. Major Burnaby relieved the situation.

'Never have believed he did it. Not for a moment,' he said.

'*None* of us think so,' said Violet, flinging him a grateful glance.

The tinkle of a bell broke the ensuing pause.

'That's Mr Duke,' said Mrs Willett. 'Let him in, Brian.'

Young Pearson had gone to the window.

'It's not Duke,' he said. 'It's that damned journalist.'

'Oh! dear,' said Mrs Willett. 'Well, I suppose we must let him in all the same.'

Brian nodded and reappeared in a few minutes with Charles Enderby.

Enderby entered with his usual ingenuous air of beaming satisfaction. The idea that he might not be welcome did not seem to occur to him.

'Hullo, Mrs Willett, how are you? Thought I'd just drop in and see how things were. I wondered where everyone in Sittaford had got to. Now, I see.'

'Have some tea, Mr Enderby?'

'Awfully kind of you. I will. I see Emily isn't here. I suppose she's with your aunt, Mr Garfield.'

'Not that I know of,' said Ronnie staring. 'I thought she'd gone to Exhampton.'

'Ah! but she's back from there. How do I know? A little bird told me. The Curtis bird, to be accurate. Saw the car pass the post office and go up the lane and come back empty. She is not in No. 5 and she's not in Sittaford House. Puzzle—where is she? Failing Miss Percehouse, she must be sipping tea with that determined lady killer, Captain Wyatt.'

'She may have gone up Sittaford Beacon to see the sunset,' suggested Mr Rycroft.

'Don't think so,' said Burnaby. 'Should have seen her pass. I've been in the garden for the last hour.'

'Well, I don't think it's a very vital problem,' said Charles cheerfully. 'I mean I don't think she's been kidnapped or murdered or anything.'

'That's a pity from the point of view of your paper, isn't it?' sneered Brian.

'Even for copy, I wouldn't sacrifice Emily,' said Charles. 'Emily,' he added thoughtfully, 'is unique.'

'Very charming,' said Mr Rycroft. 'Very charming. We are—er—collaborators, she and I?'

'Has everyone finished?' said Mrs Willett. 'What about some bridge?'

'Er—one moment,' said Mr Rycroft.

He cleared his throat importantly. Everyone looked at him.

'Mrs Willett, I am, as you know, deeply interested in

psychic phenomena. A week ago today, in this very room, we had an amazing, indeed an awe-inspiring experience.'

There was a faint sound from Violet Willett. He turned to her.

'I know, my dear Miss Willett, I know. The experience upset you, it was upsetting. I do not deny it. Now, ever since the crime the police force have been seeking the murderer of Captain Trevelyan. They have made an arrest. But some of us, at least, in this room, do not believe that Mr James Pearson is the guilty party. What I propose is this, that we repeat the experiment of last Friday, though approaching it this time in a rather different spirit.'

'No,' cried Violet.

'Oh! I say,' said Ronnie. 'That's a bit too thick. I'm not going to join in anyway.'

Mr Rycroft took no notice of him.

'Mrs Willett, what do you say?'

She hesitated.

'Frankly, Mr Rycroft, I do not like the idea. I don't like it at all. That miserable business last week made a most disagreeable impression on me. It will take me a long time to forget it.'

'What are you getting at exactly?' asked Enderby interestedly. 'Do you propose that the spirits should tell us the name of Captain Trevelyan's murderer? That seems a pretty tall order.'

'It was a pretty tall order, as you call it, when last week a message came through saying that Captain Trevelyan was dead.'

'That's true,' agreed Enderby. 'But—well—you know

this idea of yours might have consequences you haven't considered.'

'Such as?'

'Supposing a name was mentioned? Could you be sure that someone present did not deliberately—'

He paused and Ronnie Garfield tendered the word.

'Shove. That's what he means. Supposing somebody goes and shoves.'

'This is a serious experiment, sir,' said Mr Rycroft warmly. 'Nobody would do such a thing.'

'I don't know,' said Ronnie dubiously. 'I wouldn't put it past them. I don't mean myself. I swear I wouldn't, but suppose everyone turns on me and says I have. Jolly awkward, you know.'

'Mrs Willett, I am in earnest,' the little old gentleman disregarded Ronnie. 'I beg of you, let us make the experiment.'

She wavered.

'I don't like it. I really don't. I—' She looked round her uneasily, as though for a way of escape. 'Major Burnaby, you were Captain Trevelyan's friend. What do you say?'

The Major's eyes met those of Mr Rycroft. This, he understood, was the contingency which the latter had foreshadowed.

'Why not?' he said gruffly.

It had all the decision of a casting vote.

Ronnie went into the adjoining room and brought the small table which had been used before. He set it in the middle of the floor and chairs were drawn up round it. No one spoke. The experiment was clearly not popular.

'That is correct, I think,' said Mr Rycroft. 'We are about

to repeat the experiment of last Friday under precisely similar conditions.'

'Not precisely similar,' objected Mrs Willett. 'Mr Duke is missing.'

'True,' said Mr Rycroft. 'A pity he is not here. A great pity. Well—er—we must consider him as replaced by Mr Pearson.'

'Don't take part in it, Brian. I beg of you. Please don't,' cried Violet.

'What does it matter? It's all nonsense anyway.'

'That is quite the wrong spirit,' said Mr Rycroft severely.

Brian Pearson did not reply, but took his place beside Violet.

'Mr Enderby,' began Mr Rycroft, but Charles interrupted him.

'I was not in on this. I'm a journalist and you mistrust me. I'll take notes in shorthand of any phenomena—that's the word, isn't it?—that occur.'

Matters were settled like that. The other six took their places round the table. Charles turned off the lights and sat down on the fender.

'One minute,' he said. 'What's the time?' He peered at his wrist watch in the firelight.

'That's odd,' he said.

'What's odd?'

'It's just twenty-five minutes past five.'

Violet uttered a little cry.

Mr Rycroft said severely:

'Silence.'

The minutes passed. A very different atmosphere this to

the one a week ago. There was no muffled laughter, no whispered comments—only silence, broken at last by a slight crack from the table.

Mr Rycroft's voice rose.

'Is there any one there?'

Another faint crack—somehow an eerie sound in that darkened room.

'Is there anyone there?'

Not a crack this time but a deafening tremendous rap.

Violet screamed and Mrs Willett gave a cry.

Brian Pearson's voice rose reassuringly.

'It's all right. That's a knock at the front door. I'll go and open it.'

He strode from the room.

Still nobody spoke.

Suddenly the door flew open, the lights were switched on.

In the doorway stood Inspector Narracott. Behind him were Emily Trefusis and Mr Duke.

Narracott took a step into the room and spoke.

'John Burnaby, I charge you with the murder of Joseph Trevelyan on Friday the 14th instant, and I hereby warn you that anything you may say will be taken down and may be used in evidence.'

CHAPTER 30

Emily Explains

It was a crowd of people almost too surprised for words that crowded round Emily Trefusis.

Inspector Narracott had led his prisoner from the room.

Charles Enderby found his voice first.

'For heaven's sake, cough it up, Emily,' he said. 'I want to get to the telegraph office. Every moment's vital.'

'It was Major Burnaby who killed Captain Trevelyan.'

'Well, I saw Narracott arrest him. And I suppose Narracott's sane—hasn't gone off his nut suddenly. But how *can* Burnaby have killed Trevelyan? I mean how is it humanly possible? If Trevelyan was killed at five and twenty past five—'

'He wasn't. He was killed at about a quarter to six.'

'Well, but even then—'

'I know. You'd never guess unless you just happened to think of it. *Skis*—that's the explanation—*skis.*'

'Skis?' repeated everyone.

Emily nodded.

'Yes. He deliberately engineered that table-turning. It wasn't accident and done unconsciously as we thought,

265

Agatha Christie

Charles. It was the second alternative that we rejected—done on purpose. He saw it was going to snow before very long. That would make it perfectly safe and wipe out all tracks. He created the impression that Captain Trevelyan was dead—got everyone all worked up. Then he pretended to be very upset and insisted on starting off for Exhampton.

'He went home, buckled on his skis (they were kept in a shed in the garden with a lot of other tackle) and started. He was an expert on skis. It's all downhill to Exhampton—a wonderful run. It would only take about ten minutes.

'He arrived at the window and rapped. Captain Trevelyan let him in, all unsuspecting. Then, when Captain Trevelyan's back was turned he seized his opportunity, picked up that sandbag thing and—and killed him. Ugh! It makes me sick to think of it.'

She shuddered.

'It was all quite easy. He had plenty of time. He must have wiped and cleaned the skis and then put them into the cupboard in the dining-room, pushed in among all the other things. Then, I suppose he forced the window and pulled out all the drawers and things—to make it look as though someone had broken in.

'Then just before eight o'clock, all he had to do was to go out, make a detour on to the road higher up and come puffing and panting into Exhampton as though he'd walked all the way from Sittaford. So long as no one suspected about the skis, he'd be perfectly safe. The doctor couldn't fail to say that Captain Trevelyan had been dead at least two hours. And, as I say, so long as no one thought of skis, Major Burnaby would have a perfect alibi.'

'But they were friends—Burnaby and Trevelyan,' said Mr Rycroft. 'Old friends—they've always been friends. It's incredible.'

'I know,' said Emily. 'That's what I thought. I couldn't see *why*. I puzzled and I puzzled and at last I had to come to Inspector Narracott and Mr Duke.'

She paused and looked at the impassive Mr Duke.

'May I tell them?' she said.

Mr Duke smiled.

'If you like, Miss Trefusis.'

'Anyway—no, perhaps you'd rather I didn't. I went to them, and we got the thing clear. Do you remember telling me, Charles, that Evans mentioned that Captain Trevelyan used to send in solutions of competitions in his name? He thought Sittaford House was too grand an address. Well— that's what he did in the Football Competition that you gave Major Burnaby five thousand pounds for. It was Captain Trevelyan's solution really, and he sent it in in Burnaby's name. No. 1, The Cottages, Sittaford, sounded much better, he thought. Well, you see what happened? On Friday morning Major Burnaby got the letter saying he'd won five thousand pounds (and by the way, that ought to have made us suspicious. He told you he never got the letter—that nothing had come through on Friday owing to the weather. That was a lie. Friday morning was the last day things did come through). Where was I? Oh!—Major Burnaby getting the letter. He wanted that five thousand— wanted it badly. He'd been investing in some rotten shares or other and had lost a terrible lot of money.

'The idea must have come into his head quite suddenly,

I should think. Perhaps when he realized it was going to snow that evening. *If Trevelyan were dead*—he could keep that money and no one would ever know.'

'Amazing,' murmured Mr Rycroft. 'Quite amazing. I never dreamed—But my dear young lady, how did you learn all this? What put you on the right track?'

For answer, Emily explained Mrs Belling's letter, and told how she had discovered the boots in the chimney.

'It was looking at them that put it into my mind. They were ski boots, you see, and they made me think of skis. And suddenly I wondered if perhaps—I rushed downstairs to the cupboard, and sure enough there were *two* pairs of skis there. One pair was longer than the other. And the boots fitted the long pair—*but they didn't fit the other*. The toe-clip things were adjusted for a much smaller pair of boots. The shorter pair of skis belonged to a different person.'

'He ought to have hidden the skis somewhere else,' said Mr Rycroft with artistic disapproval.

'No—no,' said Emily. 'Where else could he hide them? It was a very good place really. In a day or two the whole collection would have been stored, and in the meantime it wasn't likely that the police would bother whether Captain Trevelyan had had one or two pairs of skis.'

'But why did he hide the boots?'

'I suppose,' said Emily, 'that he was afraid the police might do exactly what I did—The sight of ski boots might have suggested skis to them. So he stuffed them up the chimney. And that's really, of course, where he made his mistake, because Evans noticed that they'd gone and I got to know of it.'

'Did he deliberately mean to fasten the crime on Jim?' demanded Brian Pearson angrily.

'Oh! no. That was just Jim's usual idiotic luck. He *was* an idiot, poor lamb.'

'He's all right now,' said Charles. 'You needn't worry about him. Have you told me everything, Emily, because if so, I want to rush to the telegraph office. You'll excuse me, everybody.'

He dashed out of the room.

'The live wire,' said Emily.

Mr Duke spoke in his deep voice.

'You've been rather a live wire yourself, Miss Trefusis.'

'You have,' said Ronnie admiringly.

'Oh! dear,' said Emily suddenly and dropped limply on a chair.

'What you need is a pick-me-up,' said Ronnie. 'A cocktail, eh?'

Emily shook her head.

'A little brandy,' suggested Mr Rycroft solicitously.

'A cup of tea,' suggested Violet.

'I'd like a spot of face powder,' said Emily wistfully. 'I've left my powder puff in the car. And I know I'm simply shining with excitement.'

Violet led her upstairs in search of this sedative to the nerves.

'That's better,' said Emily, dabbing her nose firmly. 'What a nice kind. I feel much better now. Have you got any lipstick? I feel almost human.'

'You've been wonderful,' said Violet. 'So brave.'

'Not really,' said Emily. 'Underneath this camouflage I've

269

been as wobbly as a jelly, with a sort of sick feeling in my middle.'

'I know,' said Violet. 'I've felt much the same myself. I have been so terrified this last few days—about Brian, you know. They couldn't hang him for murdering Captain Trevelyan, of course, but if once he had said where he was during that time, they would soon have ferreted out that it was he who engineered Father's escape.'

'What's that?' said Emily, pausing in her facial repairs.

'Father was the convict who escaped. That's why we came here. Mother and I. Poor Father, he's always—been queer at times. Then he does these dreadful things. We met Brian on the way over from Australia, and he and I—well—he and I—'

'I see,' said Emily helpfully. 'Of course you did.'

'I told him everything and between us we concocted a plan. Brian was wonderful. We had got plenty of money fortunately, and Brian made all the plans. It's awfully hard to get away from Princetown, you know, but Brian engineered it. Really it was a kind of miracle. The arrangement was that after Father got away he was to go straight across country here and hide in the Pixie's Cave and then later he and Brian were to be our two men servants. You see with our arriving so long beforehand we imagined we would be quite free from suspicion. It was Brian who told us about this place, and suggested us offering a big rent to Captain Trevelyan.'

'I'm awfully sorry,' said Emily—'I mean that it all went wrong.'

'It's broken Mother up completely,' said Violet. 'I think

Brian's wonderful. It isn't everybody who would want to marry a convict's daughter. But I don't think it's really Father's fault, he had an awful kick on the head from a horse about fifteen years ago, and since then he has been a bit queer. Brian says if he had a good counsel he would have got off. But don't let's talk about me any more.'

'Can't anything be done?'

Violet shook her head.

'He's very ill—the exposure, you know. That awful cold. It's pneumonia. I can't help feeling that if he dies—well—it may be best for him really. It sounds dreadful to say so, but you know what I mean.'

'Poor Violet,' said Emily. 'It *is* a rotten shame.'

The girl shook her head.

'I've got Brian,' she said. 'And you've got—'

She stopped, embarrassed.

'Ye-es,' said Emily thoughtfully, 'That's just it.'

CHAPTER 31

The Lucky Man

Ten minutes later Emily was hurrying down the lane. Captain Wyatt, leaning over his gate, tried to arrest her progress.

'Hie,' he said, 'Miss Trefusis. What's all this I hear?'

'It's all true,' said Emily hurrying on.

'Yes, but look here. Come in—have a glass of wine or a cup of tea. There's plenty of time. No need to hurry. That's the worst of you civilized people.'

'We're awful, I know,' said Emily and sped on.

She burst in on Miss Percehouse with the explosive force of a bomb.

'I've come to tell you all about it,' said Emily.

And straightaway she poured forth the complete story. It was punctuated by various ejaculations of 'Bless us,' 'You don't say so?' 'Well, I declare,' from Miss Percehouse.

When Emily had finished her narrative, Miss Percehouse raised herself on her elbow and wagged a finger portentously.

'What did I say?' she demanded. 'I told you Burnaby was a jealous man. Friends indeed! For more than twenty years Trevelyan has done everything a bit better than

272

Burnaby. He skied better, and he climbed better, and he shot better, and he did crossword puzzles better. Burnaby wasn't a big enough man to stand it. Trevelyan was rich and he was poor.

'It's been going on a long time. I can tell you it's a difficult thing to go on really liking a man who can do everything just a little bit better than you can. Burnaby was a narrow-minded, small-natured man. He let it get on his nerves.'

'I expect you're right,' said Emily. 'Well, I had to come and tell you. It seemed so unfair you should be out of everything. By the way, did you know that your nephew knew my Aunt Jennifer? They were having tea together at Deller's on Wednesday.'

'She's his godmother,' said Miss Percehouse. 'So that's the "fellow" he wanted to see in Exeter. Borrowing money, if I know Ronnie. I'll speak to him.'

'I forbid you to bite anyone on a joyful day like this,' said Emily. 'Good-bye. I must fly. I've got a lot to do.'

'What have you got to do, young woman? I should say you'd done your bit.'

'Not quite. I must go up to London and see Jim's insurance company people and persuade them not to prosecute him over that little matter of the borrowed money.'

'H'm,' said Miss Percehouse.

'It's all right,' said Emily. 'Jim will keep straight enough in future. He's had his lesson.'

'Perhaps. And you think you'll be able to persuade them?'

'Yes,' said Emily firmly.

'Well,' said Miss Percehouse. 'Perhaps you will. And after that?'

'After that,' said Emily, 'I've finished. I'll have done all I can for Jim.'

'Then suppose we say—what next?' said Miss Percehouse.

'You mean?'

'What next? Or if you want it put clearer: *Which of them?*'

'Oh!' said Emily.

'Exactly. That's what I want to know. Which of them is to be the unfortunate man?'

Emily laughed. Bending over she kissed the old lady.

'Don't pretend to be an idiot,' she said. 'You know perfectly well which it is.'

Miss Percehouse chuckled.

Emily ran lightly out of the house and down to the gate just as Charles came racing up the lane.

He caught her by both hands.

'Emily darling!'

'Charles! Isn't everything marvellous?'

'I shall kiss you,' said Mr Enderby, and did.

'I'm a made man, Emily,' he said. 'Now, look here, darling, what about it?'

'What about what?'

'Well—I mean—well, of course, it wouldn't have been playing the game with poor old Pearson in prison and all the rest of it. But he's cleared now and—well, he has got to take his medicine just like anybody else.'

'What *are* you talking about?' said Emily.

'You know well enough I am crazy about you,' said Mr Enderby, 'and you like me. Pearson was just a mistake. What I mean is—well—you and I, we are made for each other. All this time, we have known it, both of us, haven't we? Do you like a Registry Office or a Church, or what?'

'If you are referring to marriage,' said Emily, 'there's nothing doing.'

'What—but I say—'

'No,' said Emily.

'But—Emily—'

'If you will have it,' said Emily. 'I love Jim. Passionately!'

Charles stared at her in speechless bewilderment.

'You can't!'

'I can! And I do! And I always have! And I always shall!'

'You—you made me think—'

'I said,' said Emily demurely, 'that it was wonderful to have someone one could rely on.'

'Yes, but I thought—'

'I can't help what you thought.'

'You *are* an unscrupulous devil, Emily.'

'I know, Charles darling. I know. I'm everything you like to call me. But never mind. Think how great you are going to be. You've got your scoop! Exclusive news for the *Daily Wire*. You're a made man. What's a woman anyway? Less than the dust. No really strong man wants a woman. She only hampers him by clinging to him like the ivy. Every great man is one who is independent of women. A career— there's nothing so fine, so absolutely satisfying to a man, as a great career. You are a strong man, Charles, one who can stand alone—'

'Will you stop talking, Emily? It's like a talk to Young Men on the Wireless! You've broken my heart. You don't know how lovely you looked as you came into that room with Narracott. Just like something triumphant and avenging off an arch.'

A footstep crunched on the lane, and Mr Duke appeared.

'Oh! There you are, Mr Duke,' said Emily. 'Charles, I want to tell you. This is Ex-Chief Inspector Duke of Scotland Yard.'

'What?' cried Charles, recognizing a famous name. 'Not *the* Inspector Duke?'

'Yes,' said Emily. 'When he retired, he came here to live, and being nice and modest he didn't want his renown to get about. I see now why Inspector Narracott twinkled so when I wanted him to tell me what kind of crimes Mr Duke had committed.'

Mr Duke laughed.

Charles wavered. There was a short tussle between the lover and the journalist. The journalist won.

'I'm delighted to meet you, Inspector,' he said. 'Now, I wonder if we could persuade you to do us a short article, say eight hundred words, on the Trevelyan case.'

Emily stepped quickly up the lane and into Mrs Curtis's cottage. She ran up to her bedroom and pulled out her suitcase. Mrs Curtis had followed her up.

'You're not going, Miss?'

'I am. I've got a lot to do—London, and my young man.'

Mrs Curtis drew nearer.

'Just tell me, Miss, which of 'em is it?'

Emily was throwing clothes haphazard into the suitcase.

'The one in prison, of course. There's never been any other.'

'Ah! You don't think, Miss, that maybe you're making

a mistake. You're sure the other young gentleman is worth as much as this one?'

'Oh! no,' said Emily. 'He isn't. This one will get on.' She glanced out of the window where Charles was still holding Ex-Chief-Inspector Duke in earnest parley. 'He's the kind of young man who's simply born to get on—but I don't know what would happen to the other one if I weren't there to look after him. Look where he would be now if it weren't for me!'

'And you can't say more than that, Miss,' said Mrs Curtis.

She retreated downstairs to where her lawful spouse was sitting and staring into vacancy.

'The living image of my Great Aunt Sarah's Belinda she is,' said Mrs Curtis. 'Threw herself away she did on that miserable George Plunket down at the Three Cows. Mortgaged and all it was. And in two years she had the mortgage paid off and the place a going concern.'

'Ah!' said Mr Curtis, and shifted his pipe slightly.

'He was a handsome fellow, George Plunket,' said Mrs Curtis reminiscently.

'Ah!' said Mr Curtis.

'But after he married Belinda he never so much as looked at another woman.'

'Ah!' said Mr Curtis.

'She never gave him the chance,' said Mrs Curtis.

'Ah!' said Mr Curtis.

BRING HOME
THE
REVOLUTION
The Case for a British Republic

J<small>ONATHAN</small> F<small>REEDLAND</small>

F<small>OURTH</small> E<small>STATE</small> • *London*

This paperback edition published in 1999
First published in Great Britain in 1998 by
Fourth Estate Limited
6 Salem Road, London W2 4BU

Copyright © 1998 Jonathan Freedland

The right of Jonathan Freedland to be identified as
the author of this work has been asserted by him in
accordance with the Copyright, Designs and Patents
Act 1988.

A catalogue record for this book is available from the
British Library.

ISBN   978-0-00-729151-9

All rights reserved. No part of this publication may be
reproduced, transmitted, or stored in a retrieval
system, in any form or by any means, without
permission in writing from Fourth Estate Limited.

Typeset in Plantin Light by Avon Dataset Ltd,
Bidford on Avon, B50 4JH

Printed and bound in Great Britain by
Clays Ltd, St Ives plc

Mixed Sources
Product group from well-managed
forests and other controlled sources
www.fsc.org   Cert no. SW-COC-001806
© 1996 Forest Stewardship Council

FSC is a non-profit international organisation established to promote the
responsible management of the world's forests. Products carrying the FSC
label are independently certified to assure consumers that they come
from forests that are managed to meet the social, economic and
ecological needs of present and future generations.

Find out more about HarperCollins and the environment at
www.harpercollins.co.uk/green

For my parents,
who taught me the meaning of home.

Contents

Acknowledgements

Initial thanks must go to the people who set me on my American journey: Peter Preston at the *Guardian*, Kevin Marsh at the BBC and Ben Bradlee at the *Washington Post*. Once in the US I benefited from the wisdom of hundreds of people, but Laura Blumenfeld, former Senator Eugene McCarthy, Curtis Gans at the Committee for the Study of the American Electorate and Andrew Kohut at the Pew Research Centre for the People and the Press all deserve special mention. Professor Seymour Martin Lipset pointed me in several right directions, not least by writing the modern classic *American Exceptionalism*, which brought together some of the key statistical data which appear in this book.

At the *Guardian*, Simon Tisdall was a generous foreign editor and Ed Vulliamy inspired at least one of the key ideas of this book, while Carol Keefer provided invaluable research and moral support, in equal measure. Alan Rusbridger showed why he is the kind of editor every journalist wants to work for: he was an early supporter of this project, and allowed me the time and freedom to make it happen.

Further help, advice and inspiration came from Sue Ellis, Robert Crampton, Adam Goldwater, Phil Hay, Allan Little, Susanna Lumsden, Jonathan Marks, Jon Mendelsohn, Rick Nye, Tanya Sillem and Keir Starmer. Robin Oppenheim and Clive Sheldon guided me on questions of law and liberty, offering sage advice. David Miliband and Deborah Hellman were kind enough to read first drafts of the text, both greatly improving what they saw.

Marc Shaw undertook the tough, dual task of researcher and sounding board – listening and debating as the ideas presented here took shape. Clive Priddle at Fourth Estate was the exemplary editor, with a knack for making the awkward suggestion – which invariably turned out to be exactly right. Emma Rhind-Tutt cleaned up and copy-edited the text, ensuring I wrote in English – and not American.

I owe the largest debt, though, to Jonny Geller of Curtis Brown. As my agent, it was he who first believed my frequent rants about Britain and the United States had the makings of a book. As one of my oldest and best friends, he also provided the constant encouragement and faith that a first-time author depends upon. It is no exaggeration to say this book would not have happened without him.

1

Introduction

ONE OF MY earliest memories is of America, even though I had never been there and never seen it. It is possible that all I knew was the word. But it was enough.

The way my parents tell it, I was four years old the day I came downstairs, dressed, packed and ready to go. I was holding a toy suitcase. No family trip was planned, and yet I was determined. 'I'm going to America,' I said. 'With grandpa.'

Apparently my grandfather – the pipe-smoking joker who had long since won my infant heart – had hatched the plan with me the previous day. Tomorrow, he had whispered, the two of us would go on a big adventure, 'To *America*.' I was to travel in his pocket.

No amount of explanation could shake me from this faith. I had packed all the essentials: pyjamas, toothbrush, teddy bear. It had to be true.

My mother and father did their best, but the truth still set off a pre-breakfast torrent of tears. I have since learned that my grandpa – whose gift for easy contentment found great pleasure in a simple joke or conjuring trick – got a stern lecture afterwards. Its themes were trust, responsibility and toddler disappointment.

Like all childhood memories, I have gathered most of the details of that story from later tellings and retellings. But one thing I remember for myself: the thrill of that word – *America*. It sounded vast and exciting, even to a four year old. The very rhythm of the name conveyed colour and plenty. As I got c the meaning became fuller. America was where it was &

1

sunny. Cowboys and Indians came from there. It was where films happened.

My father encouraged this dreaminess; after all he was infected by it himself. He had spent his youth lapping up Hollywood fairytales and had lived under their spell ever since. While other dads watched the football, mine settled in front of BBC 2's *Saturday Cinema*: Gene Kelly in a sailor's uniform, Fred Astaire in tails, and the Manhattan skyline never far away. I was the only boy I knew who could sing a song about the Swanee River.

Americana filled the house. *Time* magazine arrived each week, bringing word of the anti-war movement in San Francisco or a new kind of car in Detroit. One August day in 1974 I was told to hush for something 'very important' on television. We watched Richard Nixon announce his resignation from the presidency, 'effective at noon tomorrow'. I was seven years old.

But, along with so much else, adolescence put flight to all that. It was the 1980s and America became a dirty word. Americans had elected a witless actor as president, a man so stupid he could not speak without cue cards (or so we were told). The US was about to touch off nuclear Armageddon, and its lethal cruise missiles were all over our soil.

America was on the wrong side of everything my friends and I cared about. We clung to socialism even as it was breathing its last, and the United States was the home of capitalism. We loathed Thatcher and the Americans loved her. Our television was brainy – all *Brideshead Revisited* and the new Channel 4 – while theirs amounted to nothing better than *CHiPs* and the *Dukes of Hazzard*.

One minor skirmish I witnessed first-hand captured the mood. In 1983, McDonald's sought to open a branch on Hampstead's cherished High Street. The neighbourhood flexed its best local muscle – Tom Conti, Margaret Drabble and Glenda Jackson included – in a campaign to keep the American behemoth at bay. The war of burghers v. burgers lasted nearly ten years until the day in 1992 when the brie-and-baguette set finally admitted they were beaten, and made way for the shakes and fries.

Introduction

Litter from America

Even so, their struggle was not in vain. In their joust with Ronald McDonald, those Hampstead activists gave voice to a wide streak of British middle-class thinking. For millions of Britons, America was – and is – a vulgar, vile monster to be kept as far away as possible.

To them, the US is crass, poorly educated, obsessed with money, riven by race, plagued by extremism and filled with people who either eat too much or exercise to the point of fanaticism. They lack irony, kill each other for a nickel, invade small countries, know nothing of the world and require a credit card before they will treat the sick. Their children are either on crack, having children of their own, or sitting goggle-eyed in front of 100-channel TV with *Beavis and Butthead* on every station. America is the land of Bible-quoting fundamentalists, lamé-suited game-show hosts and gun-toting maniacs. Culturally it is a desert: theme parks substitute for history and dumbed-down slang serves for language. Politically it is even worse: kick-ass militarism, heartless corporate greed and a democracy so decayed no one votes. Bland, blow-dried candidates fight fake 'air wars' on TV and elections are sold to the highest bidder. The justice system is a joke, overrun with frivolous law-suits and billion-dollar payouts and so blinded by cash and race it allows O.J. Simpson to get away with murder. Nothing about America is moderate: it is either the obscenities of the Ku Klux Klan or the insanities of political correctness, telling Americans they can no longer call so much as a cup of coffee black.

In this climate, 'US-style' is an insult – a quick way to rubbish any new idea. 'We're becoming like America,' is a standard British lament on a par with 'We're going to the dogs.' If a politician wants to trash an opponent he need only accuse him of seeking to be 'presidential' – and it is not the presidency of France he has in mind.

Britain by contrast is an island of sanity, happily distant from the American colossus and all its excesses. To the anti-American, it is a source of pride that Britons do not subsist on burgers and that we have not forgotten how to walk as well as drive. We live in villages and pray in churches that have stood for nine or ten centuries. Our universities are ancient, and our countryside lush and lovely. We do not brag and swagger, but express ourselves with modest reserve. Our television is the best in the world, our collective sense of humour a national treasure. British political debate does not consist of thirty-second 'attack ads' but has a measure of sophistication, with the quality newspapers and the House of Commons enduring holdouts against the tyranny of the soundbite. We have standards, too. British life is sufficiently incorruptible that a UK qualification – whether it is a driving licence or a safety certificate – still means something. Best of all we have not forgotten about society. Over a century Britain has constructed a generous welfare state, one that includes the finest socialised medical system in the world – the National Health Service – and allows the children of the poor to study for free. While Americans worship Mammon, we understand that there are values beyond the material. We may not always be winners, but we have a national sympathy for the underdog and a tradition of fair play which has made Britain – in its own, understated way – one of the most tolerant and humane societies in the world.

The 51st State

This sort of attitude would be fine (though mistaken) if Britain did indeed keep its distance from the US. But it does not. In fact, we import Americana by the crateload every day of the week – into every aspect of our lives, from the way we shop, dress and talk to the food we eat and the laws we make.

Just glance at the morning paper. Start with the TV page, and notice the sheer bulk of programmes either made by or about Americans, from *Seinfeld* to *Star Trek*. Turn inside, and see how regularly the US dominates not just the foreign news pages, but every section. One edition of *The Times*, picked at random, carried two full broadsheet pages of US news (seven stories in all), a review of a new biography of Thomas Jefferson, as well as a commentary piece on the special relationship between Britain and the US. That same day's output on Radio 4 included a report on a racial discrimination claim against Texaco in the US, a *Late Book* extract featuring two characters lunching on

Madison Avenue and a short story narrated by a cockroach – with a Long Island accent. The midnight news reported that the Master of the Rolls was under fire for suggesting the introduction of 'American-style' law clerks. At 2 a.m., Radio 5 Live broadcast a full bulletin of news from a local US station – as it does every night.

And that was just one day, monitored randomly. Even as we are told that Europe is the most pressing question facing our nation, it is still America that consumes the media's interest. All the broadsheet papers run variations on the *Letter from America* format, with columnists recounting the trouble doing laundry in Greenwich Village or the price of sundried tomatoes in Santa Monica. There is apparently no market for similar musings from Vienna each week and no sign yet of a regular BBC *Letter from Bonn*.

Brits protest their disdain for Americana, yet we come back to it again and again, like moths to a porchlight. During the peak moments of the Zippergate affair that dominated 1998 – starting in January with an Internet rumour about a girl, a dress and a cigar and ending in December with the first presidential impeachment for 130 years – the British newspapers were full of little else. The cast of characters soon became household names, with Monica Lewinsky, Linda Tripp and Kenneth Starr the stuff of kitchen-table debate across Britain. The highlights – Bill Clinton's wagging-finger denial in January, his half-apology in August, the Starr Report in September – were all relayed live on British television. It was like an old-fashioned radio serial, a Dick Barton tale for the nineties, as the hero (or anti-hero) leapt free of danger only to land in a new fix in time for next week's episode. We may live 3000 miles away – but we were hooked.

And it does not need the high drama of an impeachment crisis to stir our interest in America. After the 1994 congressional elections *The Times* ran the full results of 435 House and thirty-four Senate races, along with several pages of analysis – no less than appeared in the serious American papers. In 1996 BBC TV drew level with CBS, NBC and ABC in the amount of airtime it devoted to live coverage of presidential election night. Needless to say, the Beeb rarely pays that kind of attention to any other foreign country.

Maybe we should blame the media. Perhaps excitable and outdated British editors love Americana while their readers really want to know about Warsaw or Oslo. But it is doubtful. The O.J. Simpson trial was a case in point: the British people became hooked on the fate of a sportsman they had never heard of. If Germany's biggest athlete – or Australia's or Spain's – had been charged with double murder, it is hard to imagine his case becoming a British obsession. It would have struggled to make it past the inside pages.

We look west so often, we hardly realise we are doing it. The top ten movies in Britain for 1996? Eight were from the US. The 100 bestselling books? Forty-one were American. The biggest foreign investor in the US? Britain. Head for central London and you can pick up a pair of shades at Soho's American Retro shop, or some new Levi's at the California Jeans Store. All around the country you can see kids in baseball caps – even though we do not play baseball – wearing sweatshirts promoting basketball teams they never see, from cities they could not place on a map.

British bands like Texas or Alabama 3 are at it as well, christening themselves in the holy water of Americana rather than taking the names of their real hometowns, Glasgow and Merthyr Tydfil. Sport tells the same story. Not only does American Football have its own weekly TV show in Britain (no such honour for rugby or cricket in the US), we have also imported the paraphernalia of American sporting life. How else to explain the cheerleaders and mascots prancing around at Rugby Union games or the birth of the London Broncos and the Bradford Bulls in the Super League – direct copies of teams from Denver and Chicago?

Our language is Americanised. British executives now say they have to *meet with* a client, when they used to meet them instead. Men are *guys*, women are *babes* and ambitious people *go for it*. In business the trend is most pronounced, so that now *human resources* departments *let people go* by explaining that the firm is *downsizing*. Tough on the worker, but he'd been *history* for a while. What's *that* about, you may ask. Just part of the whole America *thing*. Our literature has kept up, with Martin Amis and Ian McEwan admitting their debt to the likes of Saul

Bellow and John Updike. Howard Jacobson retreads the terrain of Philip Roth and Will Self follows a lead set first by Jay McInerney.

Even our landscape is changing, with giant, one-storey 'superstores' sprouting by roadsides all over Britain – copies of the strip malls which mar so much of the American countryside. Seven-day, all-night shopping is becoming commonplace. On the outskirts of the average British town you are now likely to find a ten-screen US-style multiplex and perhaps a bowling alley (often self-consciously called the Hollywood Bowl). In the high street, the major fast-food chains are now joined by American diners, complete with chrome fittings, a juke box in the corner and sodas and malts on the menu.

Of course, this is not new. America has been working its magic on us ever since that evening in 1887 when Buffalo Bill Cody staged his travelling Wild West Show at the brand new Earl's Court, in a royal command performance for Queen Victoria. We are told Her Majesty was – uncharacteristically – most amused, expressing shocked pleasure at the bravery of the Sioux warriors, the prowess of master markswoman Annie Oakley (the inspiration for *Annie Get Your Gun*) and the burst of audience participation in which her son, the Prince of Wales, became the victim of a mock Indian ambush on a stagecoach.

Since that day the cultural commerce has never let up. By the 1940s, GIs were bringing chewing gum and nylons to Britain while Hollywood delivered the products of the Dream Factory. In 1947 US film studios were taking more than $60 million out of the UK – enough money to combine with Britain's war debt to cause a serious problem for the country's balance of payments. A decade or so later it was rock 'n' roll, mesmerising lads in Liverpool and suburban London with the twelve-bar rhythms of the Bayou and the blues poetry of Appalachia. In our own times, the children of Chester and Chiswick pound along to the angry rap of the Bronx and South Central, mouthing the protest music of streets an ocean apart and a world away.

That habit has deep roots, too. Novelist Stephen Amidon says the parents of today's teenagers also saw the glamour in social upheavals Stateside. 'Such was the enthralment with America by the culturally hip in Britain that they even chose to fight the political battles raging over there, importing a protest movement for their own titillation. How else to explain the sight of Vanessa Redgrave and cronies protesting the Vietnam war at Grosvenor Square? American radicalism was chic, it was daring. You got to wear all those groovy clothes and sing those great songs.'

And so it has continued, containers of Americana arriving at British ports for as long as anyone can remember. Our media, our shops, our language – our very national life – are full of it. The phrase is old but no longer hyperbolic: Britain is becoming an offshore 51st State of the Union.

Best Buddies

Culture rarely travels alone: where it goes, politics usually follows. So it is that the United States has exercised a firm grip not only on the British imagination but on British government. In the years of the Cold War the connection was obvious, expressed in the slightly wishful British belief that London and Washington shared a 'special relationship' in matters of diplomacy. It is telling that the phrase is never used in the United States, for the reality has always been more one-sided than we like to admit, a fact captured by the *Financial Times* columnist, Joe Rogaly: 'As to the US . . . we have been an eager puppy, yelping our support, sinking our teeth into the ankles of its enemies, wagging our tails, anxious for the continuing blessing of our supposed best friend.'

Nevertheless the Anglo-American connection has always involved more than diplomatic cosiness. For years our politicians have looked to Washington for guidance, ideas, even rhetorical flourish. In their 1996 conference speeches, the leaders of both main parties quoted not British prime ministers but American presidents. John Major borrowed from Harry Truman to tell his party conference, 'The buck stops here.' Tony Blair preferred to adapt Franklin Roosevelt to declare, 'We have little to fear but fear itself.'

The transatlantic romance reached a high point in the mid-1980s when Ronald Reagan and Margaret Thatcher gazed doe-eyed at each other as they forged a new creed of conservatism. The bond was strong enough to endure even the frostiest days

of the Major era. Conservative ministers borrowed enthusiastically from the US, treating it as a virtual lending library of
social policy. The home secretary of the day, Michael Howard,
was especially keen. He liked California's 1994 'Three Strikes
and You're Out' law, which denied violent felons a fourth chance,
and proposed similar mandatory sentences for Britain. Howard
was equally taken by Proposition 187, by which Californians
demanded that teachers, nurses and social workers be trained
to snoop on and report immigrants whom they suspected of
being in the country illegally.

But the important new Anglo-American relationship was
forming elsewhere, one that would eventually bring the White
House and Downing Street closer together than at any time
since the dizzy days of Ron and Maggie. Tony Blair and Bill
Clinton were setting out on their own international love affair of
the centre-left. From its birth New Labour was a US-inspired
project, twinning itself with the New Democratic mission led by
Clinton. The president had barely settled into the Oval Office in
1993 before Tony Blair and Gordon Brown were touching down
at Dulles airport, eager to learn how to turn a rusty old political
machine into a lubricated election-winner. One New Labour
lieutenant, Philip Gould, had a virtual season-ticket to the White
House, huddling fortnightly with Clinton's boy-wonder adviser
George Stephanopoulos, trading memos about focus groups and
the exact contours of the 'gender gap'. An American TV news
show eventually confronted Blair on this point, playing him clips
of near-identical speeches he and Bill Clinton had delivered.
'You're almost twins,' taunted the CBS reporter, Lesley Stahl.
'Well, there are similarities, you can say that,' admitted a slightly
rattled Mr Blair. On the night of 1 May 1997, the first congrat-
ulatory call the new prime minister received – just moments
after his victory was numerically assured – was from the
American president.

The Labour government that took office hours later was
committed to an unabashedly American agenda. Installed as
chancellor, Gordon Brown pinched a US slogan to trumpet his
plan to move the jobless from 'welfare-to-work'. Later he
borrowed the signature phrase from the Roosevelt era,
describing his plan for the young unemployed as the New Deal.

When, five days after his arrival at the Exchequer, he granted the Bank of England full power to set interest rates he cited the US Federal Reserve as his model. Meanwhile, the home secretary Jack Straw was aping Bill Clinton's support for mandated bedtimes for teenagers to reduce crime and vandalism – so-called 'teen curfews'. He and Blair also demanded 'zero tolerance' for petty crime, an idea pioneered by the New York Police Department. There soon followed the appointment of a 'drugs czar', a call for directly elected mayors for the big cities and a plan for court-appointed 'public defenders'. All three ideas had originated in America.

The US influence was not confined to policy. Tony Blair moved fast to transform Downing Street into a British White House – a central hub of government, in full command of all branches of the executive. He wanted a chief of staff – just like the one who serves the president – and showed an early preference for US-style political appointees over permanent civil servants. He also adopted the American habit of plucking high-fliers from business to work in government. He even allowed his spokesman to brief the press on the record, a first for Number Ten but standard practice in the White House. Still, none of this was a great surprise. Blair had fought and won the 1997 election by raiding the arsenal of American political techniques. New Labour's Rapid Rebuttal Unit, its War Room, its focus groups and disciplined commitment to staying 'on message' – they all came marked 'Made in the USA'.

Call Customs

The American influence on the Blair project alone would justify a long, hard look at what Britain can learn from the US: if our government is determined to borrow from the United States we need to be sure it is taking the right stuff. But the sheer weight of cultural traffic across the Atlantic makes the task urgent. It is time we examined that traffic, deciding what to let in and what to keep out. We can think of it as an audit, a task for a hypothetical Politics and Culture Squad of the Customs and Excise service – necessary because the US is helping to shape our government and our society. As if that were not enough, there are five other good reasons to work out what exactly we want from America.

First, we need to resolve the screaming contradiction of our attitudes towards it. We simultaneously disdain and covet American culture, condemning it as junk food even as we reach for another helping – a kind of binge-and-puke social bulimia. The conflict was expressed concisely in a listener's letter read out on Radio 4's *Feedback* programme. She was complaining about the abundance of American short stories, plays, features and documentaries on her beloved station. 'I thought I was listening to Radio America rather than an intellectual British programme!' the correspondent fumed. 'American culture has little to offer, yet its influence is spreading across Britain like a fungus,' she went on, before adding a scolding reminder, 'We are British!'

Around the same time, Melvyn Bragg aired a two-part TV documentary about his personal love affair with America – confessing that it was now over. He had fallen in love with Elvis and John Steinbeck, Hollywood movies and cool civil rights demos. In the sixties America was the promised land. Now he saw only greed, commercialism and a grotesque gap between rich and poor. 'There's nothing left to envy about America,' Bragg concluded. It was time for Britain to issue its own Declaration of Independence – from the United States. The end credits rolled and the adverts came on. The first was for dream holidays in Florida, the second for tangy Tropicana orange juice, made with real American oranges, and the third for that passport to consumer paradise, the American Express card.

We are, in other words, in a love–hate relationship with our colonial offspring. An expert in collective psychology would have a field day, diagnosing British anti-Americanism as an inferiority and a superiority complex all rolled into one. The experts might call it the Laius Syndrome, after Oedipus's father – the affliction of the parent who loves but also envies and fears his child. Harold Macmillan had a textbook case of the disease, famously suggesting that post-imperial Britain should play Greece to the Americans' Rome, tutoring the new masters in the ways of empire. 'You will find the Americans much as the Greeks found the Romans,' Macmillan mused to a young Richard Crossman, whose notebook was never far away, 'great big, vulgar, bustling people, more vigorous than we are and also more idle, with more unspoiled virtues but also more corrupt.' Was that superiority or inferiority? Or both?

These days Macmillan's classical reference might ring fewer bells, but the ambivalence of Britain towards America lives on. In the 1990s we Brits all too often play Alfred to America's Batman – older, wiser and wittier than our American charge, but somehow slower, poorer and less glamorous. He is a muscled man of action; we are wrinkled and decrepit. The result is that same debilitating blend of condescension and inadequacy – and it is a mess. The only way to sort it out is to decide what we do and do not like about the US. Then we can start making some clearer judgements about America and what it can do for us.

Second, we should be selective about what we keep and discard from America because we *can*. We are prone to a brand of fatalism, believing there is nothing we can do about the American invasion: Coca-Cola imperialism is swallowing up the planet and we shall be another of its inevitable victims. In this view, the US hold on Britain operates like a law of nature: just as the moon determines the tides of the sea, so the Atlantic washes up on our shores – leaving a thick deposit of American slime behind.

When the head teacher Philip Lawrence was stabbed to death in December 1995, the *Daily Telegraph* succumbed to a bout of the fatalistic disease. 'Given how Britain invariably follows the pattern of America after a decade or so, the recent experience of American teachers shows how dangerous life could yet become,' the paper warned. But there is nothing 'invariable' about this or any other aspect of our national life. We shape the country we live in. Indeed, the need to extinguish such passivity from British discourse will be one of the themes of this book. We *can* choose what we want from America; we just have to start doing it.

Third, by gazing across the Atlantic we might just work out our place in Europe. For many of the lessons Britain can learn from America apply just as keenly to the Continent. The British-born US commentator Andrew Sullivan has written about Britain and America's shared passion for freedom, contrasting it with the European attachment to the strong central state: 'The most natural and challenging role for Britain in the future is staring it in the face: the economic and political liberalisation – the Americanisation, if you will – of European institutions.' Sullivan suggests that the founders of the European community consciously sought British traditions of liberty as a counterweight to French reliance on the state and German authoritarianism, to form a community that would be free of 'Gallic uniformity and Teutonic coherence'. Of course Britain snubbed those early advances, but it is not too late. With a smart eye on the lessons of America, writes Sullivan, 'some English fire could still be blown onto the embers of the European project'.

Besides, even the most dogmatic Europhile would be unlikely to argue that Britain should only look east and not west. For one thing, in the late 1990s the bloom came off the European rose somewhat, as unemployment and economic strain spread across the Continent – in vivid contrast with the thrusting growth of the US. Moreover, Britons repeatedly tell pollsters they feel as strong a link to America as they do to Europe – if not stronger. In February 1998 ICM found 61 per cent believing that Britain has more in common with America than Europe; just 35 per cent chose the Continent over the US. A Gallup survey three years earlier revealed that, in time of war, only one in ten Britons would trust France and Germany, compared to 46 per cent who felt they could rely on the United States.

Joined by language, it is still American culture we lap up. French movies are a minority taste, while American films are big box office. We watch no German TV, and speak hardly any Italian, but will stay in for reruns of *Roseanne* and *Frasier*. We recognise a photo of Bill Gates but would struggle to pick out Gianni Agnelli or Silvio Berlusconi from an identity parade. The plain fact is that, whatever the health of the diplomatic 'special relationship' between Britain and America, the cultural one is throbbing. Brussels may be trying to run our lives, but it is New York City whose skyline we recognise. Despite the moves towards European integration, we are still bound up with America – and we need to make sense of it.

Fourth, a political and cultural audit is needed because so much of what we think now is wrong – wrong about us and wrong about them. Our views of America are often based on outdated stereotypes and on a self-satisfaction about Britain we no longer wholly deserve. The result can be an anti-Americanism which makes us shut out a threat which does not exist to protect a virtue we have long lost. So we worry about US-style societal breakdown – even though property crime rates are higher in London than in Los Angeles or New York. We fear the dumbing down that comes with American culture – even though game shows are screened on primetime television in the UK but not in the US. And we fear importing America's crass commercialism – even though it is British sports teams who alter their strip to bear the name of a corporate sponsor, an action which would be regarded as high blasphemy in the US. As the former Conservative minister and cultural commentator George Walden has noted: 'Along with the most abject shlock mankind has ever produced, America has the best orchestras, the best universities, the best buildings, more top-class scientists, infinitely superior contemporary literature to our own, and (at the peak of the market) wittier and more intelligent films and television.' A thorough review of Anglo-American cultural traffic should shatter some stereotypes we have of America – and provide a new glimpse of ourselves. That, too, is one of the aims of this book.

Which brings us to the final and most pressing reason why we need to look anew at what we are importing from America: we are shipping in junk and leaving behind gold. There is much of real value to plunder from the US, but we are missing it. As acts of international piracy go, such plunder will hardly be a capital offence, for these gems were ours in the first place. The founding principles of the US were British ideas of liberty and democracy, which somehow slipped out of our hands and drifted across the Atlantic. They are Britain's very own buried treasure, stored and preserved an ocean away. Now it is time to reclaim them for ourselves.

After those schooldays in the heart of 'chattering-classes' London, I went to university, where the exposure to anti-Americanism only intensified. Now the great American satan was crushing heroic Sandinistas in Nicaragua. A fellow student became a college heart-throb by writing a folksong about the great anti-imperialist struggle – in Spanish. He performed it on Talent Night. I kept my childhood fascination with America quiet in those years; going public would have been as socially lethal as confessing a fondness for bloodsports or a warm hankering for the era of male-only suffrage. These were the days of right-on – and America was right-off.

So I suppose I carried all that British ambivalence towards America with me when I was despatched there, first for the *Washington Post* in the summer of 1992 and then for the *Guardian* a few months later. I spent four years travelling across the country, covering two presidential campaigns and the landmark congressional elections of 1994, when a Republican landslide swept away four decades of one-party control. I met suburban mothers in California's Woodland Hills and teenage heroin addicts in Seattle's Pike Street market, Christian fundamentalists in Dallas and peep-show strippers in Las Vegas – asking them about their home, their town, their country. I sat in a diner in Troy, North Carolina, and listened to the lunchtime chatter. I watched a baseball game in Baltimore and went on night patrol – in Haiti – with the soldiers of the 10th Mountain Division. I stood with the black Americans of the Million Man March on Washington and among the jackbooted neo-Nazis of the Aryan Nations in Idaho. I watched Ricki Lake on TV and listened to Rush Limbaugh on the radio. I interviewed presidential candidates and kindergarten pupils, trudging through the snows of New Hampshire and roasting in the desert heat of Arizona. I came across expat Brits nearly everywhere I went and, as I listened to their stories and examined my own reactions, I arrived at the core beliefs that make up this book. I saw a country different from the America known to most Britons, the America of New York, Washington and, most crucially, Hollywood. Different and better.

I saw a nation that has grievous problems, yet still hums with the energy of a new society, a nation that still believes it steers its own destiny, and a nation that makes most – though not all – of its citizens feel like they belong. Above all, I saw a nation that had listened to the words of a few crazy British dreamers who lived two centuries ago – and had made them real. Those radicals promised Britain a brighter tomorrow, and Britain never got it – just like a four year old who looks forward to a treat, only to be disappointed.

2

We the People

THE SUN SETS late in Florida. In the necklace of shoreline towns north of Miami, most days – even in October – hold on till the very end, their light still bright, the sky still blue. It is the same with the people. They know the jokes that say Florida is where America comes to die – God's Waiting Room and all that – but they refuse to believe it. The old folks of Florida are not ready for sunset just yet.

At the Avila condominium in Sunny Isles, one of the countless apartment complexes that make up Florida's Condo Canyon, life gets bustling early. The club room fills up before noon, a quartet of ladies clutching back-cushions as they stake out their favourite chairs. Leading the charge that October morning was Sylvia Schanker, her accent still thick Brooklyn even after twenty-three years.

'I came here because my husband was sick. He was sixty-one and he was supposed to die the day after we arrived – today he's eighty-four and he's still living!' she said with a wicked giggle. Sylvia's husband Stanley used to be a window cleaner until his asthma got so bad he had to get out. 'He couldn't breathe in New York, he couldn't work. Here he feels wonderful.'

Now in her late seventies, Sylvia plays cards nearly every day and most nights. That morning it was mah-jong, but sometimes it is pinochle, kalooki or canasta. She always puts on a dab of blusher. Her friend Sadie wears a wig, and Tessie has purplish lipstick to match her top. They all wear polyester trousers. As Sylvia talked Stanley was silent, his tongue lolling slightly. 'We've been married fifty-nine years,' she confided. 'These days we don't have conversations – we have aches and pains! I say "ooh", he says "aah".'

These two are no richer than a retired window cleaner and his wife would expect to be. They are not wealthy or well-connected or part of the establishment. Their idea of a good contact is the emergency number they ring if they fall over. And yet Sylvia and Stanley exercise real power.

That much was made clear by the president of the Avila residents' association, Marvin Manning. A former jeweller from New York who had just turned seventy, he was a perfect cross between Ed Asner and the long-forgotten British comic Harry Worth – minus a few front teeth.

Marvin occupies a unique place in condo culture because he is a civic organiser, replicating in retirement the old-time techniques of American machine politics – delivering the votes of his neighbours. In the argot of Florida politics, he is a condo commando. He does all the routine work – telephone canvassing, organising lifts to the polling station – but he also prints 'palmcards', slips of paper small enough for the condo flock to smuggle into the voting booth, reminding them which way to vote. He showed off his latest offering, a yellow square endorsing one Alex Penelas for mayor, with a reminder to 'Punch 38' on the voting machine. Marvin reckons he delivers about 400 votes that way.

To have his name printed on those palmcards Mr Penelas had to do more than tickle Marvin's fancy. He had to undergo a two-and-a-half-hour grilling from the Concerned Citizens of Northeast Dade County Public Affairs Committee, facing questions on everything from health insurance to 'beach renourishment'. His opponent had to do the same. Whichever candidate said the right things, Marvin and his fellow condo commandos would help get him elected. The committee inflicts the same ordeal on all contenders for public office, including the local congressman and the governor of Florida himself. 'It's like a job interview,' explained Marvin. 'They work for us.' And he meant it. As far as he and his fellow veteran activists were concerned, all these politicians were mere hired help – employees answering to him, Sylvia, Stanley, Tessie and Sadie.

And that is how power is understood in America. It flows

from the bottom up, not the top down. The people are in charge, and the government is their servant.

It seems a simple enough point, but its effects could not be more profound. It determines the shape of American politics and society – how ordinary citizens relate to their leaders and to each other. This apparently obvious notion – that power belongs with the people – has flourished in America, but struggled in Britain. Accordingly, it serves as the foundation for many of the ideas in this book and probably represents the core doctrine that Britain must steal from America.

American Masters

The idea of bottom-up power is written into the very founding document of American society. After the Declaration of Independence enumerated the 'unalienable' rights of man as Life, Liberty and the pursuit of Happiness, it asserted, 'That to secure these rights, Governments are instituted among Men, deriving their just powers *from the consent of the governed*'. The formal break from the British Crown was undertaken 'in the Name, and *by Authority of the good People* of these Colonies'.

Eleven years later the Constitution of the United States opened with one of politics' best-known phrases: '*We the People* of the United States, in Order to form a more perfect Union . . . do ordain and establish this Constitution for the United States of America.' Abraham Lincoln recast the idea in even clearer terms. In his two-minute Gettysburg Address of 1863, dedicating a cemetery for those who had fallen to preserve the Union, Lincoln explained that the United States was dedicated to a new idea: 'government of the people, by the people, for the people'.

In text after text it is the people who are the authors of their own destiny, they who install governments to act on their behalf. Contrast that with the document which comes closest to a British written constitution: the Bill of Rights of 1689. 'And whereas the said late King James the Second having abdicated the government and the throne being thereby vacant, his Highness the prince of Orange *whom it hath pleased Almighty God* to make the glorious instrument of delivering this kingdom from popery and arbitrary power . . .'

In other words, power in Britain comes not from the people, but from on high – with the monarch using authority on loan from God. The result is that the British system is the very opposite of the Americans': power flows from the top down, not the bottom up. The government is in charge, and the people are its servant.

In June 1995 Newt Gingrich explained all this to an audience of Republican worthies and chamber of commerce types gathered in a hotel ballroom in Nashua, New Hampshire. The animal-loving House Speaker was officially in the state to spot moose, which prowl through the hills and mountains close to the Canadian border. The press corps had followed not because it shared an interest in elk-like wildlife, but because it suspected Mr Gingrich was scouting around for a possible presidential run, New Hampshire being the first-in-the-nation state where all such campaigns must begin.

'Under the European model, God endows power to the King who lends some of it to the people,' the then Speaker explained. 'The American model endows power to the people who lend some of it to the government. It's the most radical statement of human rights in the history of the human race.'

For once the motormouth Speaker was not exaggerating. The idea of bottom-up government does indeed underpin American notions of democracy. But it is not some abstract theory, taught only in civics classes and by onetime history professors like Newt Gingrich. It informs the entire way US politics works, setting out the ideal for which the nation still strives, not always successfully. Whatever the results, the goal is clear – to put the people in charge.

Like the condo commando Marvin Manning. He regards politicians as his subordinates – and he is far from unique. During the 1996 election, Bill Clinton would leave the White House for a day's campaigning telling his aides he was off to meet the boss – meaning the voters. 'It's an employer–employee relationship,' Clinton said, more than once. He frequently referred to election day as the moment when his 'contract' would come up for renewal, as if he were a salaried chief executive facing the shareholders. In the last month of the campaign *Newsweek* magazine's cover posed the question, 'Clinton: Should We Rehire Him?'

The president brought that message to Britain when he addressed a rare joint session of the Houses of Parliament in November 1995. He told them, 'We will prevail again if and only if our people support the mission. We are, after all, democracies and they are the ultimate bosses of our fate.' (It was one of the few moments when the president was *not* interrupted by applause.)

That populist view of democracy prevails on both the left and right of US politics. In 1994 the Republicans drew up their Contract with America, knowing it would fit with Americans' view of their own government. They insisted the document was more than a British-style election manifesto. It was a binding contract of employment: if they failed to keep their side of the deal, they would be sacked by their employers, the voters.

Two years later, the party's presidential candidate Bob Dole reminded the electorate that, of course, his proposed 15 per cent tax cut would not be a government 'giveaway'. For that to be true, the money would have to belong to the government in the first place. But it did not. 'It's your money, your money, your money,' Dole would say, pounding the podium as he did so. In a gymnasium in Clarksville, Tennessee, he explained the idea as best he could. 'You shouldn't apologise for wanting to keep more of your own money – they should apologise for taking it from you in the first place.' The message is rammed home to Americans every night of the week. ABC's *World News Tonight* has a 'Your Money' slot which does not offer tips on personal finance, but rather focuses on what Washington is doing with . . . your money. 'Tonight, how the Pentagon spent thirteen hundred dollars – on a toilet seat.'

Americans teach their children that their government works for them, not the other way around. The Temps & Co recruitment agency runs a poster campaign showing the dome of the US Capitol above the caption, 'Just a reminder that even the country runs on temporary help.' Rubio's taco bar on Rosecrans Street in San Diego has a leaflet by the cash register. It is a single sheet of paper, providing the names and addresses of all the public officials at your service. In the summer of 1996 there were twenty-seven of them, starting with the San Diego County Clerk Gregory J. Smith on (619) 236-3771, working up to the

Sheriff Bill Kolender on (619) 974-2222, the Governor of California Pete Wilson on (916) 445-2841 and, just in case, the President of the United States Bill Clinton on (202) 456-1414. This is not some kind of subversive joke, or an invitation to jam switchboards for a protest. It is a standard information leaflet, found at similar outlets all over America. It aims to be nothing more than a staff directory – so that the burrito-munching customer can keep tabs on his employees, the government.

In the US, politicians are 'public servants' and they never forget who are their masters. As America's unofficial bard, Walt Whitman wrote in his epic poem 'Leaves of Grass': 'The President is up there in the White House for you. It is not you who are here for him.' Ronald Reagan spelled out the notion in a TV interview in 1990: 'The United States constitution is unique in all the countries of the world in that it isn't the government telling the people what it can and can't do; in the United States it's the people telling the government what it can and can't do.' 'Remember,' said the late Democratic Senator Edmund Muskie, whose 1972 presidential ambitions ended in tears because he made the mistake of weeping in public, 'you have a God-given right to kick the government around. Don't hesitate to use it.'

Poets and prophets, winners on the right, losers on the left – in the US they all believe the same thing: Americans have power over their own society, and the people who run it answer to them. That is not quite how it works in Britain.

British Servants

In Britain power flows in the reverse direction, from the top down. The origin of this fact is not obscure; on the contrary, we live with it still. For Britain is a monarchy. In our system, as Newt Gingrich was quick to point out, authority starts with the crown and works its way down. Clearly we are no longer ruled on the personal whim of a sovereign, but the basic monarchical structure – the very one the founding Americans rebelled against – has remained intact.

Our Glorious Revolution of 1688 did not wrest sovereignty away from the throne and allocate it to the people – which would have sent power flowing in a new, bottom–up direction. Instead it kept the old top–down arrangement. The only difference was that from now on sovereignty would reside not in the crown alone but in the more slippery notion of the crown-in-parliament. The essential fact was unchanged: as before, the people would not rule themselves, but be ruled over. They would still be subjects, not citizens – charges, not in charge. This is the historic difference between Britain and America that motivated the Founding Fathers to abandon our nation and form their own – and it endures to this day.

Thus it is Her Majesty's Government and Her Majesty's Leader of the Opposition – not ours. Members of parliament swear an oath of allegiance not to the people who elected them but to 'Her Majesty the Queen, her heirs and successors'. Our national documents are kept in Her Majesty's Stationery Office and our navy sails on Her Majesty's Ships. Our plays are performed at the Royal National Theatre, our letters sent by the Royal Mail. The serenity of an undisturbed English afternoon is the Queen's Peace; good grammar illustrates a command of the Queen's English. In America, an alleged criminal finds himself up against The People; in Britain he faces Regina. Even the words 'United Kingdom' suggest a country that belongs not to its people, but its rulers.

It is tempting to brush aside these trappings of royal dominion as quaint leftovers of an earlier era. But they are, in fact, everyday illustrations of a profound fact: control over Britain and its institutions has never been handed over to the British people. The very earth we tread proves the point. Consult the *Architects' Journal Legal Handbook*, and you will find that, 'Ultimate ownership of land in England is still, in theory, in the Crown. [In the past] the lord as "landowner" merely held an estate or "interest" in the land, directly or indirectly, as tenant from the king. A person holding an estate of the Crown could, in turn, grant it to another person, but the ownership still remained in the Crown.' To this day the proud owner of a freehold property technically holds nothing more than an interest in the land of the monarch.

Read on. 'A landowner is entitled to the minerals under his land, though all gold, silver and petroleum are vested in the Crown . . . Prima facie the seashore belongs to the Crown. If a river or stream is tidal, the soil of the bed of the river or stream belongs to the Crown, or the Duchies of Cornwall or Lancaster, where appropriate' – the Dukes of Cornwall and Lancaster being the Prince of Wales and the Queen respectively. Along with sovereignty, ownership of our country was never transferred from the king to the people. The ground we walk on, the sea we swim in and the rivers we drink from are not ours at all. We are tenants in our own land.

The Act of Settlement did nothing to alter the shape of a monarchical system which had always dispensed power from the top down: it merely replaced the personnel who stood at the apex. It took time, but eventually the king and queen made way for the prime minister and the cabinet, who assumed executive powers once enjoyed by the monarch alone. Sovereignty was thus passed not from the throne to the people, but from one ruler to another. As Andrew Marr makes clear in *Ruling Britannia*, his indictment of the failures of British democracy, even parliament has been less the voice of the people than the tool of those who would rule over them, whether the king, the barons, the landed aristocracy, the Puritans, the industrial bourgeoisie, the imperial civil service or, most recently, the modern state: 'Whenever *demos* raised its hydra-heads, during the peasant and urban rebellions, or when democrats emerged among the Cromwellian soldiery, or when radicals, Chartists, Irish men and English women challenged during the past two centuries, Parliament has been solidly with the institutions of the Old Establishment on the other side.' For centuries the grand, quasi-medieval edifice of stone, glass, slate and marble has bellowed to the vulgar masses: this is not your place. How fitting that its symbol should be a portcullis, ready to be lowered if ever the mob should get too near.

The very grammar of British politics betrays the same attitude. Tradition dictates that when the prime minister allows an election, he is 'going to the country' – as if stepping down from Westminster's Mount Olympus for the quinquennial chore of gaining the public nod. The phrase also begs a question: if the government is only now going to the country, where else has it been these last five years? In Britain we refer to state schools or council houses, while Americans speak of public schools and public housing – that way no one forgets who owns both. In the US, congressmen and presidents speak of doing the People's Business and, just to remind themselves who is in charge, they invoke, *ad nauseam*, the will of 'the American People'. Official US government literature refers to *your* government, while we speak of *the* government. When the Republicans offered a Contract with America the slogan stuck, chiefly because it is easy for Americans to imagine their Congress bound like hired hands. Tony Blair tried the same device with his Performance Contract for Britain, but the phrase never took root.

Britain, like America, has phone-in shows where the electorate can address the politicians directly. Except our programmes are called *Question Time* and *Any Questions*, implicitly inviting the public to put questions to those in authority rather than voice their own opinions. Nick Ross saw the trouble from a singular vantage point when he began presenting the nation's most popular phone-in. 'The larger problem was that listeners to the BBC seemed to think they were subordinates – they felt confined to asking questions,' he said, explaining his decision to quit *Call Nick Ross* after ten years. 'Yet plainly almost all of them had strong opinions of their own . . . For the first few months I was regularly urging: "Come on, what do *you* think?"'

In this climate, our officials soon find themselves behaving more like masters than servants. Little in our political culture obliges them to think like paid employees, or reminds them who pays their wages – a fact illuminated by the 1995 row over Winston Churchill's sale of his grandfather's prime ministerial archive. To keep this primary-source history of the man who led us in our greatest war, the nation had to fork out £12 million from the takings of the national lottery – with £1 million of help from the American philanthropist John Paul Getty. Despite this huge sum, the Churchill family is still able to charge copyright on the 1.5 million pieces of paper that make up the archive.

No such sell-off would be imaginable in the United States. American presidents leave their papers to the nation as a matter of course, usually in the form of a presidential library in their hometown. There the documents can be read within five years of a president leaving office. The tradition was started by Franklin Roosevelt, who bequeathed all his papers to the American people.

'He felt they belonged to us because he worked for us,' explained Susan Cooper, an official at the National Archives. Of course, not every president is quite so forthcoming. Richard Nixon fought a battle to the death to cling to his files, doubtless fearing yet more embarrassment at the release of transcripts from his notorious voice-activated taping system in the Oval Office. So the National Archives sued the former president, taking its case all the way to the Supreme Court – where it won. After that FDR's tradition became law. Such a notion – that a leader is but a humble servant of the people – is rooted only weakly in British life. Instead, government acts like it is in charge, with the public more of an annoying distraction than an ultimate boss – as the critic Jay Rayner smartly discovered.

Rayner learned that his favourite painting, *My Parents* by David Hockney, had been removed from the Tate Gallery and placed in 10 Downing Street on loan to John and Norma Major. This meant he could no longer see it. 'I cannot help but feel I have been robbed,' he wrote. '*My Parents* is owned by the Tate. The Tate is owned by the state. And the state is owned by me. Not all of it, mind, just the bit I pay for through my taxes along with everyone else. Which means that I am part owner of *My Parents*, the picture I have always adored.'

So the resourceful Mr Rayner asked if he could have a peek. He wrote to the Cabinet Office and – mindful that Whitehall borrows art works from dozens of British galleries to supplement the 15,000 pieces that make up the Government Art Collection – seven other departments of state as well. In each case he made the same plea, explaining that he was an art lover who would like to see the collection of which he owned a small part.

Jay Rayner did not get a reunion with his beloved *Parents*, nor even a glimpse of a pencilled drawing. The man from Downing Street told him his request was 'unrealistic', while the National Heritage department was adamant: 'Government buildings are not [the "not" in bold type] public galleries and tours of the sort you request are not possible for many practical reasons . . .' By way of reassurance, the official confided that the collection was really not worth looking at – quite 'unremarkable and undistinguished'.

Yet Rayner discovered this 'undistinguished' collection

contained a Canova sculpture, paintings by Howard Hodgkin and Peter Blake as well as several examples from the much celebrated London School. By borrowing from major galleries, Whitehall officialdom had also brightened its day with works by Gainsborough, Turner, Constable and Lowry. Nevertheless, there is no catalogue and the collection's curator is hidden from public view – apparently behind a desk in the dental section of the Department of Health.

US government offices, by contrast, make a point of opening their doors to members of the public – especially those keen to steal a glance at a favourite art treasure. They do that for the same reason politicians print their phone numbers on leaflets available at taco restaurants. They regard themselves as a public service, answering only to one boss: the people.

3

Death, Pork and the Pressure Cooker

THEY SAID IT was a good night for an execution. The air was warm and clear, and spirits high, that spring night in May 1994 when they put John Wayne Gacy to death. Quite a crowd had gathered outside the Stateville Correctional Center, the maximum-security jail in Joliet, Illinois, to celebrate the passing of a man who had strangled thirty-three young men and boys in a killing spree that lasted from 1972 to 1978. For a while Gacy had been America's most notorious serial killer, until the Milwaukee Cannibal, Jeffrey Dahmer, came and stole his title. Now he was about to die by lethal injection, and the folks outside could not have been more delighted. They sang and they danced, some wearing black executioner-style hoods, others dressed as clowns – a reference to Gacy's previous career as a children's entertainer named Pogo. It made a macabre carnival, as the crowd chanted, 'Justice, Justice, Not Too Late – John Wayne Gacy, Meet Your Fate.' Street vendors did well, too, selling T-shirts with the slogan, No TEARS FOR THE CLOWN.

Inside Stateville, a different drama was being played out. Gacy had spent his last day relaxing in his cell, smoking a cigar with a prison officer who said the killer showed not the slightest trace of remorse. His lawyers had been filing frantic last appeals, urging the Supreme Court to condemn lethal injection as 'cruel and unusual punishment', a Nazi-originated method that amounted to torture. But the justices offered no reprieve, and the prisoner hardly seemed bothered. After the discovery of several victims buried under the floorboards of his home, and his conviction in 1980, John Wayne Gacy had become one of

Death Row's celebrity residents. He had launched a new career as an artist, often drawing on his past vocation to produce work depicting clowns and harlequins. It made a chilling *oeuvre*, all those grinning faces above the signature of a child murderer. In the end, an Illinois millionaire bought the whole collection, built a bonfire and burnt the lot. He said he never wanted to see a market in serial killer chic.

Close to midnight, they led Gacy to the tiny chamber where he would die. Perhaps a jail officer called out 'Dead Man Walking' just like the movies. One of them then strapped Gacy to a table, where an intravenous tube was inserted into his right arm, releasing a powerful anaesthetic. A witness said Gacy 'swallowed hard' and stared at the ceiling when the chemicals first began flowing into his body.

The same tube should then have released two other, lethal chemicals. But nothing happened. 'There was a jelling or clogging in the line,' Howard Peters, a prison official, explained later. It did not seem to trouble Gacy, who 'took a deep breath and dozed off'. Apparently the killer did not realise his own death had hit a hitch. Eventually, after eighteen awkward minutes of fiddling and resetting of the injection machine, John Wayne Gacy was pronounced dead.

Outside there was a cheer, more dancing and much chanting. 'He got a much easier death than any of his victims,' mused a satisfied William Kinkle, the chief prosecutor who had waited fourteen years for this moment. The whole scene all but drowned out the sound of a small group of nuns who, clutching candles, had gathered as they always do on the night of an execution – to stand by the prison walls, pleading for mercy and protesting at the killing within.

The most unusual fact about Gacy's death was that anyone paid attention at all. His was the 237th execution in the United States since 1976, when the Supreme Court allowed individual states to restore the death penalty. Two decades later, state killings are carried out at the rate of nearly five a month and they have become utterly routine. They make the local TV news and the 'briefs' column in the papers, but only a quirky twist – a well-known prisoner or a strange method of killing – gives an execution genuine news value. Interest perked up in January

1996 when, in a single week, there was a death by firing squad, a semi-public hanging and a bungled lethal injection. Child killer John Taylor exercised his right to face a line of marksmen in Utah – the last state in the Union to have maintained the practice – just days after Billy Bailey was hanged in Delaware, the first time the noose had been used there for fifty years. Bailey had murdered an elderly couple, whose two children chose to watch him hang – another first. Just a few hundred miles south, hapless Virginia jailers took twenty minutes to find a vein in the body of convicted murderer Richard Townes, so that they could inject the chemical mixture that would kill him. In the end, they had to insert the tube into Townes's right foot. In Seattle, interest had focused on the case of a convict so obese, his lawyers said he could not be hanged without risking an accidental beheading. That made the news, too.

It is all pretty gruesome, not helped by the fact that capital punishment is disproportionately meted out to black prisoners over white ones. Indeed, America's continued use of the death penalty is one of those aspects of US life British progressives revile most. And yet it is an index – admittedly an ugly one – of the same fact represented by Marvin Manning and his fellow condo commandos: judicial killing is proof that, in America, the people are in charge.

Opinion polls show Americans and Britons with remarkably similar views on capital punishment. In the US, most surveys show three out of four people in favour of it, while a 1996 poll for MORI put the British figure at 76 per cent. Accordingly, the wheels of US democracy have turned and capital punishment is now practised in all but twelve of America's fifty states. Yet in Britain we do not have the death penalty. As those polls show, opponents of judicial killing have hardly won the argument among the British people. Instead our political system has simply failed to express the popular will. If the pro-execution figure was below 50 per cent, then perhaps Britain could justifiably praise itself as a society of compassionate humanitarians. Until then, what is often a cause for self-congratulation – with progressive Britons imagining ours to be a more civilised society than the US – should perhaps be a trigger for self-doubt. American democracy ensures the public get their way, even if the result is not always pleasant. The British system cannot say the same.

Death was an issue of sorts in the South Carolina Senate race of 1996. Not the death penalty so much as the mortality of the leading candidate. To get to the heart of the action, you had to drive along the Strom Thurmond Highway, close by Strom Thurmond Lake *en route* to Strom Thurmond High School. There you could have joined the celebration of Strom Thurmond Appreciation Day. Guest of honour: Senator Strom Thurmond.

The senator was then ninety-three, running for a record eighth six-year term in Congress. It had become a sport among the journalists covering the campaign to find new ways of conveying Senator Thurmond's longevity. His age was 45 per cent that of the Constitution. He ran for president when Bill Clinton was two. Of the 1,826 people who had served in the US Senate since 1789, about a fifth had served with Strom Thurmond.

He looked like a character from southern legend, with a drawl that was pure *Gone With the Wind*. His hair bottle-orange, he boasted that he began each day with sit-ups, weights and an exercise bike. He had sired his first child when he was sixty-eight, with a former Miss South Carolina forty-four years his junior. He once remarked that his undertakers would need a baseball bat to slam his coffin shut (a reference to his allegedly permanent priapic state).

In his beloved home state he had become a living monument, a leftover from the old South who once defended racial segregation and whose grandaddy, George Washington Thurmond, fought in the last battle of the Civil War. When he first ran for office – becoming Edgefield County's education superintendent in 1929 – his electorate included veterans of the Confederacy.

But still Ol' Strom was not ready to say goodbye. Now he was running – hobbling, really – for a term of office that would take in his 100th birthday, meeting voters whose great-grandparents he had once represented. Together they sat and watched a biographical video that recalled great moments from a long, long career. It included archive footage of his stint as governor and his 1948 presidential bid as the States' Rights, or Dixiecrat, candidate – championing the fight against integration. He looked old even then.

After the school choir and the current recipient of the Strom Thurmond Scholarship had finished their plaudits, the old man himself headed to the platform. Just a few steps, it seemed a long walk. The Republican senator paid tribute to the area's greatest war heroes, including William Barret Travis, the defender of the Alamo. 'He's the guy, that with 3,000 Russians threatening to attack . . .' Thurmond said. He meant Mexicans, but the audience let it go. That is how South Carolinians were with their grand old man: forgiving. (As one Democratic aide grumped during the campaign, 'All he has to do is not drool on himself and he wins.')

Afterwards the townspeople of Edgefield, a county surrounded by cotton fields and peach groves, lined up for tea, cake and a handshake with Strom. Each one had received a kindness from the senator – a water pipe fixed, a letter of condolence received – and they wanted to thank him. Occasionally he confused the women for their mothers, whom he had known forty years ago, but it did not matter – he smiled for the camera all the same. I asked him if he still enjoyed the campaign game. 'Ain't a matter of enjoyin' it,' he said. 'It's a matter of rendering good service to the people.'

And that was the truth of it. The secret of Strom Thurmond's longevity was that he practised politics the old-fashioned way, delivering for his constituents. That is why two-thirds of those queuing up to say hello that Sunday afternoon were black. Little minding that Thurmond still held the Senate filibuster record – speaking for an unbroken twenty-four hours and eighteen minutes against the civil rights bill of 1957 – the African-Americans there that day, like the rest of South Carolina, were grateful to Strom for the decades he had spent working for them. They were not fussed that, on a bad day, their senator could barely utter a coherent sentence without cue cards and was known to wander off during key committee meetings. He delivered. Sure enough, a month later, Strom Thurmond set a record, winning comfortable re-election to the place many joked had become his nursing home.

The senator was the beneficiary of a fact that might sound overblown, and whose side-effects can be lamentable, but which remains true all the same: the US system is designed to give the politician but one boss – the voters. Thanks to the separation of powers between Congress and the White House, representatives and senators are elected in their own right – not as local flag-carriers of the would-be executive. They owe little allegiance to the party leader, since they can keep their job even if he loses his – and vice versa. They do not answer to him or to national party organisations (which tend to be weak in the US), but to the people who sent them there: the electorate. It is all quite different from the British system, where the fusing of executive and legislature requires total party discipline. If MPs rebel against their own government, it will fall. As a matter of political reality British lawmakers' first loyalty must be to their party, not the people.

The contrast is plain to see, with American lawmakers declaring their independence every day. The debates on Capitol Hill may be boring, but the outcome of the votes is never wholly predictable – and the final majorities hardly ever the same. From morning to night, members of the House and Senate switch sides and break the party line in order to stay sweet with their constituents. A major piece of legislation can founder because a congressman has to placate constituents unhappy with a single clause. International trade treaties have had to be amended to take account of loggers or scallop-fishermen or cotton growers, the little people who stand between a congressman and defeat. The grizzled old Boston machine politician and onetime House Speaker, Tip O'Neill, had to cope with this fact of US political life for decades, rounding up his flock like a long-suffering shepherd, offering a deal here, a trade-off there until he had amassed the votes he needed. He later captured the entire process in his legendary dictum: 'All politics is local.'

But O'Neill's Law does not apply to Britain. Hardly ever does an MP put his constituents' interests ahead of his party; when he does, it makes headline news. Sir John Gorst found himself on the front pages in the dying days of the Major era when he resigned the Tory whip, protesting over cuts that would close Edgware General Hospital in his Hendon North constituency. He had dared side with his voters against his leaders. In Britain that episode fell into journalism's 'man bites dog' category, and qualified as news. In America, such rebellions are 'dog bites man' – they happen too often to count.

Not that the supremacy of the voters back home always leads to the best results for the country as a whole: much-needed collective action can be frustrated by the whim of a small minority. Perhaps the most graphic illustration of the problem comes from the black art known as pork-barrel politics – the antics politicians get up to in their desperation to bring home the federal bacon. Some of the most egregious cases are also the most hilarious, with public money being funnelled to absurdly undeserving causes just to win a few smiles back home. A $500,000 grant for a memorial to Lawrence Welk – a TV bandleader whose easy-listening TV specials made him a kind of US Val Doonican – mystified many, until they realised it had been stuffed into a farm bill by the honourable member for Strasburg, North Dakota, Welk's boyhood home. Senator Robert Byrd of West Virginia earned his reputation as the Prince of Pork by being utterly unashamed. Deep into his late seventies Byrd, a former Democratic majority leader and one-time chairman of the all-powerful Appropriations Committee, demanded $7 million be spent on a third US 'master clock', to be located in Green Bank, West Virginia – even though the nation's official timekeepers insisted they did not need it. More ambitiously, Byrd sought the establishment of a naval facility in his home state – even though West Virginia has no coastline and is utterly land-locked. The senator's efforts paid off. Having brought a colossal $1.5 billion in federal projects to West Virginia in just four years, Robert Byrd was re-elected in 1994 with 72 per cent of the vote. The Strom Thurmond Mall and the countless Strom Thurmond Streets dotted all over South Carolina were just as porcine in origin, all of them monuments to the aged senator's success in funnelling federal dollars back home. That is why he was able to argue in 1996 that his age and years of service were actually a plus. Through the Senate's seniority system he now chaired the high-spending armed services committee – so enabling him to spend even more of America's money in South Carolina.

It is easy to condemn Thurmond, Byrd and their fellow pork barons. Few of us would hail a career spent stewarding the federal gravy train as the vocation of a statesman. Indeed, the habitual bloating of the US budget with spending plans designed to ingratiate honourable members with their voters is an ailment which has cost the country dear, helping to inflate the federal deficit which so preoccupied Americans throughout the 1990s. The liberal commentator-turned-cyber pundit Michael Kinsley titled a recent collection of his work *Big Babies* to describe an American electorate which simultaneously wants fiscal restraint and deficit reduction even as it applauds and re-elects politicians who add just that teensy bit extra on to the budget in order to lob a juicy pork chop back to their own district. Kinsley is right. Pork-barrel politics is gross and corrupt. But he is also right to identify the electorate as the guilty party. As with the death penalty, one of the uglier features of the American landscape has come about not through an undemocratic system – but one that, if anything, grants the people *too much* say. As the scale of their election victories illustrates, Senators Byrd and Thurmond were clearly doing no more than what the people wanted. Indeed, it says much about the US system that its worst excesses stem from politicians' compulsion to satisfy the needs and desires of the people who elected them. The consequences can be troubling indeed – but they do reveal a nation that has put the people in charge.

Besides, American democracy's knack for rapid response to popular sentiment sometimes yields admirable results. It has, for example, helped certain communities – ethnic minorities, the disabled, lesbians and gays – stand alongside the heavy-weights of big business and the trade unions in exerting genuine political influence. Jewish-Americans matter enough in New York and California to urge the president to be a friend of Israel, while the 44 million Americans who claim Irish ancestry can claim some of the credit for nudging the White House towards the role of peacemaker in northern Ireland. Cuban-Americans can swing a few key districts in New Jersey and Florida, and so they are able to persuade the politicians to be tough on Fidel Castro. (The maxim that says US foreign policy amounts to little more than US domestic politics with an accent contains more than a smidgin of truth.)

Lobby groups, and the communities they represent, can get action fast in the United States. In the late 1980s, Aids activists believed there was insufficient funding for research. They brought the teenage Ryan White, a brave, bright boy who had had the disease since he was twelve years old, to testify before Congress. He died not long afterwards, but his name lived on – permanently attached to an annual allocation of cash for Aids. A decade later, voters in Hamilton, New Jersey, were distraught when seven-year-old Megan Kanka was raped and killed by a paroled child molester. They believed they should have been warned that a convicted childkiller was living in their midst. So they lobbied until a statewide, and later federal, law gave citizens the right to know when a sex offender had moved into their neighbourhood. They called it Megan's Law, and it was passed within a year of the child's death.

Less grave illustration of the phenomenon was provided by Alfonse D'Amato, then the tough-talking, spaghetti-politics senator from New York. During the first O.J. Simpson trial, D'Amato was a guest on the Don Imus radio breakfast show. Imus, who loves wise-cracking with politicos, lured D'Amato into commenting on the Simpson case, in particular the lax regime of the presiding judge, Lance Ito – a Japanese-American. D'Amato immediately plunged into his best Fu Manchu accent: 'Ahh so. Judge Eee-toh has such big eee-goh that he wanna bee on Tee Vee all time . . .' A sitting member of the chamber that calls itself the 'world's greatest deliberative body' was on the radio sounding like Peter Sellers. Within minutes, D'Amato's office was buried under a blizzard of faxes from the Japanese-American community's various representative organisations, all of them hostile. By the next day D'Amato was on the Senate floor, reading a prepared and grovelling apology to the 'millions of Japanese-Americans who have contributed so much . . .' It was the same Alfonse D'Amato who later took on the issue of 'Swiss gold', leading the battle to prise funds belonging to Jewish victims of the Nazi Holocaust from the Swiss banks. In both cases, the senator's motive was the same: he wanted the votes of Japanese-American and Jewish New Yorkers to boost his chances of re-election. Pressure groups for the two communities made sure they got their way.

Of course, sometimes the system can appear to break down. Occasionally, it seems as if the people do not get their way, with the impeachment crisis of 1998–9 the clearest example. For more than a year, Americans consistently told pollsters they backed President Clinton and did not want to see him removed from office. Yet the people they had chosen, sitting in the chamber called the House of Representatives, did not represent that view: they pressed on, voting to make Bill Clinton only the second president to be impeached in US history. The explanation for this breakdown in the usually rapid responsiveness of American democracy is not simple. Rather it comes down to the fact that Zippergate confronted the United States with a deep dilemma, setting two of the country's founding principles against each other. On the one hand, Americans believe that if they are sovereign, then their sovereign will should not be overturned: to remove a president, reversing the result of two democratic, national elections, is to challenge the very notion that 'we the people' are in charge. And yet Americans also believe that politicians are mere employees. If one of them breaks the law, he must be called to account – even if he is the president. That is why the gravest accusation the Republicans could level against Bill Clinton was the claim that he had sought to place himself above the law. As the impeachers never tired of repeating, 'In America, no man is above the law.' With those two ideals at war, both of them flowing from the same belief in the sovereignty of the people, it is little wonder that America wrestled with itself over the strange, sometimes sad tale of Bill and Monica. And little wonder that its politicians could come up with few quick answers.

In less fraught circumstances, though, the prime boast of the US system is that it responds, eventually, to the demands of the people. It is not quite that way in Britain. Public opinion can rant and rave, but there is little it can do when up against the will of the government. The 1990s roads protestors, led by Swampy and friends, became latter-day folk heroes. But they made no difference; the roadworks they sought to halt went ahead. When Margaret Thatcher wanted to abolish the Greater London Council, three out of four Londoners objected, galvanised by the palindromic slogan, 'Say No to No Say'. It did not matter; the GLC was abolished anyway. Next to no one wanted the poll tax. But it became law all the same.

The result is disillusionment and cynicism, as voters become certain that nothing they do will make the slightest bit of difference. Take Jonathan Raban, the British writer who moved from Battersea to Seattle in the early 1990s. A passionate sailor, he was drawn to the Pacific North-West in part by the splendour of the marine landscape including the 2,000-mile long 'inside passage' of inlets and naturally sheltered coastline which stretches all the way from Seattle to Juneau, Alaska. But Raban had also become involved in a local protest campaign against the proposed development of the Seattle Commons, a rundown old working district in the heart of the city. The Commons had caught the eye of Paul Allen, the man who founded Microsoft with Bill Gates. The billionaire wanted to clear the area and convert it into a giant park.

Raban had never been involved in a similar effort in Britain, even though the battle over Battersea Power Station had raged when he had lived there. He had stayed quiet. 'It was the sort of thing one might read about in a newspaper, not something one could have any effect on,' he explained. Rather than plunge into 'the soft, warm, smelly bog of British politics', Raban did nothing about Battersea. 'One's sense of powerlessness to do anything about anything in England is absolute.'

The Long Arm of the Law

In February 1992, Stella Liebeck was travelling through New Mexico. Then aged eighty-one, she sat in the passenger seat, while her son-in-law took the wheel. It was a long drive and eventually the two flagged. They decided to stop at a McDonald's in Albuquerque, to pick up some coffee from the Drive Thru' window. They pulled over, so Ms Liebeck could add cream and sugar to her drink. But as she struggled to remove the lid, the coffee spilled all over her lap. In just a few seconds she had suffered third-degree burns, the scalding hot fluid removing several layers of skin from her thighs, buttocks and genitalia. She promptly sued McDonald's for selling her a defective product – coffee served at the dangerously high temperature of 190 degrees Fahrenheit. The company said she was to blame for cradling the full, steaming cup between her thighs while in a car, and that everyone knew McDonald's coffee was served at white heat. After a two-year battle, the New Mexico jury sided with Stella Liebeck, ordering Ronald McDonald to cough up a cool $2.9 million dollars.

That case captured the American imagination, as did the action brought by the teenage boy against a bicycle manufacturer after he was hit by a car at night: he claimed nothing in the instructions told him he had to use lights after dark. A popular favourite was the case of the burglar who slipped and broke his leg while robbing a private home. He sued his intended victims, claiming their floor was a liability and they should pay.

Battles like those seem to pop up every week in the United States. The child 'divorcing' her parents. The state of Florida suing tobacco companies for the cost of treating people with lung cancer. The citizen of New York suing a theatre for 'malicious humiliation' after she was mortified to be included in a toe-curling round of audience participation during a Broadway show. The phenomenon has a name: it is litigiousness and it can seem like a national disease. Britons talk about the weather. Russians drink vodka. Americans go to court.

It is on TV, at the bookstore and in the language. Legal junkies can lap up affidavits and moves-to-strike twenty-four hours a day on Court TV, perhaps the most successful of America's niche cable channels. CNN airs half an hour of legal argument each day in *Burden of Proof*, hosted by 'a tough defence attorney and a hard-as-nails former prosecutor'. Hollywood churns out courtroom drama the way a judge passes sentences. Indeed, it is the American cinema's most enduring genre. The early ones are classics – *Witness For the Prosecution, Compulsion* and *The Caine Mutiny* – while recent models have tried to add a twist: *Presumed Innocent* had the lawyer double as the accused, *Reversal of Fortune* made the audience want the protagonist to lose. Television has kept up the habit, with *Perry Mason* in the sixties, *Petrocelli* in the seventies, *LA Law* in the eighties and *Murder One* in the nineties. Generations of Americans have grown up able to talk like the finest of advocates: 'He's leading the witness', 'You know the rules, counsellor' and 'Your honour, may I approach the bench?' Even the layout is reassuringly familiar: the shiny flat surface of American courtroom timber, the glass of water on the attorney's desk, the black/female/old judge – to say nothing of the state seal above the bench, the silent stenographer, the armed marshal. The bookshops, too, have built a good business from all these tales of dockets, stays and the boys-from-forensics. The legal thriller could well be US fiction's most reliable genre, helped along by the growing band of multi-millionaire celebrity lawyers from John Grisham to Johnnie Cochran.

Most striking, though, is Americans' interest in the courts not as voyeurs, but as participants: they are prepared to sue their doctors, their children, even their lawyers. The results can be reprehensible, with so great an emphasis on rights people forget their responsibilities. Today, sigh the critics, Americans point the finger anywhere but themselves, always playing another round of the legal 'blame game'. The Harvard professor and celebrity lawyer Alan Dershowitz coined a neat phrase for one aspect of the phenomenon: the abuse excuse. Witness the Menendez brothers, the California boys who said they only shot and killed their superwealthy parents because of years of humiliation. Or the Lebanese man who insisted he was not to blame for shooting a busload of Hasidic Jews crossing the Brooklyn Bridge: he was suffering from 'Beirut Syndrome' at the time. The culture of blame exacts a genuine cost, not only robbing America of a fortune in lost court time but altering people's ordinary behaviour, making them petrified of stepping out of line, lest they be sued. Male bosses cannot talk to female workers, so nervous are they of a sexual harassment suit; doctors avoid certain procedures – including some in the pivotal area of childbirth – for fear of possible negligence actions.

For all that, America's legal habit is not wholly a vice. In fact, it has led to the righting of some important wrongs. Some of the great advances in US civil rights took place in court – from the 1973 Roe v. Wade ruling, guaranteeing a woman's right to an abortion, to the 1954 Brown v. Board of Education decision outlawing racially segregated schools. Left to politicians, the march towards black civil rights might have been blocked for years. But judges pushed it forward. The courts continue to be a forum where the vexed social questions of the day are thrashed out and where social progress is made – often prompted by the unlikeliest cases.

In 1993 a woman whose boss had told her she had an 'ass the size of a racehorse' took her case before the Supreme Court hoping for a ruling which would determine once and for all the exact definition of sexual harassment. Teresa Harris, a former manager in a Nashville forklift truck company, had become depressed and started drinking heavily after suffering two years of repeated insults and humiliation from her employer, Charles Hardy. He called her a 'dumb-assed woman', adding that she should never wear a bikini because 'her ass was so big it would cause an eclipse of the sun'. Ms Harris and her colleagues were also subjected to the 'coin trick': the boss would demand they fish out loose change from deep in his trouser pockets. The plaintiff recalled another favourite gag of Mr Hardy's. He regularly suggested turning off the office heating, 'so that the women's nipples would get hard and be seen through their shirts'. Lower courts had already ruled that the man's conduct ranged from the 'inane and adolescent' to the 'truly gross and offensive'. What America's highest court had to decide was whether it also qualified as sexual harassment. The justices sided with the plaintiff, ruling that Charles Hardy's behaviour had indeed created a 'hostile work environment' – and therefore constituted harassment. At the time, there were few more sensitive issues in US life and Americans were anxious to have a definition they could agree on. If it had not been for Ms Harris's 'litigiousness', they might never have got that chance.

The same was true of the two Hispanic workers at the Spun Steak meatpacking factory in San Francisco, whose idea of fun was to insult their fellow workers in Spanish. In 1990 the company cracked down by imposing an English-only rule on the factory floor. The women complained that the rule discriminated against them, so setting off a legal debate on the extent to which English should be deemed the official language of the United States.

Hollywood has always understood this dimension of US justice, realising that the courthouse is the place where America fights some of its greatest causes: racial integration in *To Kill a Mockingbird*, the right to teach evolutionary science in *Inherit the Wind*, equal justice for the poor in *Twelve Angry Men*.

For good or ill, it is undeniable that Americans are wedded to the law. John Grisham says the roots of US litigiousness are not difficult to trace; they are right there in the Constitution and the Bill of Rights: 'We have all these rights that we're born with and it's like, "If you mess around with my rights, I'll sue you."' All those antagonists – the woman with the coffee burn, the boy with the bike, the insulted and insulting workers – had gone to court motivated by a similar belief: they had certain rights, and somehow those rights had been violated. Maybe their particular grievances were wacky, even downright ridiculous. But this core belief should not be dismissed too hastily, for the American culture of rights is one of the republic's sturdiest qualities, entrenching the position of the American people as masters of their own lives.

So just as Marvin Manning, the condo commando, regards the politicians as his employees so the Bill of Rights equips him with a battery of protections against any attempt the government might make to tread on his liberties. In the balance between people and authority, the latter is restrained by a Constitution which trumps any law passed by president or Congress. That document – coupled with US constitutional law, made up of past decisions of the Supreme Court – means US police cannot simply barge into Americans' homes or bug their telephones or stop them at random without running headlong into the Fourth Amendment, which asserts 'The right of the people to be secure in their persons, houses, papers, and effects, against unreasonable searches and seizures'. Any erosion of that right would be struck down by the Supreme Court. What if the US Congress sought to curb the right to silence? That would count as a direct violation of the Fifth Amendment, which insists that 'no person . . . shall be compelled in any criminal case to be a witness against himself'. It would be thrown out in a flash. Any tampering with the right to a criminal trial by jury would get the same treatment: Article III of the Constitution states clearly, 'The Trial of all Crimes, except in Cases of Impeachment, shall be by Jury.'

And yet in Britain all three of those erosions of liberty have happened, so quickly that many people barely noticed. The trouble was, Britons had no Bill of Rights to protect them or to keep their government in check. In a few swift years, the Major administration sought to remove a series of basic liberties that had taken centuries to establish. The Commons approved a bill that gave police extra powers of entry into people's homes – authority they had lost in 1763. MPs voted to allow police to bug houses and offices without the prior consent of a judge, just so long as they were deemed to be in pursuit of a case 'believed to be one of urgency' – believed, that is, by the police themselves. The Commons erased the right of an individual not to be stopped and summarily searched by police: under the revised Prevention of Terrorism (Additional Powers) Act people who fail to stop when a policeman tells them to, or refuse to empty their pockets and surrender to a full body search, can end up spending six months in jail and paying a £5,000 fine. MPs even voted to remove the ancient right to silence, allowing juries to infer guilt if the accused refuses to testify. Finally, as if to round off a bumper season in the hunting down and slaying of civil liberties, the Commons debated restrictions on the ancient right of trial by jury.

The latter right had been under assault since the 1970s, when juries were abolished for certain offences in Northern Ireland following the recommendations of the Diplock Commission. In 1986 the Roskill Commission believed panels of ordinary citizens were not capable of judging complex fraud cases, and so required specialist tribunals instead. Lord Hailsham, Sir Frederick Lawton and Lord Rawlinson suggested a property-owning qualification, while others called for age limits and literacy requirements, to ensure a better class of juror. The motive for all such proposals, according to the progressive barrister Michael Mansfield, 'is the overwhelming belief that ordinary people, given the chance, acquit too many of those on trial'. Just to be on the safe side, sometimes the judge simply dismisses the jury and hears the evidence himself.

All these erosions or outright violations of our fundamental rights happen in Britain for one simple reason: because they can. We have no hallowed piece of parchment we can brandish to block the liberty-trampling plans of a Diplock or a Roskill or a tough-minded home secretary. We can fire off a few letters to the editor, sign a petition, and finally place our trust in the liberal instincts of the House of Lords. But if the House of Commons wants to ride roughshod over our liberties by changing the law, there is little we can do. We can rely on judicial review, but that only allows judges to over-rule executive actions, not acts of parliament. Or we can look to the European Convention of Human Rights, now incorporated into British law. Even that, however, cannot be used to strike down the actions of Westminster. The British doctrine of parliamentary sovereignty leaves no room for a higher authority.

Two gaps in the British public's armour illuminate the problem particularly clearly, revealing how thin are our defences against authority. The first is the people's right to know what is done in its name. Freedom of information should be a basic component of the master–servant relationship: if government works for the public, the public surely has a right to know what it is getting up to. In America that right is pretty secure.

Take one of the least appealing aspects of US political life: the excessive role of money. The Washington trade in access and influence is pretty slimy, and Americans are rightly disgusted by it. But that disgust is fuelled, indeed made possible, by the fact that Americans are not kept in the dark over political money. They may not like the amount involved, but they tend to know where it all comes from. The law demands that lists of the big donors – corporations and individuals – be filed with the Federal Electoral Commission every quarter, after which they duly appear in the major newspapers. You only have to open up the *New York Times* to read that Steven Spielberg, Barbra Streisand and David Geffen each gave $100,000 to the Democrats while Arnold Schwarzenegger, Kelsey Grammer and Charlton Heston stumped up for the Republicans (along with, say, the National Rifle Association and the cigarette makers Philip Morris). In 1976 the US Supreme Court ruled that disclosure of donations is the one clearly acceptable regulation on politics. Its ruling quoted one of the bench's most distinguished previous occupants, Louis Brandeis: 'Publicity is justly recommended as a remedy for social and industrial diseases. Sunlight is said to be the best of disinfectants; electric light the most efficient policeman.' Brandeis's maxim has remained the working principle in the US, coupled of course with the nation's fundamental view of democracy: if politicians are public servants, they cannot keep secrets from the public.

The idea is enshrined in a law which stands in addition to the Bill of Rights: the Freedom of Information Act. It is an aid to journalists and lobbyists, citizens and activists – anyone who wants to know what government is up to in his or her name. It does not require an organised campaign or letters to congressmen or embarrassing publicity. An American (or anyone else for that matter) merely has to fill in a form, file it with whichever government agency needs to be prised open, and wait for the documents to come. The result is a handy skylight in the roof of the US government, one that has even proved useful to Britons blocked by the locked doors of Whitehall. Tam Dalyell, that tireless anorak of an MP, has frequently called on the info-gathering services of Capitol Hill and the White House to help him discover things about Britain his own government would not tell him.

For the British state much prefers darkness to light. The arms-for-Iraq affair, for example, revealed that British ministers can change their policy on a major issue and never tell parliament or the people. Sir Richard Scott, who investigated the arms-for-Iraq scandal, wrote that Whitehall had opted 'time and time again against full disclosure', and had availed itself as a matter of habit of 'the convenience of secrecy'. He laid out the full tool-kit of government secrecy, including Public Immunity Interest certificates, gag orders which ministers can slap on any policy document they feel jittery about, and the 'convention' under which ministers (of all parties) refuse to answer certain classes of parliamentary question. All this mattered, Scott wrote, because secrecy 'denies the public the ability to make an informed judgement on the government's record'. It dilutes 'the obligations imposed by ministerial accountabilty'. (If we don't know what a minister has done, how can we ask him about it?) Above all, it 'undermines . . . the democratic process'.

It is not as if British politicians are unaware of the corrosive effect secrecy has on a democracy. On the contrary, it was the very fear of democratic debate that sent the Iraqgate plotters into the shadows in the first place. Geoffrey Howe – who as foreign secretary had framed the original rules governing the supply of weapons to Iraq – admitted to the Scott inquiry that he had not wanted the change in policy to become known because of 'the emotional way in which such debates are conducted in public'. Rare is the occasion when a British politician actually confesses his utter disdain for the people he represents and for democracy itself. But with those words Lord Howe admitted that he considered the women and men of Britain either too emotional or too stupid to be allowed to know the policies executed in their name.

Iraqgate was no one-off; darkness covers our public life. Before the scandals of the 1990s made reform seem inevitable, political parties could receive hefty amounts of cash from a donor seeking influence, with the voters utterly unaware of the transaction. Even after the *Guardian* had exposed the Commons trade in cash-for-questions, the parliamentary probe into the affair was itself secret: Sir Gordon Downey investigated Neil Hamilton and other accused MPs in a closed room, with the inconvenient public kept at bay. Once the investigation was complete, the findings were still not published. John Major used the ancient power of prorogation to ensure the Downey report was not released until after the 1997 general election – once again denying the voters their right to know. Outside Westminster, the curtain of secrecy hangs just as heavily. Corporations can contemplate merger with no obligation to tell their shareholders their business plans, their workers whether their jobs are safe or either group how much the new bosses will earn.

Nor is this merely a matter of habit. The edifice of British secrecy is built on law. In 1911 a government panicked by German espionage took just thirty minutes to rush through the Official Secrets Act. The legislation may not have thwarted too many German spies but it did succeed in shutting out the British people, denying them knowledge of even the most basic aspects of their own government, including such crown jewels of national security as the menu at the Ministry of Defence canteen and the existence of the Telecom Tower. The law is now effectively redundant: these days ministers rely on the civil law of contempt and confidence to gag civil servants – but the effect is the same.

In 1996 the gulf between the US culture of openness and the British one of secrecy found grim illustration in a tale of two academics. Professor Richard Breitman of Washington's American University filed a request under the Freedom of Information Act for a hefty pile of documents from the National Security Agency. His request was granted with the release of 1.3 million pages of coded messages sent by the Germans during the Second World War and intercepted by the elite British team of code-breakers known as Ultra. The documents revealed that the Nazis were systematically killing Jews as early as 1941 – and that the British government had known about it all along. The papers had enormous significance, shedding new light on how many Jews were murdered – revising the figure upwards towards 7 million – exactly when and by whom. Three years earlier John Fox, a history lecturer at the London School of Jewish Studies, had made a request for those very same documents to be made available at the Public Records Office in Kew. He was refused. The papers were still classified in Britain, still bearing the stamp: 'Most Secret. To be kept under lock and key: never to be removed from the office.' The British authorities had kept them quiet at the time – when their release might have saved lives – and were still suppressing the truth fifty years on.

Breitman succeeded where Fox failed because of the Freedom of Information Act. That law compelled the NSA – so secretive it is known as No Such Agency – to release the papers it held, including documents acquired from London through traditional Anglo-American intelligence-sharing. Put simply, British documents could be seen in America but not in Britain. Employees of British Telecom had a similar experience in 1997. They had no idea what their company's proposed merger with the American communications giant MCI would entail until the two were obliged to file with the US Securities and Exchange Commission. Only then did they learn of the planned $2.5 billion in 'cost savings', possible code for job losses. The difference in British and American attitudes to openness meant that a UK company did not have to come clean at home, but did have to in America.

The second gap in Britons' defences when pitted against central authority is found in a freedom perhaps more fundamental even than the right to know: free speech. It is one of those cherished liberties many believe defines us as a nation.

Whatever else might be wrong about Britain, we say, at least you can speak your mind. ('It's a free country.') You can climb on a soapbox at Speakers' Corner in Hyde Park and argue for atheism or against the government, for vegetarianism or against homosexuality, as loudly as you like. Admittedly, we have no formal right to free speech, but that is only because we have no formal right to anything. Most of us would probably say that hardly matters: we know as a matter of practice that we can express our opinions without fear.

It all sounds just fine. The reality, however, is a little different. A vast range of rules exists which sharply curb what we assume to be our guaranteed right of free speech. One study counted no fewer than forty-six different statutes restricting the press. Blasphemy laws can silence any expression the authorities deem defamatory of Christianity (and, under a recent proposal, any other major religion). Race relations legislation can prosecute any statement which 'incites racial hatred'. Local authorities can ban films they consider a threat to 'public order'. Court injunctions, or more rarely, D-Notices, can halt publication in an instant, the latter being the unexplained diktats from Whitehall which usually cite 'defence' as their catch-all excuse. Ministers can silence whistleblowers with the Official Secrets Act and its legal cousins, just as they did in the celebrated *Spycatcher* case. The home secretary can ban the voice of a democratically elected politician from the airwaves on the grounds of 'national security', as he did during the broadcasting ban on Sinn Fein. Even speech we assume is uncontroversial is heavily restricted. The reporting of court proceedings, for example, is now so severely limited, with judges routinely invoking the law of contempt, that lawyers genuinely fear for the principle of open justice in Britain.

But perhaps the greatest curb on free speech comes from the laws of libel. The fact that Britain's are among the toughest in the world sounds like a good thing; instinctively many people like the idea of strong legal protection for the reputations of the innocent. But the effect is not nearly so benign. For our libel laws have functioned as a weapon of the powerful, gagging those who seek to challenge them – and denying the public the right to question their governors.

First, there is the cost. As the old joke used to have it, the law is open to everyone – like the Ritz Hotel. So if a hulking media conglomerate defames a private citizen, the individual will rarely have the wherewithal to take them on. Equally, if a small magazine or local paper irritates a corporation or a government minister the cost of a libel action can be steep enough to close them down. The result is self-censorship, with editors preferring to tiptoe around controversy all together.

Those that do dare publish are then damned by a law which doubly serves the powerful. In most countries, if someone sues a newspaper for libel he has to prove the paper's story was untrue. If he is a public figure then he has to go a step further, proving that the journalists acted maliciously. But in Britain the burden of proof is reversed: it is the newspaper which has to prove its original claim was true – often a tall order in strictly legal terms (and woefully out of date, originating in the medieval law of sedition and Star Chamber, which believed that all libels, true or not, posed a threat to public peace). If the subject of the paper's story is a public figure, it makes no difference; it counts as no defence. It was these two rules which helped Jonathan Aitken mount his long and costly libel action against the *Guardian* – before he eventually had to drop it.

The result is not only a set of rules which inhibits free expression, but a British culture with little instinct for the right to free speech. A neat example surfaced in 1997, when a fifteen-year-old girl complained to a local paper about slipping standards at her school. Sarah Briggs wrote that she was worried for her exam prospects because teachers at Queen Elizabeth's comprehensive in Mansfield, Nottinghamshire, were constantly taking time off. She argued that her school had not done enough to remedy defects identified by an official inspection, and that precious funds had been wasted on a visit by the Queen. 'Supply teachers are often late turning up for lessons because they don't know where they are supposed to be,' she wrote. 'All this wastes time. Most of us don't feel prepared for our GCSE exam next year.'

The school's response to this conscientious, thoughtful intervention by a young woman concerned for her education was immediate. Sarah Briggs was charged with bringing Queen Elizabeth's into disrepute. She was ordered to write a formal letter of apology to the head teacher and staff for 'seriously disrespectful conduct' – or face expulsion. But the teenager was adamant. She stood by her comments and refused to apologise, insisting she had simply said what she thought was right. 'I won't say sorry just to get myself back in. I'd be lying to myself. Even if teachers disagree with what I've said there is no need for them to go this far.' Eventually Sarah got back to school, her expulsion overturned by the school governors.

The striking feature of the episode was not only that it happened at all – but the lack of outrage it provoked. Several journalists' first reaction was to investigate the criticisms Sarah Briggs had made, to see if they stood up. The implication was that if she was wrong, then the school was right to expel her. Few people argued that the schoolgirl had every right to express her opinion – regardless of whether she was right or wrong. Fewer still saw that Sarah Briggs was patently not a problem child at all, but rather a star pupil – a young woman with clear, cogent views and a mature desire to air them in the public sphere.

In America she would have been invited into the Oval Office, to pose with the president as a champion of the value enshrined in the very First Amendment to the Constitution: 'Congress shall make no law respecting an establishment of religion, or prohibiting the free exercise thereof; or abridging the freedom of speech, or of the press; or the right of the people peacefully to assemble, and to petition the Government for a redress of grievances.'

That clear unambiguous statement of the right to free speech relieves Americans of the need to descend into national panic every time an ugly burst of expression – the Ku Klux Klan on cable TV, an assassin's manual in the bookshops – comes along. Nor do they have an arsenal of injunctions, D-Notices or blasphemy laws which can silence the expression of unpopular or inconvenient speech. The First Amendment reigns supreme, declaring a single, unwavering principle: free speech means free speech, even when it offends.

America's libel laws are also the exact opposite of ours. In the US it is the plaintiff who carries the burden of proof, forcing him to establish that an alleged libel is untrue. Moreover, the rules are different for a public figure or when a public interest is at stake. Ever since 1964, and the landmark case of the *New York Times* v. Sullivan, the Supreme Court has been adamant: a free press has the right and *duty* to report on matters of public import. In that case, the *Times* had criticised an unnamed police official from Montgomery, Alabama, who went on to win $500,000 from the paper – a huge fortune in those days. The *Times* appealed and the high court, in a ruling by Justice William Brennan, backed the paper: 'Debate on public issues should be uninhibited, robust and wide open and . . . it may well include vehement, caustic and sometimes unpleasantly sharp attacks on government and public officials,' Brennan declared, ruling that journalists could even make false statements in the heat of debate, so long as they were not made maliciously. The judge said that if newspapers faced massive libel payouts a 'pall of fear and timidity' would hang over them, and self-censorship would result. Such anxiety is to be avoided, since it 'dampens the vigour and limits the variety of public debate'. After Brennan, public officials seeking libel damages have to prove the accused journalists acted out of malice, with reckless regard to the truth. Such a claim only rarely holds up in court.

What it all adds up to is an American culture of rights that allows the people to stand up to authority, whether through the Bill of Rights, the Freedom of Information Act or guaranteed free speech. Litigiousness represents the uglier face of that culture, to be sure. But, just like the death penalty or pork-barrel politics, it should be seen for what it is: an unhappy by-product of what is otherwise a rather admirable feature of US life – the determination to let the people have their say – no matter how awkward or ugly their opinions – and to ensure their will is done.

4

From Normal Life to O.J. Simpson

THE NORMAL FAMILY has four members. Father is strong with broad shoulders, mother has long, flowing hair. They sit close, while their two children – a boy and a girl – sprawl lovingly across their laps. They are fit, smiling and white.

Actually, they are more a reddish shade of brown. For the Normal Family is a clay sculpture at the entrance to Normal City Hall and Normal Police Department headquarters – a muncipal showpiece for the small, mid-western town of Normal, Illinois.

The folks of Normal are used to jokes about their name; they even make some themselves. The slogan for a concert by a returning native of the town is, of course, Back to Normal. The mayor, Kent Karraker, says he accepted long ago that, unlike Minnesota or Cincinnati, his town will never spawn a world-famous pool-player called Normal Fats or an ace gambler celebrated as the Normal Kid.

The name came from the Normal University, founded last century. The college changed its name eventually, but the town never did. And somehow it fits: an average place, home to 42,219 people, surrounded by flat farmland, bang in the middle of the United States. It could be Everytown in Anystate, USA. There may be no such thing as an American norm, but if it is to be found anywhere, it is in Normal, Illinois.

The most important building around may well be Normal Community High, which comes complete with lines of lockers, jocks padded up for football and blonde-frizzed cheerleaders – all the ingredients of the American high school you would recognise from *Grease* or *Beverly Hills 90210*. It also betrays some of the uglier features of US educational life: teachers considered installing airport-style metal detectors by the school gates – machinery which is *de rigueur* in some of the big city US schools – after pupils as young as eleven were caught coming to class armed with knives and guns. Almost all the older kids testify that their peers – not them – are using marijuana, cocaine and especially acid.

Inside an afternoon sociology class the twelfth graders – seventeen and eighteen year olds – were discussing racism. The subject had acquired an extra urgency that day, because two form members had just been arrested and charged with 'felony hate crimes'. The pair had disrupted Normal life by cruising around town in a car draped in the Confederate flag, the emblem of the old deep south, shouting 'White power!' and calling out the name of the Ku Klux Klan. A black lad had grabbed at the flag and there had been a fight.

The sociology class was convinced this was part of a trend. 'The country is divided into more and more different cultures now,' said Annette Wense, earnest in her faded jeans. A few rows behind, Ted Fowler wanted to offer his own experience of racism, at the hands of affirmative action. Like a lot of other whites at that time, he believed African-Americans were getting preferential treatment. 'There's a black kid at the grocery store I work at, and he's really lazy, OK? But no one says anything, because he's black.'

On it went, a discussion touching on everything from isolationism to MTV, gently nudged along by their teacher. Few of the kids were shy; most made at least one contribution. They seemed to be the beneficiaries of a unique educational ethos – one which believed that every child had something to say. More than that, they were the obvious products of a society which encourages its citizens to let their voices be heard. For America has nurtured a noisy, often raucous public conversation. At its worst, it can be an ear-bending racket. At its best, it can sound like one of the world's most vigorously engaged democracies.

We all know Americans can talk; you only have to soak up half an hour of Jerry Springer or Ricki Lake to see young women telling a national TV audience 'How My Dad Left My Mum –

For My Boyfriend!' or watch middle-aged men sharing their secret lives as sado-masochistic cross-dressers. In New York the American fetish for self-revelation has spawned a remarkable little project, a kind of secular confessional by voicemail. Dial 212-255-2748 and you will reach the Apology Line, a place to 'Call, Listen, Perhaps Share', according to the stickers slapped on call-boxes across the city. Thousands of people have rung in, selected their category – sex, romance, humour, addiction or child abuse – and spilled their guts. Others have become hooked on the service's silent pleasure: calling in just to hear what past confessors have been saying. 'I would like to apologise to my boyfriend Harold,' says the voice of a woman. 'We've been together eleven years and I've been cheating on him for eight months.' There is less remorse in the next voice, a painter and decorator with a message addressed to the several clients whose wives he has slept with on the job. 'Let me thank you for the cheque – and the tip,' he says with a chuckle. At a rate of more than a hundred a day, men and women, workers and bosses, pupils and teachers call in, their voices reaching the Manhattan apartment of 'Mr Apology', the artist who set up the line in 1980. 'They're just burdened and they need to get things off their chest,' Mr A explains. The range has been astonishing, from the McDonald's worker who admitted he had displayed an anatomical intimacy with the product – he said he had 'dicked the fries' – to a regular called Ritchie, who claimed, plausibly, to be a serial killer. Often callers respond to other people's messages, offering their own confessions and advice – group therapy by answering machine. Calls are not of the premium-charge variety, and Mr Apology makes no money from the service. What he has created is not a business but, in its own bizarre way, a community.

For there seems to be a link between Americans' easy emotional confessionalism and the quality of their public dialogue. Americans are used to talking to each other – about their emotions, yes, but also about the country they all share. They have a thousand different ways to do it.

Pride of place goes to talk radio – the medium wave cacophony which acquired such great influence in the mid-1990s. There is some confusion in Britain about the phenomenon: we often muddle talk-show hosts – Rush Limbaugh and his imitators – with 'shock jocks' like Howard Stern. The latter are indeed shocking: Stern parades his sexual obsessions on air, asking every woman who appears whether she is a lesbian and urging female listeners to visit the studio – so they can undress, be fondled by him and his 'posse' and, on one occasion, shave off their pubic hair inches away from a microphone.

The radio talkmeisters, meanwhile, are the mainly right-wing commentators who deliver long monologues on the politics of the day. Led by the ultra-conservative Limbaugh, these hired mouths can dwell for hours on hair-splitting amendments currently passing through a House subcommittee, barely pausing for breath to take a listener's phone call. Rush himself is a one-man gabfest. 'Day one thousand one hundred and twenty-three of America Held Hostage,' he announces, counting off the days of the Clinton presidency. When the president's teenage daughter, Chelsea, was at her gawkiest, Limbaugh asked listeners why the White House kept only a cat. 'Because the Clintons already have a dog,' came the answer. He sings into his micro-phone, audibly rustles papers and drums his fingers on the desk. He begins most sentences, 'Friends . . .' and his twenty million devotees proudly call themselves 'dittoheads' – promising that their every thought is identical to his. It has proved a remarkably successful formula. One study found almost half the entire US population listening to talk radio 'relatively frequently'. Limbaugh alone draws twenty million, while a new breed of liberal big mouths are gradually breaking the right-wing lock on the AM dial. This is not Jimmy Young: there is no music, no soft consumer segments. It is undiluted politics, for three hours at a stretch.

Switch off the car radio and glance at the rear of the vehicle in front. Chances are, you will see another fixture of America's national conversation. Along with T-shirts, bumper-stickers are proof that, in America, the back of your car and the front of your chest are political platforms. 'No Castro, No Problem!' say the bumpers of heavily Cuban southern Florida; 'It's a Child Not a Choice,' declare the anti-abortionist Chevys of the Bible Belt. 'The Christian Right Is Neither,' reply the liberal Saabs of Boston. You need never be lost in America: simply check out the car in the next lane. In San Francisco, the rainbow of gay rights. In the redneck south, 'Life's a Hillary, Vote Republican.' Of course, slogans are a pretty crude form of communication, but they are evidence of a people constantly talking to each other, citizens urgently persuading, cajoling, even taunting their neighbours. So American cyclists do not just wear helmets, they wear T-shirts announcing 'One Less Car'. Movie stars are not content merely to collect their Oscars, they wear ribbons colour-coded by cause: red for Aids, yellow for hostages, pink for breast cancer.

US discourse is not all badges and five-word slogans. America also boasts a media capable of airing national debate in depth – wholly in defiance of the superficial, soundbite stereotype. The US newspapers are a case in point. While the British broadsheets rarely publish news items longer than 800 words, the *New York Times*, *Washington Post* or *Wall Street Journal* – a bestselling broadsheet which contains no photographs – think nothing of dedicating 2,000 to 3,000 words to the main story of the day, asking their readers to make the dreaded 'turn' or 'jump' to Section D, page 41, column 3. After any set-piece event – the State of the Union address, a live TV debate, a treaty signing – a full transcript is published across several pages. Events are analysed in sometimes mind-numbing depth, usually with meticulously reported details and several named sources – not for them the journalistic licence, doctored quotes and lifted facts of Fleet Street. The *Washington Post* is particularly fond of the multi-part series, run over several days, analysing a social trend or policy dilemma – often with no obvious news value. The big US papers do not wait for a politician or pressure group to demand action; that a situation exists is justification enough.

The US public dialogue spills over into the weekly and monthly press, home of the form American letters has made its own: the essay. Besides the three news magazines, *Time*, *Newsweek* and *US News & World Report*, the health of the nation is examined in the *New Yorker*, *New Republic*, *Nation*, *Weekly Standard*, *National Review*, *National Journal*, *National Interest*, *American Spectator*, *Atlantic Monthly*, *Mother Jones*, *Rolling Stone*, *Harper's* and *Congressional Quarterly* (which actually comes out each week) and the *New York Review of Books*, to name just a sample. All of these publish long, closely argued articles with enough depth and detail to make a British journalist blush.

Even these do not slake the American thirst for public debate. The US best-seller lists bulge with a brand of book that barely exists in the UK: the non-fiction polemic. With titles like *Putting America's House in Order: The Nation as a Family* or *Shakedown: How the Government Screws You From A to Z*, the flow of opinionated tomes never dries, each one a new argument for the US polity. Whether describing how the Constitution is paralysing American democracy or how an excess of law is strangling American freedom, these are the collective equivalents of the self-help manual – also intensely popular in the US – with national improvement the goal.

American television, so often derided as eye-candy – the visible evidence of a culture dumbed-down – also acts as a channel for robust national conversation. ABC's *Nightline* tackles one subject a night, and does it properly. The Sunday morning talk shows on all the main networks may be irritatingly cliquey and inside-the-Beltway, but they are substantial. During the week, primetime news-magazines like CBS's *48 Hours* or *Dateline NBC* always have at least one or two items on matters of public policy. ABC's *Primetime Live*, for example, has made a speciality of exposing politicians who take free rides on the lobbyists' gravy train. On cable TV, the noise of public discussion is even louder. CNN is drenched in politics, while just along the dial is the Cable & Satellite Public Affairs Network and its two twenty-four-hour channels, C-Span and C-Span2. The antithesis of the soundbite culture, this pair of stations – free of all advertising, thanks to a subsidy from the cable industry, and politically neutral to the point of monasticism – almost revel in their own tedium. Besides live, gavel-to-gavel coverage of the House and Senate, they also air press conferences, speeches, think-tank seminars and obscure public policy conferences. Here was the line-up on an average morning on C-Span2:

7:11 a.m.: Replay of a speech to the National Press Club on Politics and Culture by former Education Secretary William Bennett.
8:14 a.m.: The Judicial Excellence Award ceremony at

the National Centre for State Courts.
9:00 a.m.: Forum discussing a new report on national educational goals.
11:34 a.m.: Proceedings of the National Park Fundraising Subcommittee of the Senate Energy and Natural Resources Committee, live from the Dirksen office building in Washington, DC.

Delights like that are served up, without interruption, 365 days a year. There is not a soundbite in earshot, only seven-course, black tie, waiter-service soundmeals. Yet the C-Span twins have built up a near-fanatical following for their constant feed of unfiltered information. In recent years they have quadrupled their audience, so that 40 per cent of the US population now say they watch, if only occasionally. Just under 9 per cent are regulars.

The American cacophony may not amount to a latter-day Athens, but it is admirably energetic – with genuine debate triggered by the unlikeliest causes. It is as if Americans are bent on turning even the most trivial event into an occasion for collective reflection: like the runaway success of *Forrest Gump*, the 1994 Hollywood tale of the low-IQ everyman who somehow inserts himself into every defining moment of recent American history, from the birth of Elvis to Watergate. Politicians immediately clashed over whether the character – who grows from a bullied simpleton into a star football player, Vietnam war hero and eventual computer magnate – was a conservative or a liberal, while commentators attacked the movie for its depiction of a range of social ills from declining school standards to the corrosion of the American work ethic. Pat Buchanan praised *Gump* for being 'at its core, a conservative film': Forrest loves his mother, fights for his country and his greatest ambition is to have a family of his own. Liberals, meanwhile, cheered *Gump* for its political correctness: its hero is disabled, black and white are seen working together, and Forrest is raised by a single mum.

Apparently sensationalist, politics-free news stories are just as effective in prompting Americans to gaze in the collective mirror. The surreal tale of Lorena Bobbit, the softly spoken Ecuadorian manicurist who took her trimming skills a little too far by chopping off her husband's penis, was a classic of the form. At first glance, her trial in the winter of 1994 was nothing more than a freak show – its elements, sex, violence and a dismembered member thrown out of a car window and reattached in a feat of microsurgery so improbable, the mere thought of it can still make men the world over wince. But Ms Bobbit's testimony of abuse at the hands of her former husband soon had women from all over America converging on the snow-covered courthouse in Manassas, Virginia, to stand with a woman they saw as a champion of feminist resistance. For them, her story was no joke but the occasion for an honest conver-sation about how men treat women. The defendant herself understood the significance of her case. Shortly after her acquittal on charges of maliciously wounding her husband, she released a statement read by her lawyer: 'Lorena knows that many of you watching this trial have felt trapped and helpless like she did. She recommends people try to get some help. Without this change within ourselves nothing will get any better.'

As it turned out, the Bobbit affair was but a warm-up to the main event: the trial of O.J. Simpson. Outside observers saw the long, sorry saga of a black sports hero charged with the murder of his wife and her friend as a tabloid soap, a glossy example of American glamour-worship with about as much public signifi-cance as an episode of *LA Law*. They were wrong. Once one applies a broader definition of politics – to include the variety that takes a small 'p' – the O.J. Simpson case emerges as the seminal US political experience of the mid-1990s. The case had undeniable Hollywood appeal: a gorgeous blonde victim, her handsome friend, the jealous superstar husband and the *Othello* overtones of a mixed race couple. But if those had been the saga's only elements interest would soon have palled. What made one in four Americans tell pollsters they were genuinely addicted to the story was that Simpson's trial became a chamber in which the nation could debate itself. It raised the biggest questions: Can blacks and whites get along? What about men and women? Is America still a racist society? Has America turned a blind eye to spousal abuse? Is the law colour-blind? Should it be? Is justice different for the rich? Does a black man have to 'act white' to be successful? Can he ever leave the ghetto behind? Do whites still see a black man and think: threat? There were local and narrower questions, too: is Los Angeles breaking apart? Is the city's police department a haven for racists? Are blacks and Jews (who comprised the bulk of the Simpson defence team) destined to be allies or enemies? Do black women side with women or with blacks? Do cameras belong in the courtroom? Does the jury system work?

Endlessly, in the *New Yorker* and the *National Enquirer*, on talk radio and the Internet, in churches and at bus stops, on CNN and CNBC, the country debated these and a thousand other questions. When the verdict in the criminal trial finally came through on 4 October 1995 the nation stood still as it had not since the moon landing of 1969. Flight announcements at airports fell silent, office workers downed tools; President Clinton huddled with aides around a TV set by the Oval Office. Together Americans saw O.J. Simpson acquitted: blacks cheered and whites hung their heads low. And then they debated it all over again. Before O.J., the academic and lawyer Lani Guinier had called for a 'national conversation about race'. At the time the phrase had sounded like a platitude. But her wish eventually came true, with O.J. Simpson the catalyst.

Many reporters wondered why the election campaign of 1996 was such a flat affair, like a bottle of pop left open overnight. The real reason might be that the country was too exhausted. Elections are meant to trigger loud national exchanges about the issues that really matter. But the American nation had already done that in 1995, opening up wounds of race and sex that ached all the more for being exposed. After it was done, no one was in any mood to shout and scream again. And so, come 1996, they let Messrs Clinton, Dole and Perot go quietly.

The advantage of a political culture which can debate matters of national import through the medium of a celebrity scandal or a blockbuster movie is that everyone can take part. Indeed, the caricature of US culture as dumb often rests on a confusion of accessibility with shallowness. If Americans do talk to each other in simple language, it might not be because they are stupid – but because they want as many people as possible to listen.

So the twangy Texan Phil Gramm makes the case against welfare payments to the able-bodied by demanding those 'riding in the wagon get out and start pulling the wagon with the rest of us'. Whatever one thinks of the sentiment, one can but admire the clarity of its expression. Gramm's policy on crime was to stop building 'prisons like Holiday Inns'. Rival Republicans advocated a health system that was less like a government bureaucracy than a Walmart – where you could choose services like cans on a supermarket shelf. The entire party supported the arrestingly worded doctrine known as 'Three Strikes and You're Out'.

Not that the right has any monopoly on demotic language. Hillary Clinton encapsulated the case for active government in eight and eventually four words: 'It Takes a Village (To Raise a Child'). Quoting an African proverb, the first lady concisely made the argument for working together rather than leaving individuals to fight alone. The phrase took off. When the Clintons took a bus tour through Kentucky and Tennessee, the route was decorated with handmade signs attached to front porches, simultaneously announcing the name of the town and endorsing Hillary's philosophy: COVINGTON IS A VILLAGE.

The transparency of American public speech is a direct product of the country's origins. Born without fixed classes, the United States forged a language largely free of the dialects of status that mark out British English. Colloquial plain talk is the universal idiom of America, a place where professors and ball players alike refer to themselves as 'the guys'. Ethnic diversity is another key determinant. In common with other immigrant nations, the United States has kept its language simple so that it might stay intelligible to newcomers. The elaborate trills and nuances of British English are a luxury we can afford because of the relative homogeneity of our population. Americans, however, shun that kind of Latinate, polysyllabic diction, just as they dislike complex, rococo sentences, embellished with subordinate clauses, of which this is an example. Americans like their sentences simple – like this one.

It is not just a matter of vocabulary. Access to America's national conversation is also helped by the US tendency rapidly to pare down almost any question to first principles. It is as if Americans are agreed on their founding values, as captured in the Constitution; they merely have to decide how they should be applied. So while a British discussion of tax might only rarely get past a quarrel over this allowance or that exemption, in the United States it fast distils into Bob Dole's insistence that 'it's your money' against Hillary Clinton's plea that 'it takes a village'. That kind of dispute is one nearly everyone can understand.

In Britain, by contrast, discussion of our most fundamental dilemmas has tended to dwell on process, not principle. On northern Ireland: should Sinn Fein be admitted to the next round of talks only after the full decommissioning of arms or is a promise of parallel decommissioning enough? On Europe: are the convergence criteria for the single currency sufficient? The equivalent debates in America would focus on the questions at the heart of such matters: Where does Ulster belong? Should we hold on to it? Are we part of Europe or not? What kind of people do we want to be? Sceptics might dismiss such conundrums as too abstract, but it is the disputes about process which leave ordinary people cold, because they are both boring and require specialist knowledge held only by the few. When British politicians speak about 'subsidiarity' or 'convergence criteria' in Europe or 'decommissioning' in northern Ireland they are doing what closed-shop trades have always done – using professional jargon to shut out everyone else. The lesson of America is that arguments about fundamentals, like disputes over ethics, allow everyone to join in.

So much for politics with a small 'p', the day-to-day national conversation. What of Politics with a capital 'P', the formal business of candidates and campaigns? Surely any American claim to be an engaged democracy will come apart when judged by this standard. After all, to the naked eye of the outsider, US democracy looks rotten and decayed, dogged by elections that produce abysmally low turnouts and by candidates competing less on policy than on looks, charisma and the amount of cash in their pockets.

The numbers make bleak reading. In 1996's presidential contest only 48.1 per cent of those eligible to vote did so, down from 55.2 per cent in 1992 – then considered a relatively healthy year. In Britain we boast post-war turnout rates that have ranged from a high of 84 per cent in 1950 to a low of 71.5 per cent in 1997. In congressional, state and local elections the US figures plunge yet lower, rarely showing more than one in three voters bothering to visit the polling station.

There are plenty of excuses one can make. For a start, US turnout rates are calculated as a share of the total voting-age population, not just those on the electoral register (which is the British method). If UK turnout was worked out the same way, Britain's performance would look much less rosy – and the gap between the two countries would narrow dramatically. Elections are also more numerous and frequent in America. The experience of Switzerland – which also holds frequent ballots, usually referendums – suggests that if people are asked to vote often, fewer of them will. Switzerland's US-style turnout rate of 47 per cent hints that there might be such thing as 'voter fatigue' – and that Americans may suffer from it. Sociologists further believe that the lack of fixed, self-aware classes in the United States has left no class-defined political parties to match the virtual tribes found in European democracies. The Democratic and Republican parties are broadly heterogeneous coalitions, with roughly equal numbers of suburban, comfortably off supporters. They cannot mobilise a class base, like Labour or the Tories. Finally, US politicians have become hooked on negative TV advertising, which has proved remarkably effective at depressing the vote. These 'spots', in which a candidate has thirty seconds to trash an opponent, rely on a kind of subliminal manipulation: the bad guy's face in black and white, doom-laden music in a minor key, a voice-over announcing the rival candidate's affection for child-killers or for 100 per cent taxation – or some other distorted version of his position. These commercials do little to build up positive support, but work instead to persuade potential supporters of the targeted candidate to stay at home.

Still, for all the explanations, the bald fact remains that less than half of the Americans who could take part in the electoral process do so. This is a glaring weakness in American life. But it hardly reveals some inevitable, inherent flaw in the US system. On the contrary, there is a battery of available remedies – from free TV advertising for candidates to automatic registration of voters – which might transform the situation overnight. There is nothing logically pre-ordained about low turnout, nothing about it which obliges us to write off American democracy altogether. For there are other aspects of the US set-up which are surprisingly healthy – and worthy of British attention.

Take fifty-year-old Marsha Maliszewski of Battle Creek, Michigan, known to her friends as Pat. She used to work as a marketing rep for a small computer firm. But she became so worried about the state of American values she decided – despite the pressures of mothering two kids – to quit her job and work full time to make a change. She was tired of hearing about the moral decline of her town, the daily stories of degradation and crime recounted by her police officer husband. She was all too aware of the daily compromises she herself had made, little fibs that blurred the line between right and wrong. She knew she could talk the talk. But now, she said, it was 'time to walk the walk'. Everyone was always pointing the finger, blaming someone else. 'I think we all need to take back responsibility.'

So she convened a summit of teachers and clerics, business people and artists – the leaders of Battle Creek's 35,000 people – to discuss 'character'. For three days, they thrashed out a set of common values to help them make ethical decisions. Pat Maliszewski was so pumped by the summit's success that, once it was over, she resolved to take her character crusade throughout Michigan – and perhaps beyond.

She may be an exceptional woman, but Ms Maliszewski is not an exceptional case. When the measure of democratic participation is not confined to voting, but expanded to include other forms of civic activity, the US outlook becomes rather sunnier. In a recent study, the Pew Research Center for the People and the Press sought to measure American activism by assessing the political involvement of the average US citizen. They found that 29 per cent of Americans had called or sent a letter to their congressman in the recent past, 31 per cent had gone to a city or town council meeting in the community where they lived, 25 per cent had attended a public hearing, 27 per cent had joined an organisation in support of a particular cause, 17 per cent had contributed money to a political candidate, 14 per cent were members of a political party and 12 per cent had written a letter to a newspaper.

At first the Pew researchers assumed they had uncovered an

American activist vanguard amounting to nearly a quarter of the population – a busybody 25 per cent or so hassling their elected representatives, going to meetings and haranguing their local paper. That would be quite impressive in itself – but instead the Pew Center discovered a remarkable pattern: the 25 per cent involved were *not all the same people*. There was not one single group of activists getting busy, while the rest of the nation sat around watching TV. Rather the opposite. Thirty-seven per cent of Americans said they had done between one and three of the activities measured; a further 23 per cent said they had done between four and six of them; while 16 per cent reported 'regular and massive participation in seven or more of the activities'. Strikingly, only 24 per cent said they took no part in anything. In other words, three out of every four Americans engage in some form of civic activity.

The picture in Britain is not nearly so encouraging. Only 12 per cent of Brits said they had presented their views to an MP in the last two or three years, according to a similar MORI study of social and political activism in 1995. Fifteen per cent had been an officer of an organisation or a club – more likely to be a ramblers' society or fellowship of birdwatchers than anything conventionally political – but only 12 per cent had written a letter to a paper and just 5 per cent were members of a party or had taken an active part in a political campaign. Most damning of all in comparison with the US figures, when MORI asked respondents if they had done five or more of the above and other similar activities only 11 per cent said yes (39 per cent had done four or more in the US). More than a third had done nothing at all.

Americans, meanwhile, follow their politics – even with a big P – much more closely than either their notorious turnout figures or popular mythology would suggest. In 1996 it took a thirty-minute visit to a shopping mall in Marietta, Georgia, chatting with shoppers about their local congressman, Newt Gingrich, for the stereotype to fall away. The Speaker faced a colourful opponent that year, the self-made millionaire owner of the Great American Cookie Company, and there was long-shot talk of an upset.

Among the early evening customers were a computer

consultant and a car mechanic, a chiropractor and the organiser of singles' services at Marietta's Baptist church, the general manager of a health food store and a nurse, a locksmith and a housewife. It was a range that included black and white, old and young, those of high and low income. Between them, in little more than half an hour, they raised every major news event, scandal or policy position connected with Newt Gingrich in the previous year. Several mentioned the Contract with America, the manifesto which Gingrich had authored for the mid-term elections of 1994, and an equal number spoke about the 'battle of the budget' – the 1995–6 stand-off between Congress and the White House which caused a shutdown of large chunks of the federal government. Fred Woods, the locksmith, approved. 'Everything's getting leaner and meaner, except the government,' he said. 'It keeps getting fatter and fatter.'

Sandra Gerhardt, the store manager, raised the flap Gingrich had caused when he complained about having to sit at the back of Air Force One, following the funeral of the assassinated Israeli prime minister Yitzhak Rabin. That episode damaged Gingrich very badly, casting him as petty and egotistical. Ms Gerhardt thought it typical. 'He's no Alan Alda, you know what I mean? He's not a sensitive kind of guy. I can see him in the workplace as a sexual harasser or something.'

Others remembered that Newt had dumped his first wife, or proposed orphanages for the poor, or made sexist remarks about women's inability to serve in combat roles in the military, or that he had been condemned as a homophobe by his own half-sister, Candace, a lesbian activist. Soon they had collectively assembled a decent sketch of the House Speaker, probably as good as any put together by a sharp-eyed political researcher – and it came entirely from Gingrich's own voters. A quick check of the list confirmed it: what they had missed was not worth including.

Despite their couch potato image, Americans also pay fairly close attention to the set-piece occasions of their national politics. In 1992 the ninety-minute presidential debates between Bill Clinton, George Bush and Ross Perot were so popular that, by their third encounter, 97 million people tuned in – half of all Americans of voting age – far exceeding the 70 million who make up the average nightly audience for the main broadcast networks. Admittedly the figures dipped dramatically in 1996, but that signalled not voter disengagement but discerning voter judgement: by the time the debates were on TV, the audience knew Bill Clinton was cruising towards re-election and that the contest was over.

The party conventions of 1996 also garnered large audiences. Regularly panned as marathons of conflict-free tedium, the Demfest in Chicago and the Republican bash in San Diego nevertheless brought in around 25 million viewers each – not far off the record set by the Olympic Games in Atlanta which played to a peak audience of 26 million households earlier that same summer.

Sceptics like to cite America's party conventions as perfect illustrations of the degraded quality of US political discourse. Such a view is tempting: the quadrennial get-togethers do indeed look like glitzy carnivals, with their balloons, their flags, their coronation atmosphere. Unlike our own party conferences, there seems to be nothing resembling a debate, just pretty pictures for the TV audience. But such a view misses something. What is more, the easy misreading of the US party convention is to confuse once again the simple with the stupid. By defining too narrowly what counts as 'real debate' or 'serious politics', we often miss the way Americans talk to each other – the very stuff of democracy.

The Republican convention of 1992, held inside the cavernous Astrodome in Houston, Texas, was a case in point. It looked just like the movies: overweight women in sequinned waistcoats, men wearing elephant hats, stamping and cheering to patriotic standards played by a brass band. At first glance it confirmed the old cliché – a stadium-full of ridiculous Americans deluded enough to believe that a carnival was any substitute for a real political conference. But closer inspection revealed plenty of real politics. Several speakers spoke coldly about gay rights, abortion and immigration – leading to the widespread perception that the Republicans had become 'mean-spirited'. This eventually became a grave problem for George Bush's candidacy and led to the notorious 'gender gap', by which women voted Democrat by a huge margin in 1992 and again in

1996. It may have looked like a fairground, but Houston had a serious impact.

The penultimate evening was billed as Family Night in which the two candidates' wives would speak about the men they loved. Syrupy, telegenic nonsense, one might have assumed. By way of confirmation, Marilyn Quayle – whose hapless husband Dan was then vice-president – was introduced by an actor who played the title role in the TV sitcom *Major Dad*. And yet this turned out to be more than a piece of celebrity gimmickry. Dan Quayle had stirred a row a few weeks earlier by attacking the TV character Murphy Brown for choosing to have a child out of wedlock. The vice-president lambasted Hollywood for making childbirth seem like 'just another lifestyle choice' – a 'family values' salvo that later proved to be ahead of its time. Here now was Major Dad, the male head of a traditional TV family – in which children and parents happened the old-fashioned way.

Following the implicit script, Ms Quayle's speech attacked the 1960s counterculture for its dropout ethos and indirectly laid into Hillary Clinton (and feminism in general) by declaring that not all women selfishly pursued a narcissistic career; some women obeyed their 'essential natures' and stayed home, mothering their children and supporting their man. What could easily have been written off as a vacuous bit of showbiz fluff – the special-guest-star-turn by Major Dad – was actually a neat, almost subliminal message. Outsiders did not get it, but the audience in the hall and at home understood the point only too well. It was not framed in the language of Resolution 12 or Composite 43, but it was highly political. You just had to know the code.

A similar approach is needed to fathom America's penchant for personality politics, the almost cult-like fervour aroused by individuals rather than ideas. Only a fool would deny how much men (usually) and their charisma matter in US politics but, once again, it would be a mistake to condemn this habit out of hand. Admittedly, there was not much to admire in the scenes played out in Dallas in the summer of 1995, when the Texan billionaire H. Ross Perot held court at the first convention of United We Stand, the movement he had hastily put together and bankrolled during his 1992 bid for the White House.

'I'd feel I'd died and gone to heaven if Ross ran again,' said Adriane Roth, a former teacher from California who had forked out the cost of a flight, hotel room and even a $100 admission fee to join 4,000 of her fellow Perotistas – such was her devotion to the little man from Texas. Most of them were like her, desperate for the maverick computer tycoon to repeat his previous 'act of self-sacrifice' and agree, however reluctantly, to seek the presidency in 1996. Forget the jug ears and the ukulele voice, to them Ross Perot was the strongman who could turn America Inc. around. In the exhibition hall a mock stained-glass window illuminated the words, In Perot We Trust. No one seemed to take offence that Perot's name was there as a substitute for God's.

Invited – summoned, even – to Dallas was every leading politician of the day, especially those who had their own eye on the top job. Perot's game was to hint that he might step aside if his message was endorsed by someone else, and that the loyal Perot army would swing behind the anointed messenger. Since his 1992 campaign had brought in 19 per cent of the vote – despite the candidate's best efforts to shoot it in both feet, several times, with a combination of chaotic organisation, semi-racist gaffes and two false starts – the US political class knew better than to cross Ross. They believed he held the key to that crucial bloc of centrist, floating voters which tends to decide elections. They were prepared to do anything they could to win him over – abject grovelling not excluded.

'I'm frankly proud that Ross has stayed in the game, because he love's his country,' slavered the usually combative Newt Gingrich. 'We don't always agree,' the Speaker added, sending an anxious hush through the hall. 'We agree about, I guess, eighty-five or ninety per cent of the time.' An audible, collective sigh of relief. Gingrich's opposite number in the House, Dick Gephardt, hailed the Texan with a goofy grin as 'a great American patriot'. The former presidential candidate and civil rights champion, Jesse Jackson, paid the ultimate compliment a black leader can: he addressed Perot as 'Brother Ross'.

The immediate interpretation of such behaviour is obvious: the US system is so rotten, Ross Perot's enormous fortune was enough to reduce the country's political establishment to its knees. But Gingrich, Gephardt and Jackson had come to the Court of King Ross not just because he was rich, but also because he had been the first to tap into – and eventually embody – the political mood-swing of the early 1990s. Before anyone else, he had voiced the then-growing hostility to the federal government. Perot's Texas twang was like an early warning signal, alerting the governing elite to the fact that large numbers of Americans no longer trusted their leaders, assuming them to be incompetent power-grabbers who had squandered ordinary citizens' wealth, sold them out to special interests and sapped the enterprising spirit of the nation. Such talk eventually became commonplace, but Perot got there first. That is why he mattered.

And that is the way America's personality politics tends to work. US voters *do* get hooked on charismatic individuals – but only when they voice a sentiment denied expression elsewhere. In 1968 the arch-liberal senator from Minnesota, Eugene McCarthy, led an anti-Vietnam insurgency which helped speed the departure of Lyndon Johnson from the White House. McCarthy so inspired the flower children of the late sixties, they cut their hair and shaved their beards in order to canvas for him in the staid, conservative mountain country of New Hampshire. The hippies even had a slogan: 'Let's Get Clean for Gene'. Of course, the students were getting their haircut because they believed in Gene McCarthy. But they would not have done it had he not been the champion of a major, moral cause.

In 1996 the firebreathing populist Pat Buchanan ran his own insurgency, this time against 'Beltway Bob' Dole and the Republican establishment. The Buchanan Brigades – 'peasants with pitchforks', he called them – won a victory in New Hampshire and wounded Dole irrevocably. But they achieved something far greater: for more than a month Buchanan's pet issue – corporate greed and the 'downsizing' of American jobs – dominated the national conversation.

Buchanan and McCarthy are at opposite ends of the political see-saw, with Perot hopping between them. Yet, through personality politics, all three men catalysed much-needed debates and articulated anxieties that required an outlet. As the historian Ze'ev Mankowicz is fond of saying, 'People don't believe in ideas, they believe in *people* who believe in ideas.'

The Americans have long recognised that fact and come to accept it. After all, their political system requires candidates to run as individuals, rather than as standard-bearers for their party. That makes the politics of personality difficult to avoid.

Individual independence was once a feature of the House of Commons, back in its nineteenth-century golden age. These days, however, there is little scope for a single politician to have much impact, unless he becomes leader of his party. The Westminster system forces MPs to be little more than human voting machines, delegates to the electoral college which puts a government in office. A free-thinking member risks being branded as a maverick, with dim prospects for his career. The narrowness of the 'selectorate' in UK party leadership elections also prevents national movements from coalescing around individual figures. John Redwood could hardly emerge as a Tory Pat Buchanan when only 300-plus MPs had a say in his 1995 leadership battle with John Major, and fewer than 165 determined his 1997 bid for the job. It is the US 'primary' system – in which all registered voters take part – that produces a Buchanan or a McCarthy or a Jesse Jackson, speaking for the otherwise voiceless. We have no equivalent.

And so British challengers are forced outside the main parties, with the late Sir James Goldsmith and Arthur Scargill two recent examples. Their 1997 efforts might have made some headway in a multiparty, proportional representation system where both men would have had at least the possibility of influence. But in Britain, where we have lacked both the internal party outlet of the US primary system and the external outlet afforded by PR, such men are consigned to the wilderness. They become joke figures, either derided in the press or ignored. None of that would matter if only the egos of an expat businessman and a trade union chieftain were at stake. But the people they speak for, however few, get lost in the process.

It is possible that somewhere deep within the British breast lurks an uncomfortable awareness of the democratic gap between our country and the United States. For much of the British elite's apparent anti-Americanism could be read instead as a coolness towards democracy itself. It is as if the US is disliked for being too democratic, too *vulgar*. An example surfaced in early 1997 when Carlton TV staged a live, two-hour television debate on the future of the monarchy. The event turned rowdy, with much heckling and barracking from the 3,000-strong studio audience. The opinion-forming class went apoplectic, condemning the show as a zoo which imperilled not just television but the very British way of life. 'This howling and ignorant mob is a depressing omen for the future, not just of the monarchy, but of democracy as a whole,' steamed a panicked Ann Leslie in the *Daily Mail*. It was as if the white-wigged, powder-faced aristocrats of the *ancien régime* had suddenly seen the hordes storm the palace. What was most revealing, however, was the speed with which the punditocracy condemned Carlton for staging an 'American style' debate. It is as if, whenever the *vox populi* is heard, the alarmed governing classes of Britain immediately think: America.

If it is true that at some buried level we identify America with democracy – and Virgin Atlantic did promote its London–Washington service with a 'Triumph for the People' slogan, as if Britons instantly think of the American capital as a citadel of popular rule – then it is also true that, among Americans, Britain is often a byword for non-democracy. In the 1996 battle for North Carolina's Senate seat, aides to Democratic challenger Harvey Gantt voiced their frustration at their opponent's refusal to take part in a face-to-face TV debate by invoking Westminster. 'Jesse Helms is campaigning for the United States Senate, not the House of Lords,' fumed Jim Andrews, the Gantt campaign manager. 'He does not have a lifetime appointment and a peerage. He may not like it, but there's an election coming on.'

American popular culture plays a similar trick. Watching a Disney movie, it is always instructive to listen out for the accents of the bad guys – the kings and wicked dictators. In *Aladdin* both the sultan and his evil counsellor, Jafar, had Received Pronunciation English accents. So did Scar, the fratricidal usurper in *The Lion King*, his voice on loan from Jeremy Irons. Disney are masters of the subliminal association and no detail is anything but deliberate. They know the tones of England strike a chord with an American audience, reminding them of life before the republic, when they were the subjects of a faraway crown. Disney's heroes, from Aladdin to Simba, speak in an accent that is all-American – for theirs is a voice which expects to be heard.

5

Sex, Power and Getting Connected

IN THE TOWN they call Lesbianville, the shops offer a Dyke Discount, the ice-cream van is run by Sister Softee and Martina Navratilova's autobiography is book of the month. The local lingerie store has a lesbian night, and a quarter of the weddings in the Unitarian church have two brides and no groom. The listings magazine has no covergirl but a 'coverdyke', runs ads for a bookshop that stocks nothing written by men, and includes notices for the local locksmith, estate agent, lawyer and optician – all of whom are lesbians.

'Lesbianville' is Northampton, Massachusetts, a small town of 30,000 two hours west of Boston. It is surrounded by the rusty, golden trees of New England and chock-full of cafés, vegetarian restaurants and agreeably organic shops. It also has the largest concentration of gay women in America. Lesbianville is not a slur; it is the name the women of Northampton have taken as their own after the tabloid *National Enquirer* came to town and spotted '10,000 cuddling, kissing lesbians who call it home sweet home'. On sale is a phonecard bearing the slogan, 'Lesbianville, USA – A Window of Freedom'. It sold particularly well during a recent campaign by the town's women for a local by-law, extending the same legal rights to same-sex partners as those enjoyed by married and straight couples. Lesbians spoke warmly of finally finding a place where they could hold hands in the street without hearing the abuse of strangers.

Northampton has indeed embraced its gay women, estimated at anywhere between a tenth and a fifth of the local population. The *Daily Hampshire Gazette* runs wedding announcements for lesbian couples, while the Christ the King Ecumenical Catholic church will happily bless two women in marriage. 'If the commitment is there, I don't see any problem,' says the priest, Father David Gaboury. 'Christ loves us all.' The town has a Lesbian and Gay Business Guild, women-only bed-and-breakfast hotels, even a support group for lesbian ex-nuns. A gay woman serves as a judge on the local bench.

No one is really sure how all this happened to Northampton. One clue is the presence of two women-only colleges nearby, Smith and Mount Holyoke. Locals speculate that a lot of lesbians came to study in Northampton, liked it and stayed. Either way, Lesbianville has become admired throughout gay America. It is a compulsory stop for big-name gay female performers with the annual Northampton Lesbian Festival a must for kd lang, Melissa Etheridge and the rest. The local quip is that Northampton is the Ellis Island of America's gay women – every lesbian has passed through at least once.

Several thousand miles away, at the other end of the American continent, there's a haven of a very different kind. Tent City they call it, a clump of ex-army tents that houses more than a thousand prisoners on the desert edge of Phoenix, Arizona. The men bake in airless, reeking wigwams, cursing the canvas that feebly separates them from the sun.

'I'm glad they complain,' says their jailer, Sheriff Joe Arpaio. 'Maybe now they won't come back.' Arpaio boasts that he is the meanest sheriff in America, forever dreaming up new – or reviving old – ways to punish and humiliate the criminal. Not content with bringing back the chain gang in 1995, he introduced it for women prisoners a year later. Maybe Alabama got there first, but they were soft: their prisoners were only shackled at the feet. Sheriff Joe's convicts are chained to each other.

In Tent City, there is plenty of scope for Arpaio to express his unique penal philosophy. He has banned all privileges, from girlie magazines to cigarettes. Coffee is illegal and classified as 'contraband'. Food consists mainly of baloney – cold, cheap meat – after the sheriff abolished the customary three meals a day. Entertainment is minimal. At first videos were restricted to *Donald Duck* or *Lassie*, but when the inmates objected, films were withdrawn altogether. The TV is in the communal day room, Tent City's only non-canvas structure, where prisoners are now allowed to watch either the Weather Channel or the televised proceedings of the local council. 'Cruel and unusual punishment,' says Joe with a chuckle.

The sheriff is confident that his is the harshest prison regime in the US. He has lowered the cost of inmates' meals to thirty cents each – the lowest in the country. The 'prison' itself cost next to nothing because the tents, many of them veterans of the Korean war, were supplied for free. 'Some of them leak,' he says, with unmistakable pride. Sheriff Arpaio's plans include a tightening of the regime at Tent City, including a demand that prisoners 'shower and crap' outdoors. He also hankers for fifty-foot watchtowers around the perimeter, 'like a concentration camp'. His highest compliment came when he heard Arizona's felons were pleading guilty to more serious crimes – so they could dodge Tent City and go straight to the concrete state prison.

At first glance there appears to be little to unite Sheriff Joe and the good women of Lesbianville. He is a right-wing mascot; they bring the 'family values' brigade out in a nasty rash. Yet their very difference is what they have in common. Both Northampton, Massachusetts, and Maricopa County, Arizona, are not only testament to the diversity of American life, they are also products of an American philosophy which keeps power local – and which lets individual towns and cities do their own thing. If Northampton has lots of gay women, they can elect a lesbian judge, a couple of gay councillors and even introduce a local law expanding their freedoms. If Maricopa County includes lots of voters who take a hard line on crime, they can elect a no-nonsense former hardman from the Drug Enforcement Agency keen to spend his retirement slapping down a few more bad guys. And that clearly is what the people want: Sheriff Arpaio enjoys 80 per cent approval ratings in a county with a population of 2.5 million – larger than that of eighteen states. Liberals would hate Maricopa County, social conservatives fume at the thought of Lesbianville. But America is vast enough – and US local democracy so arranged – that each group can construct its own little kingdom, regardless of what goes on at the centre.

This local, decentralising instinct is written into the founding document of the republic. The Tenth Amendment of the Constitution insists, 'The powers not delegated to the United States by the Constitution, nor prohibited by it to the States, are reserved to the States respectively or to the people.' In other words, local authorities have full power over everything, unless stated otherwise. Underpinning the idea was the Founders' view that local government was more *natural*, because it was closer to the people. (Some early Americans believed local rule was not really government at all, having more in common with the libertarian ideal that individuals should govern themselves.) Indeed, so great was the Founders' determination to prevent the emergence of a single, mighty centre, they even agonised over the establishment of a national capital. Rather than elevate one part of the country over all the rest, they established a distinct Federal City, which eventually became Washington, DC. The move worked: to this day, Washington is the political capital but hardly America's most dominant city.

Of course, none of this has been straightforward – or painless. The struggle between the centre and the local – between federal and state government – has been one of the defining themes of US history. At first it was a philosophical battle, pitting James Madison's desire for a strong, central authority – a view known, confusingly perhaps, as Federalism – against Thomas Jefferson's vision of power scattered among the states. The Bill of Rights fitted the Jefferson view. Initially its strictures applied only to the federal government, not the states: it was central power that had to be restrained. Nearly a century later, however, the battle turned bloody – with a Civil War centred on a dispute over the power of the Union to impose its will on recalcitrant states. The victory of the North led to the abolition of slavery, but also to a shift in the balance of power. From that point on, the federal government gained in muscle, suddenly able to overturn state initiatives and to extend its reach further than ever before. In today's America, the debate between Jeffersonians and Madisonians goes on – with the lead roles now played by Republicans and Democrats respectively. The former argue that the slide toward Federalism has gone far enough, that it is time for Washington, DC, to cede some of its power back to the state level. These latter-day Jeffersonians have won some crucial victories, including the 1996 welfare act which shifted responsibility for the poor from the central government to the fifty states.

For all those shifts back and forth, the US has consistently maintained a level of decentralisation that marks it out among the world's democracies. Even when Federalism has been at the height of its powers – just after the Civil War, or in the FDR years – America has still been a less centralised country than almost any nation in Europe, especially Britain. When the twenty-six-year-old French nobleman, Alexis de Tocqueville, spent ten months surveying the new republic in 1831, eventually to write the classic, *Democracy in America*, he was struck by the vigour of local control in the new country. 'The strength of free peoples resides in the local community,' he wrote. 'Local institutions are to liberty what primary schools are to science; they put it within the people's reach.' De Tocqueville warned his readers not to underestimate the importance of grass roots democracy: 'Without local institutions a nation may give itself a free government, but it has not got the spirit of liberty.'

De Tocqueville's observations have survived quite well, as anyone who has driven along North Carolina's Highway 24-27 in election season has probably noticed. The road stretches from Charlotte, the state's main city, to the lush Uwharrie National Forest. Make the journey in late October and you will see elms clothed in leaves of burnt yellow, auburn, russet and gold. The fields yield cotton, the shops sell bait and the Dutch barns boast their trademark tall arches. Shelter comes from the clapboard houses, log cabins and white-front cottages. Not much has changed around there since the 1940s: still the roadside mailboxes, still the picket fences. But a few weeks before polling day, the fields and verges along the highway begin to sprout a man-made type of vegetation – signs and placards promoting candidates up for election.

WP 'Bill' Davis for NC Senate
Hayes for Governor
Re-elect Judge Tanya Wallace
Judge Raymond A. Warren, State Supreme Court

Tom Davidson, Commissioner of Agriculture
Re-elect Brady Dickson, County Commissioner
Gary Lowder, NC House
Campbell for State Auditor
Gail Myles, School Board
Brian Philip Brauns, District Judge
Jim Long, Insurance Commissioner
Judy Gibson, Register of Deeds
Tom Wicker, Lieutenant Governor
Elaine Marshall, Secretary of State
Mike Ward, State Superintendent
Tom Funderburk, Labor Commissioner
Harlan Boyles, Treasurer

That was the crop in 1996, but there is a similar harvest every election season – a long queue of people seeking jobs in their town, city or state. That so many of them – including judges and bureaucrats – have to win the approval of the people says much about American democracy. Indeed, more public offices are open to election, and elections held more frequently, in the United States than in any other country in the world. US Census Bureau figures for 1992 showed 511,039 popularly elected officials – one for every 363 members of the voting age population. The overwhelming majority of those, 491,669 to be exact, held local positions, with 18,828 in statewide jobs, half of them administrative officials and judges. One scholar estimates that, including 'primary' battles for party nominations, in excess of a million elections are held in the US in every four-year cycle.

But what is perhaps most striking is not that all these posts are filled democratically, but that they exist at all. For both their number and the range of their duties are proof that, in America, local government is a serious business. There are nearly half a million men and women like Sheriff Joe or the lesbian politicos of Northampton – people elected locally, powerful enough to make their community different from the one next door. And the muscle they flex is genuine. Each of the fifty states runs its own welfare, justice and school systems; indeed, nine-tenths of US public education is financed at state and local level. Cities and states can set their own taxes – on sales or income or both or neither – and spend them as they democratically choose. Thus the small town of Lyme on the border of New Hampshire and Vermont can levy its citizens, by agreement, to stump up enough cash to hire a local doctor, who then treats them all for free – even making house calls, virtually unheard of in America. It is their own mini-NHS. In Washington state, taxes are higher than in most parts of the US but their health care is almost a public system like Britain's. In Nevada and New Hampshire, there is a lighter tax burden and so thinner public services. The guiding principle is simple: money is raised locally and spent locally.

Sometimes local people bypass the politicians and remould their town or state directly. In the upscale enclave of Hanover, New Hampshire – home to Dartmouth College – decisions are taken at an annual town meeting, held every May in the high school gym. Any of Hanover's 9,200 citizens can come, bring motions of their own and then vote on how their community should be governed for the next year. If citizens have something urgent on their minds, they can circulate a petition and call an emergency session. Famously, Hanoverians have consistently voted to keep out McDonald's – and, unlike the good people of Hampstead, they have succeeded. New England modesty would prevent them saying it, but what the citizens of Hanover have created is a pretty close realisation of the old Athenian dream of pure democracy.

In fact, voters across the United States enjoy regular doses of direct decision-making – in the form of the referendum. Already-long US ballot forms are routinely extended with a barrage of questions on specific issues, covering their city or the entire state. One political scientist at Berkeley noted that in 1988 he was asked to vote on twenty-nine statewide propositions, five county-wide ones and eight more for the city. (He also had to choose a president, US senator, US representative, state senator and state representative as well as all the local and county officials – all told, he had to make sixty-one decisions in a single visit to the polling station.) So in 1992 the people of Colorado approved Amendment 2, denying 'special protection' to homosexuals, while the voters of Maine later rejected a similar measure. In 1996 six states debated anti-hunting laws, while six more pondered the merits of gambling. A year later the people of Oregon voted to uphold an earlier decision to legalise voluntary euthanasia. Over the years voters have ruled on everything from smoking in public places to the right of non-dentists to fit false teeth. Often these referendums are introduced by state legislatures or governors for the same reason politicians have always used them: to dodge a tricky decision. But some states have rules legally obliging officials to put certain major decisions to the people.

Perhaps the purest brand of referendum democracy is the device which is all but unique to the United States: the citizen initiative. These start out as simple petitions which, once they have gathered the requisite number of signatures (usually between 3 and 10 per cent of all voters in a given state), end up as questions on the November ballot. Anybody can launch a citizen initiative, including a regular couple like Jim and Fawn Spady. Like so many parents, they felt the schools in their area were not up to scratch. But they were not prepared merely to wait for election time to vote out the school board in Ballard, Washington. Instead they borrowed $150,000 and mounted a petition drive, balloting their neighbours on a move to allow the establishment of an independent charter school. The Spadys did not believe the politicians in the Washington state legislature would act for them. So they took action themselves. 'You have to go beyond the people in power now,' explained Ms Spady, so becoming yet another warrior in America's long battle for self-rule rather than central government.

The Spadys and people like them succeeded in placing ninety-four such citizen initiatives on ballot forms in twenty states in 1996, making it a record year. Not that the grass roots referendum is some new, flash-in-the-pan trend: the previous record was ninety, set in 1914. In California alone, citizen initiatives have led to legislation demanding that illegal immigrants be denied all but emergency public services, that affirmative action for women and ethnic minorities be dismantled at state level and that cannabis be sold for medicinal purposes to people with Aids, among others (Propositions 187, 209 and 215 respectively). When one considers the sheer futility of petition drives in most democracies, including Britain, it is a pretty impressive record (whatever one's view of the policies decided).

By allowing all these communities to do their own thing, sometimes the entire United States benefits. According to the policy nerds – or wonks, in the jargon – who are prone to drool with excitement at the thought, the fifty states act as 'laboratories of democracy'. Wisconsin tries an experiment in 'workfare'; if it is a success, the rest of the country can follow. Oregon tries postal, 'mail-in' elections. If turnout rises, the rest of the country can do the same. Perhaps the best example is crime. New York pursues 'zero tolerance', persuading criminals they will be hunted down and caught for even the most minor violations, while California tries 'three strikes and you're out', hoping to instil felons with greater fear of the judicial system by imposing tougher, longer sentences. The rest of the nation can sit back and watch, confident that whichever approach works best will get picked up (perhaps even in Britain).

Even within single states there is room for extraordinary diversity, with policy often varying from one town to the next. Take Massachusetts, the home of Lesbianville. True to the state's liberal reputation, judges there dreamed up a new way of dealing with women's crime. Instead of automatically sending all female offenders to jail, they would offer them an alternative: a compulsory course in women's literature. Under an experimental scheme, a reading list that included the Brontë sisters, Jane Austen and George Eliot became a potential sentence for all female felons except those guilty of the most serious crimes. 'It taught me patience, taught me to stick with things,' said Melanie Thompson, a convicted prostitute who surrendered to the three-month Changing Lives Through Literature course rather than go behind bars. The state's male multiple-offenders had faced punishment-by-fiction since 1991, when they were forced to read about male characters grappling with violent impulses – and then to discuss the material with staff from the University of Massachusetts' English department.

Meanwhile, a short drive away in the trim town of Taunton, there flourished a rather different approach to crime and punishment. 'Beware, you toilet-licking vipers! Hairball scum, lowlifes, punks, dirtbags, cruds – beware! Captain Good is watching you!' So begins American television's very own *Crimewatch* programme, with Captain Good as host. For thirty minutes each week, Richard Pimental – a real-life captain in the local police force – takes over Taunton's Channel 27 and rails against the criminals in his midst. 'The degenerates and lowlifes out there have been keeping us busy,' he reports from behind his mock-up police station desk, peaked cap tight on his head, his gold badge glinting in the TV light. He kicks off with the Lowlife Highlights, naming his Punk of the Week and identifying the newest members of his 'maggot patrol'. Next comes the show's most popular segment, the Sleaze Alert, where Captain Good singles out local prostitutes – before holding up photographs of their latest clients. 'This is a lady of the night, she's been charged with sexual conduct for a fee,' says the captain. 'And this is her John.' The picture shows a mug shot of an unshaven and distinctly embarrassed man, trying not to look at the camera. Then the policeman delivers his punch. 'Well, "she" turned out to be a man. The joke's on you, pal. You deserve it.'

Crimewatch has made Richard Pimental something of a celebrity in the usually well-behaved town of Taunton. People stop him in the street, and more than 11,000 locals have joined his Posse of Good neighbourhood watch scheme. Best of all, says the captain, his brand of 'shame TV' works. He claims a 65 per cent arrest rate in the cases flashed on air, and says not one of his exposed 'Johns' has ever troubled the vice squad again: they were just too ashamed. Maybe Captain Good is exaggerating. Maybe a few chapters of Jane Austen is a better way to combat crime. But, thanks to a system which allowed a university and a community TV station to try something different, Massachusetts can adopt whichever method gets the best results. It is the same nationally: Americans have used their devolved system to federal advantage, making sure the brightest ideas are funnelled to the rest of the country.

America's local diversity benefits the country as a whole in another, less obvious way. By letting each community set its own standard, the US has artfully dodged the pressure to agree a common stand on life's touchier, more divisive questions – areas where a blanket policy covering the entire nation would only alienate large parts of it. Sex is a textbook illustration of the habit.

The United States boasts that it is the sweet land of liberty, more jealously protective of individual freedoms than any country in the world. Accordingly, one can watch hardcore gay pornography on Manhattan's community cable channel or visit Hooters, the restaurant chain where all the waitresses wear tiny hot pants and the clingiest, skimpiest tops designed unapologetically to show off their breasts. At the same time, America is God's Own Country, a place with more houses of worship per capita than any nation on earth. So there is no nudity on US broadcast television (cable is different), no expletives printed in the national newspapers and, until recently, no dancing at the Baptist Baylor University in Waco, Texas (the ban was lifted in 1996). America was built on both libertarian and puritanical foundations, and the two traditions exist side by side to this day. Tension erupts constantly, but coexistence is helped by the fact that neither view ever need triumph completely. Instead, conservative values might prevail in one town or state while the permissive society reigns in another. And so in Florida, the Christian Coalition could get enough of its supporters elected to the Lake County school board to gain effective control. Once in charge, they promptly banned *Quack-Quack*, a children's book in which a duck quacks at parent figures. The school board ruled that the tale would teach children disrespect. While they were at it, they deleted all mention of condoms from an educational video on Aids prevention and adopted an 'America First' policy which would teach 'strong family values . . . and other basic values that are superior to other foreign or historic cultures'. All the while, MTV was showing videos which looked like virtual three-minute skin flicks, including one for 'Doin' It' – a rap number about anal sex. One hundred thousand Southern Baptist teenagers could fill a stadium in Orlando in 1994 under the banner 'True Love Waits' – committing themselves to virginity until marriage. 'I promise,' they declared in unison, 'to God, myself, my family, those I date, my future mate and my future children to be sexually pure until the day I enter a covenant marriage relationship.' At the same time, Howard Stern was hosting a TV special which required him to guess which of three bikini-clad contestants had had breast implants. Just as those states which want the death penalty can have it, while those who are opposed can avoid it, so America's preference for self-rule enables both its conflicting traditions of sexual morality to take root and flourish. Neither has to win.

The republic is aided in one last way by its decentralising habit. The thousands of city halls, statehouses and governor's mansions serve as 'farms of talent', rearing new generations of political leaders away from the centre. Even though the Democrats had been out of the White House for twelve years in 1992, Bill Clinton was still able to boast executive experience – as the six-term governor of Arkansas. Jimmy Carter had run Georgia, Ronald Reagan had stewarded California. By diffusing power beyond the centre, Americans benefit from a permanent feed of political talent – from mayors to governors – ready to make the move to the national level. And the traffic is not one-way. In 1990 Pete Wilson proved the centre was not paramount when he resigned from the US Senate to become governor of California – a sign that he knew genuine power lay outside Washington as well as within it.

In America, it makes perfect sense for all these cities and states to have their own governments. After all, everything in the US is writ large. The cars, the fridges, even the milk cartons are big. Little things seem to frighten Americans, who cannot bring themselves to call so much as a portion of fries 'small': it has to be 'regular'. Even the humblest hamlet insists on branding itself a 'city'. It is as if everything has had to expand, to fit the vast expanse that is America. One imagines the pioneers, daunted by the emptiness of their new, huge land, pushing westward – just to conquer the territory and fill the void.

In a country that size, it is probably inevitable that different states and regions have developed their own economies, dialects and traditions. Indeed, the decentralisation of political power in the US both reflects and reinforces a cultural diffusion that is visible in every aspect of American life. So while British business, politics, media and entertainment tend to be concentrated in London, America spreads its spoils across the continent. Everyone knows that Washington hosts the government, Los Angeles has showbiz, and New York has money. But it does not end there. Detroit has cars, Hartford insurance and Houston oil.

Boston has academe, Seattle computing and Chicago the commodities market.

Americans' first point of identification is with their city. They do not root for national sporting teams (which barely exist in America), but for their local side: Bears and Bulls in Chicago, Dodgers and Lakers in LA, Yankees and Knicks in New York. They do not read national newspapers (*USA Today* is a relative newcomer), but rely on the *Fort-Worth Star Telegram*, the *Seattle Post-Intelligencer* or the *Cleveland Plain Dealer*, depending where they live. The preservation of these quirky names – who could resist the *Times-Picayune* of New Orleans? – is evidence of an American reluctance to let local flavours be boiled away in some bland, nominally national mix.

Even television, so often blamed for homogenising culture, plays its part, nurturing American localism. The US networks are not like Britain's, broadcasting the same output across the nation at the same time. Rather they are collections of affiliate stations, one for each city. The result is that even small towns have three or four of their own stations: Baltimore and Washington, though less than forty-five minutes' drive apart, watch different TV. These channels both cater to and strengthen local identities, serving up as many as three city-centred news bulletins a night. These are not the two-minute, after-the-news efforts British viewers would recognise. On the contrary, they often enjoy better time-slots than the big-gun national bulletins produced by ABC, CBS and NBC and consistently bring in bigger audiences: 65 per cent of the US population regularly watch local TV news, compared to 59 per cent for the networks, according to figures gathered by the Pew Center for the People and the Press.

Popular culture feeds the local habit, allowing even the humblest hometowns their own mystique. Switch on the radio and you will soon hear an ode to an American place. 'Do You Know the Way to San Jose?' 'Is This the Way to Amarillo?' 'I Was Only 24 Hours from Tulsa', and 'I Left My Heart in San Francisco'. 'Long Distance Information? Give Me Memphis, Tennessee'. 'Galveston, Oh Galveston'. On it goes, one for almost every big city in America. TV producers use the same device, happily naming shows after their location: *Dallas*,

Savannah, Beverly Hills 90210. Film-makers, too: *My Own Private Idaho, Philadelphia, Mississippi Burning, Last Exit to Brooklyn, Nashville*. Even rural dots on the map of North Carolina have enough of a ring to bequeath their names to best-selling brands of cigarettes: Winston, Salem, Newport. Meanwhile, American politicians brag about their roots in the most unpromising places. Bob Dole never stopped invoking Russell, the speck on the Kansas plains where he was born and raised. Nixon was the man from Whittier, Truman the haberdasher from Independence, Missouri. In America every place has its place.

Britain presents a rather more concentrated picture. Almost all our national resources are centred on London: it is simultaneously our political, financial, media and entertainment capital. Fleet Street dominates the British press, inflicting a London bias on the rest of the country, while the broadcasters provide only a bare minimum of localised television. Our TV soaps may be set in Liverpool and Manchester but they avoid using those places as titles, preferring the fictitious *Brookside* or *Coronation Street*. Our moviemen are similarly bashful, calculating that British cinema-goers would steer clear of a film called *My Own Private Stoke* or *Leicester Burning* or plain *Middlesbrough*. Contemporary songs about the British heartland are in short supply, too: there are few pop hymns to the glories of Birmingham, Bournemouth or Bradford. It is as if our culture-makers sense a collective, squirming embarrassment at the mere mention of our towns and cities. (Tellingly, the capital is immune to this virus: from the Clash's 'London Calling' to ITV's *London's Burning*, the metropolis has a place in pop culture denied to the rest of the country.) Our politicians are just as bad. While Bill Clinton proudly cast himself as the Man from Hope, Margaret Thatcher always seemed ill at ease with her roots in Grantham – rarely returning there as prime minister – while most Britons have no real idea where Tony Blair is from at all. (John Major was the Boy from Brixton, but that's London, where different rules apply.)

Our political arrangements have, until recently, told the same story. All power has been hoarded in Westminster, with Parliament refusing to share it or spread it out. It is significant that the British word for greater local or regional control is still *devolution*, as if power belongs at the centre, even if it might occasionally be devolved outwards: a similar attitude underpins the metropolitan vocabulary which pits the 'Home Counties' against 'the provinces', quietly reasserting the existence of a centre mightier than everywhere else. A parliament in Edinburgh, an assembly in Cardiff and a mayor's office in London are all important moves towards breaking that historic, centralising habit. But there is still a long way to go.

While America's mayors and governors can raise and spend money locally, local councils in Britain have no such power. The bulk of Britain's public cash is raised by central government for the Treasury to dole out, like a monarch of old. Only one-tenth of state education is financed locally in Britain, the reverse of America's nine-tenths ratio. After 1979, the grip became even tighter as Whitehall constructed a system of central control so elaborate it would have put Stalin to shame. Rather than let communities themselves work out how much they want to spend, men from the ministry walk into every town in the country, like pin-striped tailors armed with tape measure and slide rule. They measure the 'need to spend' of every council, feed the numbers into a vast computer which then calculates the exquisitely Soviet-sounding Standard Spending Assessment or SSA. The money from the Whitehall kitty is distributed accordingly, so that councils with large obligations and a high SSA get a fat grant.

The process is staggeringly complex, factoring in extra costs for each part of England, Scotland and Wales. (Councils in the south lobby hard for a special Area Cost Adjustment, a glorified form of London weighting.) Tony Travers, the local government boffin at the London School of Economics, has joked that even the old Bolsheviks of Moscow would not have attempted Whitehall's control over local spending: 'Britain [has] needs-assessment systems that are world-beating in their ambition and complexity. No other country makes anything like the effort the British do to fine tune a service-by-service spending measurement for each local authority in the land.'

The explanations for this micro-management by London of the affairs of Oxford, Jarrow and Inverness are intriguing. Travers believes computers are partly to blame: civil servants are calculating budgets to the last penny because they *can*, thanks to technology. Boredom is a factor, too. With the empire gone, ministers and bureaucrats need something to do: 'Cumbria and Coventry have replaced Asia and Africa as the object of the imperial government's attention,' he says.

But Britain's centralising impulse goes deeper than technology and tedium; it is a longstanding force, one common to both left and right. The leading lights of early British socialism were disciples of a faith which demanded planning at the centre. In the words of the Darby and Joan of Fabianism, Sidney and Beatrice Webb: 'We cannot afford to let a town have what police it wishes, what trade regulations it prefers . . . what highways, markets or sanitation it elects, or what degree of physical health, of education and of social order it happens to appreciate.' All local decisions had to be subordinated to 'that National Minimum of efficiency without which the well-being of the whole will be impaired'. It all sounds so retro now, like ration-books or the Ministry of Works – yet this wide-eyed belief in the wisdom of Whitehall dominated post-war British thinking, eating away at the little autonomies that once enriched the country. Later the same urge to centralise animated the arch anti-socialist, Margaret Thatcher. Like the Webbs before her, she believed local authorities should bend to the will of Westminster. Furious at the independence of Ken Livingstone's Greater London Council and Derek Hatton's Militant Tendency in Liverpool, Thatcher hammered Britain's already feeble local authorities and grabbed more of the few powers they still had.

Besides that lack of power, Britain's towns and cities suffer an additional ailment: a lack of democracy. While Americans vote for everyone from the fire-chief to the proverbial rat catcher, British communities can choose their own councillors but not much else. The rest of the decision-makers – the chief constable, the judge, the hospital chief executive – are appointed, directly or indirectly, by Whitehall. While there is one elected official for every 363 adults in the US, the British ratio stands at just one for every 1,715. (Including our 659 MPs, several thousand local and county councillors and eighty-seven British members of the European parliament, we elect a total of 25,539 people in the UK.) Instead of choosing most of those who hold sway over our lives, we have government by quango, the quasi-autonomous non-governmental organisations which allow unelected people whom nobody's ever heard of and nobody's ever seen to take crucial decisions affecting all of us. When the human rights department at Essex University teamed up with the Charter 88 pressure group to draw up a 'Democratic Audit of the United Kingdom' in 1994, they found no fewer than 5,521 unelected bodies performing executive functions for the government, 4,723 of them operating locally. An entire new class has emerged, like the nomenklatura of the old Soviet Union. The Cabinet Office's own Public Appointments Unit estimated that in 1995 there were about 40,000 of them, dispensing £20.84 billion of taxpayers' money. They are, says one academic, Britain's unaccountable 'new magistracy'.

Quangos' triffid-like proliferation accelerated under the Conservatives, with their introduction of National Health Service Trusts, Training and Enterprise Councils and City Technical Colleges. All these brought with them new, unelected governing bodies, usually consisting of local worthies hand-picked by politicians and mandarins in London. Andrew Marr has usefully exposed the charming irrelevance of many of the quangos, concentrating his fire on the Apple and Pear Council, the UK Polar Medal Assessment Committee and the Consultative Panel on Badgers and Tuberculosis. He has remarked, too, on the whiff of sleaze that lingers over these outfits, wondering, for example, about the £95,000 annual salary attached to the chairmanship of the Horserace Totalisator Board, the Tote. As many as 10,000 of these quangocrats are selected each year, on a nod from Whitehall – not one of them backed by a mandate from the people. In fact, the public hardly knows of their existence. Only 14 per cent of the quangos are under an ombudsman, only one in twenty allows a member of the public to attend its board or committee meetings and a measly one in fifty is covered by rules on openness. Yet all of them are spending our money and affecting our lives.

Britain's local communities, then, suffer a double affliction: almost no power of taxation and too little representation. The result is that if Totnes wanted to be a British Lesbianville or if Birkenhead wanted a tough-as-nails crime-fighter, neither place could get their wish. They would not be able to set their own rules, nor choose the people with the power to make the change for them.

Good Neighbours – and God

Only four children are visible, but their mother insists there are six. She introduces them. Halle is two and a half, Matthew is six, Anna is eight and John is ten. They are bright children, with clear blue eyes. The other two, Grant and Mary, never appear because they are dead. In fact, they never lived. They were both miscarriages. But Mary Jo Hudson refers to them as 'my children' all the same. Grant would be eleven, Mary nearly four. Mrs Hudson is an evangelical Christian, a serious woman with a fixed gaze who believes deep in her heart that human life begins at conception.

But that is not the topic for this afternoon. Right now it is time for the four other Hudson kids to open their storybooks and practise their reading skills. Their mother will supervise, urging John to help Matthew, occasionally scolding Anna for being distracted by Halle. This is not extra work at the weekend or a refresher during the school vacation. This is the middle of a weekday, during term-time. For Mrs Hudson is teaching her children herself, at home. She is one of America's 700,000 'home-schoolers' – most of them born-again Christians, burning with a faith so great they want to hand-mould their offspring into it, away from the Sodom of the state schools. Safe behind their own front door, they can follow their own Creationist curriculum. Here there shall be no nonsense about man's apelike ancestors, no condoms handed out in Sex Ed. class. And so, in the front room of their cramped, humble home in Windsor Heights, just outside Des Moines, Iowa, Mary Jo can raise Halle, Anna, Matthew and John to know nothing of drugs, pornography and street violence. Here they learn right from wrong, good from evil. They learn that God created the world in six days – not as metaphor, but as fact.

The Hudson family is proof that in America, self-government is about more than councils and mayors. Just as local towns refuse to rely on the centre, so American individuals, families and communities are unwilling to be dependent even on local government. In areas of life outsiders might imagine to be the exclusive preserve of the authorities – education, health, welfare – Americans prefer to do things for themselves.

Alexis de Tocqueville spotted the habit more than 150 years ago. In place of the passive dependence on the central state he had seen in his native France, de Tocqueville noticed that Americans tended to rely on each other.

> Americans of all ages, all stations of life, and all types of disposition are forever forming associations. There are not only commercial and industrial associations in which all take part, but others of a thousand different types – religious, moral, serious, futile, very general and very limited, immensely large and very minute. Americans combine to give fêtes, found seminaries, build churches, distribute books, and send missionaries to the antipodes. Hospitals, prisons and schools take shape this way . . . In every case, at the head of any new undertaking, where in France you would find the government or in England some territorial magnate, in the United States you are sure to find an association.

To this day, American citizens continue to take on tasks ordinarily left to government. Education is a perfect example, with home-schoolers like Mary Jo Hudson leading the way. A more mainstream expression comes in the Parent Teacher Associations: a staggering 81 per cent of Americans attend PTA meetings at least once a year. Moreover, 39 per cent go along to sessions of the local elected school board. Many parents also volunteer in school as teaching assistants. Strikingly, one in four parents say they have helped make decisions about their child's curriculum – an encouragingly high index not only of civic involvement but of Americans' sense of control over their own institutions.

Most arresting, however, is the American approach to social welfare, regarded in Britain and beyond as one of the sacred duties of the state. Judged by that standard alone, Americans seem an uncaring nation, spending less government money on benefits and provision than almost every other industrialised nation. Of course, Americans tax and spend less anyway: while the British state, through public spending, accounts for about 40 per cent of all economic activity, the US figure is no more than 30 per cent, for all levels of government combined. But that is not the whole story. For Americans *do* spend a fortune caring for those struggling to make it through life. It's just that they do not get the state to spend their money for them: they do it themselves.

A trip around the benighted urban wastelands of Chicago is a useful eye-opener. The high-rise 'projects' of Cabrini Green or the Robert Taylor Homes have gained nationwide notoriety, conforming to every caricature of the inner-city ghetto: from teenage mums to crack babies, these desperate estates boast every social pathology you can name. Built by the legendary Mayor Richard Daley, they were designed to quarantine Chicago's poor in a place where no one would have to see them. Unseen, they would be forgotten. But not everyone in Chicago did forget. The Ounce of Prevention, a non-profitmaking organisation founded by a couple of millionaire philanthropists and several ordinary citizens, has got stuck into the slums and sink estates of Chicago and beyond. With money from individual donors and charitable foundations as well as the Illinois state authorities and the US government, the Ounce has set up dozens of schemes aimed at ending the cycle of broken families and broken lives. In the sixteen-storey Robert Taylor Homes, they run Head Start programmes of music, reading and learning for three to five year olds, as well as Early Head Start for babies aged just three months and older. Across Illinois, social workers are on hand with the Parents Too Soon scheme, which aims to prevent teen pregnancies. If they happen, it is also there to help. There are daycare centres and health clinics – two for teenagers within striking distance of the Homes. There is assistance for people abused as children, lessons in responsibility for teenage boys, and classes in entrepreneurship, teaching young women how to set up and run small businesses – an approach pioneered in the Third World. Every venture is guided by the simple belief that 'upfront investment' in social action now will save the cost of social breakdown in the future, that it costs less to build a clinic in 1999 than a prison in 2009. An ounce of prevention today is better than a pound of cure tomorrow.

All this is the fruit of private effort, nudged along by the state government of Illinois and the city managers of Chicago. And in this public-private partnership, it is clear which side is the senior partner. The state of Illinois may give a grant to the Parents Too Soon teenage pregnancy project, but it is the Ounce of Prevention which runs it – making sure its own high standards are maintained. The system works better that way, says board member Rusty Hellman, 'because we don't have all that bureaucracy to deal with'. The federal government in Washington, DC, takes the same view. When it came to award the contract for running the Head Start nursery scheme for pre-schoolers, both the Ounce and the City of Chicago put in bids. The charity beat the council and got the job.

The Ounce of Prevention does remarkable work, but it is not unique. Cabrini Green's stock of housing got a much-needed facelift a few years back when former President Jimmy Carter and his fellow volunteers with the homelessness charity Habitat for Humanity came into town. They took out their step-ladders, saws and cement-mixers and got busy. There are civic endeavours like that one all across America, often breathtaking in their ambition and scope. Indeed, statistics show Americans to be the most generous philanthropists in the world. In 1993, a whopping 73 per cent of all American households gave money to charity. Not just a few pennies collected in the cookie jar either. Those families donated an average of $880 each, racking up a national total of $126 billion. Even America's poorest gave money away: 48 per cent of those earning below $10,000 a year made a donation, on average spending $207 each. Among the wealthy, 92 per cent of those on $100,000 or more dipped into their pocket. Their average gift was $3,213.

The big corporations regard philanthropy as good business: Getty, Mellon, Carnegie and Rockefeller became household names in America as much through their generosity as their commerce. In the multi-millionaire's club, the ultimate status symbol is a charitable foundation set up in your own name. The super-rich jostle with each other to be hailed as America's Most Generous: witness Ted Turner's $1 billion gift to the United Nations, which upstaged Bill Gates's promise to spend $200 million or more wiring US schoolkids to the Internet. An average of 180 new million-dollar philanthropic institutions are created each year. Together with the corporations, they give away $15 billion every twelve months.

Sceptics might admire all this generosity, but be wary of describing it as the work of a *community*, taking on its social responsibilities. Surely big spending by foundations is just as faceless and remote as big spending by government. And yet the figures suggest otherwise. More than ninety-six cents of every donated dollar stays in the local community it comes from, and 90 per cent of all US giving comes from individuals rather than corporations seeking good PR. Besides, Americans look after each other with more than money. They give their time and effort, too. Remarkably, more than half of all Americans volunteer for charity or social service activities involving the poor, the sick or the elderly. Of that 54 per cent, the average volunteer gives up four hours a week. The old organisations – the Red Cross, Salvation Army, Scouts and American Cancer Society – can still count on unpaid workers in their millions, while the number of prison visitors has doubled since 1989 (the number of inmates has not risen nearly so sharply).

The evidence of volunteering by young people is even more startling. Habitually miscast as slackers, Generation X actually does more good work, albeit quietly, than any previous generation – certainly more than the baby boomers who made such a noise in the sixties. Detailed studies found two in three X-ers performing some form of voluntary activity – ladling out food at a soup kitchen for the homeless, removing toxins from the local river or serving night duty at an Aids shelter. Two-thirds of America's teenagers are members of youth groups, and one in two have gone door to door to raise money for a cause or organisation. Just under half have visited an elderly person in the community who was not a relative but was all alone. A similar number helped teach a child to read, while one in four had worked on an anti-drugs or anti-drink campaign.

They are people like Carrie Koop, a student at Hope College, Michigan. She and a dozen or so classmates drove eighteen hours cross country for Youth Vote '96 – a conference aimed at politicising the allegedly slack generation in time for that year's presidential election. 'In the sixties, it was civil rights or Vietnam,' said Carrie, then aged nineteen, 'but there isn't one big issue for us. There's a little bit of fixing up here and there.' Such an attitude goes a long way to explaining the pragmatic, solution-centred nature of today's less ideological politics. But it is also a neat description of the volunteer ethos that animated Carrie and her peers. All of them were involved in something, doing a bit of 'fixing up here and there'. They no longer went on marches or attended party conventions; they manned the phones at a rape crisis centre or drove a community ambulance. 'Yes, we're the MTV generation, but to say we don't care is completely false,' insisted Nina Bieliauskas, president of the Hope student congress.

Of course, volunteerism and philanthropy have their limits. Not every blighted American inner city is like Cabrini Green or the Robert Taylor Homes, irrigated with the milk of human kindness. Equally, the US belief that ordinary people should do the work of government can have some unalluring side-effects. Citizens of Fort Worth, for example, might have been alarmed to receive a leaflet in the winter of 1995 offering a strange deal. In return for a $10 contribution, the Dead Serious organisation would guarantee you a $5,000 reward in the unlikely event that you had to kill a criminal, either in self-defence or to defend your property. As soon as you sent off the $10, you would receive two Dead Serious bumper stickers warning potential car thieves that you were covered by this rather novel form of insurance. If the criminal tried his luck, you could make his day – and become $5,000 better off.

The whole scheme was possible thanks to Chapter Nine of the Texas penal code which, uniquely in the US, allows the use of 'deadly force' – at night only – to protect not just life but private property. Technically the Dead Serious plan was perfectly legal. Within a month, it had 800 recruits – delighting the group's founder, rock musician Darrell Frank. 'We are tired of being afraid,' he declared. 'We are fighting back and we will win.' A convicted burglar himself, Frank was sure he understood the criminal mind: fear of death, he explained, was the one thing that would stop a crook 'watch you bleed to death for a nickel'. The local District Attorney was nervous, describing a scheme

97

that actively encouraged people to kill as 'extremely risky'. But Frank was undeterred, keen that someone take advantage of his offer and claim the reward. 'I hope it's a woman that it happens to – an elderly woman. That would be really, really great.'

What exactly has made Americans this way? How come they are ready to carry out tasks citizens of other countries would rather leave to the police or the council? For one thing, many Americans simply see no reason why the state should be better qualified to perform the key duties of a society – education, health, welfare – than anybody else. Those three areas are the largest recipients of US corporate generosity partly because American donors trust private endeavour to do just as good a job as government. More deeply, many wealthy Americans sense an obligation to give to charity since the government asks so comparatively little of them. Knowing that US public services are weak in part because the rich are taxed so lightly, some of them feel obliged to compensate for the fact through philanthropy. The New England aristocracy made the point explicit when they founded the Boston Athenaeum in 1807: 'As we are not called upon for large contributions to national purposes, we shall do well to take advantage of the exception, by taxing ourselves for those institutions, which will be attended with lasting and extensive benefit . . .' Nevertheless, even when Americans *are* called upon for national contributions, as they have been in the post-New Deal era of relatively increased government activity, they still 'tax' themselves. Total US giving is three times greater now than it was in 1955.

But perhaps the key lies in a fact about American life fleetingly referred to earlier. 'There is no country in the world where the Christian religion retains a greater influence over the souls of men than in America,' wrote de Tocqueville, and his observation has held to this day. The US has a world-beating number of churches; even humble Normal, Illinois, has forty-four separate houses of worship. More impressive, people actually use them: church attendance has increased steadily since de Tocqueville's time, so that now 63 per cent of Americans are, in the jargon, 'churched'. The evidence can be seen, and heard, all across America. Every town has a Christian radio station; head south and you will pick up three or four. Drive on any interstate and you can stop by a church just as often as you can pick up a burger. Watch American champion athletes receive their medals or soul singers collect their Grammys and see who they thank first: usually it is the Lord God Almighty. Before a major encounter in the ring, heavyweight boxer Evander Holyfield psyches himself up by addressing 15,000 people at a gospel rally. 'God gets the praise and the glory,' he told a prayer meeting soon after he had survived Mike Tyson's infamous attempt to bite his ear off. 'He gave me the opportunity to show how a Christian is supposed to handle adversity.' The best-seller lists are crammed with religious offerings, whether the New Age fiction of the *Celestine Prophecy* or the spiritual self-help of *Chicken Soup for the Soul*. In 1996 Americans made a chart hit of a grungy foot-tapper called 'One of Us' by Joan Osborne. Chorus: 'God is good and God is great'.

Even in Sin City, the Gomorrah of the desert, you can feel the depth of Americans' yearning for something bigger. There are at least as many chapels on the Las Vegas strip as casinos, most of them of the twenty-four-hour instant-marriage variety. A must-see is the one named after Graceland. Credible culture-watchers decided long ago that the cult surrounding Elvis Presley – which has its epicentre in Vegas – is a genuinely religious phenomenon: it believes in resurrection and even has its own lay priesthood, in the form of the legions of Elvis impersonators. Something of the devotional certainly hovers above the photograph of Gary and Pam Young of Hawaii, which hangs in the Graceland Wedding Chapel. The couple's vows were read in the presence of Norm Jones, a pre-eminent Elvis lookalike. The trio stand together, bride, groom and Norm – all three dressed as the King in his latter, fatter years.

Or visit one of the Vegas cabaret extravaganzas; perhaps *EFX*, starring Michael Crawford. The 'efx' are dazzling: Crawford enters on a flying saucer, two fire-breathing dragons duel on stage; there are waterfalls, a 3-D movie and human flight. But listen closely to the lyrics. 'I am!' bellows a Crawford hologram, clearly limbering up for the role of the Almighty. 'I am Master of Celestial Light, Ruler of Past, Present and Future! I am the EFX-master!' There's more New Age hocus-pocus throughout, as the now paunchy former sitcom star orbits around the stage in an Elvis-style white suit, complete with jewel-encrusted flares.

Surveys have found no fewer than a quarter of all Americans describing themselves as born-again Christians. Healthy majorities believe in angels and – rather neatly – 66.6 per cent are convinced of the existence of the Devil. When the 1993 siege at the Branch Davidian compound in Waco, Texas, finally ended, in flames and nearly a hundred deaths, the novelist and screen-writer Ruth Prawer Jhabvala was in her Manhattan apartment watching the whole scene on television. A woman who had lived most of her life in the fervid atmosphere of India, she never-theless shook her head gently and said, 'There is no greater religious fundamentalism anywhere than here in America.'

Such fervour can look ugly, as it did at Waco and as it often does among the hardliners of the Christian right. Neither the 'pro-life' protesters who blockade abortion clinics brandishing lurid photographs of foetuses, nor the evangelical extremists who wear T-shirts declaring 'Intolerance is a Beautiful Thing', are a great advertisement for the role of religion in US life. Never-theless, it is probably America's churches, synagogues and mosques which have most energetically translated the notion of communal self-reliance from ideal to reality. One quirky example comes from South Barrington, Illinois, where the Willow Creek Community Church has won plaudits for its 'car-repair ministry'. Amateur mechanics come in to church on Saturday to repair the cars of fellow congregants who cannot afford garage charges, or to restore old bangers which are then given to the poor. Americans seem to trust the faithful to care for those who need it: nearly half of all individual charitable giving goes to religious bodies, often those that tend to the poor and the sick.

Moreover it is the exceptional nature of US religion that can claim some credit for the American belief that society should do its work at the grass roots – that collective action should come from the bottom up, not the top down. Professor Seymour Martin Lipset has described America as a nation of *sects,* in contrast with the formal, hierarchical churches found in post-feudal Europe, including Britain. While those established churches take their lead from the archbishop at the head, the American sects exist only in small, grass roots congregations with little or no formal connection to each other. Crucially, among the American sectarians – whom Edmund Burke called the Protestants of Protestantism, the Dissenters of Dissent – the first loyalty was not to one's bishop, but to one's conscience. Just as there is no American king, so there is no American Archbishop of Canterbury, nor an American Chief Rabbi. Instead the autonomous congregations of the US prefer to rely not on their leaders but themselves. That habit has extended far beyond the church door, spilling out into the very way Americans see their own society.

The Ties That Bind

Obviously all this self-reliance is good for the people on the receiving end of it, whether it be the teenage mother in Cabrini Green or the unemployed motorist in South Barrington. But the entire society also seems to benefit. For every time Americans get together to perform a task usually left to the authorities – or to do anything else, for that matter – they make a connection with each other. De Tocqueville marvelled at this American tendency to club together for shared endeavours, from the noble to the trivial. He believed this knack had spun an intricate web of local connections and social bonds, tying the young country together. He went further, insisting that the American brand of civic association was an essential ingredient in any healthy, democratic society. For de Tocqueville, social connections stood as a dense thicket, like a barricade of trees and shrubbery, between the individual and the central state; without them a people would be naked and vulnerable. 'In countries where such associations do not exist, if private individuals cannot create an artificial and temporary substitute for them I can see no permanent protection against the most galling tyranny,' the Frenchman wrote. 'In democratic countries the science of association is the mother of science; the progress of all the rest depends upon the progress it has made.'

Today's scholars agree with de Tocqueville, albeit in different language. Now they speak less of association, and more of 'civic connectedness' or 'social capital' or 'trust'. Whatever terms they use, a growing band of policy experts argue that the more people *engage* with each other – at even the most mundane level – the better it is for society. Researchers have produced striking evidence that civically engaged societies enjoy better results in education, the economy, crime and even health than disconnected ones. They have also shown that ethnic groups, tight with the communal bonds of tradition, flourish economically. Industrial districts with good ties between workers and entrepreneurs tend to prosper – Silicon Valley being the foremost example. Indeed, many economists now place social capital on a par with physical and intellectual capital as one of the key determinants of growth.

Political scientists also endorse de Tocqueville's view that the multiple strands of social connection form a cat's cradle which holds up democracy: if one is in good shape, so will be the other. A twenty-year study of regional government in Italy by Harvard Professor Robert Putnam found that areas with good, elaborate networks of clubs, associations and trade unions handled devolution well, while those with a weak civic life struggled. According to Putnam, 'Voter turnout, newspaper readership, membership in choral societies and football clubs – these were the hallmarks of a successful region.' Social capital has become a kind of Holy Grail for the policy set. Every society wants it; no one is quite sure how to get it.

Few outsiders would look to America for clues; most of them probably picture the US as one of the least 'connected' societies in the world. They have heard how the rich cower behind the closed-circuit walls of their euphemistically named 'gated communities', while the rest slouch in front of the TV munching ready-cooked meals-for-one. They know America as the land which made rugged individualism a cult, a nation raised on the myth of the lone warrior breaking from the team to hunt on his own – whether in *High Noon* or *Mission: Impossible*. The US is the country with no history of socialism, the one place where solidarity and thinking as a group were always alien. Surely America is the home of atomisation rather than civic engagement. That's certainly the view of many Brits. In the words of the *Daily Telegraph* columnist Janet Daley, 'The British are a civic-minded people – unlike Americans who are far more selfish and materialistic.'

Ms Daley finds an unlikely ally in Professor Putnam, the man who spent two decades gazing at the wondrous 'networks, norms and social trust' that add up to social capital. But that was in Italy. He has a less sunny view of his own country, detailed in a provocative 1995 essay called 'Bowling Alone: America's Declining Social Capital'. The professor argued that the country de Tocqueville had once praised was losing its talent for togetherness. He noted the decline in membership of trade unions, women's groups, the Red Cross and even the Boy Scouts. The so-called 'fraternal' organisations – remember the Leopard's Club which Richie Cunningham's dad belonged to in *Happy Days*? – had all suffered sharp drops. Taken together, the average number of associational memberships among Americans had fallen by about a quarter in twenty-five years. Americans were also becoming less neighbourly, with fewer of them socialising with the people next door. They trusted less, too – the proportion of Americans believing that most people could be trusted falling to just over one in three, from the 58 per cent figure recorded in 1960. But what crowned Putnam's argument – pushing it beyond the seminar rooms of the Ivy League and into the great media maw – was his signature image. The professor noticed that while more Americans were ten-pin bowling than ever before, bowling in organised leagues had plummeted. The only way to explain the disparity, said Putnam, was to allow for 'the rise of solo bowling'. America had become such a desolate, atomised place that grown men and women were reduced to scampering down the smooth wooden lanes of the local bowling alley alone.

Putnam suggested several potential causes for the depletion of all this social capital, so conscientiously accumulated over two centuries. He looked at everything from women's entry into the labour force to longer working hours, from Americans' increasing geographic mobility to slum clearances and corporate downsizing. Eventually Putnam identified a single, sinister cause. 'The culprit is television,' he wrote, calculating that TV was absorbing about 40 per cent of the nation's spare time. More deeply, warned Putnam, TV somehow increases 'pessimism about human nature'. It induces passivity in the viewers, rolling them up into lazy couch potatoes, too inert even to join a bowling league.

The paper sent a tremor through the US opinion-forming class, anxious that the threads of American life were unravelling. But help was at hand. In a counter-study published the following year, sociologist Everett C. Ladd knocked down Bowling Alone in a single strike. Ladd crunched the numbers, examining everything from Girl Scout membership to church attendance, before concluding that, far from draining away, US social capital was actually increasing. 'Not even one set of systematic data supports the thesis of Bowling Alone,' Ladd declared.

He found de Tocqueville's basic observation – that Americans are a 'nation of joiners' – was still true. Fully 82 per cent of Americans belong to at least one association or group, a far higher figure than in Germany (67 per cent), Canada (65 per cent), Britain (54 per cent), Italy (41 per cent) or France (39 per cent). Only Holland scores better with 85 per cent. Thus the American Association of Retired Persons grew from 400,000 members in 1960 to 33 million in 1993, becoming the largest private organisation in the world, second only to the Catholic church. Small associations are no less popular. As many as 40 per cent of Americans are thought to be involved in support groups, meeting regularly to nurture the members within. Modelled after Alcoholics Anonymous, they range from reading circles to specialist hobby clubs, each one adding to the stock of social capital.

Religion, too, has maintained its traditional role, fostering civic connections both among and beyond the faithful. Indeed, half of all America's associational activity originates in churches or religious groups. The growing Evangelical and born-again movements, for example, have built new mega-churches, vast complexes with multiple halls, community centres, even shops. With congregations of 15,000, these stadium-chapels may seem remote and impersonal – yet they have strengthened social bonds. South Barrington's Willow Creek is a much-admired example, a church where most members belong to 'cells' of fewer than ten people, a kind of support group for the devout. Willow Creek has hundreds of such clusters, for singles, old folks, women and teenagers, even some organised by hobby – all of them weaving a dense social network.

Even businesses have got in on the act, with leading US

corporations now encouraging their workers to form small, close-knit teams – whether through an impromptu picnic on a summer afternoon or by bringing out a cake to celebrate a colleague's birthday. Local communities remain among the most reliable sources of social capital. The old rural villages may be in decline, but the suburban 'block party' – where neighbours close off the road to cars, mingle with each other, drink home-made lemonade and watch their kids play ball – has plugged the gap. Indeed, the sight of a street full of people, their front doors open, spending an entire afternoon outside, has become one of the landmarks of the American suburban weekend.

In a neat rebuttal of Putnam, Ladd finally reported that the number of softball teams registered in leagues since 1967 had risen from 19,000 to 261,000. Take a Sunday walk in the park in any big city in America and you can see the evidence: office workers and thirtysomethings chugging beers and flirting while they pad through an afternoon game. So what if some Americans are bowling alone? The rest are playing softball together. As even Putnam admits: 'Even in the 1990s, after several decades' erosion, Americans are more trusting and more engaged than people in most other countries of the world.'

Including, unfortunately, the people of Britain. 'I have since travelled to England, from which the Americans have taken some of their laws and many of their customs,' wrote Alexis de Tocqueville. 'It seemed to me that the principle of association was by no means so constantly or adroitly used in that country.' A century and a half later not much has changed. One comparative study found nearly half the British people belonging to no organisation whatsoever, against just 18 per cent who remain aloof in the US. One in ten Britons is a member of an educational or cultural group, less than half the American figure. Britons are also less involved in religious groups, local community action, professional associations, youth work, protecting the environment, women's groups and health organisations than Americans. Even in areas where one would imagine the British having an edge – animal rights, the peace movement and sports – the US comes out best. Only one type of organisation claimed greater membership among Britons than Americans: the trade union.

We British not only engage less with each other we are also, perhaps unsurprisingly, less prepared to carry burdens traditionally associated with government. When it comes to social welfare, our rates of charitable giving are dramatically lower than the Americans'. While 73 per cent of US households gave, only 29 per cent of British families could say the same – each of them contributing an annual average of £196, little more than a third of the $880 given by their American counterparts. Similarly, three in four Britons do no unpaid voluntary work whatsoever, putting us at the bottom of the international league table – behind the US, Canada, France, Germany, Italy and Japan. Clear proof of our deficiency in this area was provided by the sorry tale of Care in the Community. That programme, which moved people with a history of psychiatric problems out of old, cold institutions and into the world, sounded perfect. No one liked the idea of Bedlam-style asylums; how much better for troubled people to join the community. The reality, however, was not so rosy. Many of the most vulnerable people ended up wandering the streets, bewildered and alone. They stood as dismal proof that our civic ties were too few and too weak to form the safety net which might have caught the mentally ill when they fell. Care in the Community exposed an awkward truth: the sick had lost their care, but there was next to no community.

The outlook is not all bleak. For one thing, Britain does have a history of mutual association and self-help, typified by the friendly societies and co-operatives of the Victorian era. More encouragingly, there are signs of a tentative revival in local, collective action. In a pamphlet called 'Civic Spirit', Charles Leadbeater points to the recent establishment of a patient-owned health centre in Bromley-by-Bow in east London, a community self-policing scheme in Balsall Heath, Birmingham, and the 300-house Eldonian housing estate in Liverpool, where residents have been involved in every crucial decision, starting with the very design of their homes. On one Bradford estate, residents have debated a local charter under which everyone helps everyone else, whether by getting their neighbour's shopping or giving them a lift into town.

If the experts are right – and low social capital brings

unemployment, urban poverty, crime, drug abuse, educational failure and even disease – then these attempts to build up the communal reserves are to be nurtured and advanced. The American experience seems to suggest a virtuous circle: the more communities do things for themselves, the stronger their civic connections – and vice versa. For Britain, that probably means more local government, and more grass roots action. It might even mean a town where lesbians hold hands – and prisoners while away the evening hours flicking between a twenty-four-hour weather forecast and Donald Duck.

6

Dream On: Searching for the Classless Society

IN LAS VEGAS the competition is fierce, but few could challenge the claim of the Liberace Museum to be the tackiest place in the tackiest town in all the world. You know you have arrived when you spot the two sleek china dogs standing guard in the foyer – both mementoes from the Cloisters, the Palms Spring hacienda Liberace used to call home. The dogs are unspeakably naff, but they are nothing compared with what you see inside, once you have paid the 'minimum tax-deductible donation' of $6.50 for adults, $2 for children.

Devotees of the man they used to call Mr Showmanship have constructed nothing less than a palace of kitsch, in three trinket-packed wings. The fact that the entire complex is in a shopping mall, sandwiched between a Middle Eastern Deli and a 7-Eleven, only enhances the effect.

First comes the Main Museum, housing the Piano, Car and Celebrity Galleries. Visitors are invited to marvel at the master pianist's collection of eighteen rare and customised keyboards, all looking like props from a costume drama set in imperial Austria. At the centre is Liberace's favourite grand piano, a Baldwin encrusted with thousands of mirrored tiles. Lest its discreet charms be overlooked, staff have mounted the instrument on a revolving stage.

True fans stop elsewhere, at the very piano – also a Baldwin, inlaid with gold – used at the maestro's last performance at New York's Radio City Music Hall, a year before his death in 1987. To maintain the sombre mood, a tape of Liberace's rendering of 'Bewitched, Bothered and Bewildered' tinkles gently in the background.

Next is the Car Gallery, home to Liberace's lavish collection of automobiles, including a rhinestone-covered Rolls-Royce, another Roller done up like the American flag, with rhinestones for the 50 stars, and a pink Volkswagen-Rolls hybrid – with extra rhinestones. Liberace liked rhinestones. There is one the size of a football, donated by Barron Hilton, on show in the Jewellery Gallery. Close by is the twenty-two-carat amethyst which purports to be a 'gift from the Queen of England'.

An estimated 150,000 visitors come to gaze upon this gorgeous collection each year, not all of them blue-rinsed faithful. The museum has also attracted a new breed of customer, present all over Las Vegas: the irony tourist. These are the Generation X-ers who come to Sin City for its so-bad-it's-good appeal. At the Liberace museum they make a sport of ribbing the staff about the lack of explanation, anywhere in the exhibit, for the superstar's untimely death. 'He was old, he just died,' say the guides. Aids is never mentioned.

For all that, the mood of the crowds is generous and affectionate. There is even a dash of patriotism, not confined to the performer's remarkable stars-and-stripes hot pants. The public is invited to see Wladziu Liberace's journey from humble Polish immigrant to world's highest-paid musician as the classic American story of rags-to-riches – even rags-to-rhinestones – success. Partly for that reason, visitors betray not a hint of resentment as they happily hand over good money for one purpose: to gawp at the trappings of another man's wealth.

For what is on display at the Liberace museum is more than a collection of baubles and knick-knacks, gathered by the Danny La Rue of American easy listening. Rather it is a glittering, shiny illustration of America's unique attitude to the rich, the poor and the gap between them. While other societies can crackle with class envy, the US often seems unnervingly free of the green-eyed monster. In America Bill Gates is derided as a nerd, but never begrudged his multi-billion-dollar fortune. *Fortune* magazine's Top 400 list of wealthiest Americans is meant to be placed on the mantelpiece, not pinned to a dartboard. Long before *Hello* magazine, US television's *Lifestyles of the Rich and Famous* was gazing in awe at the ranches, private jets and stretched Mercs of the super-wealthy. The message of the programme is look and learn, not look and puke. Americans show little sympathy for schemes designed to narrow the chasm between rich and poor or to dip, however slightly, into the fortunes of the very best off. Even during the Depression, Americans never made redistribution of wealth a slogan. Instead they have accepted that those at the top will earn a whole lot more than they do, whether it is the chief executive of MCI pocketing an annual bonus of telephone number proportions or Michael Jordan bagging a salary large enough to feed a small African republic.

One would imagine the reverse to be true: America the place where resentment would reach blood-boiling point. After all, the US is surely the land of grotesque inequality, where Bill Gates can enjoy his eleven-digit stash from a personal compound overlooking Lake Washington, even as trailer-park single mums feed their children from a single can of beans. It is the land of Beverly Hills and South Central, of Park Avenue and the Bronx. It is the place captured so memorably by Tom Wolfe in *The Bonfire of the Vanities*, where the rich and poor live in separate worlds, those with cash spending pots of it to 'insulate' themselves from those who have less. From air-conditioned home to air-conditioned car to air-conditioned office, they need never even breathe the same air. Bill Clinton's first labour secretary, Robert Reich, has given the phenomenon a label: 'the secession of the successful'. The comfortable can now drop out of the public sphere altogether – fleeing the inner cities for the suburbs, choosing private schools not public ones, sending their mail by courier rather than the creaky old post office.

This is not a complete exaggeration. In fact, the numbers show America to be the most economically unequal country in the industrialised world. In 1992 the richest 20 per cent of American households had eleven times as much income as the bottom 20 per cent (the multiple in Britain was seven). The poorest fifth have to get by on just 4 per cent of America's net income between them. It is now common for a US corporate chief executive to be on a million-dollar salary, earning at least forty times as much as one of his ordinary employees. In recent years the chasm has widened further, with stagnant wages causing an actual *decline* in the income of badly off Americans (an 11 per cent drop in real terms between 1973 and 1992). According to some measures, the US is simultaneously the richest country in the developed world and the one with the highest proportion of people living in poverty.

And yet Americans seem quite happy with this state of affairs. When the British Social Attitudes Survey asked workers in eight countries whether large differences in income were necessary for economic prosperity, 37 per cent of Americans said they were – far more than the 25 per cent figure recorded in Britain, or the 9 per cent in Holland. Just as striking was the 1990 poll in the *American Enterprise* journal which asked voters whether it was the government's job to narrow the income gap between rich and poor. Nearly three-quarters of Britons and Germans, and over 80 per cent of Italians and Austrians, said it was – but among Americans, just 29 per cent.

How come? The easy answer is that America is a wealthier country than all these others, and that to be badly off in the US is probably a better fate than being 'comfortable' in, say, southern Italy. On this logic, the 18 per cent of Americans defined as poor are only 'poor' in the sense that they have less than half the median income of a very rich society: in absolute terms, they are not poor at all. Economist Michael Forster took the American numbers and converted them into purchasing power in other currencies, factoring in differences in the cost of living. What emerged was striking: the wages of Americans at the bottom of the pile were relatively good. They may have been poor compared to their fellow Americans but, as a matter of raw wealth, they were doing very well. By this new measure, the US has much *less* poverty than all the countries of Western Europe, including Sweden and Germany (who score much better when poverty is defined in relation to national average income).

But such an answer is cheating a little – and it misses the more interesting point. Americans accept great inequality not just because their overall standard of living is high, but for a much deeper reason, one that forms a key part of their national myth. It is the American Dream – the belief that everyone has a fair shot at the top. Rags alongside riches are tolerable when you believe anybody can make the leap from one to the other in a lifetime. Never mind your surname, your accent or your hometown. Never mind what your parents did or how much money they had. You can reach the top. The phrase may seem ludicrous – or ironic – outside the US, but the American Dream still exercises a firm grip on the nation's imagination. The humble origins of Wladziu Liberace or Ross Perot, Michael Jordan or Bill Gates only seem to confirm the dream as reality. 'I've *lived* the American Dream,' Perot, the self-made billionaire, would say at the start of his speeches, and the crowds would always applaud. If he could do it, so could they.

You often see that same sentiment thwart left-wing candidates, railing in vain against company owners and corporate big guns. As countless old-line Democrats have discovered, it can be pretty hard to stir up class hatred in America. The workers on the shopfloor not only tend to believe the boss has earned his wad, more than a few of them picture themselves sitting in his chair one day. In 1992 and 1996 the rabble-rousing Republican Pat Buchanan – in his shirt-sleeves – did a good job of whipping up populist outrage at the fatcats of Wall Street. But the wrath never lasted. It was always dissolved by the age-old potion which makes every American employee regard himself as a potential employer. In the US, even the workers are pro-business. For low-paid Americans don't want to beat the rich – they just want the chance to join them.

The watchword is mobility. Americans do not demand equality of rich and poor, just free movement between them. What they dislike are fixed, hereditary classes – groups determined from birth and closed to outsiders. If someone works hard and has talent, then no prize should be out of reach.

That at least is the American ideal, written into the founding documents of the new nation. It forms the first, post-preamble sentence of the Declaration of Independence: 'We hold these truths to be self-evident, that all men are created *equal.*' The same conviction was ritually reiterated in the next century, in the first sentence of the Gettysburg Address: 'Fourscore and seven years ago our fathers brought forth on this continent, a new nation, conceived in Liberty and dedicated to the proposition that all men are created *equal.*' One of the Constitution's most famous phrases is contained in the Fourteenth Amendment, guaranteeing all Americans '*equal* protection before the law'.

The Founders were adamant that there should be no hereditary ruling class, like the one they had left behind in England. There should be no lords and ladies, no kings and queens. One dispute during the birth of the new republic centred on the exact title of the president. John Adams, who went on to become the second holder of the office, suggested 'His Highness the President of the United States and Protector of Their Liberties'. Others wanted George Washington to be, at the very least, His Majesty the President of the United States, if not outright King George. But it was the egalitarian purists who won the day, ensuring that the head of state would be referred to as nothing grander than Mr President.

There was a similar kerfuffle over the first inauguration ceremony, in New York on the bright morning of 30 April 1789. Washington thought the masses needed a dose of awe-inspiring pageantry if they were to accord the new, shoestring regime the same respect as the old royal one. Cannons fired salutes, and bridges all the way from the general's estate in Mount Vernon, Virginia, to Manhattan were garlanded in flowers. Washington himself was carried by an ornate state coach, in full military dress, while the ladies of the city hosted banquets that lasted all night.

The spectacle may have pleased the crowds, but the leaders of the new United States were troubled. 'I fear we may have exchanged George the Third for George the First,' muttered one senator. Thomas Jefferson was more direct, faulting the ceremony as 'not at all in character with the simplicity of republican government and looking, as if wishfully, to those of European courts'. When the time came for his own installation as president, Jefferson ordered a much more egalitarian affair. He arrived at the Capitol on his own horse, delivered his address and rode back home – dining in his usual spot at a spartan boarding house.

Jefferson had spelled out the American creed of equality in the Declaration of Independence. The celebrated sentence

quoted above goes on to state that all men share equal, 'unalienable rights, that among these are Life, Liberty and the Pursuit
of Happiness'. With those words, Jefferson fired the metaphorical
starting gun for a race in which all Americans would start at the
same point.

Of course that left no room for a blue-blood upper class,
blessed from birth with an in-built edge over the competition.
The Norfolk-born radical and pamphleteer Thomas Paine
insisted that the new United States should grant no advantage
to the 'no-ability' or any other hangers-on from 'the quixotic
age of chivalric nonsense'. Instead, rewards should go to those
who worked hard and had talent. 'Establish the Rights of Man,
enthrone equality,' Paine cried. 'Let there be no privileges, no
distinctions of birth, no monopolies.'

To that end, the early Americans set about preventing the
emergence of fixed classes, seeking ways to stop the rich simply
passing on all their advantages to their children and giving them
an automatic headstart. Education was seen as the true leveller.
If schooling was equal, then there was a chance of genuine social
mobility. In the nineteenth century Americans sought to build a
system that would give every child a common schooling. Horace
Mann and other reformers explicitly ruled out the example of
the English public schools or the European gymnasiums and
lycées, which educated the top slice of society extremely well
but abandoned everyone else. They saw where such systems led
– to the permanent division of society into an elite and a worker
class, with movement from the latter to the former all but
impossible. They decided every American child should go to
good, common schools.

One group took the argument to its logical, if somewhat
extreme, conclusion. In the early 1830s, the New York section
of the Workingmen's Party argued that the common school,
though class-integrated, was not enough. Children from poor
homes still suffered inferior opportunities because, after school,
they would return to slum housing and to parents unable to
help in their education. The New York radicals proposed that all
children above the age of six be raised instead in state-funded
boarding schools, where they would live in the same environment
twenty-four hours a day. That way the class differences between

them would be eliminated, so producing the first truly egalitarian generation. Those with energy and ability would face no barrier to their upward climb – regardless of their birth.

But the vision of America as a classless society went beyond the schemes and wheezes of a few dreamers. Historians describe the US in its first century as a place of intense, rollercoaster mobility. Great fortunes – in gold or on the railroad – were frequently won, lost and won again within a generation. The American road from rags to riches was smooth and slippery – with two-way traffic. Indeed, two unlikely observers of the infant society were struck by the absence in America of the fixed, stable classes they had grown up with in Europe. In the 1850s Karl Marx acknowledged that America would probably be among the last nations to champion socialism because 'though classes, indeed, already exist, they have not become fixed, but continually change and interchange their elements in a constant state of flux'. Writing thirty years later, Marx's partner, Friedrich Engels, described America as a country 'without a permanent and hereditary proletariat'.

Several scholars have argued that Karl Marx regarded this classlessness as a partial explanation for the weakness of US socialism. He saw that most Americans felt they had every opportunity to rise – and therefore considered themselves already members of an equal society. According to Michael Harrington, the leader of American socialism after the Second World War, Marx believed America represented a socialist society – defined in Marx's own terms of value and status relations. In this view the US had created a unique substitute for socialism, an egalitarian ideology which had delivered all that socialism could only promise. The great Italian communist, Antonio Gramsci, gave this surrogate creed a name: Americanism. He argued that America represented a new society, uniquely free of the inheritances of a feudal past that so characterised Britain and Europe. None of the rigid hierarchies of class were in place; there was no permanent peasantry and no aristocracy. This made possible a purely rational, meritocratic system uncluttered by the forelock-tugging ways of the old world. Americanism held that everyone should work hard, that nature and not people should be exploited, and that everyone

116

should have an equal chance of advancement. Michael Harrington summed it up: 'Americanism, the official ideology of the society, became a kind of "substitutive socialism". The European ruling classes . . . were open in their contempt for the proletariat. But in the United States equality, and even classlessness, the creation of wealth for all and political liberty were extolled in the public schools . . . The country's image of itself contained so many socialist elements that one did not have to have a separate movement opposed to the status quo in order to give vent to socialist emotions.'

So much for the founding ideal. But how much of the American Dream of classlessness and social mobility is reality today? At first glance, it does not look good. The big families may be shamelessly new money in origin but they are hereditary dynasties all the same. America has an aristocracy of sorts, whether it is the Kennedys, the Pulitzers or the Vanderbilts. More mundanely, the American upper middle class has succeeded in locking in its good fortune, so that well-to-do families live in good areas, where good state schools train their children for entry to the best colleges – often the Alma Mater of their parents – from where those children can repeat, and build on, the economic success they have inherited. Meanwhile the child born in the ghetto, raised by a lone parent and relying on a welfare cheque, is all but sentenced from birth to a lifetime trapped in the cycle of dependency. Little movement here from rags to riches, and not much traffic the other way either.

Yet that sketch does not tell the whole story. In fact, the modern United States can still boast remarkable social mobility. One statistic makes the case almost alone: of all the people in the bottom fifth of the US income scale in 1975, only 5 per cent were still there in 1991. To put it another way, within a decade and a half 95 per cent of the American poor were poor no more. Another study in the mid-1980s found that 18 per cent of families in that bottom fifth had moved out of it *in a single year.* Sceptics always wonder where they went – perhaps just across the boundary, into the next poorest category? No. The study found one third of those bottom-fifth families had moved up to the *top half* within a generation. From the top branches of the money-tree comes similar proof of social mobility: four out of every five American millionaires made their pile from scratch. Little wonder that only 31 per cent of Americans tell pollsters that 'what you achieve in life depends largely on your family background' – compared to 53 per cent in Britain.

Recent evidence showing a slowdown in mobility from the very bottom – with the poorest finding it harder to climb out of abject poverty – has done little to dim that confidence. You see it still, in the Americans flipping burgers or waiting tables – all of them sharing the faith that one day they will move to bigger and better things. Hollywood likes the coatcheck girl who dreams of being 'in pictures', but for every one of those there are a hundred Hispanic housecleaners saving up to put their kid through college. And every day there is another rags-to-riches story to prove it can be done, from Madonna to Magic Johnson to Bill Clinton.

These travellers on America's social escalator are people like Jon Maurer, a computer executive, fortyish, living and working in Nashua – a green, comfortable town in the south of New Hampshire. He had an accent that stopped you dead: it was unmistakably Edgware, the cadences unambiguously north-west London.

He had made the trek from the furthest tip of the Northern Line to the Granite State – from old England to New England – a few years back. He liked the climate. 'There are real seasons in America,' he said. 'Real winters, real summers.' He and his friends had organised a barbecue that afternoon at the Nashua fish and game reserve, and they were munching hot-dogs and watermelon. Maurer said he liked having leisure time and the open space in which to enjoy it.

But there was more to it than that. 'There are still a lot of opportunities here,' he said. 'I felt Britain had become pretty bankrupt, I felt kind of black about it.' Personally, Jon Maurer reckoned if he had stayed in London he would never have reached the heights he had in Nashua. 'People back home judged me by my accent,' he said. Brits assumed he was a bit wide, fine for sales but not exactly management material. In America he had been judged for himself; class and background had not come into it. 'There's no limitation on you,' he said.

It is an experience echoed by the hundreds of thousands of

migrants who have headed west. Just talk to the Brits who have made it in the US – from Ridley Scott and Alan Parker through to Tracey Ullman and Andrew Sullivan – and they all relate how America represented a liberation: finally they were taken for who they were, not where they came from. And Maurer's observation about accent is not confined to foreigners. Indeed, the weakness of the link between class and accent in America says much about the general blurriness of class boundaries in the US. Of course there are still the Brahminic lilts of New England, and a thick Bronx accent screams 'cab driver', but the tight associations that exist in Britain are absent. Most regional rhythms – mid-western or Californian or east coast – come without class labels, and they act as little bar to progress. Witness the hee-haw accents of James Carville and Haley Barbour, one a Democrat from Louisiana, the other a Republican and seventh-generation Mississippian. The two men reached the tops of their respective parties despite sounding like a couple of rednecks selling moonshine. In Britain, the equivalent – say the cockney of Jonathan Ross or the Geordie of Peter Beardsley – is fine for an entertainer, just as a rural voice can forecast the weather but not read the national news on the BBC. But imagine the chairman of the Conservative Party talking like Danny Baker. It hardly seems likely.

The usual signs and codes of class do not operate in America. Americans prefer plain speaking, using a vocabulary that varies surprisingly little across different income groups. British viewers of the Boston trial of Louise Woodward, the Cheshire teenager charged with murdering a baby in her care, were startled by the unvarnished, simple speech of both the judge and the lawyers. They bantered back and forth, remarkably free of the poly-syllabic, Latinate language one might hear in a British courtroom. They spoke like the people whose fate they were deciding, in a colloquial and unpompous voice. The freshest Americanisms often work because of their proximity to street level. If you agree to pay more for an air ticket because it will give you greater flexibility, you say you're happy to *eat the loss*. But if the salesman starts pushing too hard, he's *in your face*. If he pushes his luck, he's *history* and you're *outta there*.

The correlation between reading habits and class, so well

understood in Britain, also breaks down in the US. Both the janitor at the State Department and the secretary of state read the *Washington Post* (partly because the *Post*'s monopoly leaves little alternative). In Britain, by contrast, 'tabloid' and 'broadsheet' describe not just the shape of a paper, but the demographic status of the people reading it. With the possible exception of New York, where the *Times* and the *Post* stand at opposite ends of the social spectrum, the newspaper an American reads is a much less reliable indicator.

In the US rich and poor exist, of course – often living distant lives. But these groups are separated much less by the subtle, inherited distinctions – the tribal markings – which identify rank in the older societies of Europe. While class in Britain or elsewhere is defined by a whole battery of traits which have nothing to do with raw cash – qualities which neither come automatically with wealth, nor disappear completely when wealth is gone – America's social divide is essentially about money.

Tom Wolfe articulated the difference on a visit to Las Vegas, the city which serves as a neon-lit advertisement for America's claim to be the world's most classless society: 'At Monte Carlo there are still Wrong Forks, Deficient Accents, Poor Tailoring, Gauche Displays, Nouveau Richness, Cultural Aridity – concepts unknown in Las Vegas.' If James Bond hoofed up on the Strip he would not order a Martini, shaken *or* stirred. He would ask for a Diet Sprite in a Big Gulp cup. Despite *Indecent Proposal*, Robert Redford would not pad around in a tux. If he turned up dressed like that, the punters would either think he was nuts or ask him to change $20 for the video poker machine. The dress code in Sin City is strictly egalitarian: T-shirt, baseball cap, jeans. Las Vegas is not a classy place. How could it be? Just like America, it has no class.

Bereft of the usual signs of status – speech, manners and costume – Americans lack the machinery of deference, the tools by which one group bends reflexively before another. De Tocqueville noticed that the masses of the new United States were free of the 'servile tradition' of the old feudal societies of Europe, touching their forelock to no one. Loud and robust confirmation of this fact came at an unlikely hour, during the funeral of Diana, Princess of Wales – when the British people bowed its collective head in silence and contemplation.

There was little of either commodity in the makeshift studios of NBC News, pitched directly opposite Westminster Abbey. The US network had taken over an office building, ripped out the furniture and erected a vast video wall which served as the 'gallery' for a six-hour live special. Each screen offered a different image, 'feeds' from Sky News and ITN as well as NBC's own cameras positioned outside Buckingham Palace and among the crowds at Hyde Park.

At the centre of it all was the striking figure of Guy Pepper, widely rated as the best director in American TV news. The mere fact of his presence in London conveyed the gravity of the occasion, for 'Dr Pepper' rarely steps outside New York. Within minutes it became clear why he had become a legend: his stewardship of the broadcast would have made great television all by itself.

'OK, boys,' he began, addressing his scattered cameramen in an accent of pure, juicy Big Apple. 'Elton John is about to sing "Candle in the Wind". Guess what I want to see? That's *right*, I wanna see CANDLES!! *No*, Bob, not a woman holding a child – CANDLES! CANDLES! CANDLES! Give me somebody holding a fucking *candle* . . .'

When Earl Spencer was speaking about the sister he had loved and lost, Dr Pepper was scanning the crowd, barking into the talkback box. 'I want to see tears, Warren. T-E-A-R-S. Is no one fucking crying at this funeral? Come on, Warren, make me proud of you – give me *tears*!!' A picture of a sobbing child suddenly appeared on monitor three. 'Already seen her,' barked the Doc, recalling an image he had aired perhaps three hours earlier.

It went on like that from the moment the procession left Kensington Gardens all the way through Verdi's *Requiem* until Diana's body was finally laid to rest at Althorp. The minute's silence outside Westminster Abbey was broken only by the sound of muffled yelling, like a phonecall in a cartoon: it was the voice of Dr Pepper, leaking through the headphones of one of his hapless technicians. He was demanding shots of silence.

Only one challenge fazed this master of the airwaves. 'Who's this guy?' he would ask. 'Is that Duke Andrew, you know the

Prince of York?' A second later: 'How can she be called Princess Michael? That's a man's name.' Jeffrey Archer, a live guest, posed a terrible problem. Pepper kept calling him Lord Jeffrey. On a subsequent broadcast, on a different network, Lady Colin Campbell had to explain politely that she was not Lady Colin Powell.

For no matter how hard they try, Americans simply cannot master the intricacies of British aristocracy. Schooled from birth in the doctrine that all people are created equal, they struggle to compute a system which elevates some people over others by their very name. Born in a land where no one is Sir This or Lord The Other, Americans rebel at the very notion of titles. Their founding creed is instilled so deep, it somehow bars them from the verbal bow represented by etiquette and protocol. It is as if Americans refuse to 'know their place' – because in their society nobody is meant to have one.

Americans are clear, too, on what engine drives the escalator of social mobility: education. The very same Americans who baulk at paying taxes to close the gap between rich and poor are much happier to spend public money on schools. For nearly two centuries they have boasted proportionally greater numbers of people completing the various levels of mass education – from primary school to post-graduate research – than any nation in the world. Higher education is not an elite pursuit in the US, but massive and widespread. While Britain has about a third of its twenty to twenty-four year olds in college – more than France, Germany and Japan – America boasts a figure of 60 per cent. Despite that lead, more Americans than Europeans believe education should be thrown open wider still: 44 per cent of Americans tell pollsters there should be yet more college places for young people, against 29 per cent in Britain, and less than 10 per cent in Germany.

The politicians understand this sentiment and pander to it shamelessly. George Bush promised he would be the 'education president' while Bill Clinton won re-election by talking about school uniforms, literacy programmes and hooking up class-rooms to the Internet. In his subsequent State of the Union address, Clinton proclaimed a 'national crusade' to make America 'number one' in maths and science, a mission Hillary

Clinton compared to Dwight D. Eisenhower's mobilisation of the American people after the Soviets launched Sputnik. The Americans regard learning as deathly serious. Their kids are assigned more homework than the Japanese, and if it is not completed many schools demand a note from the parent explaining why. If the pupil is late – not absent, but late – the child has to produce another note. One Dallas woman fell foul of the rules when her child was late for kindergarten ten times. She was sentenced to ninety days of criminal probation.

Such measures may be excessive, just as the American classroom itself is far from perfect. Indeed, the worst inner-city schools and their abysmal standards are the object of enduring popular complaint: story-hungry editors are always ready to stir up readers and viewers with tales of high school graduates barely able to read their own diplomas. Universities, too, are routinely pilloried for their shallowness, for offering courses in aerobics or places to kids with a great jump-shot in basketball but not much of a record as a scholar. Nor does US education fully live up to the early ideal of common schooling. As in Britain, the well-off can pay for better teaching for their kids, by either sending them to a private school or moving into a smart area where the local schools are of a high standard. All these faults exist in the US system; it would be foolish to deny them. Yet, for all that, it is still true that education matters to Americans more than almost every other public concern, chiefly because they see learning as the key to the country's animating ideal: unhindered social mobility.

America's classlessness does not come without cost. The absence of the two major post-feudal classes – the hereditary aristocracy and the proletariat – has deprived the US of the values traditionally associated with each group: paternalism and socialism. Between them, those twin forces set up the welfare state in Europe. Starting with Disraeli in Britain and Bismarck in Germany, old-fashioned paternalists laid the foundations for a system of provision and public services which social democrats, trade unionists and socialists worked to expand. Both class-dominated groups wanted benign governments to take care of the badly off through public housing, child benefit, pensions, unemployment pay, state-funded jobs and a national health service.

But in America there was no nobility to advocate state-sponsored *noblesse oblige* – and no conscious working class to demand it. There was no group at the top offering to help those at the bottom because few Americans have ever accepted that society *has* a permanent top or bottom. The US has had no Bismarck or Disraeli, just as it has never had a mass workers' party nor a trade union movement much persuaded by socialist ideas. Both socialism and its better-dressed twin, paternalism, have been absent forces in America. The result is that the US lacks public provisions Britons and Europeans regard as basic. There is no nationalised system of health care – most Americans are insured through their jobs, while the poor and elderly have their bills paid by the taxpayer via Medicaid and Medicare respectively – and there are no universal allowances for families with children. One study found that the United States has been consistently late in the introduction of social benefits: pensions and insurance against industrial accidents both came to the US nearly fifty years after they were established in Europe. The American ideal has centred not on protecting the poor, but on giving them the chance to become rich.

Real-life illustration of this point came on an autumn evening in October 1995. It was the night before the Million Man March, and black men from all over America were heading for Washington – on buses, on planes, some even on foot. They were heeding the fire-and-brimstone call of Louis Farrakhan, the leader of the Nation of Islam and self-appointed successor to Malcolm X. The day turned out to be a festival, a reunion really. Amazingly, nearly a million men *did* come – making it the largest demonstration in US history – airline pilots and opera singers, preachers and gangsta rappers, all gathered on the National Mall at the foot of the US Capitol. Together they put the lie to the myth that a crowd of black men spelled violence. It was as peaceful as a dowagers' picnic.

The night before, the atmosphere in Washington was already building. Peewee Jackson was standing outside the DC Court-house – which, sad to say, is one place a journalist can always find hundreds of young black men to interview. Thirty years old, he was dressed like a hip-hop artist in Boss cagoule, voluminous jeans and sneakers. An oversized crucifix swung from his neck. He was discussing *the* topic of that time: O.J. Simpson, who had been acquitted less than a fortnight earlier. Like most other African-Americans, Jackson thought the verdict was right: 'I knew he didn't kill those people himself.'

The conversation moved, inevitably, to 'the System'. Could it ever be fair to a black man like O.J.? Could it be fair to a black man like him? 'I ain't got no problem, *I* finished school,' Jackson began. 'I'm a plumber, I made it. Anybody can do it. You don't need no special handouts. You don't need no help. All you gotta do is finish school and try harder. Nobody's gonna give you nothing, you know what I'm saying? You gotta do it yourself.'

He went on to explain that he had been married for eight years, he had three kids and that his role model was his mother. In just a few sentences he had demolished half a dozen stereotypes of the black American male. But the important one was his belief that education and hard work were all that was necessary for success. Like the 88 per cent of Americans who tell pollsters ambition is essential – far outstripping the 20 per cent who rate 'coming from a wealthy family' or the 39 per cent who cite 'having well-educated parents' – Peewee Jackson was a believer in the American Dream of social mobility. Accordingly, he had no interest in 'special handouts' – of either the paternalist or socialist variety. He just wanted a chance to make it.

The second potential drawback of the US pursuit of social mobility is less obvious. A society which tells its people that everyone can succeed – all they need is talent – leaves those who fail with no one to blame but themselves. The original anti-meritocrats marshalled this as a serious argument against true equality of opportunity. For the first time in human history, they argued, the poor would be unable to blame the system and would have to regard themselves as failures. Michael Young, the author of Labour's landslide-winning 1945 manifesto, and the man who actually coined the word 'meritocracy', sounded the alarm in his semi-futuristic book *The Rise of the Meritocracy 1870–2033*: 'Such widespread recognition of merit as the arbiter may condemn to helpless despair the many who have no merit,' he wrote.

The US experience suggests that 'helpless despair' is the least of the trouble. Several US criminologists have contended that America's high crime rates are partly linked to the nation's success-oriented ethos. 'In a country that stresses success above all, people are led to feel that the most important thing is to win the game, regardless of the methods employed in doing so,' writes the sage US sociologist Seymour Martin Lipset. It is no wonder that when an American teenager who sees images of $160 sneakers on TV every hour hears the Nike slogan 'Just Do It', he promptly goes out and steals $160 from a stranger. The kid simply cannot accept that he is too poor to afford the shoes; his society never stops telling him the only barrier to advancement and material wealth is his own determination. The message, says one academic, can easily become distorted into a call to succeed 'by fair means if possible, by foul means if necessary'.

That might help explain why rates for every category of crime have been estimated to be three times higher in the US than in any other developed country – a trend that has been in place since the Second World War. The figures are staggering, a key part of the major image problem America has abroad. According to the FBI, a property crime occurs every three seconds in the US, a violent crime every seventeen seconds, a robbery every fifty-one seconds, a 'forcible' rape every five minutes and a murder every twenty-three minutes. Clearly several factors, particularly the drug explosion and free access to guns, have deepened this problem, giving America a male homicide rate nearly ten times that of the European Union and an incarceration rate five times greater than Britain's. But a national myth which insists your rags can become riches – and you are a failure if they do not – must play a part.

The American Dream has one last unwelcome side-effect: workaholism. Most US employees are lucky to get twelve days' holiday a year – compared to the German average of thirty – and twelve-hour days are commonplace. It is not unusual to see a worker striding to the office at 6 a.m. only to emerge, tie loosened or skirt rumpled, locking up close to midnight. Over the last two decades, Americans have added an extra 164 hours – a full month of work – to their working year. Now time stands as one of the United States' most precious commodities. A whole industry has arisen in 'domestic out-sourcing', farming out the chores that can clutter a busy life. Hired help can range from the $25-an-hour 'paid wife' – who will cook dinner, plant roses, wait for the electrician *and* help you find your wallet – to the Nanny Link, the company which bails out people who need to employ a nanny but do not have a minute to find one. Let's Eat Already! is a Washington-based 'home-meal replacement service', whose cooks will come into your kitchen, rustle up enough dinners for a fortnight and stash them in the freezer. Script 'n' Scribble promise to send tuck parcels to your child at summer camp, even writing the accompanying 'personalized' note, while Kids in Motion will ferry junior from ballet to soccer practice. Sadly for some Americans, these enterprises – all in the business of selling time – have come too late. Visit a resort town in America and you will be struck by the number of single women in their fifties or sixties: they are the widows of men who slaved their lives away, chasing the American Dream.

Rags, Riches and Good Manners

In 1828 Fanny Trollope, mother of Anthony, took a leaf out of Alexis de Tocqueville's book and travelled to the former colonies of the New World. Unlike the young Frenchman, she was appalled by what she saw, offended above all by the sheer, unshackled classlessness of the place. In *Domestic Manners of the Americans*, she confessed herself disgusted by the 'violent intimacy' and 'revolting licence' of the new republic. Americans were so informal – so free, in fact, of the lacy niceties of status – that they were entirely without manners, the age-old semaphore of the elite.

The lady's harumphing can still be heard today, reverberating through Middle England. For a close look at British anti-Americanism reveals just how often it amounts to a suspicion of egalitarianism itself. Just as the US is often associated in the British mind with rampant democracy, so the country is also identified with the vulgarities of equality – which lots of Britons seem to dislike.

'The Radio 4 audience, which is primarily AB, is extraordinarily anti-American,' BBC producer Sheila Dillon confessed to *Vogue* magazine reporter Vanessa Friedman. An

American in London, Friedman had experienced the phenomenon first hand. 'Anti-Americanism has a tendency to run along class lines,' she wrote. 'It appears in its most virulent form among the upper classes and the media, and gets progressively weaker as it makes its way down the socio-economic alphabet.' Could it be that the Chablis-and-Tuscany set cannot stand America because of its classlessness, while the McDonald's-and-Disneyworld crowd love it for exactly the same reason?

This aspect of the British–American love–hate relationship works both ways. Snobbish Americans are often Anglophiles, regarding Englishness as a synonym for class – in both senses of the word: classy and class-ridden. The Louise Woodward trial revealed how a British accent had been a valuable asset for would-be au pairs, offering their services to American couples with young children. 'They think they're hiring Mary Poppins,' explained one US commentator. Indeed the Bristol Lounge of Boston's Four Seasons Hotel brands itself as upmarket by serving tea at four o'clock each day – complete with cucumber sandwiches, scones and clotted cream. The *New York Times* Sunday Travel section sends the same message by regularly splashing London on its cover. 'Peeks at Privilege,' promised one feature. 'Apsley House (Wellington's Prize), Spencer House (an Earl's love nest) and Leighton House (a Lord's studio)'. Countless US advertisers rely on the American identification of Britain with privilege to sell their products. Cellular One mobile phones, Taster's Choice coffee, Mueslix cereal, Leading Hotels of the World – they all use British accents, while Infiniti opted for Welsh actor Jonathan Pryce to sell its luxury cars. 'We wanted somebody who embodied a level of class, sophistication and intelligence,' said Steve Goldman, the ad executive responsible. 'Jonathan was a perfect match.' British visitors often benefit from this kind of Anglophilia – 'I *love* your accent!' – but those who stay a little longer soon learn that the more committedly pro-English an American is, the likelier they are to be an outrageous snob.

The reverse is true, too. Diehard US egalitarians do not like Britain much, seeing in our country the fixed hierarchies of class that are so unwelcome in their own. Liberal writer and policy brain Mickey Kaus once expressed the fear that widening income gaps could make America a class society 'in the English sense'. British Airways eventually dropped the old pin-striped actor Robert Morley from its adverts on American TV, partly because American viewers could not stand the British *hauteur* he seemed to personify. As mentioned in Chapter 4, Disney plays this sentiment expertly, always giving its animated kings, tyrants or overlords accents that are pure England.

The sad truth is that the animators of the Disney studios are not completely wide of the mark. Britain's feudal past *did* leave behind an entrenched edifice of class. We know its contours so well, we can trace its shape with our eyes shut. It has evolved over at least eight centuries, from those twenty-five barons who asserted their rights in the Magna Carta to that legendary *Picture Post* photograph of an Eton schoolboy in top hat and tails, alongside a few mucky-faced street urchins, all wearing rags. The system's signature, even clichéd, institutions are known to us all. Ranged on one side are the public schools and Oxbridge, the monarchy and the House of Lords, the Home Counties and the Coldstream Guards; on the other, the trade unions and working men's clubs, flat caps and whippets, beer and sandwiches, football terraces and back-to-back housing. Upper class and working class, capital and labour, gentlemen and players, officers and men – the labels vary, but they all name the same thing: a society neatly divided by class, with our politics organised the same way. It does not take a genius to spot it, but one did. 'The Englishman wants to have inferiors,' wrote Alexis de Tocqueville. 'The Englishman lowers his eyes beneath him in satisfaction.'

In this way, Britain has always been America's opposite. While the US was born free of rank, Britain has teemed for centuries with an elaborate ecology of classes and sub-classes, all incubated in a climate of deference and superiority. There has been no British Dream to challenge that order with a demand for complete mobility between social groups. The upshot is hardly surprising: 80 per cent of the sons and daughters of British unskilled workers leave school at sixteen as unskilled as their parents. The Conservatives' professional genius David Willetts offers as 'evidence of quite an encouraging degree of mobility' the fact that 10 per cent of those in the highest-income fifth of Britain's population had fathers in the bottom fifth, according to a 1996 study by the Institute of Fiscal Studies. But the same study found 34 per cent of top earners had fathers who had been in the top category. These numbers are worth thinking about; Willetts thinks they sound good. But compare them to the American figures: just one in ten of Britain's rich come from poor stock, while four out of five American millionaires are self-made. Even without statistics, people seem to know the difference in their gut. One international survey asked individuals whether they had a good chance of improving their standard of living. Nearly three in four Americans, 72 per cent, said they did – compared to just 37 per cent of Brits. Americans not only believe in mobility as an ideal; they see it as a genuine possibility in their own lives.

Of course, all this is about more than economics. For Britain has a cultural aversion to social mobility, too. Britons who manage to skip a few demographic categories usually inspire not admiration – as they might in the US – but ambivalence or even hostility. So while, in America, the Kleenex heiress or the Mars widow are happy to be known by the source of their fortune, their counterparts in Britain would be lampooned as hopelessly nouveau. The absurdity of people who have 'made it' financially being foolish enough to believe they have risen up the social scale is a source of huge amusement in Britain, and a staple of our popular culture. Think of sitcom character Hyacinth Bucket – who insists that she be called Bouquet. The entire joke rests on her desperation to be seen as middle-class; she knows that money alone is not good enough. Sitcomland's favourite pair of malapropism-prone wide boys – George Cole's Arfur Daley and David Jason's Del-Boy – get laughs because they, too, regularly dare venture beyond their station. When the fictional Derek Trotter finally did make his millions – discovering a precious timepiece in his lock-up – he became miserable. He missed the struggle of the old days. The message seemed to be: you can make a ton of dough, but in Britain you can never truly change rank. NBC's *Friends* may be middle-class, ABC's *Roseanne* low-income, but no US sitcom plays on the intricacies of status quite the way the British do. (American popular culture prefers to toy with race and ethnicity: think of Eddie Murphy's black man turned Wall Street banker in *Trading Places* or

Gregory Peck's *faux* Jew in *Gentleman's Agreement*.)

Our attitudes to the real-life rich and famous are tellingly different, too. Britons are famously afflicted by the tall poppy syndrome, the urge to cut down anyone who gets 'too big for their boots' or 'has ideas above their station' (to name but two English phrases inherently hostile to social mobility). Those who have made their own fortunes – from Andrew Lloyd Webber to Alan Sugar – fast become either joke- or hate-figures, exposed to a disdain that rarely descends upon the likes of Viscount Linley or the Duke of Westminster. It is as if we are wary of those who have dared skip over class boundaries, lines that are too deeply etched in the British landscape to be ignored.

The absence of a British Dream of social mobility might go some way to explaining the relatively weak emphasis our country has placed on mass education. In contrast with those first US meritocrats, who saw the classroom as ground zero in the battle for equality, Britain preferred a system which delivered an excellent service to the elite but not much to everyone else. Hence the public schools, which bestow an instant advantage on the children of those who can pay. (Progressive-minded, middle-class parents try to get round this basic unfairness by sending their children to state schools, but there a different injustice prevails: selection by house price, with 'good' areas enjoying good schools.)

A perennial target of the class warrior's ire are the two universities which dominate Britain's national elite. Graduates of Oxford and Cambridge – while just 2 per cent of the total university output – can pick up 40 per cent of the jobs on offer in the civil service and 73 per cent of those in the Foreign Office in a single year. Among ambassadors, law lords, appeal court judges and the quangocracy, Oxford and Cambridge still claim unassailable majorities. For the rigorous meritocrat, those figures do not, in themselves, represent a problem: elite institutions are quite tolerable, so long as they are open to those with the greatest talent, not just the 'right' background. Unfortunately, Oxbridge cannot quite make that boast. State schools account for no more than half of the annual intake, proof that fee-payers enjoy disproportionate success. Moreover, the state schools which send pupils to Oxford and Cambridge are often those in 'good', well-to-do areas. The middle class has retained a virtual lock on Oxbridge, suggesting that background is still as relevant as merit in the race for advancement in British life.

Perhaps most revealing of all is our relative lack of interest in nursery education. All committed egalitarians are hard-liners on this issue. Like the New York section of the Workingmen's Party, they realise that genuine social mobility requires an equal start in life, and that means nursery school. Yet Britain, which has more single or working mothers than most western European countries – and therefore a greater need – provides less nursery education than any of them. To be precise, in 1996 fewer than 50 per cent of British toddlers enjoyed a publicly financed place at a nursery school, compared with 77 per cent in Germany and 95 per cent in France. In the US the federal Head Start programme, providing pre-school learning to those who cannot afford it privately, is almost sacrosanct. Few politicians of either left or right would dare challenge its claim on public funds.

There is, perhaps, some compensation for Britain's historic lack of mobility and the durability of the country's class system. While America lacked a High Tory elite and a permanent proletariat – and so was denied paternalism and socialism – we had both. For centuries Britain was blessed with a patrician class who wanted to care for those below, and a *hoi polloi* who looked to their betters for sustenance. Such terms are Greek to the Americans, but in Britain they have defined much of national life. In the latter half of the twentieth century these two classes – embodied by the Conservatives' Rab Butler and Labour's Hugh Gaitskell – joined forces to form the consensus known as Butskellism. Together they constructed and sustained a welfare state which – along with a mild redistribution of wealth – sought, if not exactly equality, then at least a slight narrowing of the gap between rich and poor.

The goal this approach never aimed at was social mobility. While the Americans strove to open up the upper reaches of society to those below, Britons concentrated on cushioning those at the bottom – hence Britain's post-war history of spending healthily on welfare in one form or other, but relatively much less on education. One Nation Tories of the old school regarded it as their aristocratic duty to improve the lot of those less fortunate than themselves, but they were not particularly keen to shift them up the social order. Intriguingly, many of the early Labourites felt the same way. They called for more pay and better services for the working man – but they did not insist upon his right to become middle or upper class. Such a right would, of course, have amounted to the effective elimination of fixed classes. The fact that neither paternalists nor socialists demanded any such thing meant that both groups – including the most passionate self-proclaimed egalitarians – ended up upholding and reinforcing Britain's class system.

Indeed, several of early socialism's greatest luminaries shared with the English aristocracy a distinctly condescending view of the common man, one which contained no desire to see him scale the social ladder. One has only to scan the writings of the Webbs, George Bernard Shaw and assorted Fabians – several of whom also flirted with eugenic theory and unashamedly racist attitudes toward immigrants. So while Shaw mused that 'the overthrow of the aristocrat has created the necessity for the Superman', the Webbs yearned for a society dominated by a scientific elite, with power in the hands not of the masses, but of the expert. As Beatrice Webb wrote in her diary in December 1894, 'We have little faith in the "average sensual man"; we do not believe that he can do much more than describe his grievances, we do not think that he can prescribe the remedies.' Many of these public-school socialists believed the greatest contribution they could make was their own intelligence – in short supply among the proletarian 'nitwits and bozos' who then made up the Labour Party. The leading Communist and editor of the *Daily Worker*, J.B.S. Haldane, had little time for 'the curious dogma of the equality of man'. As far as he was concerned, 'we are not born equal, far from it'. The young Bertrand Russell was so anxious that the high-calibre gene pool of the elite should not be muddied by the working class, he suggested that the state issue colour-coded 'procreation tickets': those who dared breed with holders of a different-coloured ticket would face a heavy fine. In an unpublished 1913 essay called 'Population', the father of Labour economics, John Maynard Keynes, argued for legalised birth control on the grounds that it would reduce the 'proportion of the population born from those who from drunkenness or ignorance or extreme lack of prudence are not only incapable of virtue but also incapable of that degree of prudence which is involved in the use of [contraceptive] checks'. For Keynes the working class consisted of men and women too drunk or stupid to know what was good for them. Such prejudices were not so shocking in early Labour circles, not when the conflict between left and right often resembled a civil war within the English ruling class. A leading firebrand of the time once quipped that he only joined the Communist Party because he did not make the First XI at Eton.

Until 1979, then, the British ideal was that the 'haves' would help the 'have-nots', with the government as the most reliable middleman. The arrival of Margaret Thatcher destroyed that consensus. She took on the forces of paternalism – the wets in her own party, the BBC, the Church of England, the universities, even on occasion the House of Lords and the royal family – and set out to crush socialism, declaring the trade unions nothing less than 'the enemy within'. The Thatcherite vision proclaimed that government would no longer act as a vast steamroller, levelling the playing field of life. The rich would have less of their income redistributed to the poor via taxes and the welfare state. Thatcher herself may have gone, but the essence of her creed remains in place.

What is left is a gap where a British ideal of equality should be. The old, semi-feudal approach – where those on high protected those below – has all but vanished. Perhaps we need a new egalitarianism, one which fits the real world but which might also inspire idealism and conviction. The American belief in genuine social mobility – where the journey from rags to riches is not only possible but encouraged and celebrated – might be the right place to start.

7

From Fruit Salad to American Pie

WHITNEY HOUSTON ONLY had to speak, and her audience would cry out. 'That's right,' they chorused, like a congregation at one of the city's countless black churches. 'Hmm-hmm, say it, girl.'

Except this was not a church, but a cinema. And Whitney Houston was not preaching, but starring in *Waiting to Exhale*, the movie version of a novel about four black professional women and their search for a good man. A scene that had been played out across America was now underway in Washington's Union Station cinema. 'Go girl!' cried the audience in unison as Bernadine – played by Angela Bassett – emptied out her cheating, no-good husband's wardrobe, dumped all his Armani suits in his open-top BMW, splashed on a full can of petrol, struck a match and torched the lot. 'That ain't right,' muttered some of the men in the cinema. But the women were unanimous. 'Do it, girlfriend,' they told the on-screen Bernadine, who had just learned her husband was leaving her – for a white woman.

For the next ninety minutes the cinema never had more than a half-second of silence. '*Ha*llo,' the audience called as love interest Wesley Snipes first came into view. 'Swing, girl,' they urged as the portly Gloria wiggled her way past a new suitor. Every twist of the plot was greeted with loud commentary from the people in the stalls. 'I wouldn't shake that man's hand,' heckled one woman, as Bernadine made peace with her ex after winning a hefty alimony settlement. And if it was not words, it would be whooping, clapping and cheering – from the opening titles to the final credits.

Waiting to Exhale was a rare phenomenon. African-American

women hailed the film as 'our Million Man March', their answer to the all-male rally that had filled Washington a few months earlier. Groups of black women – mothers and daughters, friends and colleagues, church groups and book clubs – had been packing out cinemas, engaging in the call-and-response of a revivalist meeting. To an outsider, it seemed a remarkable event.

But to the managers and ushers of the Union Station cinema, this was business as usual. They have got used to the audience-participation tradition of the mainly black community they serve. A sign headlined 'YAKETY-YAK!' reminds movie-goers of the 'two-shushes' rule: be warned about noise twice and you are out. There is even a little cartoon just before the main feature, showing a stick man made of a reel of film. He does a little jig before placing his finger over his lips. 'Shushhhhhhh!' he says, before the words 'SILENCE IS GOLDEN' materialise above him.

You do not see that message so often in the Janus, the Uptown or the Avalon – or any of the other movie theatres in the mainly white North West quadrant of Washington. Cinema noise is apparently not such a problem there. And there are hundreds of little differences like that, separating the two communities who share America's capital. Black Washington has shops, fast-food outlets, even hairdressing salons that would never be seen in white North West – and vice versa. That is how it looks across much of the US – black and white Americans living wholly different, separate lives.

Even that most American of pastimes – watching television – is affected by a kind of apartheid, with blacks and whites tuning in for entirely different programmes. A striking study of TV ratings found that the top ten shows watched by whites and the equivalent list for blacks had not a single show in common. Not one. When the list was expanded to the top twenty, only one programme made it on to both the black and white charts: *Monday Night Football*. So *Home Improvement*, the sitcom about the host of a television DIY show, could simultaneously be the favourite among whites and rank a lowly twenty-nine in the black countdown. Meanwhile, the all-black *Living Single* was the top-rated show among African-Americans – but came in 103rd among whites. *Martin* and *Moesha* have almost no white faces, while *Friends*, *Seinfeld* and *Roseanne* feature no one who is black. The trend is so pronounced that even programmes which are regarded as US national institutions – like the Sunday evening news magazine *60 Minutes* – are, in reality, all but unseen by 12 per cent of the population. The advertisers have not taken long to adjust to the situation. Burger King and Coca-Cola have realised that to reach America's 30 million black consumers they now have to produce special 'black' ads, with African-American actors and voice-overs, for screening during black programmes – commercials which the dedicated *Frasier* or *X-Files* fan might never see. If television is the way modern societies communicate, black and white Americans are simply not talking to each other.

But the problem is not confined to TV. The races are also divided by economics – with the median white income nearly $13,000 larger than the equivalent figure for blacks – and by geography, each community living in separate neighbourhoods from the other, visiting its own shopping malls, buying its own products. Perhaps the starkest indicator is romance. While America's other ethnic minorities are marrying across communal lines, only 12 per cent of new black marriages in 1993 involved a white partner – and that was hailed as a four-fold increase on the 2 per cent figure recorded in 1970.

None of this will come as any surprise to those who believe race shows America's ugliest face: America as the land of the ghetto and gangsta rap, lynch mobs and the Klan, Louis Farrakhan and the LA riots. It is the nation which fought a civil war over the enslavement of blacks, enforced *de facto* apartheid until the 1960s and lives with an unofficial version of it even now. Indeed, race seems to invalidate every one of America's claims to be an enlightened society. The US brags about the vigour of its democracy – yet black Americans say they are effectively disenfranchised, with millions unregistered and shut out to this day. Americans boast that theirs is a society in which heredity does not count – yet for 400 years black Americans have been judged on the single feature they inherit: the colour of their skin. They are told they live in a classless society – yet they have historically been treated as something even worse than a class: a caste.

The heart of the problem lies in the exceptional nature of African-American history. Uniquely in a population which is self-selected, black Americans did not *choose* to come to America. They were dragged there in chains. They were not fleeing persecution or famine, like the Jews or the Irish, or chasing their dreams like the Italians or the Poles. They were plucked from their homes, stashed in the holds of slave ships, and sold into bondage. They did not sail in the *Mayflower* or gaze adoringly at the Statue of Liberty, the lady with the ice-cream cone torch who welcomed in generations of refugees from every corner of the globe. Malcolm X borrowed a lyric from Cole Porter to say it better than anyone: 'We didn't land on Plymouth Rock. Plymouth Rock landed on us.'

The pain has not faded with time. Black men wear T-shirts that come straight to the point: 'OVER 400 YEARS OF SLAVERY, YOU'RE DAMN RIGHT I GOT AN ATTITUDE.' African-American politicians still draw on the imagery of the plantation, the Big House and the 'massah'. Spike Lee calls his film company Forty Acres and a Mule, after the compensation package promised to the four million slaves freed after the Civil War. One group of campaigners has gone further, demanding that the offer be honoured at today's prices – precisely $198,149 for each black American alive today. The National Coalition of Blacks for Reparations in America, or N'cobra, has filed a series of federal law suits claiming that the US government should make up for the economic exploitation of their ancestors and for the 'fundamental injustice, cruelty, brutality and inhumanity' of captivity. Some descendants of the slaves refuse to pay income tax, insisting that it is the state which owes *them* money. 'This country got rich off our sweat and we have never been paid what's due. It's time to set things right,' explained seventy-year-old Valena Conley, the great-grandchild of an enslaved cotton-picker, then seeking $110 million in compensation. 'There is a sickness among our people,' explained N'cobra's Charles King, 'a sickness of the mind that is a residual of our state of bondage.'

If the United States was a Shakespearean character, slavery would be its tragic flaw. It was America's greatest crime, one whose reverberations echo down the centuries, felt even now. Some sociologists believe every one of America's current pathologies can be traced back to the black–white divide. But it was a tragic flaw in a deeper sense, too. For America's treatment of its black minority marked a fateful exception to an otherwise noble ideal. As Jesse Jackson told the crowds at the Million Man March, the United States' founding document originally applied to white property-owning males only. 'There is a structural malfunction in the Constitution,' he thundered. 'That's why we have a burden today of two Americas, one half slave, one half free.' Jackson was not saying the Constitution was worthless. Quite the contrary: he was lamenting the fact that America's sacred text of liberation and equality did not apply to everyone. The Founders themselves were aware of their blind spot on race, and how dearly it would come to cost them. In 1781 Thomas Jefferson contemplated the bondage in which white men held blacks and wrote, 'I tremble for my country when I reflect that God is just.'

Jefferson and Jackson agree: it was not the American ideal that was at fault – simply black Americans' exclusion from it. This is a crucial distinction. For although the race war between black and white is the United States' gravest defect, it should not obscure an American ideal which has made the US the most ethnically diverse society on the planet – and the most patriotic one to boot. The American brand of national identity has both unified the country and lent it a sturdy form of 'can-do' optimism – surprisingly free of the aggression associated with nationalism elsewhere in the world. The key lies in the way Americans see themselves.

Waving the Flag, Building the Barn

It was the third of July, the day before Independence Day. The location was not grand, just Room 507 of the Arlington, Virginia branch of the US Immigration and Naturalization Service – a standard-issue office building, on an ordinary shopping street. With a lectern at one end, the American flag at its side, this was the 'ceremony room'. Here a collection of strangers from strange lands would incant an oath, a pledge and an anthem – and so become citizens of the United States.

There were sixty-eight of them, their faces as diverse as the country they were joining: an aged Vietnamese man, his face creased like fine paper, a young Dutch blonde, a black Muslim woman, a Yorkshire housewife. Before the afternoon was out, each would become an American.

'Welcome, new citizens!' a clerk called out, like a real-life Lady Liberty. The room was so crammed, friends and relatives were kept outside, filling the corridor. One man managed to squeeze through to take a picture of the six-year-old Albanian boy his daughter had just adopted. The new grandfather presented the child with a balloon, bright with the stars and stripes.

An official took the register, which sounded like a roll-call at the United Nations: an Abdullah and a Fernando, a Murphy and a Kim. He checked they had all gone through the requisite interview where they had declared, among other things, that they had neither sold their body for sexual pleasure, nor been members of a communist party nor wanted a dictator to rule the US. The new citizens had swotted up on all this in advance, thanks to a government manual explaining the basics of American civics, history and culture – including pictures of the Liberty Bell and the Lincoln Memorial and lots of little quizzes to test their knowledge. They were told to put all that democratic learning to good use and register to vote. 'The forms are just downstairs.'

Then came the moment to cast the magic spells which would turn this ethnic fruit salad into American pie. The high priest and sorcerer would be the branch's district director, William Carroll. He began by telling the citizens-to-be that he had personally naturalised 72,000 immigrants. 'I know an awful lot of you out there,' he said. 'I love being out and about, saying hello, seeing how you're doing and how you're succeeding here in America.'

But today, he promised, would be an especially wonderful day. 'Really a new birthday, a *re*-birthday in a new homeland, that offers to you as new citizens the great gifts of freedom and liberty.' He reassured them that he, too, was a product of immigration, a second-generation American, half-Irish, half-Italian, raised on the fifth storey of a brownstone in south Brooklyn. Like them, he grew up speaking a foreign language. Like them, his family ate food their neighbours found strange.

They called it 'worms' or 'grass', but now, he said, Americans pay 'top dollar' to eat calamari and pesto. In the gentlest way, Carroll was telling his audience to endure the taunts and insults that might come their way; for they would pass. He recalled that his grandfather used to say: 'I could have gone to Spain but I never could have become Spanish; I could have gone to England but I could never have become an Englishman.' And yet, Carroll explained, 'he truly became an American in the 1890s, as you will truly become Americans today.'

It was an extraordinary sight. Immigrants, elsewhere tolerated and often loathed, were being embraced by an official of the United States government. Dark-skinned foreigners were not being cast out, but ushered in. They were not all young, skilled and employable, but included children, the old and the infirm – people who elsewhere would be rejected as burdens on society. William Carroll went further. He told these newcomers not only how lucky they were to be accepted as Americans, but how lucky America was to have them. 'This is a wonderful opportunity for these United States. Because it is people like yourselves who continue to make this nation the most prosperous in the history of mankind. We've received outstanding cultural benefits and wonderful intellectual gains from people such as yourselves.' He knew how hard it had been 'to leave the land of your heritage, the land where your ancestors are buried'. But now he wanted them 'to not just live in America but, please, become part of America. I know it's hard to believe, but *you* are America'.

Then, their right hand over their heart, their English broken, they sang out the anthem of their new country. 'Oh, say, can you see, by the dawn's early light . . .' There were tears in every eye, a lump in every throat. Finally, the new citizens were handed their green certificates of naturalisation; they looked like A4-size dollar bills. Janice Green from Doncaster said she felt more emotional than she expected, that now she realised it was 'goodbye England'. Birgitte D'Antonio from Maastricht in Holland was thrilled to be part of the 'best country' in the world. Fatjon, the Albanian, played with his balloon.

As they turned to leave, William Carroll had one more request. 'Retain your culture,' he urged them. 'It's very important. It's really the tapestry that makes America. I certainly wouldn't give up my Italian or my Irish culture – especially my Italian food, as you can see from my size! Good luck and happy Fourth of July.'

It is hard to square that little scene – and the thousand like it, played out in US immigration offices every day of the week – with the history of racial tension between American blacks and whites. William Carroll's words of inclusion, not only tolerating diversity but welcoming it, could have been written by a campaigner against racism and prejudice – and yet here they were, spoken warmly by a government bureaucrat. How is that possible in a land where white once enslaved black and where the two still live separate lives? The answer lies in America's golden rule – the one to which black America was the fateful exception.

The Canadian-born writer Michael Ignatieff has drawn the contrast between 'ethnic' and 'civic' nationalism, defining the first as the primitive desire to reawaken some mythologised past and the second as the reformist urge to build a new society, one which will enable its people to live *in* the world, not apart from it. American national identity is clearly a stranger to Ignatieff's first category. It cares nothing for blood-and-soil mumbo-jumbo; there is no such thing as an 'ethnic American'. Instead Americanness is an *idea*. In the words of G.K. Chesterton, 'America is the only nation in the world that is founded on a creed.' It is significant that America's greatest symbol – the Statue of Liberty – is a monument to an ideal, not a person. As one of America's foremost political pundits, E.J. Dionne, writes: 'It is the rare patriotic orator who emphasises the bloodlines, backgrounds or ethnicity of the Founders. They are celebrated – and thus we celebrate ourselves – for sharing not blood, but ideas: ideas about human freedom, self-government, individual initiative and mutual assistance.'

Americans are reminded daily that their society did not emerge from some ancestral murk, but was deliberately *created* in a revolutionary, ideological act (most choose to forget that an entire culture already lived in the 'New' World). To requote those words of Abraham Lincoln's, 'Four score and seven years ago our fathers brought forth on this continent a new nation, conceived in Liberty, and dedicated to the proposition that all men are created equal.' It is a striking thought: unlike most societies, the United States had a start date and a *reason* – a project which defines and coheres American national identity to this day.

For Americans regard themselves as more than a lump of people who happen to share the same land mass. They see each other as members of a society created for a purpose, a team bound together by a common goal. Hollywood captured the idea in the movie *Witness*, the Harrison Ford thriller set among the Pennsylvania Amish. Americans still talk about the barn-building scene, where the entire community joined together to raise a new structure in a matter of hours. In that Amish village, American cinema-goers liked to imagine they saw the entire United States. Even now, more than 220 years on, Americans regard their revolution as ongoing, a work in progress. Hence the words of Vice-President Al Gore to the pumped-up crowd that gathered on the steps of the Old State House in Little Rock on election night in November 1996: 'Add your voices and your talents to our grand experiment in self-government.' Or the sparkling rhetoric of that long-ago Democrat, Adlai Stevenson: 'This is our heritage and this is our true glory; we are a people, I tell you, that is just beginning its high adventure on this continent.' No matter that the nation is in its third century; it is still an experiment, just beginning.

The effect is extremely potent, inducing in Americans a sense of themselves as a single, coherent community. Ralph Reed, the boy-faced former mastermind of the Christian Coalition, used to insist on the right of religious folk to air their views in the 'public square' – imagining the United States as one giant village. Televised encounters of politicians and voters are called 'town meetings'. In one such event at San Diego during the 1996 presidential campaign, a woman asked Messrs Clinton and Dole how 'we are going to bring the country back together, be all faces around the table, the new American family'. Never mind that there are 250 million of them; she imagined they would all have room. Even the way Americans say their own name so often – from TV shows called *American Journal, America's Most Wanted* and *America's Funniest Home Videos* to car ads for garages claiming to be 'America's favourite dealer' – is part of the same habit. It first strikes the outsider as naked jingoism or, at best, a mark of a nation insecure in its own identity, like a three year old who delights in shouting his own name. But, like those images of the public square or the national kitchen table, the linguistic tic of self-naming is really an assertion that America is a society – fractious as a family, but bound together by a common aim.

What America enjoys is the patriotism of common purpose – a rare phenomenon with one particularly appealing quality. It is an inclusive faith. Bloodlines, birthplace, even language are not required. All an outsider need do is join the ongoing American mission, the 'high adventure' – simply by signing up for Chesterton's 'creed'. In the words of President Clinton: 'If you believe in the values of the Constitution, the Bill of Rights, the Declaration of Independence, if you're willing to work hard and play by the rules, you are part of our family, and we're proud to be with you.' It is that simple, spelled out in black and white.

The civic nationalism of the United States enables it to regard new arrivals, like those crammed into Room 507 of the Arlington branch of the INS, not as a threat or potential dilution of the country's character, but as new recruits to the national project. That is why they must first mug up on the basics of democracy and liberty, the rudiments of the 'creed'. Indeed, newcomers occupy a central place in the American myth. The US prides itself on being a nation of immigrants, with its foremost symbol, the Statue of Liberty, standing not only for freedom but refuge and welcome. We have all seen the flickering archive footage showing boatloads of ragged European refugees, their faces drawn from a hellish voyage, craning to get a glimpse of the colossus of New York harbour. Inscribed at the base of the statue, the sonnet words of Emma Lazarus:

> *Give me your tired, your poor,*
> *Your huddled masses, yearning to breathe*
> *free,*
> *The wretched refuse of your teeming shore.*
> *Send these, the homeless, tempest-tossed to me,*
> *I lift my lamp beside the golden door.*

To this day, America casts itself as a promised land where the world's dispossessed will be gathered in like exiles. The great migrations are commemorated and celebrated, officially and in popular culture. From *West Side Story* to *The Jazz Singer*, the American popular song has lauded the immigrant journey, whether in Leonard Bernstein's 'I Like it Here in America' or Neil Diamond's 'Coming to America'. In the 1990s, movies like *Mi Familia* or *The Perez Family* have come forward to tell the stories of the newest migrants, the Hispanic-Americans. But the older communities are not forgotten. In 1995, the 150th anniversary of the potato famine was marked with more zeal in the US than in any country outside Ireland. Lectures, exhibitions and academic forums were convened wherever any of the 44 million Americans who claim Irish lineage live, each retelling the story of the famine as *American* history – explaining how the potato blight compelled up to 1.8 million Irish to flee to the New World. It is perhaps no surprise that one of the United States' most visited attractions is the museum on Ellis Island – the nineteenth-century clearing house for newcomers from Ireland, Italy and all of old Europe. The now restored medical examination rooms, holding areas and baggage halls bustle with families keen to see where their migrant journey ended – and where their American journey began. It is as if the US has developed a kind of reverse imperialism: instead of conquering the many peoples of the world, it has allowed itself to be conquered by them. One geographer has described the United States as the first 'world colony', one land settled by all the peoples of the planet.

Admittedly, there have been lapses from the ideal, most notoriously in the run-up to the Second World War when too many refugees from Nazi Germany were turned away. In recent years, too, there have been moves to curb immigration, especially in the border states of California, Texas and Arizona. But these efforts have tended to focus on illegal immigrants, the wetbacks who cross the Rio Grande in the dead of night, not immigration *per se*. Besides, most of these attempts have been overturned in the courts. Overall, the United States continues to welcome legal new arrivals at a rate that puts other nations in the shade. In 1996 alone, America processed a record 1.3 million new citizens – 0.5 per cent of the American population.

Immigrant roots are often a source of embarrassment in other countries: Jan Ludvik Hoch felt obliged to morph into Robert

Maxwell, and Roland Walter Fuhrhop into 'Tiny' Rowland, lest anyone doubt they were truly British. So did Lithuanian-born Larushka Mischa Skikne, reborn as actor Laurence Harvey and Ukranian Louis Winogradsky, who recast himself as TV mogul Lew Grade. Even our very own royal family sought to hide their foreign origins: how else did the Battenburgs become Mountbattens? It is not that way in America. There the Warsaw-born John Shalikashvili could rise to the top of the US military and feel no pressure to pasteurise his name into one his fellow countrymen could pronounce more easily. Shalikashvili's predecessor as chairman of the joint chiefs of staff was equally prone to boast, not hide, his origins outside the United States. 'My parents came to this country as immigrants over seventy years ago,' proclaimed retired general and Gulf war hero Colin Powell at the 1996 Republican convention in San Diego. 'They came here, as had millions of others, with nothing but hope, a willingness to work hard and a desire to use the opportunities given them by their new land – a land which they came to love with all their hearts . . . They found their dream in America, and they passed that dream on to their children. Here, tonight, over seven decades after they landed on these shores, their son has been given the privilege of addressing the Republican party.' The general won huge applause, his speech an eloquent reminder of the romance Americans attach to the act of immigration. 'New land', 'dream', 'these shores' – it is the language of fairytale. It is hard to imagine the British army being led by a black child of immigrants. Harder still to picture him at the Tory party conference, reminding everyone of his origins. Yet here was the equivalent event, taking place on a hot August night in California.

For a permanent rhetoric of inclusion prevails in America, one which celebrates ethnic diversity as a net asset. It is often clumsy, often contrived, but America's public conversation strains itself to bring in, not keep out. In December shopkeepers say 'Happy Holidays', lest 'Merry Christmas' make non-Christians feel excluded. When the US Postal Service issued its two stamps for Christmas 1996, it made sure one of them showed the multi-coloured candles of the menorah, the traditional candelabrum of Chanukah. The American post office said it planned the Festival of Lights stamp as the first in a series 'designed to honour the country's increasing cultural and ethnic diversity'. Even the cheesiest TV ads make sure the faces on show are Hispanic, Chinese and Italian as well as milky white. Political correctness is part of it, but advertisers also know that an ethnic mix conveys a sense of vitality, inclusion and, dare it be said, colour. President Clinton said he wanted his first cabinet to 'look like America'. Sure enough, he appointed lots of women, several African-Americans and a couple of Hispanics.

Inevitably, perhaps, some Americans fear immigrants' pride in their own heritage has gone too far, so that now there is more emphasis on what divides US citizens than on what unites them. They mourn the arrival of the hyphenated American – whether it is of the Japanese-American or Irish-American variety – preferring plain old 'Americans'. According to these critics, the US has strayed from its historic role as a melting pot, a society which could mix a hundred old identities and forge a new one. For them, the 'diversity' ethos has led to balkanisation, as ethnic groups develop such strong, separate identities they quarantine themselves away from the rest of society. Pessimists cite the rising number of American campuses where students from minorities choose to live only with each other, in a system of voluntary segregation. Rhode Island's Brown University has a Harambee House for African-Americans, its name taken from the Swahili for 'the coming together of community'. There is also an Hispanic House, French House, Slavic House, East Asian House and German House. Campuses all over the US have likewise bowed to students' demands and organised dorms by race and ethnicity. The historian Arthur Schlesinger has warned of 'tribalisation', while one senior Republican urged Americans to look to Quebec and even Bosnia to see where all this sharpening of ethnic identities would lead.

Nevertheless, there is plenty of evidence that the melting pot is still in good working order. People may panic that 17 million Americans count Spanish as their first language, 1.2 million speak Chinese and 800,000 Tagalog. But the more important figure is the one that shows 97 per cent of Americans speak English well. For all the angst about Bosnification, only 1 per cent of all US federal documents are printed in languages other than English. Moreover, with the exception of the black community, Americans are marrying out of their own racial or religious group more than they are within it. Jews are typical, recording intermarriage rates of up to 57 per cent.

Along with the melting pot, the US fulfils another of its cherished national myths: its promise to turn immigrants' rags into riches, to sweep them from dockside to poolside in a generation. Statistics show that immigrants – including the West Indians who in Britain are often the butt of racist accusations of indolence – are more prosperous after fifteen years in the US than native-born Americans of the same socio-economic category. One example: 40 per cent of Mexican-Americans, a community composed almost entirely of immigrants, are now in white-collar jobs or beyond. The US egalitarian ideal of social mobility is realised daily by the new arrivals who come to America – and make it.

The US looked kindly on diversity from the very start. The Declaration of Independence included a plea for more immigrants to come and help build the new republic. In 1790 George Washington told the Jews of Newport, Rhode Island, that all Americans shared equal 'liberty of conscience' but that the Jews would not be tolerated – because 'toleration . . . of one class of people . . . by another' was an inherently patronising idea which had no place in a free United States. The Jews would not be second-class citizens, but as American as anyone else. For the Founders, it was straightforward. Americanness was not about race or roots, but membership of the society and sub-scription to the creed. Of course, such a definition automatically shuts out anyone deemed to be an enemy of the American project: in the eyes of the McCarthyite witch-hunters of the 1950s, Communists were un-American – never mind that they were born and raised in the United States. But mainly this civic, rather than ethnic, identity serves to include not exclude. So Hispanic teenagers and Asian-American kids can wear stars-and-stripes sweatshirts – and mean it. They feel no confusion, for they know what American values are: they are them.

The great American error – the one for which they have paid in the blood of a civil war, a thousand lynchings and two centuries of racial tension – was to extend this ideal only to those who *chose* to come to the United States as immigrants, shutting out those who were dragged into the country against their will, as cargo (along with those who were already there). Black and Native Americans were never given the chance to sign up to the 'creed', to join in the high adventure. Their fate was to be the exception to an unprecedentedly humane rule.

For those who were and are included, America's patriotism of common purpose is strong indeed. The camaraderie of a collective mission helps explain the poll numbers which show Americans among the most patriotic nations on earth. Gallup found Americans were more willing to fight if their country were at war, and generally more patriotic, than citizens of thirty other nations. In recent surveys, 75 per cent say they are proud to be Americans, with that figure rising to 98 per cent among young Americans. Four out of five Americans go further, saying they want to do something to serve their country.

More telling than any statistic, though, are the displays of national feeling. You cannot miss them – starting with the flag. It is everywhere, hanging in every public building and plenty of private homes. It is on Ralph Lauren sweaters and a thousand movie posters. It stands to attention in the school principal's office, and watches over concerts, ballgames and conferences, like a silent blessing. From the front porch to the rear bumper, the Americans display it and never tire of it. For them, the stars-and-stripes is a thing of beauty and enduring style. As the painter Jasper Johns proved, it needs no embellishment. Indeed, Old Glory is handled with quasi-religious reverence. As anyone who has seen a military funeral will tell you, a meticulous ritual exists for the folding of the flag – corner by corner, so that not one inch of it should ever be profaned by a touch of the earth. Flag-burning remains perhaps the most provocative gesture available to any American rebel – tantamount to spitting on a Bible.

The national anthem inspires similar devotion. Stand with the crowds at any public gathering and see how they sing their hearts out. Not for them the head-bowed mumbling of other countries; they really sing, belting out the words: 'Oh, say, does that star-spangled banner yet wave, O'er the Land of the Freeeeeee, And the home of the — braaaave' The crowd holds still for a second, shakes from its brief immersion in national consciousness and raises its eyes – its mood palpably lifted. The flag, the anthem, even the *name* of their country can make Americans teary-eyed. A lazy advertising copywriter or politician's aide knows the most reliable applause button is simply the word 'America'. As a casual expression of approval, whether for a delicious ice-cream in New Jersey or a spectacular sunset in New Mexico, Americans will say, 'Is this a great country or what?' Most of them truly believe America is the finest place on the planet, God's own country. Hardly any of them ever leave, and those that do usually come back. In the language of advertising, it is the ultimate in brand loyalty, with the stars-and-stripes as the definitive corporate logo.

The American brand of civic or idealistic nationalism has an extra ingredient, besides inclusivity. America's status as the *created* society, coupled with the belief that the nation is engaged in an ongoing project, gives its people an extraordinary sense of control over their own destiny. 'We built this place,' Americans seem to say. 'We can rebuild it how we please.' From left to right, Americans are firm in the belief that each generation shapes its country anew. When the star of the Iran-contra scandal, Colonel Oliver North, sought to become the US senator for Virginia – so joining the very body he had defied – the phone number for his Republican campaign HQ was 703-CHANGE-IT. When the liberal lion of New York, Mario Cuomo, stirred the 1984 Democratic convention in San Francisco it was by sketching a vision of a better America and by insisting that, 'It will happen – *if we make it happen.*' In this conviction, both sides are faithful to America's founding creed, whose central message one British academic has aptly summed up as, 'You don't have to receive a world: you can make a world.'

It is a cliché to describe America as the can-do society, but this is why the phrase has meaning. In surveys, clear majorities of Americans believe there is no limit to what their nation can do. Nearly two thirds agree that, 'As Americans we can always find a way to solve our problems and get what we want,' and well over half believe there are no 'real limits to growth in this country today'. Individuals share this gospel of possibility, unable to see any limit to their potential. The sheer energy and ambition of Americans has been well documented, their unabashed conviction that only hard work stands between them and their dreams. Underpinning it is the collective conviction that Americans themselves are on a forward journey, to a bright future of their own making. Thus Americans can fight and win two world wars, put a man on the moon and bag enough Nobel prizes to boast a new American Nobel-ity – but still believe their best is yet to come. Few understood this faith better than Ronald Reagan, who used a catchphrase from Al Jolson to tap into Americans' precious sense of future possibility. With an encouraging punch of the arm and an avuncular wink, Reagan would promise Americans what they believed to be true: 'You ain't seen nothin' yet.'

Peaceniks and Globocops

That's all very well for the Americans. Perhaps their patriotism *is* idealistic, inclusive and optimistic at home. But that has surely not been the record abroad. In the mind of the average British liberal, at least, the US has a sorry history of invading small countries, meddling in Latin America and the Middle East, kicking ass and generally acting as an unelected world policeman – Globocop. People saw the Americans bomb Tripoli, invade Grenada and cover Greenham Common with cruise missiles; they remember Ronnie Reagan blithely joking in a radio address that he was launching an all-out assault on the Soviet Union: 'We begin bombing in five minutes.'

And yet aggressive militarism does not feature much in the real-life United States – not even among the men and women of the US military. A visit to the Marine Corps base at Camp Lejeune, North Carolina, is instructive, revealing lines of young men and women, wrapped in identical winter gear, trudging in formation across a waterlogged field, each rhythmically piercing the ground with a metal pole. It looks like some weird Highland sport, or a mass litter clear-up involving lines of volunteers with pogo-sticks. It is actually an exercise the Marines used to conduct in Norway, to learn how to find the body of a fallen comrade, buried under snow. But cutbacks have meant fewer trips to Norway – and resourceful commanders have had to make do with imaginary snow back home.

In the old days, the soldiers of Camp Lejeune practised such things in readiness for battle with the Communist bear in the snowy wastes of Europe. Now so straightforward a war seems fanciful, obsolete outside the storylines of Tom Clancy. Just ask the pole-prodders. Do they imagine an enemy when they are acting out this scenario? 'No,' replies Sergeant Barbara Bruington. Does she know who her enemy is? 'Honestly?' she asks. 'No.'

Still, it seems a good life at Camp Lejeune. The houses are neat, there are several health clubs and a cinema showing films that are only slightly out of date. Despite the name, Camp Stores do not consist of a tin shack containing blankets and boots, but a swank American shopping mall. Known as the MWR – Morale, Welfare, Recreation – it contains everything from Burger King to Estée Lauder. What is missing on the base are gung-ho spirit and bloodlust. 'In the old days, we knew who was the good guy,' said Sgt Bruington. 'Now, a lot of times, when the wars come up we don't even know what we're fighting for.' The military top brass had made no secret of its lukewarm enthusiasm for the most recent missions – nation-building in Somalia, upholding democracy in Haiti. The soldiers themselves seemed just as tepid about their emerging role as part peacekeeper, part fire-fighter. One section at Camp Lejeune had just learned that of thirty eligible recruits, none had chosen to re-enlist.

On this point, the people in uniform are marching in step with the civilians they are paid to defend. For the knee-jerk, 1980s image of the Americans as latter-day imperialists, anxious to kick some foreign butt, looks woefully wide of the mark. The truth is, Americans do not really want to go anywhere – especially not now that the communist 'threat' is gone. Operation Restore Hope, the 1993 mission to save the starving of Somalia, is a case in point. The moment eighteen US Rangers were killed – and their naked bodies dragged through the streets of Mogadishu – the venture was all but over. Popular support, once at 84 per cent, simply evaporated. Once US lives are at risk, most Americans are extremely reluctant to get involved. In the language of the military analysts, the only acceptable use of force today is the 'zero-casualty' mission. Politicians speak of the 'Dover test' – Dover being the air force base where body bags are brought home for burial. These days very few missions pass the Dover test.

So while British troops were despatched to the Gulf for Desert Storm and to Bosnia with barely a peep of public dissent – the politicians sent them, and off they went – in America, George Bush had to fight for months to persuade his countrymen to repel the aggression of Saddam Hussein. While the British parliament rolled over in a show of the 'bipartisanship' invoked in all overseas crises, the US Congress was distinctly wobbly – with the Bush White House obliged to offer multiple assurances that force would only be used as a final resort. The Senate's most heavyweight voices on military matters – including the chairman of the armed services committee – all voted against the use of arms.

The pundits call this US allergy to military entanglements the Vietnam Syndrome. After that trauma, Americans fear any foreign adventure could fast become a 'quagmire', just like Vietnam. The phrase was bandied around in 1994 when President Clinton urged Americans to intervene militarily in Haiti and again in 1995 when the administration encountered fierce resistance to US involvement in the former Yugoslavia.

But this aversion to armed action actually pre-dates the Vietnam war. A study by Sol Tax of the University of Chicago concluded that the war in Indochina only aroused the *fourth* biggest opposition movement in US history: huge numbers of Americans had previously refused to fight in the anti-British war of 1812, the Civil War, the First World War and Korea. Peace movements have existed since the republic's birth and, until relatively recently, conscientious objection was almost exclusively an American phenomenon. Moreover, when Americans do eventually go to war, they have to be convinced a moral purpose is at stake. Mere national interest is not good enough. In Somalia it was feeding the hungry, in Haiti the removal of a brutal dictatorship, in Bosnia the halting of a second genocide in Europe. Seymour Martin Lipset attributes this moralistic, 'utopian' approach to foreign policy to the Protestant, sectarian roots of the country. The American Protestants – with their grass roots congregations, rather than state-backed hierarchies – have always demanded individuals obey their consciences, not the state. Wars have to be sold to them as moral missions – fighting what Ronald Reagan called the Evil Empire, for example – otherwise they will not go. In this context it is easy to understand the American bafflement at British attitudes to Northern Ireland: there is no way Americans would have acquiesced in a near thirty-year troop presence in a war-zone with almost no public debate.

The merit of such military reticence is debatable, but it is at least hard to reconcile with the international image of the US as a kick-ass brute. Even outside the theatre of war, there are few signs in America of the aggressive nationalism so familiar in Europe and elsewhere. There are no American football hooligans – or baseball thugs or basketball louts. At ice-hockey games the most vicious violence is on the rink. One never sees 'America' supporters, draped in the stars-and-stripes, knocking back cans of lager – chiefly because the United States almost never competes as a nation. Instead it tends to play itself at sports of its own invention. Hence baseball's so-called World Series is actually an event confined to North America. The serious sporting rivalries are among the big cities – the Dallas Cowboys, the Cleveland Indians, the Seattle Mariners – serving to reinforce those strong, local identities, rather than pumping up the blood of patriotism. There is no US national baseball team, no all-American football squad. The nearest equivalent is the US side in tennis's Davis Cup or the so-called Dream Team in Olympic basketball, but even they hardly stoke a surge of jingoistic chest-beating: when the latter played Argentina in the Atlanta games, the American tabloid papers did not rattle off 'Twenty Things You Never Knew About the Argies'.

The explanation for this apparent mildness of national temper towards foreigners might not be all flattering. The simple fact is, Americans are not that interested in abroad. Their general knowledge of the world beyond the US can be laughably bad. Witness the students at the University of Arizona who thought Fidel Castro was the leader of the Palestinians and who identified Imelda Marcos as a brand of perfume. For most Americans, the US is the world. That's why ABC's *World News Tonight* shows no embarrassment at being a twenty-two-minute bulletin with rarely more than two and a half minutes dedicated to coverage away from home. One CBS broadcast featured a round-up of stories 'from around the globe': the datelines were Cape Canaveral, Sacramento, Des Moines and Miami.

In 1992 Andrew Kohut, of the Pew Center for the People and the Press, surveyed 3,500 Americans to test their awareness of current events. Kohut found his results 'depressing'. Asked to name the TV show that Dan Quayle had attacked for glamorising single motherhood, 65 per cent were able to volunteer *Murphy Brown*. When the same group was asked which former communist country was facing a prolonged civil war among its various republics, only 21 per cent said Yugoslavia. An earlier survey asked Americans to rate the 'most important story' of the month. Twice as many people chose the trial of Mike Tyson for rape as the break-up of the Soviet Union. 'The public is really consumed with its own problems,' sighed Kohut.

George Demko spent a career grappling with America's congenital insularity, as chief geographer of the US State Department. He says Americans have 'mental maps' in which home towns are central, with the rest of the world 'getting hazier as you move out'. Family roots outside the US ensure a place on the mental map for the old country, as do holidays abroad. Otherwise it has to be something really special. 'The oil and hostage crises worked to increase the Middle East's visibility on the mental map,' says Demko. 'Even so map stores were besieged during the Gulf War by Americans who had no idea where the Gulf was.' He blames 'lousy geography' teaching in US schools.

But others believe America's foreign blind spot, like its military isolationism, is simply in the nature of the country. Spanning a whole continent, the US has little need of outside distraction. Instead, from the beginning, Americans have been obsessed with their own mission. According to the academic geographer Donald Vermeer, 'Those that came here had to have an inward orientation to move westward. That consumed all their interest and energy. We were a new people, without any real external threat. And discovering gold and oil made us say, "To hell with the rest of the world." We felt self-contained. We still have that. I suppose it's the immaturity of a young country.' With a project inside, Americans feel little need to knock heads outside. This can be frustrating for foreign allies seeking US engagement in military ventures. But as another example of the side-effects of a civic nationalism, it might just count as a positive virtue.

Skinheads, Old Maids and the Cricket Test

Britain is rather different. We feel our country existed long before we got here. It was not built by a set of radicals and dreamers; it was not animated by a founding idea. Rather it evolved a millennium ago, gradually, and shrouded in Wessex fog. It exists, like a fact of nature. Our buildings are old, and our legends even older. Our streets wind and stretch, each with its own idiosyncratic name; they do not run in numbered or alphabetical straight lines like the deliberate, started-from-scratch grids that characterise every American big city. We have no Founding Fathers whose faces we can carve into Ben Nevis. We have no start date, a fact which once led columnist Neal Ascherson to ask, 'When was Britain?' (Neither the Roman conquest, nor 1603's union of the crowns nor even 1707's union of parliaments quite fit the bill.) Such confusion is the fate of the evolved, rather than created, society. The Americans enjoy the neatness of dates: 1776 for the founding of the republic, 1787 for the drafting of the US Constitution, 1789 for its formal ratification. When was America? It is not a question any American would ever need to ask.

Britain has no start date and no founding purpose. There was no British Revolution, and there is no ongoing national project to bind the society together. Perhaps the empire performed that task once but, now that it has gone, few Britons know which goals they all share. The obvious corollary is that our nationalism slides quickly into Michael Ignatieff's ethnic category. Ignatieff draws this sorry conclusion himself, recalling in *Blood and Belonging* that British patriotism has historically been xenophobic (hostile to the French, the Irish, the Jews and now, most keenly, the Germans); rural, not urban; and romantic in its hankerings for a pre-industrial world gone by. Yet for today's Britain the 'ethnic' tag seems highly inappropriate. If we did once, we share the same blood no longer. We are too ethnically rich for that, ranking as one of the most diverse states in Europe.

Moreover, few of us find a national identity based on ethnicity very appealing – not now, after the century of Nazi Germany, Bosnia and Rwanda. But nor can we easily lay claim to a civic nationalism, not when we struggle to identify any uniquely British civic ideal to be nationalistic about. The result is muddle – and it is not confined to chronology. To Neal Ascherson's question, we could legitimately add others. *What* is Britain? All the British Isles or just the British mainland? Will it always include Scotland? Is Northern Ireland separate? And: *Who* is British? Only those born here? Or do we include newcomers? What do we mean by British values? 'When we say Britishness, do we actually mean whiteness?' asked Suzanne Moore, the self-described 'woolly, liberal' columnist, on hearing of a proposal to teach British identity in schools. At the heart of the problem is the hardest question of all: What is Britain *for*?

The lack of a clear answer has one particularly unhappy result. With no British creed, we have no entry mechanism for outsiders. We cannot follow the words of President Clinton and say, 'Sign here and you will truly become British,' because there is no real national project in need of recruits. So we end up with the reverse of America's attitude towards ethnic diversity. Secure in their homogeneity of ideals, they regard heterogeneity of complexion as an asset. Bereft of a civic faith, we are uncertain of our national culture and worry that newcomers will 'swamp' our essential Britishness (which none of us can really define.) For them, immigration is a promise. To us, it is a threat.

The extreme expressions of this sentiment are well known, from the anti-'alien' trade union movements at the turn of the century through Oswald Mosley's British Union of Fascists in the 1930s to the National Front and British National Party, via Enoch Powell and his 'rivers of blood'. Less familiar, perhaps, is the extent to which mainstream British policy and opinion has habitually closed its doors to outsiders. When France took in three million foreigners between the wars, Britain admitted just 250,000. We offered shelter to only a handful of refugees from Nazism, and took in fewer migrants from our former colonies than either Holland, Belgium, France or Portugal did from theirs. The only brief let-up came after the war, when West Indians were actively recruited to help rebuild British industry. But the door was slammed shut once more in 1962, with the Commonwealth Immigration Act.

In fact, we are so closed to newcomers that for the past century we have been a net *exporter* of people. The strenuous efforts made by successive London governments to ensure only a few thousand Hong Kong Chinese would come to Britain following the handover to Beijing is just the most recent example of hostility to immigration. The fact that the people involved were renowned for their enterprise, family values and education – precisely the kind of newcomers America strives to recruit – made no odds. (As it turned out, the US went out of its way to bring in the people of Hong Kong, specifically doubling the number of visas available – making room for 190,000 new immigrants from the colony.)

Of course, Britain's history and geography make it very different from the US. Ours is not a settler nation, and living on a densely populated island means there is simply less room for new people. All the same, the sheer iciness of the British attitude towards immigrants is striking. While William Carroll and his team organise a tear-jerking ceremony for new citizens, the British authorities offer nothing. New Britons do not come together in a branch of the Home Office, sing their new national anthem and hear a warm speech of welcome. They do not weep in the embrace of relatives and of their new country. Instead they get a standard letter from a civil servant in the Home Office (Nationality Division).

> Dear—,
> I am writing to let you know that on present information we propose to grant this application for British citizenship.
> Before we can register/issue a certificate of naturalisation, however, you/your client . . .

Heartwarming. The immigrant then has to take an oath of allegiance in front of a JP or lawyer, before waiting a month to receive the certificate – in the post. No ceremony, no big moment.

Once settled, the new British citizen will not find himself

surrounded by that permanent rhetoric of inclusion which so marks out the United States. TV adverts will not feature an ethnic mix as a matter of course, nor will the staff of newspapers or the cast of soap operas. Politicians will not vie to be photographed with children of many colours, as they do in America. And when a Conservative backbencher refers to 'black bastards', as David Evans did in 1997, he will not be forced on to the floor of the House of Commons to apologise, *à la* unlucky impressionist Senator Alfonse D'Amato but will be lauded by several national newspapers for daring to say out loud what many Britons 'really feel'. The immigrant is unlikely to hear a public official repeat Mr Carroll's appeal for newcomers to retain their culture. Instead he might encounter Norman Tebbit's notorious 'cricket test', demanding that new Britons drop all allegiance to the old country. West Indian support for the Caribbean touring sides of the 1970s and 1980s clearly irritated old-fashioned Britons like Tebbit. And yet when Hispanics cheered Latin-American teams during the 1994 World Cup, hosted in the US, most Americans assumed it was all part of the fun. (Indeed, the *Washington Post* has now become one of several major US newspapers to run a full page of sport in Spanish.)

Britain's lack of a civic or idealistic nationalism affects more than immigrants. It saps the patriotism of everyone else. With no shared mission to celebrate, national pride can seem vacuous if not plain nasty. Small wonder that our own flag is hardly ever seen in Britain. It flew tall during the Second World War, but after that it was slowly lowered – its descent doubtless accelerated by the withdrawal from empire and the humiliation of Suez. It remains resilient as a subversive or ironic symbol, whether in the RAF target-shape pioneered by the parka-wearing mods of the 1960s or as a punk declaration of war a decade later. The Cool Britannia fad of the mid-1990s saw the Union flag flutter once more – first as the colour scheme of Noel Gallagher's guitar, then as a mini-dress for Geri Halliwell, when she was still a Spice Girl. In both cases the red, white and blue was used more to evoke the Swinging London ethos of the sixties than as an expression of British patriotism. Still, for many progressives the flag is forever associated with the fascist boot boys of the 1970s. Ethnic minorities confess they cannot help but see it as a threat since, in the old phrase, 'There ain't no black in the Union Jack.'

Britain's national anthem poses similar problems. Many Britons, especially younger ones, feel only squirming embarrassment at the sound of 'God Save the Queen'. When it appears at the closedown of the night's television, it often sounds plain ridiculous. The Sex Pistols tried to use it the way they had the flag – subversively – but the best we can usually manage is the solemn mumble, as regularly performed by our national soccer team. Perhaps the chief problem is that the song is not about us, but *her*. 'Send her victorious, happy and glorious . . .'

Sometimes all this discomfort can lead dangerously close to self-hatred. The headline in the London *Evening Standard* during the 1996 Olympic games – 'Why Are We So Useless?' – echoes the record-collecting narrator in Nick Hornby's novel *High Fidelity*, who despairs at the unromantic mediocrity of Britain. 'The Seven Sisters Road', he laments, 'is not Thunder Road.' Even our leaders are infected by it. No less than the Archbishop of Canterbury, Dr George Carey, remarked: 'We're a pretty ordinary little nation and yet we don't realise it.' Only 54 per cent of us say we are proud to be British, and less than half of us tell pollsters we want to do something to serve our country. British English does not feature the phrase, 'Is this a great country or what?'

Lacking the patriotism of common purpose, Britain is denied the optimistic self-confidence that comes with it. Unexpectedly perhaps, Winston Churchill's words during the Battle of Britain are a case in point: 'If the British Empire and its Commonwealth last for a thousand years, men will still say, "This was their finest hour."' As more than one commentator has noted, those words aroused our nation at the time, but doomed us ever after. They enshrined in us the belief that, whatever else we achieved, our best days were behind us. It is hardly surprising that patriotism in Britain often seems like a passion for the past. When John Major wanted to stir our national pride, he spoke of 'long shadows on county grounds, warm beer, invincible green suburbs, dog lovers and pools fillers . . . old maids bicycling to holy communion through the morning mist'. A world gone by. British business and culture are just as guilty. In the pre-landing video screened on Heathrow-bound flights from the US, British Airways would show a montage of castles, palaces, royal parades, Beefeaters, Oxbridge colleges and a couple of cathedrals – with scarcely a modern image in sight. The BBC and major independent TV producers play the same game, churning out costume drama as if it were going out of fashion. Poor Jane Austen has been adapted to within an inch of her life (including versions of books she did not even write). Our penchant for *faux*-classical architecture and pedestrianised retro town centres is all part of a heritage fetish in which today is a mere evocation of yesterday. Sometimes Britain can seem like a widow still turning the pages of her sepia-tinged wedding album, unable to face the world outside her window.

The result is that on a bad day Britain can feel so fixed in the past, change seems all but impossible. The very architecture of our landscape, filled with streets and squares and buildings that are centuries old, blesses us with a rootedness we all cherish – but it can also lead to a sense that we have inherited our society, we cannot create it afresh. The American fondness for architectural innovation, exemplified by the adventurousness of downtown Chicago or the business district in Houston, can be exhausting in its unrelenting novelty – but it sends the opposite message. Too many Britons feel as if the grooves and channels of British life have already been carved; all they can do is negotiate their way around them. Put crudely, the ambitious Brit hopes to find his place in a system that already exists and seems to have existed for ever, while the ambitious American hopes to change it – or even build a new one. Our language contains hints of this fatalism: 'Grin and bear it', 'Like it or lump it' or 'Ours is not to reason why'. The famous stiff-upper lip is an attempt to make a virtue of this same vice, but the quality speaks of passivity as much as stoicism. American English, meanwhile, demands action and, in the face of strife, not forbearance but resistance: 'No guts, no glory', 'No pain, no gain' and the obvious 'Go for it'. While the US rejoices in its status as the can-do society, Britain can often feel like the opposite: the can't-do society.

In this context it is perhaps inevitable that 49 per cent of Britons told Gallup they would emigrate from Britain if they could. Their chosen destinations were either America or other created, settler societies – the blank slates of Australia, New Zealand or Canada. Those are new nations, setting no limit on what an individual can achieve. Britain rarely feels like that. It is not a blank page, more like a book that was written long ago.

The absence in Britain of a US-style idealistic nationalism has one last consequence: our patriotism can be far from benign to outsiders. The expansionist history of the empire has led many liberals to regard national feeling as a dangerous force, like a virus to be kept safely corked. Occasionally it leaks out, almost always prompting revulsion among progressives. Few can forget the 'Gotcha' triumphalism of the Falklands war or the anti-German drumbeat of the tabloid papers during the Euro '96 soccer championship – 'Football War on Germany' in the *Daily Mirror*, 'Watch out Krauts, England are gonna bomb you to bits' in the *Daily Star*, 'Let's Blitz Fritz' in the *Sun*.

A particular wariness is reserved for the patriotism of the English. Unlike the acceptable national pride of the Scots and the Welsh, English nationalism is assumed to entail an aggressiveness which shuts out minorities at home and beats heads abroad. Some of the more zealous Eurosceptics have tarnished patriotism's good name yet further, associating it with a pettiness and xenophobia few find attractive. Several thoughtful voices have warned that if greater national expression for Scotland and Wales weakens the Union, then English nationalism could be released anew – freed of the restraining influence of Britishness. Most of them have seen this as a cause for alarm, presuming that such a force could only be thuggishly right-wing. But the American example suggests another way. An idealistic, civic nationalism, animated by the camaraderie of a shared project, can be inclusive at home and either indifferent or a force for good abroad. It can also instil a sense of optimism and sky's-the-limit possibility. For Britain that might mean putting aside the empire-building of old and replacing it with a new goal: the construction of a new society at home.

8

Taming the Beast

THE AIR IS so silent, and the snow so white, that for a moment you could believe you had died and gone to heaven. It is as if God himself has tucked in his children under the smooth blanket of snow that lasts from November to March, year in year out. For in Montana, that pristine pocket of America just above Wyoming and below Canada, nature has crafted a landscape beautiful enough to make you weep. Tall pines scrape the sky, reflected in cool, mirror-clear lakes. Mountains and valleys are dusted in Christmas-card snow, like the finest sugar. Everything is dipped in a piercing blue light, at rest and quiet.

Yet somehow, amidst this peace, the talk is of war. Men in combat fatigues are arming themselves, preparing for the confrontation to come. Citizens' militias have sprung up, ready to do battle with the evil force threatening their God-guaranteed way of life. Their enemy: the US government.

They are gathering in the high-school gym in the tiny Montana hamlet of Noxon. Several hundred concerned citizens have trudged through the snow to hear the newly formed Militia of Montana defend the state's fierce, freedom-loving tradition. From the podium they will hear warnings of the coming threat from Washington, DC. Like a latter-day George III, the federal government has become a tyrant, they are told, poking its nose into every aspect of ordinary Americans' daily lives, demanding ever higher taxes, passing ever more intrusive laws.

The event is hosted by the Militia's founders, the Brothers Trochmann, John and David. The former is the talker of the family, a flinty, biblical character with a fine doomsayer's grey beard. He explains why Bill Clinton's efforts to restrict guns are a clear sign that tyranny is on the way. 'Gun control is for only one thing,' he warns. 'People control.'

Next there is a slide show, with documents and photographs detailing how the federal authorities are constructing the apparatus of dictatorship. Excessive taxes, expanding regulation, a planned national identity card, a rumoured 'bio-chip' – an electronic barcode to be secretly implanted in the buttocks of every US citizen – all are designed to help Washington subordinate the American people.

The ex-soldiers, car workers and teachers in the gym are rapt as Trochmann and assorted guest speakers show stills of military hardware being shipped across the United States bearing UN – and even old Soviet – markings. They hold up obscure documents purportedly showing how America is to be carved up into ten manageable regions. A murmur of recognition ripples through the room at the mention of the mysterious black helicopters, circling above middle America, spying on the innocent. Some militiamen whisper about the strange numbers on the back of road signs which will one day be used to shepherd the masses into forty-three concentration camps for political dissidents. These, they insist, are already under construction. Others confide that the New World Order has plans to annihilate 80 per cent of the US population.

Outside the hall, brother David is hawking the tools of resistance. He is minding a stall, selling US army manuals on survival, booby traps and guerrilla warfare and even the notorious *Anarchists' Cookbook*, which offers ten easy steps to make a bomb. David's personal favourite is the 'zapper', a truncheon developed by the German army, capable of delivering an electric shock of 160,000 volts. 'That'll put you down on your knees right away,' he says, with a salesman's pride in his product. As he speaks, punters in jeans and lumberjack shirts examine videos with titles like *America in Peril* or *Battle Preparations*. Their wives check out the sachets of freeze-dried food, ideal for surviving in the wilderness on the run from the Feds. One couple agree they 'could get by' on the elk and deer they already hunt. John Trochmann says darkly, 'When the enemy comes, they'll learn how we've prepared.'

Up until then the American press had either ignored the militiamen or depicted them as a Dad's Army of weekend soldiers, middle-aged men with middle-aged spreads huffing and puffing in the remote countryside. They were boys with toys, playing war games. But the reality was much less cuddly – as events were later to prove. On 19 April 1995 a truck bomb blew apart the Alfred P. Murrah federal office building in Oklahoma City, killing 168 men, women and children. As a reflex, Americans first blamed faraway Arabia, assuming only the bearded villians of the Middle East would dare break the heartland of the Middle West. But then, with the arrest of the blond, blue-eyed Timothy McVeigh, came the dread realisation that the killer lurked within. A graduate of the US militia movement, yes, but also a decorated veteran of the Gulf War – one of their own.

At first, people scrambled to peer into the paramilitary netherworld that had spawned McVeigh. Then they spread the blame a little wider. Experts rushed forward to explain that the Oklahoma bombers were not maniacs from beyond the pale, but merely the most extreme advocates of a right-wing, anti-government creed which had long been mainstream. President Clinton joined in, condemning the 'loud and angry voices' on the right who had created the climate in which McVeigh and friends had been incubated. His unstated targets were talk-show hosts like Rush Limbaugh or the convicted Watergate dirty trickster turned broadcaster, G. Gordon Liddy – both of whom had made a good living demonising the federal government and the people who work for it. Limbaugh once told his twenty million listeners, 'The second violent American revolution is just about – I got my fingers about a quarter of an inch apart – is just about that far away.' Liddy, meanwhile, was fond of echoing the militias' invective against the Bureau of Alcohol, Tobacco and Firearms, whose unhappy task it is to regulate the American angry white male's three favourite things. Just weeks after Oklahoma, Liddy was on air advising his audience how best to kill ATF agents. 'Head shots,' he insisted, 'head shots.'

But the blame would not stay on the extremist fringes. It kept spreading outwards, like ripples on a lake. For it was not just the far right which had made a religion of hostility towards central government. Ronald Reagan himself had coined the catechism of the faith in his 1980 Inaugural Address, when he declared that 'Government is not the solution to the problem; government *is* the problem.' Years later Reagan's Republican disciples kept up the attack. Even the former president's heir errant, the disgraced Colonel Oliver North, got in on the act. When he sought to become a senator in 1994 he described Washington, DC – the home of the US government – as 'Sodom on the Potomac'.

Soon there was another suspect wanted for Oklahoma besides Timothy McVeigh. He was the mystery fugitive known only as John Doe 2. The term was grimly appropriate, for in US parlance John Doe is Joe Bloggs, Mr Average – the American Everyman. The term fitted because, in truth, neither the far right nor the Republicans had ever had a monopoly on American anti-government fury. On the contrary, suspicion of the central state is an all-American tradition – one which underpins almost every other American ideal, including those most admired by progressives. Take, for example, the militias' talk of a 'shadow government', a conspiracy by the military-industrial complex. That was not original. Rather, it was borrowed from the left-wingers of the 1960s, particularly the Black Panthers and the peace movement, who depicted Lyndon Johnson and Richard Nixon as tyrants heading illegitimate regimes, lying to their own people. It was the left, not the right, which first cast the CIA, FBI and assorted government agencies as a dark enemy within.

Indeed, in the early days, it was the Democrats who were the anti-state party – a tradition set in train by the libertarian Thomas Jefferson and extended in the 1820s by Andrew Jackson. The first Democrats associated a strong executive with the monarchical and aristocratic ways of Britain – a pattern not to be repeated in the new republic. Later it was the trade unions – always identified in Britain with state intervention – who were particularly suspicious of government meddling. In the 1930s the American Federation of Labor – ancestor of today's AFL-CIO, the US equivalent of the TUC – was a syndicalist movement, seeking power for the unions, not the state. Many outsiders have long assumed that because US trade unions were anti-socialist they were right-wing. In fact, the AFL was an extremely militant organisation, often violent and willing to strike. As one historian of the movement has put it, 'It was not conservative, but rather a militant anti-statist group.'

The AFL's more radical comrades, the revolutionary Industrial Workers of the World, were also opposed to socialism – because it bestowed too much power on the state. They were anarchists instead. The IWW flame was rekindled in the 1960s by the New Left, in particular by the flower children and their movement against the Vietnam war. Those young activists shared their forebears' anti-government instincts – exhibiting none of the discipline and hierarchy of the more authoritarian European left. The radical left groups which have existed in the US have tended to be of this anarchistic variety, chiefly because American progressives usually believe that what the state gives, it can also take away.

One shining illustration of the American left's deep scepticism towards government came in 1971. The National Taxpayers Union called for a dramatic reduction in the welfare responsibilities of government – a move backed, predictably, by several right-leaning free marketeers. But, despite its name, the National Taxpayers Union was not some neo-conservative pressure group. On the contrary, its board included three luminaries of the New Left: Noam Chomsky, Marc Raskin, who headed the radical Institute for Policy Studies, and Karl Hess, former editor of the left-wing magazine *Ramparts*. Their idea was to devise a system of tax credits for any individual or group who helped out people on welfare. Contributions would be knocked straight off the donor's tax bill – a genuine cut, rather than a mere deduction from their taxable income. That way the citizen would be giving to the needy *directly*, bypassing the state.

So it stands to reason that the figure in mainstream American culture whose views most closely resemble those of the anti-government right is not a Republican, but the left-wing film-maker Oliver Stone. His production line of conspiracy movies, in which shadowy men meet on frostbitten mornings to plot against their own country – usually on the steps of the Lincoln Memorial – is a perfect example of what author Richard Hofstadter famously called *The Paranoid Style in American*

Politics, a style which spans both ends of the ideological spectrum.

Indeed it is the liberal artistes of Hollywood who have done most to perpetuate the American tradition of anti-government suspicion. In movie after movie it is not Moscow or Baghdad that is the real enemy but Washington, DC. No charge is too outlandish – so long as the state is the suspect. In *Independence Day*, suited officials at the Pentagon keep the 'fact' of a 1947 alien invasion from the president himself. In John Grisham's *Pelican Brief* the trail of lies and killing leads all the way to the Oval Office. In *ET*, it is the government and its allies in the dreaded 'military-industrial complex' who are out to destroy the adorable little alien. Even super-patriots like Tom Clancy and Sylvester Stallone cast Washington as the bad guy. In *Clear and Present Danger*, the steel-jawed Jack Ryan discovers his bosses are in cahoots with South American drug dealers. Eventually he has to testify against his own government. Rambo, too, was betrayed by the CIA – along with all those other American heroes missing in action in Vietnam. That war, like the Watergate scandal, occupies a special place in the conspiracy theorists' universe. Both events appeared to confirm what were once the darkest fantasies of the left. Overnight, pinko invective became American received wisdom.

Michael Medved, the ultra-conservative film critic with a fine line in Yiddish-ised one-liners – he calls TV's favourite sci-fi series *Star Drek* – believes the trend began in earnest in the 1970s. After the Church Report into excesses by the Central Intelligence Agency, 'the CIA became a three letter abbreviation for evil', says Medved. 'In fact there were far more films in which the CIA were bad guys than the KGB.' Despite the image abroad of Hollywood as a worldwide distributor of gung-ho American patriotism, few American movies ever root unhesitatingly for the US government. The preferred hero has always been the lone maverick, betrayed by an official agency and fighting for good on his own. In *Mission: Impossible* Tom Cruise joined the likes of Jack Ryan and Rambo, doing battle with the leaders of his own side. The message is the same in all these yarns: love your country, but do not trust the government. Or, as the 1970s bumper sticker used to put it, 'QUESTION AUTHORITY'.

One Dallas tourist attraction does brisk business cashing in on the sentiment. The Conspiracy Museum is just opposite Dealey Plaza, round the corner from the Texas School Book Depository, near the grassy knoll. It is right in the heart of the mother of all conspiracies: the assassination of John F. Kennedy.

The museum gift shop makes the most of its location, selling T-shirts with 'WHO KILLED JFK?' on the front and 'NOT LHO' on the back. Anyone naive enough to believe Lee Harvey Oswald actually murdered America's best-loved president will be the object of intense tutting from the museum staff. Everyone knows LHO was the 'patsy'.

The Conspiracy Museum is fast becoming a fixture on the Dallas death tour. After a visit to the Sixth Floor, where tourists can lean out of the very window where the patsy aimed his rifle, it is a must. Not that it purports to tell the real story, only all the different versions available. 'That's the beauty of the assassination of JFK,' beams curator Ron Rice. 'If you don't like the story, you can write your own. He can be shot two thousand different ways.'

Which makes for a pretty confusing museum. On display are countless maps, boards and charts featuring lines and strings to depict 'trajectories' and 'acoustic echoes'. It is like being inside the graphics unit of a homicide department. But it is not all Kennedy. There is an interactive CD-Rom with the low-down on every plot and plan cunningly concealed throughout American history. Touch the screen on Abraham Lincoln, and wonder, 'Was John Wilkes Booth really John St Helen?'

The paying public lap it up. Alice Holinbeck, a middle-aged lady from Florida, was thumbing through a copy of the *Grassy Knoll Gazette* as she whispered her theory that conspiracy was no museum piece – it was with us right now. 'Look at Vince Foster,' she said, referring to the White House lawyer officially deemed to have committed suicide shortly after Bill Clinton took office. 'That's a bunch of garbage.' Nor, Ms Holinbeck confided, were the government telling the truth about Waco and Oklahoma City: an alliance of European bankers and globalists were behind both events. 'They have a grand scheme,' she explained intently.

Such distrust of the nation's highest officials, and of

government itself, is utterly commonplace in America – extending from popular culture to politics, from left to right. The World Values survey found majorities of Americans less willing than Germans, Britons, Austrians and Italians to let their government set wages or prices, create jobs or reduce the working week. And Americans are not hypocrites: just as they do not want government interfering in their lives, nor do they want it to look after them. Polls find them hostile to state meddling in social matters like smoking in public places or the wearing of seat belts. It is not that Americans do not see the value in, say, car safety. On the contrary, it was a US campaign, led by consumer rights guru Ralph Nader, that pushed carmakers to fit seat belts worldwide in the first place. Nor are Americans blasé about the risks of cigarettes: they have ostracised smokers with notorious zeal. No, the reason why only 49 per cent of Americans – compared to 80 per cent of Britons – believe the wearing of seat belts should be required by law is simple and stubborn: they cannot stand the state telling them what to do. That is why any policy discussion in the US is always conducted on two levels. First, does this idea have merit? Second, even if it does, is this a legitimate task of government? Or will it increase yet further the reach of the state?

Americans pick up the attitude early. When the city fathers of Washington, DC, established a curfew for teenagers – demanding they be off the streets and tucked up in bed by 11 p.m. – the kids immediately rebelled. A visit to the 7-Eleven in suburban Tenley Town proved the curfew was having precisely the opposite effect to the one intended: at the stroke of eleven, Washington's boys and girls came out to play. 'What curfew?' asked one, not really joking. 'Most of us don't follow it,' said Kathy, sixteen years old and tiny in the driver's seat of her mum's big Acura car. As midnight approached, the kids kept coming – barefoot girls and whiskery boys in grungy shorts long enough to reach their ankles. 'I think it's a matter of principle,' explained David Brunner, keen to be out during this, his last week of school. 'I don't think the government should say where you can be and when. I have certain inherent rights, like the right to stay out as late as I want.'

The 7-Eleven crowd might not be the best illustration of

Americans' government-phobia. For one thing, the much-loathed curfew was a local decision, not a central one. For another, young David Brunner's talk of rights was slightly wide of the mark since, as a minor, there were plenty of 'inherent rights' he did *not* enjoy. Even so, his words, like those of his friends, are testament to the strength not only of the US culture of rights, but America's enduring scepticism about authority. Those teenagers were all good-hearted, bright people. But the line from Tenley Town to the commandos of Montana is more direct than either side would ever guess. For suspicion of the state is nothing less than a national faith, as old as the republic itself.

America's origins made it this way. The United States was founded in rebellion against an overmighty ruler, by people determined to escape the grip of strong government. 'The history of the present King of Great Britain is a history of repeated injuries and usurpations, all having in direct object *the establishment of an absolute Tyranny over these States,*' thundered the Declaration of Independence. The Founding Fathers were adamant that no such dominion would ever take root in their own land.

Accordingly, the Declaration and, more specifically, the Constitution were deliberate mandates to weaken the government and strengthen the governed. Hence the separation of powers, with lawmakers placed in one corner – the Congress, and the executive in another – the White House. Lest there be any confusion, the two were kept physically separate – one at each end of Washington's Pennsylvania Avenue.

The Founders did not stop there. Once they had chopped the beast-of-government's head in two, they moved to tie it down and lock it in a strong cage. They installed the Supreme Court as a third branch of government, to act as an extra check on the other two. They split the legislature into two elected chambers and installed different election timetables for each of them – and a different one again for the president. Just to keep things interesting, they set up an elaborate series of rules about who could overrule whom and when. Like the child's playground game of 'paper, scissors, stone', it takes a feat of memory to recall what beats what.

The final result is a system which threw out the British-style hierarchical pyramid, topped by a monarch – or surrogate monarch, in the form of the prime minister – and replaced it with an object of much messier geometry, purposely weakened by built-in conflicts. The object of the game was to keep the central executive in its place: the first constitution, the Articles of Confederation, took the game so seriously it had no executive at all, just a Congress to pass laws.

Thus, despite his title, an American president is not nearly as 'presidential' as his counterparts abroad, including the occupant of Number Ten Downing Street. He cannot attempt to make war alone without triggering a row with Congress. Indeed, the battle over war powers is one of the most enduring tensions between Capitol Hill and the White House, with Congress demanding the right of veto over military activity (the issue at the heart of the Iran–Contra scandal). Unlike a British prime minister, the US executive's term of office is fixed in advance. He cannot call the election when it suits him; polling day comes around on a predetermined date whether it helps or hurts him. Nor can the American president hold on to power indefinitely. The Constitution rules that he serve only two consecutive four-year spells in office, and similar term-limits restrict the governors of the various American states. No American politician is allowed the delusion that he is indispensable or that power belongs to him alone.

The president is limited in his patronage, too. He can appoint no one, not even his own cabinet; he can only nominate, subject to the approval of the Senate. This is no mere formality, as the long line of defeated nominees can testify. Selected by a president of one party, hopefuls often face a grilling before a Senate committee dominated by the other. Those who survive that ordeal then have to win a vote of the entire chamber. The need for Senate ratification applies to the president's judicial appointments, too, including federal judges and members of the Supreme Court.

Despite their apparent complexity, the purpose of all these rules is simple – to keep the executive from dominating either the legislature or the judiciary. Both are to retain their independence, always. Any attempts by the administration to meddle in the judicial process usually ends in high cost to the meddlers – a lesson Richard Nixon learned too late. The president faces just as much resistance from the legislature, where his influence is confined to mere persuasion. He cannot impose a whip on congressmen and senators, three-line or otherwise. In direct contrast with Westminster, neither the US president nor the members of his cabinet have so much as a seat in the legislature; instead, they are quarantined away, at the other end of Pennsylvania Avenue. There is one more profound difference. The American president is powerless to determine the membership of the second chamber. While a British PM could always appoint new members to the House of Lords, seats in the US Senate are allocated by the people alone, in democratic elections.

The thread of principle running through the entire machine of US government is that power should not be concentrated in the executive, but spread around. Congress is allocated authority in its own right, distinct from the presidency. So it is Capitol Hill which writes the annual US budget, setting the levels of taxation and earmarking where the money will go. The Hill has its own Congressional Budget Office which dukes it out with the executive Office of Management of the Budget. It is no rubber stamp.

The whole is a scheme of almost mathematical beauty, a system of checks and balances so finely calibrated that after two centuries no one element has gathered power all to itself. A bill might pass in the House of Representatives, but it must also win the approval of the Senate and be signed by the president. That gives him power of veto, but it does not make him invincible: both houses of Congress can override the presidential veto so long as they have a two-thirds majority. At a stroke, the authors of the American system devised a mechanism to prevent the tyranny of the majority – at least the tyranny of the simple, arithmetic majority. If anything, the US system gives a power of veto to the minority, the one-third of representatives who can say no.

Like the final weight in a three-part scales, the judiciary can swing in and knock down laws or decisions of both Congress and president which it deems unconstitutional. And, unlike their

British counterparts, justices of the Supreme Court need not fear that governments will simply go back and change the rules. The only way an American politician can tinker with the Constitution is to amend it – and that takes two-thirds of both Houses, the signature of the president *and* the approval of state legislatures in at least thirty-eight of the fifty states. Any change with that much support – and the process can take up to seven years – is likely to represent the settled and popular will. Otherwise, the Bill of Rights reigns supreme, defending the constitutionally guaranteed liberties of the individual or minority even when they are unpopular. If US public opinion suddenly turned against, say, blind people, and a state governor, president or Congress was elected on a manifesto promising to persecute them – the blind would nevertheless be protected. The Supreme Court would speak for them, in the name of the Bill of Rights.

Americans seem perfectly happy with this kind of machinery, a central state which, according to one scholar, is more limited in its powers than any in the world, bar Switzerland. Two centuries after George III, the old arguments for weak government still exercise a firm grip on the American imagination; the threat of monarchical rule still sends a shiver down the collective spine. Even the slogans of the revolutionary war live on, their target no longer the Redcoat Army of King George but the reviled agencies of Washington, DC. Car number plates in New Hampshire bear the war cry, 'LIVE FREE OR DIE', while patriots still fly flags depicting a fierce serpent and the eighteenth-century warning, 'DON'T TREAD ON ME'.

At election time Americans remember their history, occasionally using their ballot deliberately to weaken their government by dividing it. Armed with several votes at the polling booth, Americans have learned the art of 'ticket-splitting' – picking a president of one party and a congressman of another. Ticket-splitters tell pollsters they are not voting that way by accident, but because they actively want a divided government and weak central state. Despite years of moaning about Washington 'gridlock' – with each side vetoing the other and paralysing the system – the voters repeatedly prefer to share out power rather than place it all in the hands of one party. That might explain why five of the six administrations prior to Bill Clinton's first term in 1992 saw control of Washington split between the two main parties, one end of Pennsylvania Avenue in the hands of each. In 1996 the electorate pulled off a classic: giving Republicans both Houses of Congress even as they re-elected Clinton the Democrat to the presidency. Republicans had urged precisely that outcome in TV ads warning voters not to give Bill Clinton a 'blank cheque' in the form of a Democratic Congress. The strategy, which tacitly admitted Clinton was bound to win, was designed to play on the long-held American fear of a too-powerful executive. And it worked.

Occasionally the US has wavered from its wariness of central authority. The Great Depression prompted a change of heart as Franklin Roosevelt pushed for a state role in economic planning and social welfare. FDR's New Deal introduced a raft of government programmes – from the National Recovery Administration to the Tennessee Valley Authority – which enlarged the federal bureaucracy. The legacy of that era lives on, in a Department of Agriculture which provides nearly one bureaucrat for every three farmers and in a federal tax code which runs, at last count, to seven million words. The White House itself expanded in this period, ballooning into the famous 'Imperial Presidency' – muscular enough to deal with the consecutive crises of the Depression, the Second World War and the Cold War against communism.

Now, though, that post-1930s expansion in government looks more like a sixty-year exception than a new rule. The US executive has begun to shrink back to its original, minimalist proportions. Indeed, Republicans hailed their congressional landslide in 1994 as a return to the Founders' conception of small government and a reined-in state. They argued that the post-Depression period had been an aberration born of crisis, and that it was time to restore the natural, American way of doing things. Bill Clinton got the message, agreeing to sharp cuts in public spending and the removal of a welfare safety net which had been in place for six decades. The state activism of FDR and the post-war period was abandoned. As Clinton himself declared in 1995: 'The era of big government is over.'

All this scepticism of the state can seem desperately unappealing, especially to those British progressives who insist that the problem with contemporary life is that there is too little government activity, not too much. The US brand of anti-authoritarianism can seem particularly ugly when its ambassadors are the camouflaged fanatics of the militia movement, their finest hour the bombing of 168 innocents in Oklahoma City. And yet to dismiss the American attitude to government outright would be a mistake. For it might well be the thread that links the other defining aspects of US society – including the country's most admirable qualities. From popular sovereignty to the Bill of Rights, local autonomy to the American Dream – the Founders' determination to tame the beast of central control has helped shape the United States of America.

Before and After: A Trip Around Britain

It is always fun to watch American tourists in Britain, to see them eyeing our nation through a video camera, multiple gadgets strapped around their waists, ooh-ing and ah-ing at the palaces, castles and stately homes which remain our public face. For many it is like Disneyland, only real: all the legends of angry kings and beheaded queens, pretty princesses and sickly princes – as if England were a land of fairytales. Americans come from cities so new, they sometimes struggle to find a building that has been standing for more than a few decades. In Britain they can tread on soil fairly squelching with history.

But for some there is an extra pleasure: when they visit Britain, they visit their past. They know they are from the New World; across the Atlantic they can see the Old one. They have learned about it from watching BBC costume dramas on public television's *Masterpiece Theater*, or films like *The Madness of King George*. But how much better to see the genuine article. Best of all, we have hardly changed a thing.

Of course, the country itself has altered drastically since the eighteenth century, but the system Americans remember is still there, preserved at perfect humidity like a precious museum piece. So Americans learn that in the old world they were not citizens but subjects of the British crown. As Britons still are. They read that dukes and marquesses, lords and ladies formed one half of the nation's legislature, exercising power over laws simply by virtue of their birth. In the last year of the twentieth century, they were still there. They remember hearing how back in the olden days their rights were never written down and could be snatched away by an over-mighty master on a whim. In Britain, it is still that way. It must almost be comforting for the visiting American to see how little has changed. US history teachers must be particularly grateful. Like those pairs of photographs showing the slimmer-of-the-year before and after a diet, Britain's constitutional arrangements represent a real-life 'before' picture – with America as the 'after'. We live in the place they left behind.

While the jealous guarding of liberty against the ambitions of the state was hard-wired into the American mindset from the start, Britain has retained a more deferential stance towards authority. Britons are happy enough to attack this government or that one, but government itself enjoys a fairly lofty position in our national life. For the best part of the twentieth century, paternalists on the right and socialists on the left have looked to the state for answers and blamed it when things went wrong. Whether it is Rottweilers that bite or kids strung out on drugs, it is a British reflex to demand action from the government, usually legislation. If a heavy snowfall causes traffic delays or England loses a Test series, a minister will soon be hauled on TV or radio to explain himself. One compulsively naughty boy triggers a crisis at the Ridings school and the nation demands a response from the education secretary. Even the behaviour of the supposedly private utilities – including the pay of their top executives – is seen as a legitimate subject of complaint to Whitehall.

Those on the Thatcherite right of British politics may be determined to roll back the state, yet none of them shows the loathing for government on display in the United States. They may want reduced taxes or a little more privatisation, but they do not describe civil servants as tyrants plotting the enslavement of their own countrymen. Nor are there many British counterparts for the survivalists of Idaho and Montana, who have discarded their car registration plates and driving licences, and even come off the national electricity grid, to sever their last connections to the reviled central state. One small measure of the gap between Britain and America is the UK debate over electoral reform. Opponents warn that proportional representation will lead to coalitions, and therefore weak government. The beauty of the first-past-the-post system, they chirrup, is that, no matter who wins, the British people are guaranteed a strong administration – able to do what it likes without the support of others. In America, such an argument would be offered by the other side – *against* our current system and *for* PR.

Britain's political machinery, whether as cause or effect, serves our penchant for strong government perfectly. Of course, much of Westminster's power has been eroded recently, whether by the global economy or the European Union – both of which tend to make laws of their own. But within the terms of our own system, the central state still exercises remarkable control.

The phenomenon starts at the top, with the overweening might of the executive – an arrangement rooted in our monarchic past. A British prime minister can act like a king because he has inherited a king's powers. This is not rhetoric, but constitutional fact: the bulk of the royal prerogative has been handed from the palace to Downing Street. The result is a British premier who enjoys a power scholars freely describe as absolutist, with only the most meagre restraint. On his own he can deploy troops, requisition ships and otherwise make war – a crown prerogative in which parliament, astonishingly, has no official role. That same prerogative gives him and his ministers plenty of powers which require not so much as a nod towards the Commons. The chancellor's budget decrees an extra tax on beer or cigarettes or petrol and, lo, at the stroke of midnight, it is done. Backed by a parliamentary majority, the PM can close schools, build roads and sell off public industries. In striking contrast with the US president, he can even determine the terms of his own employment. The power to dissolve parliament and call an election means the prime minister decides when his stint in office should end – an enormous tactical advantage over his rivals, equivalent to a running race in which one of the contestants fires the starting gun. What is more, he faces no limit on how many terms of office he can serve. As Margaret Thatcher famously promised, a British prime minister can 'go on and on and on'.

But what makes the British system truly extraordinary is the executive's power over the other branches of government – those pointedly kept separate in the US and elsewhere. It exerts decisive influence over the judiciary, most obviously through the lord chancellor's appointment of judges and the home secretary's determination of parole, pardons and even, on occasion, sentencing. Armed with a Commons majority and tight party discipline, Downing Street also controls the legislature – giving it the power to write the very law of the land. The prime minister has even been able to determine the make-up of one of the legislature's two chambers, through his gift of seats in the House of Lords. All other potential sources of power, including local authorities, are ultimately just as subordinate to the centre: when the Labour-controlled Greater London Council took its own independent line in the 1980s, Margaret Thatcher abolished it at a stroke. Directly or indirectly, the people who govern Britain are chosen by the prime minister, from government ministers to the chairmen of our country's countless quangos. Downing Street's patronage is so great, even a putative Archbishop of Canterbury has first to get a thumbs-up from Number Ten.

Pundits hesitate to call such a set-up presidential, partly because power is believed to rest not merely with the prime minister but with the entire government, especially the Cabinet. But since the people who sit around that table every Thursday morning owe their position to the boss – and can be dismissed with a glance – they, too, are mere assistants to the prime minister, with no constitutionally enshrined power of their own. As Geoffrey Howe admitted in his notorious resignation speech in 1990, the old-fashioned notion of Cabinet government, in which colleagues act collectively, is rendered 'futile' if the prime minister is sufficiently bent on getting his, or her, own way. The board of UK plc has only one chairman and chief executive, and it is near-impossible to move against him.

Yet theory would have us believe the British system is the very opposite. The doctrine of parliamentary sovereignty is supposed to grant all political power to the *legislature*, with the executive as its subordinate. On this logic, whoever controls parliament controls the government. It seems pretty democratic:

the People's House able to sack a prime minister and his Cabinet on a straight up-or-down vote of confidence.

That may work as a description of the British system, but only technically. Our own experience tells us that, far from being a curb on the power of the prime minister, the House of Commons is the very source of his domination. Once a party commands a majority in the Commons, it holds on to it with a discipline so tight the practice is even *called* whipping. MPs are herded and bullied through the division lobbies like sheep in a pen, merely to deliver the goods for the leadership which rules them. The legislature is reduced to a rubber stamp, a law-making machine in the employ of the government.

The enfeeblement of parliament has now become a cliché, its frequent irrelevance as visible as the rows of green benches empty at all hours except for the weekly knockabout of Question Time – enjoyable theatre, but a mainly useless method of oversight. (These days the more serious work of scrutiny is increasingly left to the likes of *Newsnight* and the *Today* programme.) Voters know that an opposition or backbench MP is all but powerless, while for years Britain's young and talented influence-seekers headed for careers in the City or the media, dismissing Westminster as a retreat for the impotent. Parliament's standing has suffered yet further as Britain's own laws begin to take second place to those of the European Union, a shift recognised by the British judiciary's admission that when an act of parliament clashes with a directive from Brussels or a ruling from Strasbourg, it is EU law that rules.

As if functional redundancy were not bad enough, the parliament of the mid-1990s also showed signs of ethical decay. The cash-for-questions affair and the series of scandals that marred the closing years of the Major administration soured an already bitter public taste. By 1996 a European Union poll found Britons had less faith in both their government and parliament than the people of any member country bar Portugal. Just under half of us felt we could not rely on the House of Commons to make decisions in our interest. Even the Italians had more faith in their legislature.

This, then, is the shape of the British system. A mighty executive with effective control over all branches of government, including the almost toothless legislature which is supposed to hold it in check. Walter Bagehot believed this 'near-complete fusion of the executive and legislative powers' to be the 'efficient secret' of the British system, ensuring strong government. But the warning voices were always there. Edward Gibbon, a keen student of the corruptions of concentrated power, wrote in his *Decline and Fall of the Roman Empire* that 'the principles of a free constitution are irrecoverably lost' when legislative and executive authority converge too closely. In 1765, Sir William Blackstone, the greatest legal mind of his day, cautioned that merging the two branches of government 'would be productive of tyranny'. More than two centuries later Lord Hailsham, a renowned jurist of his own time, sounded the same alarm, issuing his oft-quoted prediction that Britain was moving towards an 'elective dictatorship'. When *The Economist* issued its own call for constitutional reform, it neatly summed up the problem with a pocket cartoon, showing a hand over a ballot box, popping in a voting slip marked 'I give all power to . . .'.

For more than two centuries, the Atlantic has separated two radically opposed views of government. On one side America, where a weak central authority is seen as a positive virtue. On the other a European ideal – typified by France – which looks to a mighty central state. One follows Thomas Jefferson's dictum that the government which governs least governs best. The other adheres to a pattern of state control set by Napoleon Bonaparte, with all power emanating from the centre. For most of our history, we Britons have leaned closer to Bonaparte than to Jefferson. We have lived with the virtually unrestrained central government rejected by America's founders all those years ago. They loudly insisted that changing that system was the first step towards creating a free society. Now, at long last, it might be time to listen.

9

Ten Steps to the Revolution

THEY ARE A diverse bunch – the condo commando in Florida and the lesbians of Northampton, the Liberace fans of Las Vegas and the immigrants reborn on the Fourth of July – all living their own lives, unlikely to meet each other. Yet they are bound together. For each one of them tells the story of a core American value – and those values are themselves connected. Indeed, none of them can be fully realised without at least one of the others. Taken together they form the 'creed' identified by G.K. Chesterton, even the ideology described by Antonio Gramsci: Americanism.

It is this set of ideals from which Britain might learn – even if the United States has fulfilled none of them completely: the goal is the American dream, not every dot and comma of the American reality. Still, it is a hefty shopping list. In an era when there is much talk of a New Britain, perhaps it can also serve as a set of directions – a roadmap to the future.

1. Popular Sovereignty

The place to start is America's fundamental view of power. Adopting it means turning our current doctrine on its head – declaring that power does not flow from the top down, but the bottom up. It would be that 'most radical statement of human rights' lauded so warmly by Newt Gingrich. The British people would be placing itself in charge, insisting that government is its servant, not its master. It would be learning the central lesson of the American Revolution, declaring that it is We the People –

not the Crown, nor even Parliament – who are sovereign.

Such a declaration would be profound indeed, requiring a shift in the way we understand both our democracy and our society. For sovereignty in Britain currently rests not with the people, but with a much trickier concept: the crown-in-parliament. It is this notion of parliamentary sovereignty which results in Britain's trademark concentration of power. For it declares that parliament is supreme and can brook no rival – not the will of the people, not even the law. If a statute stands in the way of the government, ministers can simply change it, even when the obstacle in question is common law, evolved over centuries. The conservative philosopher Friedrich Hayek understood the danger when he warned, 'The triumphant claim of the British parliament to have become sovereign, and so able to govern subject to no law, may prove to have been the death-knell of both individual freedom and democracy.'

Traditional defenders of the British system dismiss such talk as pure alarmism. Parliament is elected by the people, they insist; its sovereignty can surely amount to nothing more than the indirect expression of the people's will. But it is worth remembering that a parliamentary majority is not the same as a popular one. Tony Blair won only 44 per cent of the votes of the British people in 1997, yet that translated into a 179-seat advantage in the Commons. In fact, no party has won more than 50 per cent of the votes cast since 1935 – and, remember, these are percentages not of the total adult population but merely of those on the electoral roll. Yet the doctrine of parliamentary sovereignty allows them untrammelled power. Clement Attlee nationalised in the 1940s with a 48 per cent mandate; Margaret Thatcher privatised in the 1980s on the strength of 44, 42 and 43 per cent votes in her three election victories. Those who believe parliament is identical with the will of the people are making a tall claim.

Even if one concedes that voters at least have the final say on polling day, it remains true that once a Commons majority is in place, it can do what it likes – no matter what the people think. Blended with the crown, it and it alone is sovereign. As Jean Jacques Rousseau witheringly wrote more than two centuries ago, 'The English people believes itself to be free; it is gravely mistaken; it is free only during the election of Members of Parliament; as soon as the Members are elected, the people is enslaved; it is nothing.' We seem to understand that truth ourselves. A 1995 MORI poll found 85 per cent of Britons believed ordinary voters had 'little or no power' over public policy. Just one in a hundred said they had a 'great deal' of influence.

This then is reformers' first task: to challenge the traditional British notion of parliamentary sovereignty – so often lazily used as a synonym for democracy – and move towards the great American innovation, popular sovereignty. We have to break the habit of centuries which allows no authority above or even beside parliament, and declare that it is the people – not the House of Commons – which must be sovereign. Such a move will mean going far beyond the terrain usually staked out by constitutional reformers. But as those first Americans understood, popular sovereignty is the foundation of democracy. It is the principle on which a new constitution for Britain should be built, the idea which connects and coheres all the democratic changes we so urgently need. For it alone will make us the owners of our own country.

2. More Democracy

Few would ever object – at least not out loud – to calls for greater democracy. If the people are in charge, then clearly they should take the crucial decisions affecting them. But, under the surface, there runs a thick streak of British ambivalence towards the rule of the people. One can see it in the dire warnings of 'mob rule' which greet any proposal for direct democracy, or in the instant criticism levelled at politicians who consult opinion polls or focus groups – even in the high-brow disdain for large circulation newspapers and big box-office films. If a TV programmer wants people to watch his station, he is immediately accused of sinking to the lowest common denominator. Some traditional High Tories are bold enough to admit their lukewarm commitment to democracy. Sir Peregrine Worsthorne happily describes himself as a reactionary who still harbours doubts over the wisdom of the Great Reform Act. Even that champion of the classless society, John Major, once let the mask slip while explaining his resistance to a referendum on the Maastricht Treaty. He said the issues involved were 'highly complex' and that the electorate might be swayed by 'irrelevant' distractions when they came to make their decision. Such condescension betrayed an almost nineteenth-century low regard for the fickle, unscrubbed mob.

Not that the left's record is much better. It was a Labour minister, Douglas Jay, who wrote that, 'In the case of nutrition and health, just as in the case of education, the gentleman in Whitehall really does know better what is good for the people than the people know themselves.' Jay's heirs today are the fairweather democrats, those well-intentioned liberals happy to rely on undemocratic means when they aid their own cause – whether it be a favourable ruling from an unelected judge or a benignly paternalistic vote in the House of Lords. The textbook example is parliament's refusal to restore the death penalty, despite colossal public demand for its return. Few campaigners against capital punishment seem troubled by that democratic deficit. Witness Clive Stafford-Smith, the indefatigable British-born lawyer, now living in Louisiana. He has dedicated his career to the defence of death row prisoners – noble work, saving human lives. But when, during a BBC debate on the death penalty, he was accused of frustrating the people's will, Stafford-Smith did not hesitate to admit, 'I don't care about the people's will.'

Few liberals take the opposite view, urgently seeking to persuade their fellow voters of the rightness of their cause, eager to submit their views to a national debate, strong in the conviction that they would win. Too few of them acknowledge that the real victory over capital punishment will come not just by banning it, but by winning the argument among the public. The model here is Vermont or Massachusetts or any of those ten other liberal American states – places free of the death penalty because that is what people have chosen and voted for, again and again. In those twelve states, liberals do not rely on the protections of a kindly elite, saving the people from their worst instincts. Instead they have abandoned judicial killing because democracy has spoken. In Britain we are without it because democracy has not been heard.

Perhaps death row is not the greatest advertisement for a vigorous democracy, while others might find the power of pressure groups, the grease of pork-barrel politics and the dominance of charisma equally unappetising. But these are hardly legitimate grounds for the rejection of greater democracy. Just as genuine believers in freedom of speech follow Voltaire, and support the freedom to express even those ideas they find repulsive, so full-blooded democrats have to back the system even when it yields outcomes they despise. For British progressives that might require an intellectual, even emotional leap. It will mean looking beyond this policy or that and returning to first principles: if we truly believe in democracy then we must construct a system which lets the people decide. Such a transformation will not make outright victors of either left or right. Democracy applied consistently in Britain would probably disappoint the left on capital punishment, but please them on handguns or fox-hunting. It might upset the right by extending self-rule to the English regions, but delight them by safeguarding the monarchy. What would emerge would not be the politics of left or right but of British democracy, rigorously applied. If the results turned out to be contradictory, so be it. It would merely be proof that the system was working, accurately reflecting the complex people it served.

The Americans have a set-up which, for all its flaws, works by letting the people decide. Some of the machinery might be worth shipping across the Atlantic – starting with the ballot box. The principle should hardly need to be stated: in a democracy, direct elections are the obvious way to select people for public service. Education authorities, health trusts, magistrates – they should all be directly elected by the people they hope to serve. Those who disagree need a strong case: in a democracy the burden of proof rests on those who believe voters should *not* decide, not the other way around.

Allied to this core democratic principle is the question of accountability. If the voters of North Carolina decide Tom Funderburk has done a poor job as labor commissioner they can throw him out next time. In extreme circumstances – where an office-holder has been exposed as corrupt, for example – voters can even demand, through a petition, a special 'recall' election, summoning the offender back home before his full term is out. By comparison, a Briton unhappy with the people who oversee hospitals, schools, training, housing or urban development – to say nothing of the police and the courts – is powerless. Not only do we have no idea of quangocrats' qualifications or policies before they start, we have no way of making them answerable to us once they are in place. Elections are the straightforward solution.

They offer another advantage, too – ensuring the governors look more like the governed. America's mayors, judges and sheriffs include women and ethnic minorities because the people vote for them. A clear example is the diversity of the US judiciary. The reason why the black or female or Asian judge is such a staple of American TV courtroom drama is that they actually exist in real life – elected at the ballot box. Britons often lament the homogeneity of the nearly all-white, all-male, all-Oxbridge British bench: at last count there was just one woman on the Court of Appeal, with thirty-four men; of the ninety-nine judges at the High Court, only seven were women. Elections might produce a more varied complexion, just as they have in the US. Similarly, direct election is a sure way to keep judges in touch with the people they serve. The unworldly m'lud who has not heard of reggae can survive on the British bench; but he would be swept aside if he had to face the people.

The election of judges is instructive, if only because it probably marks the limit of people's appetite for democracy. Many Britons would reject such a move, preferring Solomonic wisdom, rather than desire for re-election, to be the guiding motive of the judiciary. But here, too, the US precedent can be of help. The Americans elect only local and state judges. Federal judges and members of the Supreme Court – all those responsible for interpreting the Constitution – are not elected, but nominated by the president and ratified by the Senate. Such a mixed approach represents a good compromise, removing the risk of populist excess while remaining true to the principle that public jobs should be allocated through democracy, not patronage. Britain could use a similar combination for its most sensitive appointments.

Besides the allocation of public jobs by election, there is another American democratic device we might want to borrow: the referendum. Especially in its citizens' initiative form – when a mass petition is enough to get a question on a statewide ballot – there is no purer form of democracy. Some complain that the US has taken referendum democracy too far, to the point where even the most trivial questions – like Idaho's debate on false teeth – are put to the people. Traditionalists argue that such matters, along with the weightier ones of immigration, gay rights and drugs, are precisely the questions which politicians are paid to decide. Representative government is threatened, they say, if direct democracy takes its place too frequently. It is this view which underpins Britain's traditional resistance to the plebiscite. The American position is different, holding that too much public participation is better than too little. It is the same tension that exists between parliamentary and popular sovereignty. If we are serious about shifting from one to the other, and letting the people decide, then a change in our attitude towards referendums is in order. America shows that, at the local and regional level in particular, they can be a vigorous addition to democratic life.

Beyond the mechanics of popular decision-making, Britain will need to alter much of its cultural landscape if it wishes to be a fully engaged democracy. Until recently, the noisy public conversation heard in America was alien to Britain. We were more reserved, less able to air our differences – and certainly our feelings – aloud. In recent times, that has seemed to change. The response to the death of Princess Diana has been analysed at great length, with many observers regarding that remarkable week as an overnight conversion by the British to the gushy confessionalism of the US. That might be an exaggeration. Instead, the events of September 1997 seemed to reveal a subtler change, one that had been in train for a while. For British people *are* becoming more expressive, especially the younger ones. You only have to tune in to today's radio phone-ins and contrast them with the programmes of a decade ago. Fewer callers feel obliged to limit themselves to asking a question. Now they are quite happy to offer their own opinion. The informality of much British life – typified by the prime minister's call-me-Tony request to his Cabinet colleagues – is part of the same shift. We are getting better at talking to each other, both as individuals and a society – certainly a pre-requisite for a mass-participation democracy. Even so, the American experience suggests we still have some way to go.

3. A New Republic

If the name of the game is popular sovereignty, then the British people needs to wrest control from the combined force now in charge: the crown-in-parliament. Some changes to parliament are suggested below. But what of the other half of this constitutional double act? It is a touchy subject, even among radicals. It was not so much as mentioned in Labour's manifesto in 1997. And yet the crown is at the heart of Britain's problems with sovereignty, democracy and equality.

To the first Americans it was obvious: in a democracy there could be no place for heredity. It was the people who were sovereign, not one social caste. The notion that power could be conferred by blood alone struck them as absurd, and they were determined to be rid of it. In the new republic, there would be no royal dynasty and no formal role for an aristocratic elite. Heredity violated the fundamental American notion of equality which held that any citizen could reach the top, regardless of their genes. As Thomas Paine argued in *The Rights of Man*, it was people of talent, not high birth, who should lead the country. For Paine, a hereditary governing class was 'as absurd as an hereditary mathematician, or an hereditary wiseman, and as ridiculous as an hereditary poet laureate'. He lambasted the British system, which reserved both the throne and the upper house for persons selected by bloodline. That was more than two centuries ago. Yet on the brink of the third millennium, the very same system was still standing. Two-thirds of the 'triple cord which no man can break', as Edmund Burke described the holy trinity of crown, nobility and Commons, were still determined by nothing more than the vagaries of paternity.

Traditionalists insist that today's monarchy enjoys merely ceremonial and symbolic power, that reformers are wasting their time attacking harmless pageantry. Such a view is either ignorant or disingenuous. Although she arrives at parliament in a gold coach wearing a storybook crown, the Queen is not just a bauble. She has both power and significance. Only electoral fluke has prevented the situation in which the monarch would have to exercise that power: a hung parliament. Faced with deadlock at the polls, the unelected Elizabeth Windsor would decide herself which party leader should be allowed first shot at forming a new government. If Her Majesty decided no administration could be assembled, she would have the authority to call fresh elections. This is more than symbolic influence, yet it exists with not so much as a nod to democracy. How would the Queen make up her mind? Who are the courtiers who would offer Her Majesty 'advice'? Who chose them? It sounds like paranoid Francis Urquhart territory, but this is not fiction. As recently as 1931, the King handpicked a prime minister during a time of political and financial crisis. (In the words of Harold Laski, '[Ramsay] MacDonald was as much the personal choice of George V as Lord Bute was the personal choice of George III.' MacDonald's emergence at the head of the National Government was 'a Palace Revolution'.) According to the veteran student of Whitehall, Peter Hennessy, the Queen has had at least five similar moments of decision since 1949, crises triggered by prime ministerial resignations or narrow election results. A dead heat at the polls would immediately see the Queen drawn once more into politics, flexing a muscle no weaker for being so rarely seen.

Not all royal power is exercised by the monarch. The prime minister can govern like an absolute ruler because he has appropriated the royal prerogative: as Her Majesty's First Minister, he has inherited her powers to rule the United Kingdom. No republic starting from scratch would ever grant such powers to a president. But in Britain they were already there, bundled together and tied with purple string. They were simply passed from one hand to another in the Glorious Revolution. If Britons want to reform the elective dictatorship which concentrates more power in the hands of the British prime minister than almost any comparable executive in the world, they will have to attack the source of that power – the crown.

Even putting aside both the residual powers the Queen exerts herself and the crown prerogative bequeathed to Downing Street, monarchy would still matter. Those who dismiss it as purely symbolic make a mistake: symbols count. US politics is all but conducted through the language of symbols; even in Britain they exercise a grip which stays firm long after more literal powers of law and statute have grown feeble. The trouble with royalty is that it symbolises two of our ugliest traits. By conferring enormous status and wealth on one family, the monarchy enshrines the worst values of a semi-feudal class society. Britain cannot sincerely tell its people it is a meritocracy, with full social mobility, when the head of state is selected by birth. Worse still, the crown symbolises the very essence of our political culture – declaring loud and clear that power in Britain flows from the top down, with the throne at the summit of the pyramid. So long as the head of state belongs, automatically and irreversibly, to a single, pampered family we can but be subjects of their kingdom, not citizens of our own land. This diminishes us as a people. As Malcolm Turnbull, the founder of the Australian Republican Movement, said after Bill Clinton had raised a glass in honour of 'Her Majesty, the Queen of Australia', those words made Australia 'just a little bit less of a nation'.

The grand American experiment in self-government began with a break from royalty. The Founders understood that democracy could not breathe if sovereignty lay with a single, unelected family and that it had to be transferred to the people. If Britons are truly to own their country, they need to do the same. Like a child who grows up and leaves home, it is time we issued our own Declaration of Independence – from the House of Windsor. As the most successful nation in the world to have thrown off the British crown, the Americans can show the way.

The US precedent is particularly useful in reassuring those fearful of abolishing the monarchy. Older Britons are often scared by the mere word 'republicanism' (even when they are not associating it with the IRA). They imagine public beheadings for the beloved royals, the severed heads of Charles or Philip rolling into a basket carefully placed by the guillotine. Such lurid fantasy has held back the cause of the republic nearly as much as the tendency of British reformers to shy away from the question. Though it may seem obvious, republicans need to say out loud that their historical guide will not be the Jacobins of 1789 but the first Americans. They did not execute George III, they simply proclaimed their desire to be free of him. The Windsors would still live, but they would follow the precedent set by King Haakon of Norway, who once remarked that the only thing he was allowed to poke his nose into was his handkerchief.

To the pragmatic royalist argument – that kings and queens boost tourism – the United States also serves as handy rebuttal. Tourists flock to Washington to admire the trappings of democratic rule just as much as they come to London to gawp at the vestiges of absolutism. There are queues around the White House at all hours, and permanent homage to those shrines of self-rule: the Washington, Lincoln and Jefferson memorials. The French precedent is perhaps even more apt. The Palace of Versailles continues to attract seven million visitors annually – more than two centuries after anyone lived there. There is no reason to imagine that Windsor Castle or Buckingham Palace would be any less popular. Besides, their current magnetism can be overplayed: recent figures show that the twenty most visited tourist attractions in Britain did not include a single royal destination. Top of the chart was Blackpool Pleasure Beach, with Alton Towers, Morecambe's Frontierland and Chessington World of Adventures all coming in ahead of the monarchic sights. Windsor did have one place in the top twenty – but it was Legoland, not the castle, romping in at number eighteen.

Moreover, the US stands as proof that a head of state chosen by the people can still inspire the awe and respect once aroused by monarchy. The Americans love their presidents and worship the presidency, no matter how much tabloid slime is thrown at it. In celebrating the office, if not the man, they celebrate themselves – the system they have built and their own experiment in self-government. That is why they make myths of FDR and JFK, tell folk tales of Washington's cherry tree and Lincoln's log cabin, and carve the faces of their greatest leaders in the granite rock of Mount Rushmore – where they can pay homage, as if to ancient gods. They obsess over the First Family and make movies in which the president is a cross between James Bond and a comic-book superhero (think of the fighter-pilot commander-in-chief in *Independence Day*, Michael Douglas's turn in *The American President* or Harrison Ford's portrayal of an Indiana Jones of the skies in *Air Force One*). If the US is any guide, democracy and lustre are far from incompatible.

Not that Britain would have to follow the American lead all the way and install a US-style executive president. The scope of the prime minister's powers means he is quite presidential enough as it is. Indeed, it is debatable whether Britain would need to replace the monarchy with a new, separate head of state. The head of government could take on both tasks quite comfortably, as he does in the US or South Africa. If people cannot accept the prime minister as head of state, there are plenty of alternatives. Candidates could be selected by national ballot or a vote of parliament. Simplest of all would be the elevation of the Speaker for the handful of state occasions where Britain needs a figurehead other than the prime minister.

Letting go of monarchy will not be easy. For older Britons especially it occupies a key place in our national heritage. Whatever their origins, a lot of royal traditions now feel like our own (the Queen's Christmas broadcast comes to mind). In a world that is increasingly uniform, we will be losing something distinctly British. But we need to see that feeling for what it is – the comfort of familiarity and nostalgia. Those sentiments are not to be dismissed, but they should be weighed against their cost. Monarchy instils fresh generations of Britons with a feudal history of inequality in which they are mere subjects. By gently putting the whole institution to bed, we shall be declaring that there is only one sovereign in our land: ourselves.

4. Separation of Powers

Establishing a British republic will leave one piece of unfinished business. It concerns the second of the three elements in Burke's 'triple cord': the nobility. As we entered the twenty-first century, one half of our legislature was still dominated by a class whose status was conferred at birth. It may be amusing for a Wyoming tourist to see the 'hereditary lord admiral Malahide and adjacent seas', as the Tenth Baron Talbot is properly known, but it makes a mockery of Britain's claim to be a democracy, still less a meritocracy. If the British people are serious about taking charge of their own society, then they – not a blue-blood caste – must supply both the head of state and the membership of a second chamber. The United States insisted on both rights long ago.

Defenders of the House of Lords used to speak of the need for a wise, reflective body able to revise legislation. They were right, but they were simply making the case for a second chamber, not for an hereditary one. They argued that an upper house filled with party placemen would be a dread prospect. They were right again, but that is an argument against patronage, not a defence of bloodline. Both their demands would be amply satisfied by a democratically elected second chamber – much like the US Senate.

Such a major change could not happen in isolation. A second house with its own electoral legitimacy would pose a serious challenge to the current dominance of the Commons. Equipped with genuine muscle, it would break Britain's age-old concentration of power – which bundles the branches of government into a single, mighty centre – and move closer to the US system, where power is spread around. The enduring British preference for strong government would doubtless lead traditionalists to reject any such division of power, anxious that it would weaken the executive. Hostility on these grounds is always greatest among those whose party occupies Number Ten. Many Labour supporters who used to rail against the autocratic executive when the Tories were in Downing Street fell strangely silent once it was their man in charge. But clear-sighted democrats need to ask which works better – Britain's 'fused' system or the separated powers of America – no matter who is in the job.

Critics of divided government – including many Americans – bemoan the 'gridlock' it can cause: voters elect a president on a set of promises, only to see him stymied by a hostile Congress. Legislation gets stuck, so that even the humble Brady Bill – imposing a mandatory five-day waiting period before the purchase of a new gun – was blocked for seven years. It is as if the American law-making beast suffers from a dire and chronic constipation.

This can be irritating when the frustrated law is one you care about. But gridlock has its advantages, too. The built-in restraint of a separated powers system can prevent impulsive, ill-thought-out plans – 'panic legislation' – from becoming law. Witness the fate of Bill Clinton's counter-terrorism bill, proposed days after the bombing in Oklahoma City. Determined to be seen as a man of action, the president suggested the FBI be given increased wire-tapping and surveillance powers, to prevent future Oklahoma-style crimes. Civil libertarians immediately saw the dangers, as did some cooler heads in Congress. Despite the hot blood of those days, when bodies and children's toys were still being pulled out of the wrecked Alfred P. Murrah Building, the bill was not rushed through. An alliance of Democratic and Republican libertarians used their Constitution-given right to be difficult and won a delay, allowing time for the bill's worst excesses quietly to fall away.

Contrast that with Britain's Dangerous Dogs Act of 1991, devised amid the outrage that followed a spate of Rottweiler attacks on small children. That bill barrelled through parliament like a toboggan on the Cresta run. The Opposition could do nothing, and no Tory would break party discipline to stop it. The result was an unwieldy and costly law which created as many problems as it solved, and which had to be humanely put down in 1997.

It is not only in cases of emergency that gridlock can come in handy. A spasm of paralysis can be especially useful when a politician's grandest scheme is at stake, Margaret Thatcher's Community Charge being the classic example. Widely loathed during its trial run in Scotland, the 1990 poll tax inspired a nationwide movement of civil disobedience captured in the borrowed Dario Fo slogan, 'Can't Pay! Won't Pay!' The tax was regarded as illegitimate, even by traditional conservatives. Yet there was nothing inside the parliamentary system to block it. The people were driven to extremes, finally resorting to a riot in Trafalgar Square. Even then, it took the tea-room putsch that toppled Margaret Thatcher to kill off the policy once and for all.

The poll tax would never have made it past a middle-ranking think-tank in America. Congressmen anxious to save their own skin – and with re-election never more than two years away – would have voted against it. If they had not, a few Senate hearings taking evidence on the pilot scheme would have rapidly exposed its flaws. If somehow it had become law, it would have been struck down by the Supreme Court as an unconstitutional restriction on the right to vote – which it surely was. Like a silver ball on a pinball machine, the poll tax would have been buffeted on the cushions and bells – the checks and balances – of the US Constitution until it had fallen into oblivion.

Bill Clinton knows the process only too well. The jewel of his first administration was to be his proposed overhaul of the US healthcare system. It never even came to a vote in the Senate and it did not deserve to. Its heart was in the right place – seeking to provide basic medical cover for all – but it called for a comically complicated bureaucracy. Written down, it read like a parody from a Soviet political satire, complete with panels, committees, sub-panels and sub-committees – all that was missing was a People's Commissar. Rendered as a diagram, it looked like a circuit board for the space shuttle. The fact that it was drawn up in secret by Hillary Clinton and a few of her wonkish friends hardly made it more attractive. Republicans branded the healthcare reform a relic of the old Eastern Europe, while Democrats struggled to be more than tepid. The always direct Texan Senator Phil Gramm warned that the Clinton plan would 'pass over my cold, dead political body' and was eventually able to declare it 'deader than Elvis'.

The separated powers of the US did to healthcare reform what the fused system of Britain could not do to the poll tax – it stopped a bad law in its tracks. Moreover, the US filter mechanism operated even in the absence of conventional gridlock: the healthcare débâcle happened in 1993–4 when the Democrats controlled the White House *and* both houses of Congress. The episode was proof that, in America, the brakes work even when a single driver has control of all parts of the vehicle.

The secret of divided government's success in restraining

ideas too extreme, too stupid or both can be expressed in a single word: scrutiny. Defenders of the British system like to trumpet the accountability it offers, obliging the prime minister and his Cabinet to appear before their fellow MPs in the House of Commons. Nothing like Question Time exists in the US, they boast, adding that Ronald Reagan would have wilted under the rowdy barracking Thatcher faced twice a week for eleven years. Below that surface, however, parliament's record as a scrutineer is not good. The serial failure of MPs to weed out flaws in legislation is well known, with the pension reforms of 1986 often cited as a particularly inglorious example. It was not as if honourable members had failed to spot the countless problems in the bill; they saw them all too clearly. They were just powerless to do anything about them. In recent times, parliament's weakness as a watchdog has been dramatised through its failure to punish or even notice the corrupt and rotten behaviour of government ministers. The sleazy antics of Messrs Hamilton and Aitken were uncovered beyond Westminster, through the endeavours of an inquiring press. In the arms-for-Iraq affair ministers failed to tell the truth to MPs, and got away with it. Both scandals served as proof that parliamentary scrutiny of the executive had broken down, a view shared by Sir Richard Scott, who investigated the whole sordid, Iraqgate mess. Scott concluded that executive power had been abused, thereby lending 'substance to the charge that the constitution has become an elective dictatorship'.

In the United States, Congress is always on the prowl, its eyes and ears open. Admittedly, the separation of powers means the president – who has no place in the legislature – is not routinely grilled by congressmen in the chamber. But, as Bill Clinton learned through painful experience, that hardly puts the White House beyond the scolding reach of Capitol Hill. Besides the 'nuclear option' of impeachment, Congress is armed with its own committees, staffs and budgets – all aimed at holding the executive to account. Congress can summon cabinet members and lower-level administration officials – including the head of the military, the chairman of the joint chiefs of staff – to appear in televised hearings to report to the committee that oversees their work. Not for them the half-hour Punch-and-Judy of

Question Time; the interrogation can last hours, with questions of mind-bending detail. The congressional record on policing sleaze is also impressive, a reputation burnished by Capitol Hill's dogged pursuit of the Watergate scandal.

On any of these measures, then, the US system appears to serve its people better than Britain's: it filters out panicked or extreme legislation and keeps the executive branch properly supervised. It works by separating powers, not concentrating them – the efficient secret of American democracy which moved Professor Gary Wills to remark that of the two treasures of American civilisation that would endure through human history, one was the US Constitution (the other was jazz). The old British claim that divided or 'weak' governments damage the health of their nation looks suspect when one considers the United States: the country continues to dominate the world economy and to enjoy a standard of living that is the envy of the planet. In the US, at least, divided government appears to have done little harm and plenty of good.

If Britain wants to learn that lesson, the first move will be to use Westminster the way it was intended: as a parliament of two chambers. The executive would remain, as at present, in the House of Commons. But legislative functions would be shared with a democratically elected second chamber. As in the US, the upper house would represent larger constituencies: while the Senate is made up of states, Britain's might consist of regions. Such a set-up would both avoid duplicating the local responsibilities of the Commons and fit well with any future acts of devolution, by providing regional parliaments with a direct counterpart at Westminster. The key step would be the 'staggering' of elections to the second chamber, with some seats up for grabs during a general election and others fought in 'off years' – when there are no ballots for the Commons. (The Americans contest one-third of Senate seats every two years.) Opposition parties would often win those off-year elections, as they do in most mid-term polls. As a result, the second chamber would frequently have a majority of a different political colour to that of the Commons.

At a stroke Britain would have adopted a system of separated powers, with the second house serving as an automatic check and balance to the executive. That, after all, is the whole point of a two-chamber system – a system we exported to the world, but which we allowed to rot at home. Panic legislation promoted in the Commons would run into a roadblock in a democratically elected second body, legitimately empowered to do more than demand a period of reflection (the effective limit of the Lords' current power). Ideological grandiosity would be blocked, too: the poll tax won a majority in the Conservative-led Commons, but it would have fallen in an elected chamber of the regions which, thanks to the mid-term pendulum effect, would almost certainly have been in Labour hands.

The executive would finally face some genuine scrutiny – not just the gentle squint over the shoulder allowed by the current system. The present Westminster committees are too often poodles of the majority party. In a genuinely bicameral apparatus, committees of a Conservative-controlled second chamber could be vigorous watchdogs, able to hound members of a Labour government, and vice versa. No longer would we hear the pressure group drumbeat for a 'new independent body' or an 'immediate judicial inquiry' to monitor some aspect of the executive's conduct or work, whether on MPs' ethics or the safety of football grounds. Suddenly those demands could be met within parliament itself, by a second chamber committed to watching over the executive. It is a clear index of Westminster's decline in the public esteem that serious scrutiny is seen as a task for others – judges or the great and the good – rather than our own elected representatives. In the US activists always demand *congressional* investigations – a sign that they trust the task of executive supervision to the legislature. Our doctrine of fused power and parliamentary sovereignty has led Britons to believe they cannot trust Westminster to perform the same function. Separation of powers would restore that trust.

A second house could also take on the ratification and rejection of appointments to senior public posts, including Cabinet ministers and senior judges – granting a measure of independence to the former and democratic accountability to the latter. In the Commons such hearings would be a mere formality, with the governing party's in-built majority guaranteeing approval for all its choices (one can picture the love-in as ambitious backbenchers queued up to lavish praise on their own party's choice for a Cabinet post). But hearings in a potentially hostile, elected second chamber would be meaningful. As the US Senate's televised interrogations have shown, such a procedure also adds a healthy dash of sunlight to public life.

Replacement of the House of Lords will require the removal of an equally decrepit part of our system: the post of Lord Chancellor. Even before Derry Irvine compared himself to Cardinal Wolsey it was clear that this most ancient office was a medieval leftover. For the Lord Chancellor is the embodiment of the concentrated or 'fused' powers which Britain ought to remedy. He is simultaneously head of the courts, Speaker of the House of Lords and a senior member of the Cabinet. In other words, he occupies commanding positions in the judiciary, legislature and executive – and he is not even elected. In a democratic system of separated powers there can be little justification for clinging on to such an anachronism – no matter how fine his robes.

If we made these changes, our political culture would be transformed overnight. In place of an elective dictatorship crushing a powerless opposition would come a new, and ultimately less adversarial, politics. The prime minister would no longer rule with a royal sceptre, but would have to negotiate across party lines, building alliances with opponents. The old pendulum-rhythm of British politics – in which power changed hands and the country changed direction – would be broken, as politicians, often in spite of themselves, were forced to govern in the national interest. Centrists who have long hankered for the European style of coalition-building, consensus politics – complete with horseshoe-shaped chambers – would see their dream come true. The irony is, they do not have to copy Europe to get there: such politics already exists on Capitol Hill, in a system evolved directly from our own. (The US example suggests that this style of consultative politics does not rely on proportional representation; the Americans have come close to it with a first-past-the-post electoral system much like our own.)

The establishment of an elected second house would give

democrats everywhere cause to celebrate. Instead of granting all power to whichever party gains a majority once every five years, a two-chamber system with off-year elections would ensure Britain is governed by a set of 'rolling majorities' – representatives elected at different times during different public moods. Paradoxically, the greatest supporters of this shift to popular sovereignty should be parliamentarians themselves. Critics will rightly see a second chamber as a challenge to the sovereignty of the House of Commons. But parliament itself will be revitalised. No longer a glorified museum piece, with rubber-stamp debates and toothless powers of scrutiny, its debates will suddenly matter. The Commons-based executive will have to work hard to assemble a majority in the second chamber, fighting for each vote. It will be a throbbing centre of dispute and argument, a forum where the nation can genuinely thrash out its differences. All this could culminate in the most dramatic change of all: parliamentary politics might, at last, become *exciting*.

It is easy to lose sight of the big picture when discussing such matters. It can fast become a closed, hair-splitting discussion of the mechanics of 'constitutional reform', rather than a heated conversation about the way we govern ourselves. But that is what such changes are really about. By setting up machinery to keep the government in check, we will be asserting our own role as masters of our own society. Accepted but outdated notions of parliamentary sovereignty will give way to a new concept for Britain: the sovereignty of the people.

5. A Culture of Rights

All this democracy will need a counterweight. For when we speak of 'the people' suddenly taking charge, what we mean is the *majority* of the people. What of the minority? The US Founding Fathers were aware that popular sovereignty could soon collapse into the tyranny of the majority, happily passing laws that suited its purpose but which trampled on others. Their solution was to enshrine John Locke's notion of truly limited government. This held that the will of the majority was not always sovereign, that it could govern only certain aspects of people's lives. Specifically, the majority could not infringe on personal liberties. Even if the government was fully democratic, and truly represented the will of the majority, those fundamental freedoms were to remain inviolate.

To this day the Bill of Rights and its custodians, the Supreme Court, stand up for the reviled minority against the clamour of the rest. When American neo-Nazis wanted to march through Skokie, Illinois – home to hundreds of Holocaust survivors – the disapproval was universal. But the neo-Nazis' First Amendment right to free speech meant they, not the majority, prevailed. In the federal set-up of the United States, the Supreme Court is especially necessary. It is there to ensure that none of the fifty states violates any of the constitutionally enshrined rights of their citizens. Historically that has often led to the court forcing social progress on more recalcitrant regions of the country – like the Bible-belt states who were obliged by 1973's Roe v. Wade decision to allow women the right to an abortion. The most dramatic instance came in 1957 when President Eisenhower flew the 82nd Airborne Division into Little Rock, Arkansas. The Supreme Court had ruled that all American schools had to be racially desegregated – even if a majority of Arkansans thought otherwise. It took troops to enforce the Constitution, and to defend the rights of the black minority, but defend them they did.

If British citizens are to establish popular sovereignty, they too will want safeguards for the minority. As local and regional self-rule expands, the case becomes especially urgent – a point which the incident at Little Rock graphically illustrates. A Bill of Rights will be vital to ensure basic rights across the whole country.

Some will argue that this is a need we satisfied long ago. After all, we wrote the Magna Carta when the rest of mankind was still in loincloths; our 1689 Bill of Rights came a full century before the French drew up theirs. Both stand as precious gems in our national heritage, even landmark documents in the evolution of humanity. But neither work as clear rosters of our rights as individual citizens living in Britain today. The Magna Carta is concerned with the relationship of twenty-five barons, the king and the church. Its language is all but impenetrable: 'No clerk shall be amerced in respect of his lay holding except after the manner of the others aforesaid and not according to . . .

All counties, hundreds, wapentakes and trithings shall be at the old rents without any additional payment, except our demesne manors.' And few of its ideas seem progressive eight centuries on: 'No one shall be arrested or imprisoned upon the appeal of a woman for the death of anyone except her husband.' The 1689 document is not much better, defining the liberties of parliament rather than people – 'That the freedom of speech and debates or proceedings in Parliament ought not to be impeached . . . ' – and culminating in a genuflection by Westminster before the throne – 'All the people aforesaid most humbly and faithfully submit themselves, their heirs and posterities for ever . . .'

Our rights, like our constitution, are wreathed in a fog of aged common law, custom and precedent. In the sleepy days of consensus maybe that was sufficient. But in recent years we have learned, all too painfully, that rights which are left vague or unstated are not rights at all – but can be snatched back by government in a heartbeat. Witness the Major administration's alteration to the 1689 Bill of Rights, made solely to enable the disgraced Neil Hamilton to proceed with a libel action. The roots of the problem are the monarchical origins of our system. Citizens have rights; subjects have to be content with entitlements, privileges strictly limited by the royal prerogative. Britons fall into the latter category, granted only as much autonomy as the crown allows – an indulgence which can be taken away on a whim.

The options are pretty clear. We can stick with our current system of common law traditions and unspoken conventions, which crumble like sandcastles before the onslaught of a determined government. Or we can insist that individuals deserve not entitlements, but rights – liberties that cannot be touched.

An immediate solution is provided by the incorporation into British law of the European Convention on Human Rights. It not only spells out some basic freedoms, it has the added advantage of placing a seal on the fact that European law is already supreme in British courts. But it is far from perfect. Most of the key rights are subject to so many qualifications, they are hardly guaranteed at all. Even if the Convention was more robust, incorporation would not be a complete answer. For the value of a bill of rights goes beyond its utility as an at-a-glance guide to civil liberties. The very *process* of drawing up a statement of rights is valuable, forcing a society to decide which values it shares and where the limits of majority power should lie. Such a dialogue would touch on everything from abortion to euthanasia, privacy to freedom of the press. By simply importing a pre-written document from Strasbourg we will have skipped that process – like a person who goes to sleep a child and wakes up an adult, having skipped the adolescence in between: it might be quicker and less awkward, but the transition to maturity is less complete. We Britons have not grown up in a culture of rights. A debate over our very own liberty charter – not one borrowed from others – would be a useful start.

Yet, even without that national discussion, the relatively bland European Convention arouses unease in traditionalists. If Britain is to build on it – and give it genuine clout – then those objections will have to be tackled head on. Since the chief complaints are based on the US experience, the American Bill of Rights should prove a highly relevant model.

First, critics warn that any charter of liberties poses an automatic threat to parliamentary sovereignty. Acts passed in the House of Commons would no longer be supreme, but could be struck down if deemed incompatible with the bill of rights. Westminster would suddenly be subordinate to a higher authority. For traditionalists, who regard parliamentary sovereignty as a sacred ideal, this is too much to bear. Many of them, including some at the highest levels of the Labour government elected in 1997, wobbled, suggesting instead the so-called New Zealand model. This would reduce the bill of rights to little more than a set of guidelines. If a statute clashed with it, the courts would simply notify parliament of the problem; they could not strike down the offending law. Braver hearts argue that an incorporated European Convention be treated the same way as EU law: when judges face a conflict they should always uphold the Convention, while still recognising parliament's ultimate right to throw out the entire document if it so wished.

This is a neat dodge, but unnecessary. For all such criticism reveals is a failure to understand the original, Lockean point of a bill of rights. Its whole purpose is to place certain liberties beyond the reach of the majority represented in parliament. If that challenges parliamentary sovereignty, then radicals should celebrate, not apologise. Limiting the authority of parliament is not a drawback of a bill of rights. It is the goal. For that reason, the European Convention should occupy the same place in Britain as the Bill of Rights does in America. It should be the restraint of last resort on both legislature and executive, a champion for the minority against the majority. It should be 'entrenched', able to strike down any laws or government decisions which violate it. The lighter touch of the New Zealand model all but defeats the object of a bill of rights. If we are to look abroad for inspiration, it should be across the Atlantic.

Such talk instantly prompts a related anxiety. Will an entrenched rights charter not give enormous authority to the judges who enforce it? Surely such a document will take all the key dilemmas of the age out of politics and into the courts. Life-or-death questions of medical ethics, sexuality and race will no longer be determined by democratically elected politicians but by a closed, job-for-life set of robed wise men, suddenly empowered to interpret a document with greater authority than parliament itself. The US seems to confirm such worries. The thorniest American debates of modern times have been settled by the Supreme Court, including decisions on affirmative action for minorities, the legitimacy of single-sex education and the nature of religious freedom.

Such fears are, unfortunately, out of date. Britain's judges already take pivotal decisions of life and liberty, just like their counterparts in the US. Through the process of judicial review, they already strike down actions taken by government ministers, quangos and local authorities – anything, in fact, except acts of parliament. The difference is that, while American judges are guided and limited by a written constitution, ours have no such restraint. A charter of liberties would plug that gap. In other words, the British judiciary will enjoy fewer unfettered powers *with* a bill of rights than they do without.

None the less, there is something perverse about an unelected judiciary exercising even that restricted power in a democracy. If a top rank of judges is to act as custodian of Britain's constitutional liberties – formally empowered to slap down the government when it violates the constitution – then it will have to be chosen more democratically. It will no longer be good enough for the bewigged m'luds to emerge, chosen by a network of old boys who went to the same school and the same Oxbridge college. After all, it is not only their technical ability that is relevant; their political and moral views are of legitimate public interest, too. The US system offers a solution. Selecting those members of the American judiciary who rule on the Constitution through a blend of presidential nomination and Senate ratification injects just the right dose of democratic accountability into the US Supreme Court, while life-tenure insulates it from the daily gusts of public opinion. Members of a new, British constitutional court could be chosen by a similar procedure, starting with nomination by the prime minister in the Commons followed by open hearings and ratification in an elected second chamber. The upper house would, accordingly, lose its function as the highest court of appeal – a current anachronism which, in any case, violates the separation of powers by merging legislature and judiciary. Organised this way, the shift to a bill of rights should give those nervous traditionalists nothing to fear. Far from politicising a non-political judiciary, it would simply democratise an already powerful one.

The second fear of a bill of rights is inflexibility. Opponents worry that rights which we assert now will be written in stone, while those we leave out will be ignored for ever. Times and mores change, yet we risk being saddled with a document too brittle to accommodate those changes. The majority of the future will be bound by the majority of the past. The US Constitution appears to be a case in point, starting with its second amendment: 'A well-regulated Militia, being necessary to the security of a free State, the right of the people to keep and bear Arms, shall not be infringed.' That, say the critics, might have made sense in the days of Redcoats, Paul Revere and muskets, but these days the right to bear arms amounts to a licence for Uzi-wielding hoodlums. In this view, serious gun control is impossible because the Constitution has locked America into a 1776 view of arms which cannot be broken.

But this is poor logic. If Americans wanted to be rid of the bullet, the Constitution could not stop them. Of course, changing it is hard; that is the whole point. Yet a straightforward process does exist for amending the Constitution and the Bill of Rights. Prohibition is the obvious example. When Americans wanted to ban alcohol, they passed the Eighteenth Amendment in 1919. When they wanted to drink again, fourteen years later, they simply had to pass the Twenty-first Amendment and it was done. In short, America's attachment to the bullet cannot be blamed on an inflexible Constitution. Rather it originates in America's founding struggle against an armed superpower – Britain – when the right to bear arms was an essential guarantor not only of liberty but of the right to stay alive. The belief that a gun is the last line of defence against an overmighty government lives on, under the skin of the American people. It is this which underpins America's gun culture. If it changed, the Constitution would be supple enough to change with it.

Finally, many Britons fear that establishing a culture of rights will import to Britain an outbreak of that quintessentially American disease: litigiousness. But America's stampede to the courts might owe less to the Bill of Rights than it does to the more mundane fact that going to court in America costs nothing. The 'no-win, no fee' system – universal in the US, but only narrowly in use in Britain – coupled with the no-cost rule, which frees losers of any obligation to pay winners' legal costs, means an American can launch a court case as a gold-digging expedition, confident that if he loses he will not pay a dime. Of course, there is a value to a legal system fully open to everybody, but the US experience suggests the no-cost rule acts as an invitation to litigation. By ensuring that losers still pay, and that the poor remain covered by some form of subsidised insurance against costs, Britain could establish a culture of rights while still avoiding a rash of US-style law fever. Besides, Americans' readiness to go to court is not all bad. We have seen already how US law suits can push forward the boundaries of civil rights, forcing decisions which ultimately serve the common good. Britain needs to devise a funding mechanism which would help that type of litigation – by continuing to allow legal aid for all judicial review cases, for example – but would limit public support for more frivolous actions. Of course, law suits can be noisy and irritating. But that noise is the sound of a free people, asserting its rights and liberties. If we hear a little more of it in Britain, it might not be such a bad thing.

Even if we go ahead and entrench the European Convention, the task will not be complete. There is some reinforcement Britain should make to the document, drawing on America's tradition of free speech. One of the reasons why the US is a land of such wide extremes – from the Klan to political correctness, televangelism to Howard Stern – is that all sides are allowed a hearing. Restricted expression keeps everyone within the cosier, narrower banks of the mainstream. Free speech is much more difficult to manage, as Judge Lance Ito discovered during the O.J. Simpson trial: the right of the media to write and broadcast what they wanted forced his jurors into a year-long quarantine and made his courtroom a three-ring circus.

But free speech need not collapse into anarchy, as the US illustrates. For even the First Amendment allows freedom to be tempered with responsibility. As the jurist Oliver Wendell Holmes famously remarked in 1919, 'The most stringent protection of free speech would not protect a man in falsely shouting fire in a theatre and causing a panic . . .' With that as justification, direct challenges to public order, including explicit threats to kill the president, can and have been outlawed. The law of conspiracy punishes the speech of villains plotting a crime. Child pornography is banned because its production requires the commission of a further criminal act. In other words, the United States' commitment to free speech does not leave it defenceless against evil. It merely requires hard, compelling evidence before it will tolerate any restriction on free expression – harder and more compelling than the standards set in Britain.

Similarly, looser libel laws do not inevitably foster an irresponsible press, suddenly able to smear individuals with impunity. After all, when it comes to aggressive vigour, few US newspapers can hold a candle to the British tabloids. For America's relaxed rules apply only to coverage of *public* figures: private individuals defamed in the media still have the law on their side. In fact, they have greater protection than most of them ever use. Forty-three American states have privacy laws on their books, allowing compensation for gross and unreason-able violations where there is no legitimate public interest.

Extra comfort comes from that US no-cost rule which – coupled with the no-win, no-fee system – allows individuals who believe they have been libelled, and small publications who are accused of it, to be unbowed by the fear of expensive litigation.

There are two specific moves for Britain to make. First, we must formally establish our right to free speech. The European Convention's Article Ten is a step in the right direction, but it allows far too many exceptions (including the right of governments to ban any expression considered harmful to 'public morals'). Britain should go further, with a more unambiguous statement of its own. Added to it would be a Freedom of Information Act, premised on the belief that since government works for us, we should have the right to know what actions it takes in our name.

Second, we must reform our libel laws so that they are no longer biased in favour of the powerful. That will mean shifting the burden of proof from the defendant to the plaintiff and allowing for a public interest defence. Lest we forget, free speech is a serious matter. Maybe children should be seen and not heard, but adults have the right to speak out, even the right to offend – balanced by the adult obligations to use that freedom responsibly. Americans already enjoy that badge of political adulthood. It is time we caught up.

But for Britain truly to establish a culture of rights will require action outside the law. Indeed, it will mean resorting to law less often. It is striking that when Americans come across something they do not like, they only rarely demand that it be banned – the reflexive response in Britain. Americans prefer the consumer boycott. So when tapes surfaced of senior staff at Texaco trading racist and anti-Semitic jokes, black Americans threatened a boycott of the company's petrol stations – a threat withdrawn only when Texaco paid out a multi-million dollar 'goodwill gift'. Lesbian activists came up with a novel way of venting their anger at Sharon Stone's depiction of a bisexual murderess in the steamy thriller, *Basic Instinct*. Rather than demand the film be banned, they picketed cinemas, armed with placards bearing the slogan 'KATHRYN DID IT' – thereby giving away the end of the plot. The American preference for the boycott over the ban is typical in a country which opts for citizen action over state intervention. But it is also a sign of a deeply entrenched culture of rights. Instinctively Americans shy away from anything that might compromise the liberty of someone else. It is an attitude we might benefit from in Britain.

6. A Written Constitution

Once they had declared the sovereignty of the people, and secured the rights of the minority, the early Americans had one last innovation: they wrote it all down. This was more than an administrative gesture. The Founders understood that a written constitution was, in itself, a crucial component of popular sovereignty. These days a written constitution can seem an obscure demand, the abstract desire of scholars. But the first Americans knew it was as fundamental as any of the reforms it would codify. They believed they needed it the same way a person who buys a house needs a set of deeds – as proof of ownership.

More deeply, they understood that a written constitution – irrespective of its content – was critical for popular sovereignty simply because it would let the people know how their system worked. If knowledge is power, then a people ignorant of its own political machinery is powerless. The rebel Americans saw how Britons had been kept in the dark by their unwritten constitution. They resolved that a truly sovereign people would not tolerate mystery in a system that was supposed to work for them.

Once again, Thomas Paine was the pioneer. He lamented that the British system was as full of baffling arcana as the rules of a clandestine masonic lodge. From the procession at the state opening of parliament – with the Silverstick-in-Waiting, the Mistress of the Robes and various Pursuivants – to the timing of elections, ancient mystery was everywhere. Paine believed all the tinsel and paraphernalia of 'tradition' was used by the aristocracy to dazzle the people, to blind them to the truth of democracy. It served to intimidate them into believing that government was a complex, unknowable task best left to an anointed priesthood of others. For Paine, flummery and ermine served to shut people out. A straightforward document, setting out the rules of the game, would let people in. Paine was hopeful: 'The age of fiction and political superstition, and of craft, and mystery is passing away.'

But Paine was too much the optimist. The trappings of superstition which made government seem unknowable in his time endure to this day. Britain still has a Lord Great Chamberlain and a Lord Privy Seal, Orders in Council and the Prorogation of Parliament – elements of the political system which remain utterly opaque to the ordinary voter. The Mori poll of 1995 found two in three voters knew 'just a little' or 'hardly anything' about the way parliament works, while slightly more were in the dark about the British Constitution. Three out of four felt ignorant about the House of Lords. Depressingly, a clear majority, 55 per cent, said they knew little or nothing about their rights as citizens. Britons rely instead on the small academy of constitutional scholars, the Robert Blakes and Lord St Johns of Fawsley, who get to play witch-doctor as they stare into the black and somehow perceive the secrets within. Meanwhile the rest of us feel disenfranchised and alienated, ignorant of the basic system which governs our lives.

In a more mature polity, Paine believed, there would be no need for the fog of ritual. 'There is no place for mystery, nowhere for it to begin' when the people rules itself, he wrote. The 'crafts of court' are left behind. Writing a century later, Walter Bagehot also believed that monarchy and the 'dignified' elements of the constitution could be jettisoned if the electorate was sufficiently advanced to accept a republic neat and undisguised: 'Where there is no honest poverty, where education is diffused and political intelligence is common, it is easy for the mass of the people to elect a fair legislature. The idea is roughly realised in the North American colonies of England and in the whole free States of the Union.'

Bagehot's observation holds good even today. In the US, there is no mystery and nowhere for it to begin. Americans know their way around their own system. They learn their Constitution in school, and venerate it thereafter. It inspires a near-religious reverence, its authors accorded similar status to the writers of the gospels. The major amendments are known

212

by almost everyone and even the obscure ones have a following. During the O.J. Simpson trial, as LA detectives testified about their initial search of the accused's home, a debate started on the Fourth Amendment, banning 'unreasonable searches and seizures'. When Hawaii's courts allowed same-sex marriages, Americans turned to Article 4, which demands each state lend 'full faith and credit' to the laws of the others. (Under that clause, if Harry and Tom got married in Honolulu, they would have to be recognised as a legal couple in Harrisburg or Hartford.) On the stump in 1996, Bob Dole would reach into his pocket and produce the text of the Tenth Amendment, which keeps most power at state, not federal, level. There is even a Tenth Amendment Movement, tapping into that perennial American suspicion of government and aiming to keep Washington within its constitutional limits.

The US Constitution lends an unusual clarity and coherence to the American national conversation. Any new proposal or policy can be instantly measured against the original goals of the nation as codified in the Constitution. A call to ban a violent or pornographic film is immediately discussed in terms of the First Amendment. Any attempt to give fewer rights to immigrants than native citizens is instantly weighed against the Constitution's guarantee of 'equal protection' before the law. The result is a great leveller. With no hidden body of knowledge decipherable only by experts, all Americans can take part in their collective discussion. Everyone can see what is in the Constitution; it is there in black and white.

Britain should learn the lesson. We need a written constitution to break the mystique once and for all, to make government simple, transparent and accessible to everyone. The superstitious nonsense of a constitution written in invisible ink, which so incensed Thomas Paine, is still with us, exerting the same effect now as it did then – casting government as the exclusive preserve of a set of initiates rather than of the people. We need to assert that this is *our* country; we have a right to see the rules by which it is organised. They should be laid out on paper, containable in a booklet small enough to fit in a pocket. Schoolchildren would read it and learn about the country they live in – and own. They would soon realise that there is no more to understand than what they see in front of them, no expertise they need in order to take part. They would come to believe they have as much say as anyone else, an essential condition for any genuine democracy. With mystery banished, Britons would see their system of government for what it is: not a holy relic or a law of nature, but a working apparatus susceptible to repair and even dramatic reconstruction if the moment requires it.

Traditionalists warn that such a document will sacrifice the flexibility of our current, unwritten arrangements. But who benefits from such flexibility? Is it the people – or the politicians, who can do what they like, without restraint? With a written constitution, any changes have to be debated in the open, rather than undertaken inadvertently, incrementally or, worst of all, by stealth. All three situations have occurred in our own time, from the erosion of ancient rights of the accused in the criminal justice system to the transfer of key powers to the European Union.

Furthermore, the US actually offers a way to maintain flexibility and keep the Constitution as a living, evolving document. We could learn from their system of amendment and revision, perhaps demanding two-thirds majorities in both houses of parliament coupled with the approval of three-quarters of the regional assemblies around the country. Such a stiff requirement would certainly represent an improvement on our current situation, where a single party with a simple majority in the Commons – and usually less than 50 per cent of the popular vote – can, if so minded, violate even our most basic liberties.

7. Local Power

Putting the people in charge will require one enormous change in our political culture: a vast switch of emphasis from central to local government. As the lesbians of Northampton and the sheriff in Arizona know well, genuine popular sovereignty means placing power with the people – in their own backyard. Moves towards self-rule in Scotland and Wales and a mayoralty in London represent a good start. The US, with its mini-parliaments in each of the fifty states, is a useful guide to how the distribution of power could go further. Since we do not have a president in London, we will probably avoid installing US-style executive governors in Edinburgh or Truro, but the idea of democratic assemblies for each nation or region in Britain – with one or two chambers, it is up to them – is hard to oppose.

The next step will come in the cities. America has shown that directly elected mayors not only ensure accountability but also eliminate the facelessness that so often bedevils low-profile local councils. An individual held responsible for a town or city – whose re-election and reputation depends on bins being emptied and streetlights that work – will demand the clout to do his job properly. Britain's cities should expect nothing less. We could spread democracy further, electing chief constables and all local officials in control of sizeable budgets – just as they do in the US. What competition is to economics, elections are to politics: they give people an incentive to work harder.

Like their American counterparts, Britain's new regional and city-wide authorities should have tax-raising powers – even if they barely use them. The American rebels taught the world that there is no taxation without representation, but the reverse is also true: without power of taxation, there is not much representation. If local authorities cannot raise or spend money, they fast become impotent (the precise fate of British councils in recent years).

All this will help – and be helped by – a change in the culture. Here, too, we might follow the US lead, spreading our cultural treasures more evenly. There was no unarguable case for staging the Millennium Experience in London or for locating all our finest museums in the city. We should encourage the American habit of local specialisation, in which different cities are allowed to dominate different fields. Those who believe such diffusion and autonomy is possible only in a country as large as America – and that centralisation is inevitable on an island as small as ours – should remember our past.

At the beginning of this century and the end of the last, Britain's cities were proud, muscled places, confident enough to build the ornate libraries and grand town halls which still stand today. Andrew Marr has described how Joseph Chamberlain in

Birmingham and leaders all round the country equipped their cities with gas, pavements, drinking water and streetlighting. They set up electric companies, trams and trains. Glasgow, Tunbridge Wells and Hull each had their own municipal telephone companies (the latter still does). Labour-led councils innovated a tradition of municipal socialism, opening public baths, wash-houses, art galleries and even cinemas. Leeds, Cardiff and Sheffield were the industrial powerhouses of their day – the Midlands the Silicon Valley of the nineteenth century, Manchester the Seattle. They had wealth and status, and their proud, distinct cultures grew accordingly. Economic times have changed. Several of those big cities, like so many of the people who live in them, have been made redundant. The industries which were once their *raisons d'être* have either moved on or vanished altogether. Inevitably, those economic changes have helped rot the British cities, like damp in an old house. But our political culture has made matters worse.

This is the challenge today. For all its rhetoric about rolling back the frontiers of the state, Thatcherism actually extended the reach of central government, crushing local autonomies wherever it saw them. The task now is to reverse the centralism of our politics, our economy and our national culture. Not everyone will applaud such a shift away from the centre. Critics on the left, for example, might raise the question of equality and fairness. Local government expert Tony Travers identifies a 'shared assumption in Britain that local public services should be broadly similar throughout the country'. If local authorities go their own way, then poor areas will have less money to spend on rubbish collection and schools just because rich people do not live there, while wealthy towns will collect fatter taxes and have all the best parks, teachers and streetlights. That seems plain unfair. As with the National Curriculum or universal health care, we want everyone to have a claim on the same services, no matter where they live. Perhaps that means local diversity and nationwide equality of provision are incompatible goals, that more independent communities will always be more unequal communities. Maybe Britons will simply have to choose between diversity and equality.

It is a serious problem, and one Americans continue to

wrestle with. Children in Massachusetts *do* have more money spent on their education than their counterparts in Alabama. But there are some instructive attempts at solving the problem. Local jurisdictions can be drawn so as to include a mix of rich and poor neighbourhoods. That way one can subsidise the other. The city of Charlotte, North Carolina, used to get a raw deal because rich people worked in the city but lived – and paid taxes – outside it. The tax base got smaller and smaller, with only the poor of the inner-city paying into the public coffers. Charlotte solved the problem by stretching out its boundaries to take in the suburban hinterland, so embracing all those reluctant taxpayers. Taxes on sales or on businesses can work a similar magic, ensuring commuters and even tourists make a contribution to the upkeep of a community. Properly configured, even a poor area can raise enough cash to provide services as if it were a much richer one. The US model also shows that central government need not be out of the picture entirely: federal cash can be, and is, used to bring poorer states in line with their better-off neighbours.

Besides, it is not as if the British system – under which Whitehall gives finely calibrated allocations to local authorities – is a model of fairness. It may sound equitable but it can also be oppressive, hurting the very communities it purports to help. As Travers points out, 'soon after they were perfected as measures of need, [Standard Spending Assessments] were pressed into service as *de facto* limits on each council's budget'. In other words, they became excuses for 'capping', with Whitehall barring democratically elected councils from drawing up their own budgets and setting their own rates of tax. Under the British system, the people of Lyme in New England would not be allowed to pay a bit extra on the rates to hire their own doctor. Lyme Council would be capped for even trying. Like all standardisation, a one-size-fits-all approach to local spending cuts both ways – ensuring one area does not get too little, but denying them the right to have more.

Which leads to the second likely objection to local autonomy. Critics on the right fear the result will be a string of mini-Stalingrads raising taxation across the land, the exemplar being the 'Tartan Tax' levied by a self-governing parliament in

Scotland. Yet such fears are illusory. For one thing, local authorities in Britain already levy funds from their constituents through the Council Tax – they are just not allowed to keep or distribute the money as they see fit, even though they have been elected. It is a ludicrous situation, in which they have responsibility, but no power. Local democracy would remedy that situation – not by asking councils to raise more money, but simply allowing them to spend the money they already bring in.

The American experience should bring the tax-wary critic further peace of mind. There, in the most tax-averse nation in the world, states (and some cities) have the right to levy a duty on sales and even their own income tax. They spend the money providing for the local people who elect them – so reducing the workload of national government, which can then afford to tax less. Thus a New Yorker may pay three sets of taxes: a city levy to the Big Apple, state tax to Albany and federal tax to Washington, DC. Even so, he will still pay less tax overall than his counterpart in Britain. The difference is that his money is spent where it is raised – locally. A similar system of autonomy would not necessarily make Britain a more heavily taxed country, but it would make it more diverse – no longer a nation groaning under a leviathan of central bureaucracy as it is now.

The third fear of devolution is emotional. Traditionalists fear that expanded autonomy for Wales, Scotland and the English regions will lead to the break-up of the Union. Once again, they should look to America. People in Texas or Virginia or California enjoy the institutions of self-government in their states, but consider themselves no less American. Indeed, the federal structure of the United States has actually strengthened national unity by preventing any one region from feeling subordinate to another (the Civil War erupted when that understanding broke down). Anyone in Scotland during the long years after 1979 would agree that it is that sense of subordination, and *lack* of autonomy, which endangers a union's integrity. Americans see no conflict between their state identity and their Americanness, chiefly because the latter evolves out of the former: after all, it is the United *States*. In Britain, where even limited autonomy has been so long denied, local and national allegiance are in conflict. A MORI poll in 1995 found that 34 per cent of Scots and 21 per cent of the Welsh felt more Scottish or Welsh than they did British, while similar numbers did not feel British at all. The American model shows that when people are allowed to express their particular identities, their national allegiance is only enhanced.

The final objection dwells on timing. All this talk of decentralisation makes no sense, say the sceptics, when Britain is edging towards ever closer integration with the European Union. Power is moving upwards, to Brussels, not downwards to Bristol or York. But such a view misses something crucial to the European project. Eurocrats speak enthusiastically of a 'Europe of the Regions' and of 'subsidiarity' – the notion that power should be exercised at the lowest level possible. That means whichever decisions are not taken at Brussels will be handed on to Halifax or Huddersfield, not Westminster. The visionaries of Europe see a future in which some power goes to the centre, but much more goes to the communities – much as it does in the federal United States. Greater local autonomy inside Britain fits that vision perfectly.

8. Civil Society

Taking charge will mean breaking another long-held British habit. We will need to curb the instinct which makes us look to the state, not ourselves, to solve our problems. For popular sovereignty entails not only rights but responsibility: if we are masters of our own society, then it is up to us to make it work. During most of our history we have looked upwards – first to the crown and then the state – as if to a benign parent, ready to scold us when we have been naughty but also obliged to look after us, 'from the cradle to the grave'. That needs to change. We have to see that habit for what it is – a feudal leftover, a relic from the time when those at the bottom looked to their masters for succour. Even the cherished welfare state has its roots in the old class system, in which a permanent elite felt obliged to tend to a permanent proletariat. The paternalists and socialists who built it were people of the noblest intentions, but their creation turned too many of us into passive recipients – as grateful for a state handout as subjects on a Maundy Thursday, bowing their heads to receive a purse from a kindly king. We need to make the move from passive to active, from subject to citizen – from political infancy to adulthood.

For many Britons this will be a hard step to take. After Oklahoma City, America's traditional hostility to the state is hardly enticing, while our own trust in government has seen us construct a health service and welfare state of which the Americans can only dream. We have spent a century equating the state with compassion, believing that if there is a social need, government should meet it. Any retreat from public provision is immediately condemned as a betrayal of government's sacred obligation to protect the weak. But a move away from central authority need not be a mandate for callousness. Instead it could mean shifting the burden of care off the state and placing more of it on our own shoulders. The goal is a smaller welfare state – embedded in a welfare nation.

In America the state is not the only outlet for good deeds, and taxes not the only means by which people look after one another. Ordinary Americans help in the provision of education and welfare, independent of government. They show that care, like power, does not always flow from the top down. British liberals get squeamish when they hear such talk. Words like 'charity' and 'voluntary endeavour' evoke images of the Dickensian workhouse. But such anxiety is unwarranted. For British radicals have their own, distinguished history of mutual aid, separate from central government. The author of the 1945 Labour manifesto, Michael Young, has recalled that before the party made a fetish of state ownership, it pursued a philosophy of self-help, embodied by the Victorian Friendly Societies, the Sick Club, the Slate Club, the Co-operative Society, the trade unions and the building societies. It is true that some of the latter have recently cut loose from their roots as mutual associations, but the idea of mutuality remains sound. Young suggests a return to the reciprocal ethic in housing, and in health and education. Britain's 1,500-plus self-help medical groups could be involved in the NHS, while parents become more active in the classroom. Local government, says Young, should be more truly local, with smaller neighbourhood councils reflecting and nurturing a sense of communal identity.

Such ideas, spearheaded by the people Young calls 'social entrepreneurs', represent a real future for British radicals. Of course, many tasks will remain the province of central government, as they should. Defence is the most obvious example. Economic data also show that healthcare is provided more efficiently by public rather than private means. (America's system of private medical insurance is one item we would clearly not wish to bring to Britain.) The state will sometimes be the obvious lead investor in industrial enterprises requiring risk and vision, two qualities in scarce supply among our notoriously short-termist financial elites. The US offers plenty of examples of 'pump-priming' by the federal government, most visibly in businesses related to research and new technology. But where ordinary citizens can take on tasks traditionally left to government, they should.

A virtual circle could develop. The more we rely on ourselves, the smaller our need for the state; the smaller the state, the more we will learn to work together. The pattern works in reverse, too, as Alexis de Tocqueville saw all those years ago: 'The more [the governing power] stands in the place of associations, the more will individuals, losing the notion of combining together, require its assistance: these are causes and effects that unceasingly create each other.'

De Tocqueville noticed a further phenomenon: when citizens shoulder duties ordinarily performed by the government, they develop a fuller, richer civil society. Where once was a single, thick vertical connection tying individuals to the state, countless horizontal threads are sewn, linking people to each other. The American experience certainly suggests a link between a weaker central authority and increased 'social capital'. British progressives have recently become more alive to the importance of civic connectedness, an impulse which has led some of them towards communitarianism. But communitarians often flounder on how best to *achieve* the apple-pie goal of stronger communities, many of them reduced to nostalgic pleading for the return of the activist central state. The US suggests another route – offering at least two ways to replenish the nation's stocks of social capital.

The first centres on the policy moves government and others can make. Dan Coats, a Republican senator from Indiana, once proposed a package of eighteen bills designed to strengthen civil society, chiefly by an intelligent combination of tax breaks and subsidies. Mentors and parents would get help teaching 'character' to their kids, while neighbourhood groups and grassroots bodies would qualify for financial aid. The US tax code would reward donations to charity, in order to encourage new ways of providing care and welfare for the needy, distinct from the top-down, bureaucratic provision of the state.

Away from Capitol Hill, local policymakers can have an impact, too. The American introduction of community colleges – small mini-universities serving a town or city and often majoring in supplemental, adult education – has helped cultivate new social ties. A favourite example comes from San Luis Obispo, a modest farming town about four hours north of Los Angeles. Town planners there debated a proposal demanding all new houses be built with front porches, so nudging neighbours to sit on the stoop, talk to each other and gradually form a community. Industry can also play a role, not least because the workplace represents one of the crucial 'associations' of modern life. Many enlightened US corporations have sought to transform their firms into communities, complete with value system – expressed in a mission statement – personal loyalty and ties of trust binding employees to each other. These can sound Big Brother-like, especially when workers find themselves under pressure to form friendship networks with clients. But they are proof that companies are beginning to realise the value of social connection. They should be encouraged to extend that logic beyond their own factory gates, to recognise the worth of connectedness in the wider community – which is, after all, their market. British chief executives might think twice about replacing corner shops or village post offices with vast 'superstores' – for such moves can only rupture precious civic links which are, ultimately, good for business.

The second step is less obvious. Britain's churches, synagogues and mosques should move away from the top-down hierarchies of old – which have always reflected the pyramid structure of the British state – and move towards the looser, grass-roots congregations found in America, which have done so much to boost civic connectedness. For the Church of England this will entail a truly radical move: disestablishment. While Sunday attendance is at rock-bottom in the established, state-backed Church of England, worship is at mass levels in the unestablished, independent churches of America. Britain's Anglicans might also gain new energy by breaking free. Their action is not only bound to add to the stock of social capital, it will also serve as confirmation that power does not always have to flow from the top down – even in the house of God.

Besides, disestablishment has other virtues. As the first Americans understood, separation of church and state is essential to preserving religious liberty. It also makes ethnic pluralism a little easier to achieve, by ensuring that no faith is elevated above any other. Church disestablishment in Britain would end the current unequal practice which grants Anglican bishops seats in the House of Lords by dint of their office, but leaves out leaders of other faiths. Besides being an ugly blurring of spiritual and legislative powers, this practice enshrines religious inequality. We need to end it – if we have not radically transformed the upper house first.

It defies all our prejudices and fifty years of received wisdom, but trimming back the state could make Britain more of a society, not less; one that is more caring, not less. It means shaking off the last, feudal vestiges of *noblesse oblige* and serf-like expectation and deference. In their place can develop a new resolve to do things ourselves. In defiance of the 1980s, we would be declaring that there *is* such thing as society – and we are it.

9. The Classless Society

If we move away from the old paternalistic welfare state, we will need not just an upsurge in civic endeavour but a whole new approach to equality. Our starting point should be the American Dream and its commitment to social mobility. That ideal insists everyone should have an equal shot at success: 'Old or young; healthy as a horse or with a disability that hasn't kept you down; man or woman; Native American, native-born, immigrant;

straight or gay', as Bill Clinton once put it. No matter who you are, you should have a fair shot at all life can offer – regardless of the way you talk, the colour of your skin or your parents' money. That is the American Dream.

Could Britain adopt a similar vision? It may have to. How else could Britain justify its increasing abandonment of the old welfare ethos, except by expanding social mobility? Put simply, it is only legitimate to deprive a man of a handout if you give him a hand-up instead. Either society protects the weak and the poor or it allows them the chance to become better off. Those are the only two moral choices. To give up one duty without taking on the other is to create the worst of both worlds. In a smart 1995 pamphlet, 'Meritocracy and the "Classless Society"', the thinker Adrian Wooldridge urged his fellow Conservatives to realise that, if opportunity was not extended, the entire Thatcherite project would be rendered ethically suspect: 'The task now facing the right is to use the concept of merit to complete and civilise this revolution . . . making sure that everybody, regardless of parental wealth or family connections, has a chance to get ahead. The last fifteen years will have been a terrible failure if those who prospered under Mrs Thatcher are allowed to pull the ladder up behind them.'

Constructing a British Dream of genuine social mobility is not pure fantasy. On the contrary, this US-style conception of equality fits our instincts. Take a close look at what most Britons actually mean when they speak of an equal society. They do not hanker for sameness or uniformity; few sincerely believe that a road-sweeper should be paid the same as a brain surgeon. On the contrary, most of us accept that human beings have different talents and should be rewarded accordingly. We object if the reward seems disproportionate – hence the outcry when heads of the privatised utilities pay themselves huge bonuses simply for having the good luck to run a monopoly company – but we do not object to merit-based pay in principle.

What sticks in our craw is not inequality *per se* but unfairness. We do not mind some people having huge fortunes, so long as we think they have earned them. In its most obvious form, this is a rejection of the hereditary principle: that someone gains huge wealth and privilege on production of their birth certificate just seems wrong. We may not begrudge Richard Branson his millions, but many of us do have a problem with the Duke of Westminster. Few Britons are clamouring for Paul McCartney to pay 98 per cent tax on the royalties of 'Penny Lane', but we are reluctant to fork out for the Queen's yacht or to repair her castle. The Victorians drew a distinction between the deserving and undeserving poor. We have quietly revived the idea, applying different standards to the deserving and undeserving rich. It is not all about desert, however. We do not resent winners of the national lottery, even though they have hardly 'earned' their instant fortunes. The key point is the fairness of equal chances. Once we are satisfied that everyone taking part has an equal shot at the top – as they do in the lottery – then we can tolerate the widest inequalities, as they do in America.

The challenge for Britain is to construct a society of equal chances, one that sets limits on no one. In policy terms, it will entail a move away from benefits and towards opportunities, from handouts to hand-ups. As Neil Kinnock once explained, people 'do not want feather-bedding, they want a foothold. They do not want cotton-woolling, they want a chance to contribute'. One American aphorism expresses the difference well: Give a man a fish and he'll eat for a day, teach him *how* to fish and he'll eat for life. In crude terms, while British prime ministers from Benjamin Disraeli to James Callaghan fretted about feeding their subjects, the Americans wanted everyone to be able to feed themselves. While we spent more money on welfare, they spent more on education.

Traditionalists of the old left have always considered the American opportunity-centred approach to be the soft option. But that is scarcely true. Opening up British society to full social mobility would require massive investment in education – the starting line in the running race of life. Next, Britain would have to spend substantial amounts training adults, enabling them to reach their potential. Such a project would, of course, mean removing the headstart some in our society enjoy over others: no titled aristocracy, no monarchy, no House of Lords. It might also entail a shake-up of the armed forces, the public schools, Oxbridge and all the other citadels of privilege – from the officer class to the closed boardrooms of the City. No more glass ceiling penning in women, no more prejudice holding back blacks: there can be no room for discrimination in a society that wants everyone to have an equal chance of success. For the sake of consistency, the government would have to apply these same meritocratic principles to itself. No more quangocrats appointed by a friendly word in the ear; instead, fully open, fair competition for all jobs.

Those still doubtful of such a project's radical credentials should chew on three thoughts. First, the bulk of spending would have to be directed at the least skilled and poorest – those most inhibited from shinning up society's ladder. That means diverting money to bad schools in bad areas and to technical training for those who do not choose the academic path. Second, the emphasis on a hand-up rather than a handout would only apply to those whose problem is a lack of opportunity. That is not everyone. Some people – the chronically sick, the elderly or even lone parents who want to stay home with their children – do not need work, but help. A civilised society would still provide it, whether via the state or from the people themselves, through more local, voluntary endeavour. Third, establishing genuine social mobility will require sacrifice from the well-off. The middle classes have tended to do very nicely out of the old welfare state. Because they can afford to live in good areas, their children have gone to good schools. Those same kids have then gone on to higher education at least partially subsidised by workers whose children never get near a university. White-collar types know their way around the NHS, too: they can usually fill in the forms and use the right telephone manner to get the treatment they want. Despite the best intentions of the paternalists and socialists, the experts agree that welfare spending aimed at cushioning life at the bottom has ultimately served to reinforce the advantages of the middle class. They will have to give up some of those privileges if opportunities are to be extended.

A British Dream of social mobility will also require an end to dogma. Education is the most important area, and will also be the most controversial. Some are bound to say equal chances means common schooling for all – closing down the public schools, and investing enough money in today's 'sink' institutions to make them as good as any in the land. Others might condemn such action as old thinking, seeking to impose a grey uniformity on all Britain's children. They might argue for a return to academic selection, allowing children with sufficient ability to go to the best schools they can – regardless of where they live or their parents' income. After all, selection already exists – by wealth in the private sector and by house price in the public. Adrian Wooldridge and others suggest absorbing the public schools into the state-funded sector, which would then provide a rich range of different schools, all pitched at different academic abilities. There could be centres of excellence, not only academically but also for children with aptitude in technology, science, the arts or sport. The only relevant criterion for advancement would be the child's needs and ability – not their class and birth.

Wooldridge provocatively calls for the return of the IQ test, as the only mechanism which could factor out the advantages of background and good tutoring, so removing the middle class's current advantage to make room for a wholly classless, merit-based system. The experience of Solihull in the early 1980s illustrates how radical such an idea would be. When the council in that Birmingham suburb proposed the return of formal academic selection, well-to-do parents rebelled. They had bought expensive houses in an expensive area and regarded places in good schools as part of the package. As Wooldridge drily observes, 'they would not tolerate working-class children taking those places just because they happened to be good at passing exams.' A society committed to full-blooded social mobility might require a dramatic change in attitudes.

10. A New British Identity

If Britain were to take the nine steps outlined above it would automatically take the tenth: it will have constructed a shared project, and with it a nationalism of ideas, not blood.

A British patriotism which looked to the present and the future, not the past, would have an enormous effect. If America is any guide, our national pride would become deeper, more inclusive at home, less aggressive abroad and richer in optimism and possibility. The lesson of America is that such a nationalism is of the civic kind, based on a set of ideals. Put simply, when we have a national project, we will have national pride.

Sceptics will wonder how Britain could possibly develop an idealistic nationalism of this kind. After all, ours is not a created society. We live in an ancient land, not a deliberately constructed community. No one would pretend that Britain is brand new. Still, we can use the end of the twentieth century and the beginning of the new millennium as a fresh start, as the moment to embark on a national project. Ringing the changes would amount to just such a mission. Asserting that sovereignty rests with us, the people; reshaping our institutions so that power flows in the right direction; removing the vestiges of feudalism so that a classless society becomes a genuine possibility; in short, forging a new country – all this would change the way we feel about Britain and each other. In the language of liberation movements, we would be reclaiming our nation.

Such a process can have a powerful effect on patriotism. Look at South Africa, where blacks switched from loathing their national institutions to loving them – simply by making their country their own. We are not in the business of abolishing anything as grotesque as apartheid, but we need to sweep away a post-feudal order and declare, like the new South Africans, '*Mi Smo Narod*' – a phrase which means both 'we are a *people*' and 'we are *the* People'. Then we can engage together in the adventure they call *masakane*, the building of a new nation.

The new South Africa, like the new United States two centuries earlier, understood the importance of symbols for such a collective endeavour. Along with their new constitution and bill of rights, they designed a new flag and wrote a new anthem (a highly symbolic blend of the old Afrikaner standard and the music of the African National Congress). Britons could do the same. We could have a national competition for a new flag, one that does not stand for our imperial past but for our democratic future, one not associated with fascism but which black, Asian and all Britons can regard as their own. The Union flag is not a holy relic; it is a man-made symbol we choose to use. King James I created a first version in 1606, and today's banner was only designed in 1801, when the cross of St Patrick was added following the union with Ireland. It makes perfect sense that, as we throw off our feudal past and declare ourselves citizens not subjects, we should mark the occasion with a new flag.

The same goes for our current anthem, which barely deserves the name. It is less a national anthem than the bleat of subjects, begging to be dominated ('Long to reign over us . . .'). It is not a celebration of ourselves, but a hymn to an unelected ruler. We could stage an open contest challenging Britain's poets and songwriters to find a new anthem – along with a flag – to mark the new millennium.

The beauty of a nationalism of ideas, rather than blood, is that it allows an equal place to everyone who joins it, whether their family has lived in Britain a thousand years or none. In practice that is less likely to lead to a radical reform of our immigration laws than to a shift in attitude to the 4.5 per cent of our population which is not white. The Americans realised long ago that, far from being a burden on the state, immigrants usually boost the economy of the country they join, and powerfully enrich its cultural life. We should heed George Washington's words that tolerance is not enough, that it is but a poor substitute for warmth and celebration. In this enterprise we have one historical advantage over the Americans. We are not cursed with a legacy of slavery in our own country. It is undeniable that Britain's industrial revolution was funded by the sweat of African slaves and on the plantations of the Caribbean, and that at one point Britain benefited from the produce of around one million people held captive around the world. But the fact that slaves were not kept *inside* Britain on anything like the American scale means that the experience has not affected us the same way. We are not haunted by it, and nor does it doom our chances of racial harmony. As a result, black–white relations often appear much smoother in Britain than in America. While they do not marry across racial lines, we do. Forty per cent of black Caribbean men under thirty-four, and 20 per cent of black Caribbean women of the same age, were living with a white partner, according to the 1991 UK census. To cite an apparently trivial example, TV's *Blind Date* happily pairs contestants of different races, while the equivalent shows on US television will only match blacks with blacks, and whites with whites. American sitcoms and TV drama obey the same convention.

In other words, the story of the black British community is closer to that of America's Hispanic, Jewish or Italian immigrants: they are all people who *chose* to move in search of a better life. Britain is free of the built-in contradiction bequeathed to the US by the slavemasters of the past. We can take the American ideal of ethnic diversity, centred on a national project, and go one better than the first Americans – by extending it to everyone.

A Liberal Reunion

It is a full list – ten steps that would alter Britain profoundly. They form a coherent whole in the shape of the United States, which has bound them together in the creed Gramsci called Americanism. Viewed through a British prism this agenda can seem a pretty mixed, if not confusing affair: it is left-wing on some questions – demanding abolition of the monarchy and the House of Lords – but right-wing on others – urging a move away from the central state and towards the voluntary sector.

There is indeed something for both left and right in such a programme. Before the twentieth-century infatuation with the state and central planning, liberty was always the project of the left. Freedom was the rallying cry of the first radicals, whether they were the heroes of the Peasants' Revolt, the Levellers, the Roundheads, the Whigs, the nonconformists or the Chartists. To tame the state, and win greater liberties for the people, might represent a break with the left's recent past – but it would be a reunion with its earliest roots.

For the right, the conversion to Americanism should be just as natural. Margaret Thatcher dedicated herself to rolling back the state from the economy; curbing the power of the state over ordinary Britons' lives should mark the next logical step. The reforms on offer here – from directly elected mayors to abolition of the crown prerogative – would achieve precisely that goal, draining power away from the centre.

But the deeper point is that the old labels of left and right are increasingly out of date. Relics of the Cold War era, they fail to capture the distance by which politics has moved on. Surveys of young Britons reveal a whole new world view, one that defies the easy polarities of the past. This next generation is fiscally conservative but socially liberal, wary of state intervention and high taxes, but open to diversity of race, sexuality and family life. In short, they want more freedom, economically and personally. The smart money says the politics of the next century will be dominated by libertarianism.

If that is right, then it will represent for Britain not so much a new wave as a return to our roots. For what the doctrine of Americanism may amount to is an idea whose name has become so distorted as to lose all meaning: liberalism. Applied to the economy, liberalism translates into a preference for the market over the state. Applied to society, it means shifting power away from the centre and closer to the people themselves. What the founding Americans understood was that for the creed to make any intellectual – and indeed moral – sense, it had to include both.

British liberals have only ever gone half-way. In the nineteenth century, the Manchester School took up the economic liberalism of *laissez-faire*, but left political and social reform to others, chiefly the Liberals. The left, meanwhile, abandoned liberalism altogether, looking instead to socialism. In our own time, Margaret Thatcher revived economic liberalism but she, too, had little stomach for the political implications of her programme. She could not see that once she had opened up the economy, society would have to open up, too. For more than a hundred years economic and social liberalism have been kept apart.

Now might be the time to reunite these twins, separated in their infancy. The triumph of market forces under Margaret Thatcher locked economic liberalism firmly in place. Now it must be joined by political liberalism for the triumph to be complete – and legitimate. To have one without the other is to have the worst of both worlds: none of the paternalistic protections that justify a strong government, and none of the freedoms that legitimate a weak one.

The Americans understood all this long ago. In a turn-of-the-century visit to the United States, H.G. Wells – who besides his mastery of science fiction was no slouch at political analysis – concluded that only one ideology ruled in America, and that it animated both Republicans and Democrats. It was liberalism, as pioneered in Britain. In *The Future in America*, published in 1906, Wells described the ideal, understanding that it was a movement not only of *laissez-faire* economics but of political reform: 'The liberalism of the eighteenth century was essentially the rebellion . . . against the monarchical and aristocratic state – against hereditary privilege, against restrictions on bargains. Its spirit was essentially anarchistic – the antithesis of Socialism. It was anti-State.'

Wells's words still ring true today, as a clarion call to British radicals of every stripe, beyond the timeworn labels of left and right. From now on the British political contest will be between progressives and traditionalists, with representatives from both of the old sides, left and right, in each camp. Reformers will need to follow the American lead and reunite the two halves of liberalism, to build on the state-taming work already complete in the economy and extend it to politics. That means a rebellion against the top-down 'monarchical and aristocratic state' which still stands, and against the hereditary elite that continues to exercise power within it. That will be painful for the right. But it also means a rebellion against the top-down methods left over from state socialism. The left needs to see its century-long flirtation with Marxism as a false seduction, in which state-centred Bonapartism was the real suitor. We need to recover our own freedom-loving tradition, one inherited from the liberalism of Locke, the anarchism of Shelley and a thousand dreamers in between. We need to reclaim the ideas that were born in Britain but which only flourished in the United States. They are ours, and we want them back.

10

Bringing it all Back Home

AT THE END of America is Seattle. Perched on the edge of the
continent, where the north-west corner of the United States
melts into the Pacific Ocean, it is an ultimate place – the last
frontier. For those who have followed the age-old call – go west,
young man – Seattle has always marked the end of the journey.

The early pioneers made their trek west in seventy- or eighty-
mile spurts, failing at each stop. No matter how bad it got – with
each new farm turning to dust – they refused to turn back.
They struggled on, from the hardness of the Dakotas and the
emptiness of Nebraska, across the Rocky Mountains, on to the
big skies of Montana and the hilltops of Idaho until they finally
found a place that was neither dry nor hostile: the lush, verdant
expanse they called Washington state. 'The greenness, the
abundance, the fertility of the soil was matched by the
abundance of jobs and hopefulness they found here,' says
Jonathan Raban, who has written a history of the men and
women who, like him, headed west. 'Everyone in Seattle has a
memory of some dusty homestead back east where they failed
and which drove them here.'

The west occupies the same place in the American
imagination to this day: here, despite failure everywhere else,
you can make it. A century ago, the lure was gold. Today's
prospectors come in search of less tangible riches: cyberspace,
cappuccino or grunge.

Tom Hertzog came to Seattle to play Nintendo. Unfeasibly
boyish for thirty-two, he has the sparkle-eyed enthusiasm of a
video-game fanatic which, by his own admission, he is. He wears

jeans, a sweatshirt and long, seventies-footballer's hair – the uniform of the science nerd.

He first became hooked on Super Mario, Pilot Wings and Solar Striker when he was introduced to Nintendo by a college friend and fellow pizza-delivery man (picture Beavis and Butthead). Soon every available minute of the day and night was spent twiddling the joystick and rapid-fire buttons on a Nintendo Entertainment System. 'You could easily say I was obsessed,' he says.

After college, Tom worked at a dead-end job selling wholesale electrical supplies. His girlfriend could see he hated it, so she suggested he chase his real dream. 'Where's Nintendo?' she asked. The answer was in Seattle.

Never mind they had no jobs to go to, the couple quit and headed west. They laid down their savings as a deposit on an apartment, while Tom spent nearly four months looking for work. The money was about to run out when his dream came true. Nintendo hired him as a temporary 'game-counsellor', manning one of the company's bank of telephone help lines.

As a Nintendo samaritan he would answer the frustrated cries for help of fellow fanatics, struggling to crack the fifth level of Donkey Kong or break the secret of Earthbound. Soon Tom was promoted, so that now he works as a game tester, rooting out the gremlins in new products. 'I'm obviously in heaven,' he says. 'I get to play games all day long.'

Tom is chewing the fat during a lunch break at Nintendo's headquarters in the Seattle suburb of Redmond. His colleagues are dressed just as relaxedly as he is: there is not a necktie in the building.

Nintendo HQ is cradled within the Microsoft 'campus', as Bill Gates fondly refers to the heart of his empire. It is a village of clean, glassy structures pulsing with cyber-ideas, flickering with the light of computer screens and new gizmos. The techno-campus is silvery and sleek, just as the futurists of old Hollywood might have imagined it, but the workers are not clad in shiny bodysuits. Instead, they are in the civic costume of Seattle: torn jeans, rock-band T-shirts, multiple body-piercings.

There are people like Tom throughout the city – young fortune-seekers who have trekked westward armed with nothing but the rumour of promise. They would never use such hokey language – they are far too post-modern and ironic for that – but what Tom and the other Seattlites are living is the American Dream.

You might hear about the friend of a friend who arrived, aged twenty-four, and leased an espresso cart from one of Seattle's burgeoning gourmet coffee retailers. He was in at the start, so he got shares in the company. Now, aged twenty-eight, he is a millionaire – testament to the success of the Seattle phenomenon that has reshaped the American high street: the cappuccino boom which has put a 'speciality' coffee house on every US corner.

Or you might run into Alex Cronin – in Seattle just a few months, but already hooked. A migrant from Colorado Springs, he is now studying atomic physics at the University of Washington, which would probably pass for a British red-brick campus were it not for the striking, snow-topped view of Mount Rainier, visible from every angle.

Alex's speciality is precision measurements, particularly the study of parity violation (don't ask). He is also a committed rock climber, enthralled by the rock-and-ice mixture of the Cascade Mountains. He likes the open space of the Pacific North-West, but since he has arrived he has had an idea. 'I was listening to the radio and hearing about how Seattle needed a new metro or tram service and I thought, "Hey, I could devise my own transport system."' Like millions before him, Alex had seen the west as a blank page – and believes anything is possible.

But the people of the Pacific North-West are living the American Dream in a sense that goes beyond mere can-do spirit and rags-to-riches success. They have, for instance, taken advantage of the American philosophy of power to construct a socialised health system in Washington state akin to Britain's NHS – an example of a community doing things for themselves. They have set a lead in ethnic diversity. Despite a tiny non-white population, for years Seattle had a black mayor and in 1996 the voters of Washington elected Gary Locke, the first Chinese-American to serve as a state governor.

Perhaps above all, Seattle is a beautiful place where people seem to lead contented lives. At the weekend there is kayaking on Lake Washington, skiing across the Canadian border or hiking up Mount Rainier. Scuba divers say the octopuses off Seattle are heart-stoppingly large, and the windsurfing and white-water rafting are always good. Best of all, these natural wonders are never more than a drive away; for the superfit, local buses come fitted with racks for mountain bikes. Seattlites say they live in an urban paradise.

Maria Nelson loves it. Dominican-born with fine Latin good looks, she used to live at the other end of the continent, in chilly Burlington, Massachusetts. Back then the east coast was in the grip of a slump and in 1991 the downturn hit home: her husband, a biomedical technician, was laid off. Neither had been to Seattle before, but they succumbed to the same impulse which has gripped Americans for generations. 'We decided to pack up our things and go west,' she says. 'We were ready to jump into anything.'

Neither Maria nor her husband, both in their thirties, had any idea what they would find, but they left anyway – happy to follow a national tradition and start their lives afresh. Their faith was rewarded. They both found work within weeks, and now their mortgage is lower and their earning power greater than ever it was back east. Their children can play outside with a rainforest a drive away, the mountains in view and Lake Washington a cool, cobalt-blue pool at the heart of it all. Maria said she was as content as she ever dreamed possible. 'I don't really know what I was looking for,' she smiled. 'But I've found it.'

Happy endings like Maria Nelson's do not happen every day, but they are a useful reminder of what the American adventure has actually achieved – not in the abstract terms of political programmes, but for real people and their lives. The sceptic will doubtless wish the Americans luck, but say that their revolution is *theirs* – it is not anything we could emulate. To suggest grafting the American ideal onto the British body politic is pure folly; it would just never take. We are who we are; we can be no other.

And yet the beauty of an American-inspired project for Britain is that it does not require us to change our nature at all. On the contrary, it demands the very opposite: that we become true to ourselves. Because this is not about becoming America.

This is about making Britain the nation it was destined to be.

For the American ideal is our own. It was crafted by people who were either British, of British parentage or who had grown up under British rule – reacting to the British system of government. Their ideas flowed directly from the finest traditions of British radicalism. Indeed, many of them saw their ideas as a programme for all of Britain, not just the colonies – only to find themselves rejected by their own countrymen.

Thomas Paine, who has been cited throughout, is the epitome of the phenomenon. He was born in Thetford, Norfolk, and, although he dedicated his life to the new republics of America and France, he remained an Englishman to his death. He may have written *Common Sense*, a bold demand for independence for the colonies, and immediately become the chief propagandist of the American revolution. But his best-known work, *The Rights of Man*, was written as a rebuttal to Edmund Burke in a dispute not about the future of faraway lands but of their own nation.

Thus was America formed by England's finest. William Penn, a London-born Quaker and a passionate advocate of freedom of conscience, first sought to work his magic in his native land. His reward was four prison sentences, including one stretch in the Tower of London. So Penn left England and tried to nurture his doctrine of religious freedom and limited republicanism in the more hospitable climate of the new world. He applied to the crown for a grant of land and received a slab on the east coast, with himself named as supreme governor. And Pennsylvania was born.

America's history was written by such men: George Washington, the descendant of John Washington of Northampton, himself the fruit of the De Wessyngtons of Durham; Ben Franklin, whose family fled to New England in 1682 in search of religious freedom; John Adams, the heir of refugees from England who found a haven in Massachusetts in the 1620s.

But the American revolution had English lineage that went beyond mere blood. Its core ideas were rooted in English radicalism. The Declaration of Independence itself is a document about Britain, its long litany of grievances directed against the British king – 'He has dissolved Representative

237

Houses repeatedly... imposing Taxes on us without our Consent.' The Declaration was little more than a rewrite of the *Two Treatises on Government*, authored nearly a century earlier by the great English philosopher, John Locke. Here, for example, is the Declaration's key proposition:

> All men are created equal, that they are endowed by their Creator with certain unalienable Rights... That to secure these rights, Governments are instituted among Men, deriving their just powers from the consent of the governed.

Here is how Locke had put it in 1689:

> Men being free, equal and independent, no one can be put out of estate and subjected to the political power of another without his consent.

The Declaration's author Thomas Jefferson made no pretence to originality, stating explicitly that, 'I did not consider it as any part of my charge to invent new ideas.' Rather he was seeking merely to codify into law Lockean social contract theory. Of course, John Locke had not gone as far. He was no republican, for a start. But in justifying the accession of William and Mary and the Glorious Revolution of 1688, Locke had challenged the old, absolutist concept of sovereignty. No longer did divine ordination, hereditary succession and passive obedience give the crown power. Rather, he argued, sovereignty was on loan to the monarch from those he ruled. It was a profound shift, detaching the throne's legitimacy from God. Whatever Locke's intentions, the *Two Treatises* established for ever the notion of power flowing from the bottom up. As one scholar has observed, 'By the time Jefferson and the Founding Fathers needed to justify their revolutionary actions, most Americans had absorbed Locke's work as a kind of political gospel.'

It therefore made perfect sense that when George III tried to exercise arbitrary rule over the colonies – acting as if still backed by the divine right of kings – the Americans argued that the king was overstepping the mark, a mark implicitly agreed in England's Act of Settlement of 1689. They insisted the Glorious Revolution had already established a legal basis for limiting royal power. So when the Declaration of Independence proclaimed 'That whenever any Form of Government becomes destructive ... it is the Right of the People to alter or to abolish it, and to institute new Government', the American rebels asserted that they were simply following the principle of 1689 to its logical conclusion.

Of course, there is a big difference between limiting royal power and abolishing it. But, significantly, most Britons saw the connection between the American action and their own a century earlier. Even the ultra-traditionalist Edmund Burke was loath to condemn the colonists: he confessed that a defeat for the rebels would be a defeat for liberty, and that they had acted on the same principles which had underpinned England's own Glorious Revolution. Britain's radicals were more full-blooded in their support. They saw the new United States as the embodiment of everything they had been preaching, and as proof that radical reform need not lead to anarchy and bloodshed. Thomas Paine believed it was only a matter of time before 'the principle of [America's] government, which is that of the equal rights of man', would come back to its natural home in Britain and make 'rapid progress in the world'. Outsiders, too, understood that America represented the fulfilment of English dreams of liberty. As so often, de Tocqueville put it best: 'The American is the Englishman left to himself.'

Yet we did not make those dreams come true in our own land. Instead, we cast out the great prophets of freedom who went on to become heroes in America. We jailed William Penn, most famously during the landmark trial of 1670 when he and William Meade were tried at the Old Bailey for addressing an unlawful and tumultuous assembly. The determination to punish Penn's views on religious tolerance was so great that the jurors were locked up for two nights without 'meat, drink, fire and tobacco', deprived even of a chamber pot, as the Recorder insisted, 'We shall have a verdict or you shall starve for it.' When the jury refused to convict men they believed innocent, the jurors themselves were fined and imprisoned. Thomas Paine got similar treatment in 1792, when he was drummed out of the country, sentenced to death *in absentia* and so barred from ever coming back. A Chelmsford mob had burned Paine's effigy under a banner that declared 'BEHOLD A TRAITOR! WHO, FOR THE BASE PURPOSES OF ENVY, INTEREST AND AMBITION, WOULD HAVE DELUGED THIS HAPPY COUNTRY IN BLOOD!'

There are good historical reasons why we did not take to revolution when our American cousins did. In those critical years between 1750 and 1780, Britain reaped consecutive bumper harvests – and, as every schoolchild knows, a full stomach is no condition for revolution. More importantly, Britain suffered no real political crises or disorder until 1820: by limiting the power of the crown in 1688 we had pre-empted the kind of troubles that would dog the French monarchy a full century later. Prosperity and stability combined to drain Britain of revolutionary imperative at a time when revolution was sweeping both Europe and America. So, in one of the great ironies of our history, our very success in gaining a little liberty early denied us the chance to win a lot of liberty later.

There is a tragic quality to this story, akin to Moses' leadership through the wilderness but ultimate failure to see the promised land. We showed the world the way of freedom, but never found it for ourselves. As *The Economist* has observed: 'The key concepts pioneered by Britain which have so much influenced the growth of democracy elsewhere – the separation of powers, the notion that basic liberties must be protected from the power of the state – were born of Parliament's battle to restrain the monarch in the 17th and 18th centuries; but they were never firmly established in Britain itself. Other systems copied the best things in the British tradition; Britain let them wither.'

So America describes itself as the land of the free, yet liberty is a British creed. The founders of liberalism – Hobbes, Locke, Mill – were British. Our country's freedom-seeking tradition produced not only the republicanism of Thomas Paine, but also the proto-feminism of Mary Wollstonecraft, with her *Vindication of the Rights of Woman*, and the anarchistic libertarianism of William Godwin. Our great poets, Blake, Shelley and Coleridge, were intoxicated by the scent of extreme liberty (all under the influence of Godwin); indeed, Shelley is hailed as the greatest of anarchist poets. Our religion has been infused by the ideals of dissent and nonconformism. Even the early English socialists, including Robert Owen and William Morris, and trade unionists spoke in a libertarian tongue that set them apart from their European comrades. Nor is this an exclusively English legacy: let us not forget 1320's Declaration of Arbroath, where the Scots effectively appointed their own king – so becoming the first to insist on a bottom-up flow of power.

To requote Adlai Stevenson, this is our heritage and this is our true glory. British radicals need to immerse themselves once more in this deep spring of anti-authoritarian and libertarian thought. For it is ours. The wilfully provocative would say the British left's flirtation with Karl Marx and other European visions of state-controlled socialism was a century-long detour, an aberration from our true instincts. Freedom of the individual and the withering away of the state – this is the stuff of which British radical dreams have always been made. (One scholar believes Marx was inspired to coin the 'withering away' slogan by the early British socialist economist, William Thompson.)

Britain's progressives have let their inheritance be stolen. But it was our entire nation which lost its birthright – to America. This book has sought to show that, despite the old cliché, Britain *did* have a revolution. The trouble is, we had it in America. The Founding Fathers were English radicals, who took a revolution intended for us and shipped it across the Atlantic. With it they exported our rightful destiny. It is time to bring it back home.

Select Bibliography

1. Introduction

Blood, Class and Nostalgia, Christopher Hitchens, Chatto and Windus, 1990

'The Europeans', Andrew Sullivan, *The New Republic*, 12 February 1996

'Fear and Loathing in Europe', Ian Buruma, *The New York Review of Books*, 17 October 1996

2. We the People

The Pelican History of the United States of America, Hugh Brogan, Pelican, 1985

American Exceptionalism, Seymour Martin Lipset, Norton, 1996 (See particularly cross-national polling data from the World Values Survey, cited throughout)

Ruling Britannia, Andrew Marr, Michael Joseph, 1995

The State We're In, Will Hutton, Jonathan Cape, 1995

Land Law, Kate Green, Macmillan, 1989

3. Death, Pork and the Pressure Cooker

The Power Game, Hedrick Smith, Random House, 1988

'We're a half-free press', Alan Rusbridger, *Guardian*, 8 February 1997

Adventures in Porkland: How Washington Wastes Your Money and Why They Won't Stop, Brian Kelly, Villard Books, 1992

4. From Normal Life to O.J. Simpson

Why Americans Hate Politics, E.J. Dionne, Simon and Schuster, 1991

Washington Babylon, Alexander Cockburn and Ken Silverstein, Verso, 1996

The Vocal Minority in American Politics, Pew Research Center for The People & The Press, 1993

'Feasting on C-Span's Unedited Feed', Blaine Harden, *Washington Post*, 9 May 1996

State of the Nation 1995, Research for the Rowntree Reform Trust, Mori, 1995

Pressure Group Politics in Modern Britain, Introduction by Peter Riddell, Social Market Foundation, 1996

5. Sex, Power and Getting Connected

Democracy in America, Alexis de Tocqueville, Doubleday Anchor Books, 1966

The Federalist Papers, Alexander Hamilton, James Madison, John Jay, ed. Clinton Rossiter, Mentor, 1961

'Bowling Alone: America's Declining Social Capital', Robert D. Putnam, *Journal of Democracy*, January 1995

'The Data Just Don't Show Erosion of America's Social Capital', Everett C. Ladd, *The Public Perspective*, June/July 1996

Shifting Engagements: Lessons from the 'Bowling Alone' Debate, John Clark, Hudson Briefing Paper, Hudson Institute, October 1996

Trust: The Social Virtues and the Creation of Prosperity, Francis Fukuyama, The Free Press, 1995

Sharing the Journey: Support Groups and America's New Quest for Community, Robert Wuthnow, The Free Press, 1994

The Time Bind, Arlie Russell Hochschild, Henry Holt, 1997

Civic Spirit, Charles Leadbeater, Demos, 1997

Social Capital: a fragile asset, Peter A. Hall, Demos Collection 12, 1997

6. Dream On: Searching for the Classless Society

The Great Gatsby, F. Scott Fitzgerald, Penguin, 1990

Literary Las Vegas, ed. Mike Tronnes, Henry Holt, 1995. (See Tom Wolfe's *Las Vegas (What?) Las Vegas (Can't hear you! Too noisy!) Las Vegas!!!!*)

Socialism, Michael Harrington, Saturday Review Press, 1972

Letter from America, Alistair Cooke on presidential inaugurations, BBC Radio 4, 17 January 1997

Reflections on the Republican Revolution, Tim Hames and Alan Grant, Social Market Foundation, 1997

Meritocracy and the 'Classless Society', Adrian Wooldridge, Social Market Foundation, 1995

Blair's Gurus, David Willetts, Centre for Policy Studies, 1996

Measuring the Mind, Education and Psychology in England, c.1860–c.1900, Adrian Wooldridge, Cambridge University Press, 1994

'Eugenics and Progressive Thought: A study in ideological affinity', Michael Freeden, *The Historical Journal,* 22, 3 (1979), pp. 645–671, Cambridge University Press

'Lost essay reveals "racist" Keynes', Sarah Ryle, *Guardian,* 31 January 1997

7. From Fruit Salad to American Pie

Passage to America, Terry Coleman, Hutchinson, 1972

American Immigration, Maldwyn Allen Jones, Chicago, 1960

The Fate of Hong Kong, Gerald Segal, Simon and Schuster, 1993

Conflict of Loyalty, Geoffrey Howe, Pan Books, 1995

British Immigration Law: Simple Guide, Akbar Ali Malik, Unique Books, 1992

Ethnicity in the 1991 Census, Vol. 1, ed. David Coleman, HMSO

On Living in an Old Country: The National Past in Contemporary Britain, Patrick Wright, Verso, 1985.

8. Taming the Beast

The Frozen Republic, Daniel Lazare, Harcourt Brace, 1996

'Britain's Constitution', *The Economist,* 14 October 1995

The English Constitution, Walter Bagehot, Fontana, 1963

9. Ten Steps to the Revolution

Constitutional Reform in the United Kingdom, Frank Vibert, Institute of Economic Affairs Inquiry No. 18, September 1990

King George V, Kenneth Rose, Weidenfeld and Nicolson, 1983

Can Congress Revive Civil Society?, Dan Coats, Policy Review, January–February 1996

'Roots of Revival', Michael Young, *Guardian,* 19 March 1997

10. Bringing it all Back Home

History of the American Revolution: Britain and the loss of the Thirteen Colonies, John Alden, Macdonald, 1969

The American Revolution, Edward Countryman, Pelican, 1987

A Struggle for Power: The American Revolution, Theodore Draper, Little Brown, 1996

The Glorious Cause: The American Revolution, 1763–1789, Robert Middlekauf, Oxford University Press, 1982

Liberty and Prosperity: Political Ideology in Eighteenth Century Britain, H.T. Dickinson, Weidenfeld and Nicolson, 1977

Edmund Burke: His Political Philosophy, Frank O'Gorman, George Allen and Unwin, 1973

The Thomas Paine Reader, eds. Michael Foot and Isaac Kramnick, Penguin, 1987

Anarchism, George Woodcock, Pelican, 1963

The Making of the English Working Class, E.P. Thompson, Victor Gollancz, 1963

The Declaration of Arbroath, ed. James Adam, The Herald Press, Arbroath, 1993